Land of Promise, Land of Tears

Jerry L. Twedt

authorHOUSE®

AuthorHouse™
1663 Liberty Drive
Bloomington, IN 47403
www.authorhouse.com
Phone: 1-800-839-8640

Published by AuthorHouse 1/3/2012

ISBN: 978-1-4678-7399-4 (e)
ISBN: 978-1-4678-7401-4 (hc)
ISBN: 978-1-4678-7400-7 (sc)

Library of Congress Control Number: 2011960728

For my Great-Grandparents
Ole and Helena Branjord

Acknowledgments

I would like to thank my brother Harris J. Twedt Jr. (better known as "Pete") for answering many questions about farming, raising hogs, family history and for just being my big brother. I also wish to thank his lovely wife, Viola Mae, for providing material on the history of Saint Petri Church and for explaining how to prepare Komla and hagletta. More thanks goes to Arlen Twedt, who has researched the lives of the early Norwegian pioneers and the history of Story County, Iowa. He was a great source of information on everything from where fords were located to the site of the Branjord family farm. Still more thanks goes to Judy Branjord Stephenhagen for her help on the Branjord genealogy. She is our family historian.

The library in Story City, Iowa has my thanks for providing the history of Fairview, which is now Story City. And a big "mange takk" to the Vesterheim Norwegian-American Museum in Decorah, Iowa for sending me information on how infectious diseases were treated in the mid-nineteenth century. A tour of the museum gave me a wonderful feel for how the early pioneers lived.

However, my biggest thanks must go to Barbara, my companion, best friend and wife for fifty years.

Chapter One

"Berent! Berent Branjord! Where are you?" Helena called as she stood, hands on hips, in the cabin doorway. She listened carefully for the telltale giggle of her mischievous four-year-old, but heard only the squawking of two angry blue jays circling overhead. "Berent! I don't have time to play this game. Answer me!"

He did not.

Helena's dark blue eyes narrowed. Her full, generally upturned lips became a straight, narrow line. She studied the barn and hog house, which squatted like sagging haystacks forty yards to the south. No movement. "He could be there," she thought, "but the little stinker is afraid of the two sows. No, he is most likely in the corncrib." She stepped out onto the small porch, shading her eyes from the afternoon sun, and looked west to the log corncrib Ole and Big Per Larson had erected a year ago March.

"Berent, come here or I'm getting the big wooden spoon!"

Her threat was answered by a rooster, who flapped his wings and strutted atop the chicken coop just south of the crib. Helena glared at the bird. "I don't need any remarks from you," she said as she walked the twenty yards to the crib.

The fresh prairie grass tickled her bare feet and, despite her anger at Berent, she smiled. After all, she reminded herself, it was a beautiful April day. So, to celebrate, she raised her long gingham dress above her calves and enjoyed the soft spring breeze, although it made her feel slightly sinful.

The corncrib was not Berent's hiding place, nor was the wagon parked beside it. Helena looked east past the seeded oat and wheat fields to the Skunk River woods. He certainly had not walked the quarter mile to reach the river, had he?

Fear began to replace anger. There were all sorts of animals in the woods: weasels, muskrats, mink, fox, even wolves. But most feared of all were badgers. A shiver went through her. She hated badgers. Four years before, in 1865, a badger had carried off a two-month-old infant from a basket sitting in the doorway of a cabin in Hardin County.

She turned quickly to the north, where her husband Ole was plowing the corn ground. The movement sent her long blond hair, which was done up in a loose, single braid, flying over her right shoulder, coming to rest on her right breast. Even though Ole was two hundred yards away, she could see the matched pair of bays straining to pull the steel plow blade through the deep, black soil. To the west was nothing but prairie that seemed to go on forever. Was Berent out there? Alone? Lost?

Helena took a deep breath, forcing herself to count to ten. Berent wasn't lost. He was hiding. The little stinker was just hiding! She had an idea. "Berent, I see you hiding behind the cabin. You come out now!"

There was a short pause, then, from behind the outhouse, which was north and west of the cabin, stepped a curly-haired blond boy wearing a faded calico dress that by some miracle had survived his older brother and sister. Helena knew it would never survive Berent. "You do not, Mama! I am not behind the cabin. You can't see me there!"

"Well, I can see you now. Get into the cabin!"

Berent put his hands on his hips and stomped his right foot. "You didn't find me, Mama. You cheated!"

"I wasn't playing. You can play hide-n-seek with Oline and Martin, not with me. When I call, you come! Understand?"

"But Oline and Martin are in school. There's nobody to play with," Berent moaned.

"That's no excuse. You do not hide from me. Now get into the cabin or I'll get the big wooden spoon!"

Berent stuck out his lower lip but began walking to the cabin door. "You don't play fair, Mama. You cheat."

Helena watched him and, despite her anger, smiled. He was always into something but was such a delight. She fought the urge to snatch him up in her arms and squeeze him until he giggled.

Berent squatted on the cabin porch, crossed his arms, and glared up at his mother. "You cheat."

"So you've told me," Helena said, tousling the boy's hair. "Want a drink of water?"

"No!"

"Suit yourself." Helena smiled, entering the cabin to prepare supper. "It must be four o'clock," she thought, wishing again they had a clock. She loved clocks. Especially chiming ones. She loved doing things by the clock. There was comfort in the precision of it: eating supper at six, going to bed at nine, getting up at five. Helena sighed. A clock was a luxury they could not afford.

A box elder bug had the effrontery to scurry across the plank floor. Helena grabbed her broom and swished the bug out the door, past Berent's left ear, and onto the ground. The four-year-old immediately pounced on the bug.

"Don't you bring that bug back into the house!" Helena ordered.

Berent retrieved the dead insect and returned to the porch, where he resumed his monumental pout.

"House," Helena muttered. She had called the cabin a house. How she wished it were a house. A real house with rooms. Rooms with doors. Doors that could close, giving a person private space for private thoughts. She sighed again. Would she ever have a real house? Ole promised she would. But thirty-two years of life had taught her that promises, no matter how sincere, were as substantial as a morning mist over a Norwegian fjord.

"Stop it!" she scolded herself. Then thought, "If the Lord wishes us to have a house, he will provide a house. Blessed be the name of the Lord." After all, what did she have to complain about? The cabin was larger than most, sturdy, well caulked, with a shingled roof, a plank floor, and a loft. It was so much better than the hovel in Hardin County. Helena shuddered. No! She would not even think about their two years in Hardin County.

Enough of this! It was time to start supper.

Helena was correct about the cabin being sound. It was also well designed. In fact, due to her and Ole's hard work, it was considered one of the finest log cabins in north Story County. The cabin faced south, with a solid door in the center and windows on each side of the door. Reaching from the doorway to the inside west wall was a bench built into the south wall, in front of which was a plank table. At the head and foot of the table were store-bought captain's chairs. Tucked under the table were three stools.

The west wall was dominated by the fireplace and Helena's most prized possession—a small cook range. In the northwest corner was a sink which drained into a large wooden bucket. Next to the sink, resting on a tree stump, was a pail of drinking water. Along the north wall were two clothing trunks, a spinning wheel, a churn, and a mostly empty bookcase.

Ole and Helena's rope bed, which lay against the east wall, had a mattress stuffed with prairie grass and corn husks and was covered with worn sheets and a quilt Helena had made while still in Norway. At the foot of the bed was a trap door that opened to the root cellar, and next to the trap door was a ladder that led to the loft where the children slept.

The southeast corner and the south wall up to the door were devoted to Ole's cluttered workbench. It was also the bane of Helena's existence and the cause of numerous sharp words and sour looks. Near the door were pegs on the wall for winter coats and capes, beneath which was a rack of overshoes made of buffalo and muskrat hide, and the children's wooden shoes. The only leather shoes belonged to Ole and Helena, and, as much as possible, were saved for church and special occasions. As in most Norwegian rural log homes, the center of the cabin was empty. This was the work space for everything from churning butter to spinning yarn to mending harness.

Helena added kindling to the cook range. Ole had bought it from a neighbor in Hardin County whose wife and daughter had died. The man was returning to Norway. It had cost most of their savings, but had proven to be a godsend. Cooking on it was so much easier and faster than using the fireplace. The range even had an oven, which she planned to use to prepare johnnycake for supper.

Helena put the last of the kindling into the stove. "Berent! I need you to bring in some wood from the pile."

There was no answer. Nor was there anyone sitting on the porch. Her four-year-old was again among the missing.

"Berent! You answer me!" Helena shouted as she rushed out of the cabin. The boy was nowhere to be seen. Red-faced with anger, Helena turned the corner of the cabin and looked at the outhouse. This made her angrier. The outhouse had no door—yet another bone of contention with Ole. He had promised to build a door but had never gotten around to it. Not having a door did not bother him. As he said, "There is no one out here but family." He did not understand her need for at least some privacy.

Then Helena spied Berent on his way out to where Ole was plowing. She was about to call him back when she saw he was carrying the water jar to his father. Her anger subsided, but she could tell from Berent's walk that he was still boiling. She laughed and shook her head. "Little man, I'm afraid you've inherited my temper," she said, then walked back into the cabin.

Berent

Mama cheats! She said I was hiding behind the cabin and I wasn't! That's not fair! I'm going to tell Papa. He told me never to cheat. I don't cheat! Well, sometimes I peek when I play hide-n-seek with Oline and Martin. But that's not really bad cheating. Besides, they hide where I can't find them. They always find me. Martin says that's because I always hide in the same place. But I like to hide there! It's not fair!

I hate being the youngest. I'm going to tell Mama to buy a baby. Not a little one like Mrs. Thorsen has. You can't play with him. All he does is cry and poop. Mama should buy one who can run and play, but he has to be littler than me.

There's a worm! Oh, he got away. I like to follow the plow because I find lots of worms. Mama doesn't like worms. I'm going to tell Papa she cheats. Maybe he'll spank her. But not too hard. I don't want her to cry. I saw her cry once. Some lady's baby died. I don't like to see Mama cry. I'll tell Papa not to spank her.

Chapter Two

Doll and Lady strained to pull the plow through the rich soil, turning its blackness to the sun. Ole enjoyed plowing. He loved the smell of the earth as it folded over like a page turning in a book. And even though his arms and shoulders ached from holding the plow and his legs were tired from the walking, he felt the promise of a fresh beginning—a new crop.

Ole still marveled at the depth of the soil. In Norway, a farmer did not so much plow the ground as scratch at it. Solid rock lay only inches below the thin layer of dirt, whereas here in Iowa, the topsoil went halfway to China.

Of course, cutting through the prairie grass for the first time required a steel plow and several teams of oxen. The story was that, in places, ten teams of oxen were required to break the ground. The most he had seen were four teams. Ole considered himself lucky that the farm in Hardin County and these forty acres in Story County had both been broken when he purchased them. There was still prairie on three sides of him, but that land had already been sold. There was no way for him to expand.

Ole reached the end of the field, turned the horses, and was about to set the plow when he saw Berent coming with the water jar. He smiled. A drink of cold water would be most welcome. Ole slapped the reins and set the plow, meeting up with Berent about fifty yards down the field.

"Whoa," Ole called. The horses gratefully stopped. "Well, what do we have here? Are you my favorite water boy?" Berent nodded. Ole continued, "Let's see, what is your name again? Oh, yes—Herman!"

"My name is not Herman! It's Berent! You know that, Papa."

"You don't say. Well, you look like a Herman to me."

Berent stomped his foot. "I'm Berent! And Mama cheats!"

"Mama does not cheat," Ole answered, becoming serious.

"Yes, she does! But I don't want you to spank her."

Ole removed his old, floppy hat and wiped his forehead with the sleeve of his homespun gray shirt. "That sounds like a good idea. I won't spank her."

"But she still cheated. She said I was behind the cabin and I wasn't. I was hiding behind the outhouse."

Ole studied the angry little face and did his best not to laugh. He failed.

"It's not funny, Papa!"

"No, I'm sure it's not. Why don't you give me a drink and we'll talk about it."

Berent handed the jar to his father. It was empty. "There's no water in the jar, Berent."

The boy looked surprised. "Mama forgot to fill it."

"Mama didn't know you were coming, did she?"

Berent stuck out his lower lip and shook his head. "I wanted to tell you she cheated."

"Enough of this cheating business!" Ole said, his voice becoming hard. "You were hiding from Mama again, and she didn't know where you were. I've told you not to do that. Mama worries about you. Do it again and I'll swat you with the big wooden spoon. Understand?"

Tears filled the boy's eyes as Ole handed him the empty jar. Berent turned for home, his shoulders slumped. Ole tried not to smile. Again he failed. Like his wife, he found it difficult to stay angry at his youngest child. "Berent, I'm almost finished. Do you want to ride on Doll?"

"Yes!" Berent answered, a huge grin replacing the tears. He dropped the water jar and held up his arms to be hoisted onto the horse's back.

"No, no. You're going to have to carry the jar."

Berent quickly scooped up the water jar. "Can I ride Lady instead of Doll?"

"No. Lady doesn't like to be ridden when she is in harness," Ole replied, picking up Berent and setting him on Doll's broad, sweaty back. This was nothing new to the gentle animal; however, she still gave Ole a look that said, "I really don't need this."

Ole patted her neck. "It's just for one more round, Doll. We're almost done."

Berent looked down at his father. "I think Lady would let me ride her if I wore pants."

"Don't start about wearing pants," Ole said. "That's between you and your mother."

Ole placed the tied reins over his right shoulder and under his left arm, then picked up the plow handles. "Get up!" he called.

"Get up!" Berent repeated, clinging to Doll's harness with one hand and the water jar with the other.

The horses, like any good team, moved as one. The plow knifed into the soil, which surrendered and folded over in defeat. Within twenty minutes, the work was done. Ole again removed his floppy hat and wiped his brow. Berent mimicked his father. "We sure worked hard, didn't we, Papa?"

"We sure did." Ole chuckled. "Let's go home."

Ole laid the plow on its side and, without urging, the team started for the farmstead. He was a contented man. The oats and wheat were sprouting. The spring rains had been plentiful, and the corn-ground plowing was finished. Perhaps, God willing, 1869 would be a year to remember.

Ole

I still can't believe the soil in this country. In Norway, you farm rocks. Oh, there are rocks here. My aching back will confirm that. But these rocks can be dug out, leaving rich land to work. You plant the seeds and the crops seem to jump out of the ground! Last year my corn was knee high by the fourth of July. Amazing. And the grains! I harvested twenty bushels of oats per acre and eighteen bushels of wheat.

If I can have another good year, I'll be able to keep two more sows. And then, let's see, if the four sows could average eight to a litter, that would be thirty-two pigs. I could keep three or four of the gilts and a boar, sell the rest at five cents a pound, and I would have nearly enough to buy eighty acres, and then …

Whoa, Ole. Slow down. You're getting way ahead of yourself again. The corn is not even in the ground; the wheat and oats are just peeking through; and only God knows whether we will have enough rain, or too much rain, or tornados, or hail, or wind, or, God forbid, locust like we had in Hardin County.

Don't think about Hardin County. Helena almost died. So did I. Bad years. Don't think about them.

The good years are ahead. This will be one of them. I can feel it. Eighty acres. I'd have to get another team of horses and a hired man. The team could be a problem. I don't want any plugs on my farm. But the hired man would be no problem at all. There are single men arriving from Norway every day. He could sleep up in the loft with the children.

Ah, there I go again, making plans out of thin air. I can't help it. That's what this country does to a man. Just look at what has been done in just twenty years! Doubling the size of a farm is not a fool's dream. Hans Twedt has done it. So have Jake Jacobson and Jonas Duea. I can do it! And when the boys get older, I can double it again. Can you imagine Ole Branjord owning one hundred and sixty acres? No one in Norway would believe it. Especially that old skinflint Hallstead. He told me I was crazy for coming here. He said I would starve or be killed by wild Indians.

My, my. One hundred and sixty acres. Wouldn't that be something?

Chapter Three

"Whoa!" Ole called, bringing Doll and Lady to a halt by the corncrib.

"Whoa!" Berent repeated.

Helena stepped out onto the porch. Berent waved, his feud forgotten. "We're home, Mama."

"So I see."

"I hear you cheat," Ole said, the ends of his lips turning upward and disappearing behind his salt and pepper mustache.

"Now don't you start," Helena said.

"Papa's not going to spank you." Berent grinned.

"I'm glad to hear it."

Ole lifted Berent off of Doll. "He asked me not to."

Helena smiled. Ole had never struck her and she knew he never would. He was much too gentle to do that. He even found it difficult to spank the children. Not that he was weak. He could out-work any man she knew, with the exception of Big Per Larson.

She admired her husband as he pushed his floppy hat back on his head. Ole was not tall, standing no more than five feet nine inches, but he had broad shoulders, strong arms, and a slim waist. At thirty-nine, his brown hair was beginning to thin and his beard was flecked with gray, but his body was still hard and smooth to touch. Helena blushed slightly. Perhaps it was sinful, but she did enjoy touching his body.

"I see Berent brought you water."

Ole laughed. "Well, he brought me the water jar."

"Berent!" Helena scolded. "You know you have to put water in the jar."

Berent looked down at his bare toes. "I was mad."

"Taking an empty jar out to your father was silly," Helena said, shaking her finger. "Let this be a lesson to you. People do stupid things when they get mad."

Berent did not look up. He just nodded. Ole patted him on the shoulder and said, "Why don't you go to the well and get me a drink?" The boy answered with a grin and ran to the barn.

Helena returned to the cabin as Ole unhitched the horses and removed their harness. After wiping it down with an old burlap sack, he hung the harness on pegs inside the crib. There was no tack room. That, in turn, was because there was no real barn. Ole spat in disgust. He hated his barn. In fact, he did not even call it a barn. To him, it was a hovel.

"The barn" was little more than a glorified lean-to, with the lower walls made of sod and manure and the upper structure a conglomeration of vertical poles, in between which was packed prairie grass. The open end faced south and was partially enclosed but had no door. Above was a thatched roof, which was in constant need of repair.

During the winter, when snow banks surrounded the sides and a thick layer of snow covered the roof, the building was remarkably warm and friendly, but during the spring and summer rains, doing chores was damp and unpleasant. Having a real barn, made of lumber, with horse stalls, cow stanchions, and a haymow, was Ole's dream.

Ole wiped down the horses with the same sack he had used on the harness and started for the barn. Berent met him with a jar half-filled with water. "Thank you," Ole said, pausing to take a long, refreshing drink. "My, that's good," he added as he handed the jar back to his son. "Take the jar back to Mama and see if you can help her."

"Can't I help you?"

"Well," Ole said thoughtfully, scratching his beard, "you could help me feed the sows."

"I'll help Mama." Berent gulped and bolted for the cabin.

Ole laughed. Since being chased by an angry sow, Berent wanted nothing to do with pigs. If Ole wanted Berent out from underfoot, all he had to do was mention doing something with the sows and the boy disappeared faster than snow in June.

Ole led Doll and Lady to the artesian well by the barn, where the two horses dipped their soft muzzles into a large wooden tub of water. The tub served as a drinking fountain for the horses, a cooling tank for the milk can, and, in summer, a place to give small children a quick, cold bath. But it was just the first step in Ole's carefully constructed water system.

Shortly after buying the farm, Ole had piped a naturally flowing well. Below the spigot, he placed the tub with a six-inch, U-shaped cut in the top. He then tilted the tub slightly and put a piece of tin into the slot, which in turn allowed the overflow from the tub to run into a ten-foot-long log trough that was placed just inside the pasture fence. A second trough caught the overflow from the first and carried water to the pigpen. This arrangement allowed all the farm animals to have easy access to fresh water.

"That's enough for now," Ole said, and then led the horses around the barn to the pasture gate. After being released, Doll and Lady walked a few steps, then lay down and rolled. It was their way of massaging sore muscles and wiping away the day's sweat.

Ole was about to shut the gate when he heard the unmistakable sound of cowbells. He looked west and saw his two older children, Oline, age eleven, and eight-year-old Martin, herding home the family's two cows. All of the cows from the nearby farms were released after the morning milking to graze on the open prairie. It was the responsibility of the children to find them and bring them home at the end of the school day.

The children were walking twenty feet apart, their body language announcing that they were having another of their frequent sibling spats. Ole sighed. Again he would be called upon to be judge, jury, and enforcer. As the cows reached the cabin, Oline ran inside. A smile appeared on Ole's face. Perhaps he would be spared having to play Solomon.

The two cows, a mix of Holstein, Shorthorn, and God knows what, walked into the pasture and straight to the water trough. Their names were Maud and Mabel, so designated by Oline, who had found the names in a book. Martin, his expression more serious than usual, stopped by the fence, unwilling to look Ole in the eye. He was wearing a homespun shirt and dark pants, both made by his mother.

"How was school today?" Ole asked as he shut the gate.

Martin's head snapped up, his blue eyes flashing. "I didn't do it on purpose, Papa!" The boy had his father's dark hair, round face, and hazel eyes, but had inherited his mother's temperament.

"Didn't do what?"

"Show up Mr. Tuleffson."

"Oh yes you did, Martin Branjord!"

Martin and Ole turned to see Oline, her long blond braids streaming behind her, running toward them. In her right hand were what looked like two twigs. Martin groaned. "Not the truth sticks."

Inwardly agreeing with Martin, Ole watched Oline skid to a stop before him. Her beautiful oval face was set in a frown, and the dark blue eyes that came from her mother were angry. Something had riled her usually placid personality. She handed Ole the truth sticks. "Martin showed up Mr. Tuleffson on purpose."

"Did not!"

"Did too! And he got us all in trouble. Everybody has extra spelling to learn and a whole page of math to do. Even the first graders!"

"I didn't do it on purpose!" Martin shouted.

"Yes, you did! I saw the look on your face. You thought you were so smart because Mr. Tuleffson gave the wrong answer."

"The right answer was in the book. He doesn't even read the book!"

"No more!" Ole said, in a voice that silenced both children. He looked down at the sticks and rued the day he brought them home.

A year before, Ole had been in the general store in Nevada, the county seat, when a novelty drummer had been showing his wares. The truth sticks consisted of a ten-inch twig with bark removed, notches cut into the top, and a one-inch long, quarter-inch wide piece of wood loosely screwed into one end. With another twig, he rubbed the notched surface, and the small piece of wood twirled like a propeller. The drummer asked in a dramatic voice if this was the town of Nevada. He then rubbed the notched stick and the small piece of wood rotated to the right, which meant yes. Next, he asked the stick if a small boy, watching with big eyes, was forty years old. The small piece of wood rotated to the left. Everyone in the store applauded. Ole bought the truth sticks, learned from the drummer how to make them work, and brought them home. Ever since, if there was a question of veracity, one of the children would get the all-knowing truth sticks.

The problem, of course, was that the operator was not all knowing; however, Ole had learned the chances were good the truth resided with the child who demanded the sticks be used.

"Oline, tell me what happened," Ole said.

"Mr. Tuleffson was teaching history to the sixth grade. He said the American Revolutionary War ended in 1781. Mr. Smarty here stood up and said it ended in 1783. Mr. Tuleffson said he was wrong. Martin said it was in the book."

"And I was right!" Martin said proudly.

"Yes, but Mr. Tuleffson got mad and assigned us extra work! The big boys were ready to beat you up!"

"Papa, Mr. Tuleffson doesn't even read the book. He just says stuff."

"You weren't supposed to be listening!" Oline replied. "You were told to read a chapter in your third grade reader."

"I've read the whole book three times!"

Oline stomped her foot. "Oh, you're impossible!"

Ole asked, "How did you know the war ended in 1783?"

"The answer was in the history book," Martin said. "Mr. Tuleffson left the book open on his desk during recess."

"And you had to show him up! You did it on purpose! Papa, use the truth sticks!"

Both children looked up at Ole, Oline with anticipation and Martin with resignation.

"Truth sticks," Ole said as he rubbed the plain stick over the notched one. "Did Martin show up Mr. Tuleffson on purpose?"

At first the "propeller" did not move, then it began to rotate to the right.

"See!" Oline shouted. "I was right!"

Martin looked down at his toes, saying nothing. There was no fighting the truth sticks.

Ole handed the two twigs to Oline. "Put the truth sticks away and go help your mother."

"Are you going to spank him?" Oline asked hopefully.

"No. But he will have to milk both cows."

"Ah, Papa!" Martin groaned.

"Good!" Oline cried, giving Martin a look only a big sister can give a little brother. She then ran to the cabin, holding the twigs high in triumph.

Ole looked down at his son. "Why, Martin? There are just two weeks left of school. Why are you causing trouble?"

"I'm not causing trouble. Mr. Tuleffson doesn't like me."

"Do you think embarrassing him in front of the whole school is going to make him like you?"

Martin kicked the ground. "No. But he's not a good teacher."

"He's not a teacher at all. He's just an eighteen-year-old boy who agreed to finish out the year when Mr. Amenson got sick. He's doing the best he can."

"No, he's not!" Martin argued, his anger returning. "He gets the wrong answers when he does math. He can't spell. In English class, he gives the wrong meanings for words. And in history, he doesn't read the book!"

"Do you think it is your place to correct him?"

Martin opened his mouth to answer, thought better of it, and looked down at his feet. "No, sir."

"No is the correct answer. He is the teacher. You are the student. Why didn't you go up to him after school and point out the mistake?"

"I did that last week!" Martin cried. "He got mad, called me a smart aleck, and told me not to bother him again."

Ole knelt down in front of his son. "That was wrong of him. But you are wrong too. Martin, God has blessed you with a good mind. You read far ahead of your age group. But that doesn't mean you have the right to embarrass your teacher or your classmates. Next fall you will have a new teacher. Now, promise me there will be no more trouble."

The boy made a face like he had just tasted a lemon, then slowly nodded his head.

Ole stood and patted Martin on the shoulder. "Good. Get the pail and milk the cows."

"Both of them?"

"Yes. And don't look like such a martyr. They are just about dried up. Next week we'll stop milking altogether."

Martin began walking to the cabin, then paused. "Milking is woman's work."

"Oh? Who told you that?"

"Lars. His mother and sisters do the milking. Why doesn't Mama milk?"

"Because she doesn't want to," Ole replied. "When we married, she told me milking was something she would never do."

"Why?"

"I don't know. But I do know that on this farm, the men do the milking."

Martin blinked several times as a surprised look replaced his frown. It was the first time he had been included when the word "man" was used. His shoulders squared and his chest expanded as he continued on to the cabin.

Ole watched him with both pride and concern. Martin was a joy and a worry. He was smart. Perhaps too smart. He had been reading the Bible for over a year and was trying to read the English newspaper that was published in Nevada. Martin could speak and understand English better than either he or Helena. Where did he get his brains from? His mother? Yes, his mother.

Ole walked to the hog house, shaking his head. When Helena had become pregnant with Oline, he had worried about his children being slow. Now he was faced with a child who was exceptionally intelligent.

Martin

I know what to expect when I reach the cabin. Mama greets me with the big wooden spoon in hand. But it isn't so bad. She talks to me about being disrespectful, then whacks me once on my bottom. Berent cries. I don't know why he is crying. I'm the one getting hit. Oline pretends not to watch, but I see her looking out of the corner of her eye. Sometimes Oline can be a big tattletale! Mama didn't really spank me because she doesn't like Mr. Tuleffson either. She knows he is a bad teacher.

I change into my old clothes. The shirt is too small and has a rip that Mama sewed together. The pants have holes in the knees. I hate pants with holes in the knees. Someday I'm going to have lots of money and never wear pants with holes in them.

I pick up the milk pail and walk to the barn. Maud and Mabel are standing at the empty feed bunk. They are the only animals in the barn. The horses and two yearling calves are grazing in the pasture, while the four sheep lie in the shade of a big old tree. I don't know what kind of sheep they are. I don't think Papa knows either. Papa and Big Per Larson sheared the sheep a week ago, and they still look like they have been skinned. Berent thought that was what the men were doing, and he howled like a wild Indian. Mama had to take him into the cabin, but she was smiling. The sheep have given lots of wool to be carded and spun into thread.

The cows look at me, waiting to be fed. Stupid cows! They eat prairie grass all day but still expect some corn and oats. I go to the feedbox, open the heavy lid (I couldn't even lift it last year), and scoop out a mixture of corn and oats into the feed bucket. After feeding the cows, I put ropes around their necks so they cannot just get up and leave, and then pick up the stool and milk pail and begin to milk Maud. Papa is right about the cows going dry. Milking will not take long.

Why did the Elders have to pick Mr.Tuleffson to finish out the year? He just likes to hit us with his willow switch. He's no teacher. He's not even smart. I wish I weren't smart. People look at you funny when you're smart. If I weren't smart, Mr. Tuleffson wouldn't pick on me. Mama says most teachers like smart students. Not Tuleffson! He hates me. I can see it in his eyes when he looks at me. He purposely asks me questions I can't answer, then laughs. But I showed him today! Oh, did his face get red. Then I laughed. I know I shouldn't have. I couldn't help it. I know he'll find an excuse to hit me tomorrow. But I won't cry. I'm not going to cry.

I wish I were dumb like Nels. No, not really. He's too dumb. Maybe like Christian. He's sort of in the middle. That's it. Next year I'll be like Christian. He's in the grade where he belongs. I wish I belonged. Where do I belong? Maybe I don't belong anyplace.

Chapter Four

Ole dumped half of a pail of oats and corn into a trough for the two sows. He had already fed the market pigs. As he straightened up, he hit his head on a crossbeam. "Ouch!" he cried, rubbing his head. He then muttered, "Someday I'll have a real hog house."

The hog house was a smaller and lower replica of the barn. Ole was forced to bend over to enter. This was especially a problem when he had to clean out the manure. Thankfully, the pigs relieved themselves in the front, leaving the straw bedding in the back perfectly dry. Pigs were much cleaner in their personal habits than cows, horses, or sheep. Smarter too.

Ole left the hog house. From where he stood, he could see into the barn, and witnessed Maud swishing her tail across Martin's face. The boy yelped and muttered angry threats at the cow. Ole laughed. Maud was adding to the punishment. There would be no need for him to get the big wooden spoon, which was a relief. He hated spanking the children.

The bellow of oxen drew Ole's attention east to the stage road that ran along the Skunk River. A wagon, pulled by a familiar team of oxen, was turning off the road and starting up the slope to his farm. Ole chuckled as he began walking to the cabin. He had to warn Helena to set an extra plate on the table.

Helena also had heard the oxen and was standing in the doorway. Ole pointed east. Helena laughed, nodded, and went back into the cabin. It was not unusual for Big Per Larson to pay a visit around suppertime.

Ole watched the approaching oxen and the large man standing in the wagon box. Big Per was six feet, six inches tall, but that was not what made him *Big Per*. There were a number of men in the community well over six feet tall. No, what made Big Per *Big Per* was his heft. Huge arms, the size of a girl's waist, were attached to shoulders an ax-handle wide. Beneath the shoulders was a barrel chest, and below that was a gut attempting to match the chest. Providing a foundation for this impressive assemblage of bone and muscle were two long legs requiring pants cut twice the normal size in the upper thighs. Big Per was the strongest man in Story County, perhaps in the state.

"Ole!" yelled Big Per in a tenor voice that was somewhat surprising in such a large man. "I see you're done plowing."

"Finished this afternoon," Ole called back with a grin, knowing full well what was coming next.

"You would have been done two days ago if you had used oxen."

Ole laughed. "Not with those two critters you're driving."

"Oh! Did you hear that boys? You're being insulted. But don't pay any mind to Ole. He's just a horse lover."

Oxen versus horses had been an ongoing, friendly argument since the two had become neighbors. They had liked each other from the first meeting, and the friendship had been cemented when Ole and Helena helped Per through the grief of losing his wife.

The oxen plodded into the farm yard and stopped without direction near the barn.

"Good afternoon, Per," Ole said.

"Good afternoon yourself, Ole," Big Per answered. He then grunted as he stepped from the wagon onto the front wheel and eased his massive bulk to the ground. "Getting old," he added.

Ole said, "Not you."

Big Per snorted. "My knees tell me I'm right and you're wrong. Mind if I water Buck and Pride?"

"Not at all. Can you stay for supper?"

"Supper?" Big Per said, scratching his full black beard as his brown eyes widened in feigned surprise. "Is it that late already?"

"Yes, it is," Ole answered, trying to keep from smiling. "So there is no sense for you going home to a cold stove and empty cabin."

"Well, if you insist."

"I do."

Both men laughed and Big Per slapped Ole lightly on the shoulder, driving the smaller man back a step. "You're a good man, Ole Branjord. I thank you."

Ole nodded and helped Big Per remove the yoke from "the boys." After watering the beasts, Per tied them to the wagon while Ole brought some hay.

"Well, let's get washed up," Ole said. "I don't know about you, but I'm hungry."

"Now that you mention it, so am I," Big Per replied, leading the way to the water tub.

The two men rolled up their sleeves and washed their hands, faces, and necks. Big Per was dressed identically to Ole in a gray homespun shirt and black pants. This was no surprise as Helena had made the shirt and pants for both. Martin came out of the barn carrying a half-full pail of milk just as the men finished up washing. He grinned. "Hello, Mr. Larson."

"Hello yourself, Martin. I see your pa has you milking."

Martin nodded as he held the pail up to Ole. "Papa, should I get the funnel?"

Before he could answer, Ole saw Berent come running from the cabin, funnel in one hand and milk pitcher in the other. "No need. Helena is sending your brother."

Big Per slowly shook his massive head. "I swear, Ole, that woman can read minds."

"I've known that for years." Ole grinned.

Berent came to a skidding stop. "Mama wants some cold milk for supper."

"I thought she might," Ole answered, taking the pitcher from Berent. He placed it on the ground, lifted the milk can from the cool water, and poured the milk into the pitcher. Before returning the can to the tub, he emptied the fresh milk from the pail into it. "Here," he said to Berent as he handed him the pitcher. "Do you think you can carry this to Mama without spilling?"

"Yes, Papa," Berent said, turning carefully toward the cabin.

"Wait a minute," Ole said. "You haven't said hello to Mr. Larson."

Berent stopped and looked over his shoulder. He eyed the huge man with more than a little fear. "Hello, Mr. Larson," he mumbled.

"Hello yourself, Mr. Branjord."

Berent turned around, a surprised look on his face. "I'm not Mr. Branjord. Papa is Mr. Branjord."

"You don't say," Big Per said, raising his heavy black eyebrows. "With that long beard of yours, I thought you were Mr. Branjord."

Martin giggled. Ole chuckled. Berent frowned. "I don't have a beard. Papa does."

"You don't? Well, I'll be a monkey's uncle!" Big Per scratched his beard. "Then this man is Mr. Branjord and you are Jacob."

"No!" Berent said, stomping his foot. "I'm Berent!"

Ole saw Berent's lower lip begin to quiver. "Mr. Larson knows who you are, Berent. He's just teasing you. Take the milk up to Mama."

Berent scowled as he walked to the cabin. Big Per grinned, revealing a missing front tooth. "He's a good one, Ole. Like his big brother here."

Martin blushed. He was not used to compliments. In the Norwegian community, a "not bad" was the best that could be expected for a job well done. Everyone knew getting the big head was a mortal sin.

"Thank you, Per." Ole said with pride, but did not add what he was thinking. *Indeed they are.* That would have been bragging. Instead, he slapped Big Per on the shoulder. "Let's eat!"

Chapter Five

Helena wiped the perspiration from her face before opening the oven door and removing the pan of johnnycake. She placed it on the back of the stove, where sausages sizzled in a cast-iron skillet.

"Mmmm, that smells good," Berent said, perched atop the large chest decorated with a rosemaling design.

"Yes, it does." Helena smiled.

Oline wrinkled up her nose. "It's a good thing. We have it enough."

Helena's smile vanished. "If you don't like it, young lady, you can go to bed without your supper!"

"I like it!" Oline said quickly, her stomach growling. "I just wish we wouldn't have it so often."

"Umph!" Helena muttered, thinking she too wished they would not have it so often. She also wished they ate less salt pork, cornmeal mush, buttermilk mush, sour milk mush, and all the other mushes! But at least their bellies were full, unlike in Hardin County. "Is the table set?"

"Yes, Mama."

Helena gave a quick glance at the table. The flatware, pewter mugs, and pewter plates were all in place. "You forgot the molasses."

"Oh, sorry," Oline replied, taking the pitcher from the sink and running it to the table just as Big Per, Ole, and Martin entered the cabin.

"I have brought a guest for supper," Ole said.

Big Per grinned, his hands behind his back. "Ole insisted I stay."

"Well, I should hope so!" Helena smiled. "You are most welcome, Mr. Larson."

"I thank you, Mrs. Branjord," Big Per said as he pulled a ten-pound bag of flour from behind his back. "And here is a little flour. I'm sure you can use it."

Helena clapped her hands. "Oh, Per, how thoughtful. I am almost out. Thank you."

Big Per's smile was so broad, his eyes crinkled. Pleasing Helena Branjord was a major joy in his life. He actually blushed. The big man had always been somewhat shy around beautiful women, and to him, Helena Branjord was a beauty. "You are most welcome. Maybe you can bake me biscuits sometime."

"I'll do that right after supper. You can take them home with you. Now, sit down and eat before everything gets cold."

While Helena brought the food to the table, the children took their places on the bench, Ole pulled his chair up to the table, and Big Per sat on two of the stools across from the children. When Helena was seated in her chair opposite Ole, she looked at the children. "Say blessings."

Everyone bowed their heads. The children said in unison, "Bless this food, oh Lord, that thou hast so bountifully provided us. Amen."

The adults added their "Amen" and the eating began. Conversation was limited to "please pass" and "could I have some more." Within minutes, the johnnycake and the heap of sausage patties resided in six contented stomachs.

"Ah, Mrs. Branjord, that was delicious," Big Per said. "Many thanks for the meal."

Helena blushed slightly. "You are welcome, Mr. Larson."

"Indeed, it was delicious." Ole nodded with pride. "I do believe you make the best johnnycake in Story County."

"Mama makes the best johnnycake in the whole world!" Berent said, turning to his mother. "But we ran out of molasses."

The three adults looked at the boy and burst out laughing.

"That is because most of it is on your face," Big Per said.

"It is not," Berent replied, putting both hands over his face.

Helena quickly grabbed the boy's arms. "Don't touch anything!" She then wiped his face and hands with a damp washcloth, which had been placed on the table for this very purpose. "There! That's better."

"Mr. Larson," Martin said, "Andrew told me in school that his papa's wagon got stuck in a slough yesterday and you lifted it out."

"Oh, it was nothing," Big Per replied. "The back wheels were in the slough. I just lifted and the horses pulled the wagon out."

Berent looked in awe at the big man. "Papa says you're the strongest man in the whole world."

"Does he now?" Big Per said, scratching his beard. "Well, I've heard there is someone stronger than me."

"Who?" the children said in unison.

Big Per looked at each child before saying, "A fellow named Berent Branjord."

Oline and Martin groaned. Berent clapped his hands and laughed. "I'm not strong like you."

"I think you need to prove that. Let's arm wrestle."

Berent grinned from ear to ear as he crawled over Oline to stand opposite Big Per. The plates and mugs were moved and Big Per placed his right elbow on the table. Berent immediately grabbed Big Per's hand in both of his and began pulling. Grunts and growls came from both participants.

"Pull, Berent!" Martin yelled.

Big Per's arm began to move back. Oline became excited. "Pull harder!"

Berent's face became red with effort, but the big arm refused to budge. Then slowly, the arm moved forward into a vertical position. "Help me!" Berent cried. Martin and Oline grabbed hold of Big Per's arm, almost tipping over the pitcher of milk, which Ole rescued and held. The children strained, but Big Per's arm remained as straight as the trunk of an elm. The children were panting when, with seemingly little effort, the arm moved forward until it touched the table.

The children groaned. Big Per laughed. "You kids are getting stronger."

"Oh, they're strong enough." Ole smiled. "Except when there is work to be done."

"Speaking of work," Helena said, "you three can help me clean up and wash the dishes."

The children sighed as the adults stood up. Ole picked up his pipe and tobacco from the mantel over the fireplace. Big Per pulled the same from his pocket, and the two men walked out onto the porch. They were greeted with early twilight, the sun nothing but a huge orange ball in a nearly cloudless sky.

Both men sat on the bench to the left of the door, lit their pipes, and puffed in contented silence. There was neither need nor desire for conversation. The work of the day was completed, a soft breeze promised a gentle night and a sparkling tomorrow, and their stomachs were full. What more could two men ask?

After nearly ten minutes, Big Per emptied the dead ashes from his pipe. "Ole, when are you going to break those two acres of prairie to the west?"

"I figure right after threshing."

"August is hot."

"I know. But there is no good time to break sod. Will six oxen be enough?"

"We'd be better off with eight. I've got four and I'm sure we can get Ben Lura's four."

Ole nodded, knocking the ashes from his pipe. "A fellow told me they were using ten teams north and west of here."

"Ahhh," Big Per snorted. "I've heard that too. But I'd have to see it to believe it. How can you control twenty oxen?"

"I have no idea." Ole laughed. "You're the oxen man."

"If they were using ten teams, they were breaking ground with horses, not oxen," Big Per said. He was about to continue when he saw a ragged gray animal come from behind the crib and carefully advance to the cabin. "Well, I see the ugly beast is right on time."

"And I'm glad of it," Ole replied. "He is the best watchdog in Story County."

"He's more wolf than dog," Big Per muttered as he refilled his pipe. "I tell you, Ole, one day he'll turn on you and kill every small animal on the place."

"I don't think so. He's been guarding the farm every night for over a year."

"Where does he go in the day time?" Big Per asked, lighting his pipe.

"Don't know. He's always gone by sun up."

The large, scruffy wolf-dog lay down about twenty feet from the men and put his scarred face between his front paws.

Big Per asked, "Have you touched him yet?"

"No, and I don't ever expect to," Ole answered as he lit his pipe and recalled the animal's arrival.

Three-year-old Berent had announced the event on a warm spring day. "Doggie!" the boy cried from the cabin door, then ran toward the barn. Helena quickly followed. What she saw was the back of a long-haired, gray animal lying on its side about ten feet from the artesian well. "Don't touch the doggie, Berent!" she ordered.

Berent paid no attention. "Nice doggie," he said, gently petting the matted fur.

"Berent! Step back! The doggie might bite you."

The tone of his mother's voice made the boy retreat. Helena warily circled what she thought was a dog. "Shoo!" she yelled. "Go away!"

The animal remained still. Helena stepped closer, believing the beast was dead. But as she approached, the eyelids opened and the unmistakable yellow eyes of a wolf glared at her.

"Oh!" Helena cried, stepping back. The animal attempted to rise, but fell back with a whimper.

"Oh, dear Lord," Helena said.

"Doggie sick, Mama?"

Helena nodded. "Yes, Berent. Doggie is sick."

"Mama make him better?"

"No, I don't think so."

Helena could now see the wolf-dog had been in a tremendous fight. Blood saturated his coat and chunks of flesh hung like flaps from his side. What should she do? She wished Ole was home, but he and the two older children had taken freshly churned butter to the store in Fairview, two miles north. Tears came to Helena's eyes. She hated to see anything suffer.

As Helena stood frozen, Berent walked to the well, picked up an old, round pan, dipped it into the tub, and carried the water back to the animal. Although he spilled most of it, he set what remained in front of the wolf-dog. "Doggie thirsty," Berent said.

Helena looked at her son with amazement and thought, "Why didn't I think of that?"

Berent knelt down in front of the wolf-dog. "Doggie drink," he said.

The animal raised his head, looking into the eyes of the little boy. Berent smiled. "Doggie drink," he repeated as he pushed the pan under the wolf-dog's powerful jaws. Helena's eyes widened with fear, but the massive head lowered and a parched tongue began lapping up the water.

Helena watched for a moment, then ran to the barn, where she picked up a discarded grain sack. She soaked it in the tub and spread it over the wolf-dog's wounds. "There. That should cool you a little."

"Mama fix doggie." Berent grinned.

"Mama will try," Helena replied. "You get him some more water."

While Berent filled the pan, Helena retrieved ointment from the cabin and spent the next hour cleaning and salving the wounds. The wolf-dog appeared to understand that these two creatures were attempting to help him. He lay still and only growled once.

When Ole arrived home, his first reaction was to put the animal out of its misery; however, the children's pleading and the tears in Helena's eyes put a quick end to that idea. Actually, he took little convincing. First, he hated to kill a helpless animal, and second, he was convinced the wolf-dog would die without any help from him.

The next morning, Ole discovered the animal was not only alive, but able to snarl at him when he attempted to refill the water pan. The wolf-dog also snarled at Oline and Martin. Only Helena and Berent were able to touch him. They repeated their roles of the previous day and presented him with scraps of salt pork. Berent petted him and said, "He is a nice doggie, Mama."

"Yes." Helena smiled. "He is a nice doggie. A little ugly, but a nice doggie."

It was at this moment that the wolf-dog mix, a beast who would strike fear in the hearts of animals and men alike, received the unlikely name of "Doggie." For a week, Helena and Berent nursed and fed Doggie. Ole became more worried each day the beast became stronger. He was about to forbid any more contact, when Doggie disappeared. Berent cried, but the rest of the family, including Helena, were relieved.

That was the end of the story, or so Ole thought, until one evening a few weeks later when Berent went running from the cabin. "Doggie! Doggie!" he cried. Ole and Helena leaped from their chairs but could only watch as Berent threw his arms around the wolf-dog's neck. Doggie responded by licking Berent's face. The boy giggled. "Doggie back!" Helena ran back into the cabin and returned with a leftover piece of ham, which she held out to the animal. Doggie licked her hand before snatching the meat.

Doggie's coat was still scruffy, but the numerous bites had healed, and he had gained weight and strength. The patient had not only survived, but flourished. His tail wagged furiously until Oline attempted to pet him. Fangs were exposed, accompanied by a deep snarl.

"Stay back!" Ole warned. "He's adopted Mama and Berent, not the rest of us."

"Will he ever like me?" Oline asked, stepping back to her father's side.

"Maybe not. He's a wild animal," Ole answered. Fear and worry mounted as he looked at the beast. There was little doubt Doggie was capable of killing every animal on the place, to say nothing of the humans who shared their lives.

However, in the weeks and months that followed, Doggie became the farm's protector, not destroyer. He never allowed anyone but Helena and Berent to touch him, but it became obvious he considered the entire family part of his pack. Each night he would arrive at dusk, circle the farmstead, and mark the territory as his. When the sun rose, he was gone. During the time of Doggie's watchful presence, not so much as one chicken had been lost to predators.

Big Per puffed on his pipe, staring at Doggie. Not much frightened the big man, but he had to admit the animal's yellow eyes sent chills down his spine. Berent came out of the cabin carrying a plateful of table scraps and salt pork. "Hi, Doggie. Here's your supper."

Doggie rose and wagged his tail. The boy set the plate on the ground and hugged his friend. Big Per pounded the ashes from his pipe, spat out some tobacco juice, and put the pipe in his pocket. "Ole, have you ever tried spanking Berent when that beast is around?"

Ole chuckled. "I may be blockheaded Norwegian, but I'm not that dumb."

"I didn't think so," Big Per said, standing up from the bench.

The instant Big Per moved, Doggie stopped eating, his body tensed, and his ears went flat against his head. He glared at Big Per, who responded in kind. "Don't you give me that look, beast. I'm just leaving." Per's eyes softened as he turned his attention to Berent. "Take good care of your Mama and Papa, Mr. Branjord."

"I'm not Mr. Branjord," Berent replied, hands on hips. "I'm Berent!"

"Oh, that's right. I keep forgetting." Big Per laughed as he took a circular route away from Doggie and walked to his oxen. Ole followed and helped hitch the oxen to the wagon. Big Per was clamping on Buck's yoke when Oline came running with a basket of freshly baked biscuits. "Don't forget these!"

"Thank you, Oline," Big Per said, taking the basket. "And thank your mama. I'll think of both of you when I enjoy them."

Oline smiled and dashed back to the cabin.

Both men watched her run. Big Per said, "She getting more like Helena every day."

"I know. And thank God for it. I wouldn't want her to look like me."

"Amen to that!" Per said as he placed the basket on the wagon seat.

"Are you going up to the ford?" Ole asked, knowing the answer.

"Bah! Fords are for horses." Big Per snorted. "With Buck and Pride, I can cross the Skunk most anyplace I want."

"Well, you be careful. I don't relish having to harness my horses just to pull you out of the river."

"That will be a cold day in hell," Big Per said, climbing into the wagon. Buck and Pride did not wait for a command to go. "Thank Helena again for supper."

"I'll do that," Ole called. "And next time bring your violin."

Big Per waved. Ole walked to the cabin.

Helena

Ole is asleep. How does he do it? He's asleep as soon as his head touches the pillow. He can ask me a question and be asleep before I finish the answer. I'm just the opposite. I stare into the dark for at least half an hour before falling to sleep. But I'm not staring into the dark tonight. There must be a full moon. I think I could sit by the window and read.

Ole is snoring. Not a big, nasty snore; it's more like a low purr. I don't mind his snoring. It actually helps me get to sleep. I find it comforting. Maybe he sleeps so well because he works so hard. Ole's not as big as some, but nobody outworks him. Not even Big Per can outwork him.

Poor Big Per. He is so lonely. But there is little chance of him finding a new wife. Women are in short supply. I don't even know a single woman over twenty, and no young woman is going to be interested in a man nearly fifty. Oh, wait! I forgot about Frida. But Per isn't that lonely!

He needs a woman, though. Sometimes he looks at me like I'm a piece of sugar taffy. It's good he is such a sweet, gentle thing. He could be scary if he were not. Maybe God will provide a nice woman for him. Dear Lord, if it be thy will, find a good woman for Per. Now, I don't want some poor man to die just so Per can marry his widow. But if he is going to die anyway, Per is a good person. You think about it. Thy will be done. Amen.

"Mama?"

"What is it, Berent?"

"Oline rolled over on me."

"I'm sure she didn't mean it. Go back to sleep."

There is silence for a moment, but I know what is coming next.

"Mama, can I sleep with you and Papa?"

I am right. "No, Berent. You're too big for that."

"Please?"

Ole opens one eye. "What's the matter?"

"It's Berent. He wants to sleep with us."

"Again?" He rolls over and props himself up on his elbow. "Berent, go to sleep! Hear me?"

"Yes, Papa."

Ole plops back on the bed and is immediately snoring. There is silence. Berent wanting to sleep with us started about a month ago. He had a bad dream and I made the mistake of letting him come down from the loft. Another mistake. Why do I make so many mistakes with my children? Why can't I be like my mother? Oh, Mama, after all these years, I still miss you. Rest in peace. I wonder how my sister is doing? Her letter in March said everything was fine. But I could tell it had been a hard winter. I hope they had enough to eat. It could not be as bad as the year I left. Whole families starved that winter. Poor Finland. Poor, beautiful Finland. Will I ever see it again? Will I ever see my sister again? Not likely. Stop crying, Helena! You have it so much better than she does.

Why can't I get to sleep? It is so stupid to lie here awake. If it is so stupid, Helena, then get up!

I slip out of bed and walk to the door, hoping Berent has gone back to sleep. There is no sound from the loft, so I open the door, snatching my cape as I walk out onto the porch. The air is cold. I wrap the cape around me and stare at the moon. It appears to be so close. When I was small, Papa told me that if I went out of the house at night when there was a full moon, the moon would fall and crush me. I grip the cape more tightly. It is silly, but I am still a little afraid to be outside when the moon is full. Then why am I standing here?

I am about to go back inside the cabin when I feel something brush my leg. It is Doggie. He sits on his haunches and I scratch behind his ears. "How do you sneak up on a person like that, Doggie? At times, you are downright scary."

He answers me by backing up a few steps. He just lets me touch him for a short time. Only Berent can treat him like a normal dog. Berent can hug him, lie on him, and even pull his hair, for which I am grateful, especially since Berent has started this hiding business.

"Do you watch Berent during the day? I never see you, but I'll bet you are not too far away. I just wish you were as protective of the other two."

Doggie opens his mouth as if he is smiling. He has done this many times, and I always return his smile with one of my own. It's foolish, I know. But it does seem to please him.

I look up at the moon and shiver. I now realize why I can't sleep. It was this time of year. The moon was full. It was cold. Oh, so cold. I was holding her in my arms. She was so small. I hugged her. She looked up at me and … stopped breathing.

No! I will not think of Nettie! There is too much work to do!

I hurry back into the cabin, but do not go to bed. I open the big chest and pull out my box. It is a small box, made of dark wood, given to me as a child by my father. In it I keep my treasures. Not that there are many. I take the box to my rocking chair and sit. I look down at the painted flower on the top. It is my one and only attempt at the art of rosemaling. I'm afraid it is rather a poor attempt, although Mrs. Lessing praised me. Maybe when the children are older, I can try again.

I open the box. I see the *solje* Ole gave me, a brooch that belonged to my mother, a large comb for my hair, two colorful glass necklaces that I'm too embarrassed to wear, a pair of black leather dress gloves that I hope someday to wear, and a lock of soft blond baby hair tied with a pink ribbon. Nettie's hair. My most prized treasure.

Oh, Nettie. You were so small.

Chapter Six

Ole drove Doll and Lady up to the door of the cabin. "Hurry up or we'll be late for church," he called from the driver's seat of the wagon. He was wearing his black suit. Actually, his only suit. Ole was quite proud of the suit, even though the seat of the pants and the elbows of the coat were shiny and worn. He had married Helena in this suit. It was the only one he had ever owned.

The two boys raced from the cabin; Martin was dressed in a white cotton shirt and black pants, and Berent was wearing a light green cotton dress that reached his ankles. Both were barefoot. Martin ran past Berent, jumped up on the rear wheel, and hopped into the wagon. "I won!" he cried.

"You cheat!" Berent wailed.

"I do not! I gave you a head start."

"Not a big enough one. And you wouldn't beat me all the time if I had pants."

Berent began to climb up the wheel but was stopped by his father. "Come up front, Berent. I'll help you up."

Berent walked to the front. Ole reached down and swung the boy up into the wagon. Berent grinned. "That was fun, Papa."

Ole smiled. "You are getting so big I won't be able to do that much longer."

Helena and Oline walked from the cabin, each wearing a dress of blue. Oline's was a powder blue, Helena's more a royal. Helena also wore a matching bonnet and her only pair of leather shoes. Unmistakable pride filled Ole's eyes. Oline was getting prettier every day, and Helena was beautiful. Even after giving birth to four children, she had a figure that made men look twice.

"It shows, Mama," Oline grumbled. "Everyone will see it."

"Well, everyone saw you tear it last Sunday," Helena replied. "I sewed it the best I could."

"What's wrong? Ole asked.

"Oline tore her dress last Sunday playing tag after the service," Helena answered, helping her daughter climb into the wagon.

"The dress looks fine to me," Ole said.

Oline sank down into the straw. "Oh, Papa! Everything looks fine to you. Mama, can't you make me a new one?"

"Next winter," Helena said as she walked around to the front of the wagon. She held out her hand and Ole helped her up to the seat. Ole marveled. Helena even looked graceful climbing into a wagon.

"Thank you, Mr. Branjord." Helena smiled.

"You are most welcome, Mrs. Branjord," Ole replied with a bow of his head.

Both laughed.

Oline was still pouting. "I'll bet Elsa has five new dresses. Why do her folks have so much money?"

Ole slapped the reins, putting Doll and Lady into motion toward the stage road. "Because her grandfather owns a bank in Norway, that's why."

The trip to Saint Petri Lutheran Church took the Branjords north past the settlement of Fairview, across the Skunk River at the ford, and then back south and a mile east to the church.

Saint Petri sat atop a small hill overlooking the river. Constructed in 1864, the white frame building glistened beneath the late morning sun. It had five arched windows on each side and a bell tower, on which was a high steeple. The church was surrounded by a white picket fence and was by far the tallest building in north Story County. The settlers were rightly proud of their church. All had sacrificed money, time, and talent to build it.

The churchyard was filled with wagons disgorging families, who streamed into the building. The church could seat four hundred and, on most Sundays, was nearly full.

Ole pulled Doll and Lady to a halt beside Big Per's oxen. The children scrambled out while Ole tied the horses to the rear wheel of Per's wagon. There was no way Buck and Pride were going to move until their owner forced them to. He then helped Helena down from the seat and felt the tension in her body. He knew the reason why. He felt the tension himself. "Maybe things will be better this week," he said.

Helena sighed. "I doubt it. I'm almost afraid to talk to anyone."

"I know. It is such a shame."

Helena took Ole's arm and they walked to the church door. There were smiles, waves, and softly spoken greetings, but no hugs or kisses. Norwegians avoided public shows of affection. The procession into church was a reverent, almost stately affair. Sadly, included with the smiles, greetings, and waves were the frowns, furtive glances, and questioning looks of a congregation about to come apart.

Inside, Ole and Helena separated, Ole joining the sea of black coats sitting on the right, and Helena and the children sitting with Julia Twedt and her brood on the left. Julia smiled and pulled four-year-old Joseph to the far side of her. Experience had taught her and Helena to keep as much distance as possible between Berent and Joseph. What mischief one could not think of, the other could. The two boys waved and grinned, as if plotting what they would do after the service. Julia turned Joseph's face forward.

Julia was a quiet, pretty woman of thirty-one, but her lined face and black winter dress made her look older. Helena thought, "It is no wonder she looks tired. She is stepmother to two and mother to five." Two-year-old Sam snuggled next to her. One-year-old Carl sat sucking his thumb on her lap. Stepdaughter Hattie, thirteen, sat to her right, then eight-year-old Abel and seven-year-old Jane. Helena could not even imagine the problems of raising seven children in a small cabin.

"I want to sit next to Able," Martin whispered.

"No, you know the order," Helena replied, seating Berent to her right and Martin and Oline to her left. Oline sat by Jane, which the seven-year-old enjoyed, but secretly Jane would have liked to sit next to Martin.

With the children settled, Helena glanced across the aisle. Ole was sitting by Big Per. In the same pew were Hans Twedt, Julia's husband; his son, fifteen-year-old Ole; John Mehus; Paul Thompson; and the Sheldahl brothers, Lars and Rasmus. The men sat placidly, deep in their own thoughts. Helena diverted her eyes to the picture of Christ rising from the tomb on Easter Sunday, which hung behind the altar, and ground her teeth. It was not fair that women had to deal with the children by themselves. Men sitting on the right and women on the left was a custom brought from Norway, and it was a custom the women of Saint Petri were petitioning to change. The Yankees sat as families in their churches, so why should not the Norwegians? It was good for families to worship together. And the children always behaved better when their fathers were in arms' reach.

Helena calmed herself by studying the painting of Christ rising from the tomb, which served as a focal point and a constant reminder that Jesus was core of the Christian faith. Helena could not judge the painting as art, but did feel the power of the artist's depiction. Here was her Lord, the God who loved her, rising from the grave, conquering death, and saving her from her sins. Looking upon the painting always sent shivers down her spine. But today, the feeling of elation quickly faded. The painting had become another bone of contention. To some, it was too fancy, too high church.

Surrounding the picture was a carved walnut frame made by Reverend Amlund, who also had constructed the altar rail and the pulpit out of matching wood. All agreed the end result was stunning and a source of pride. It was further agreed that if Reverend Amlund decided to leave the ministry, he could make a good living as a cabinetmaker.

Inga Lyngen, dressed in a beautifully made yellow cotton dress and matching bonnet, rose from her chair and crossed to the pump organ, where she began to play the prelude. Helena relaxed and smiled. She loved the organ, but knew others did not. For some it was too expensive and too high church. Helena thought the music was the best part of the service. So did Oline, who was half standing so she could see Inga's hands float across the keys.

Inga was a striking young woman in her late twenties. Unlike many Norwegians, she had dark hair and brown eyes. She was talented, bright, sweet, and lived in a large frame home just outside Fairview. Had it not been for her husband, every woman in the congregation would have envied her. As it was, they only felt pity.

There was a commotion in the back by the door. Helena did not turn her head. She knew who it was. Her hands clenched into fists. Emil and Hanna Signaldahl and their daughter, Elsa, were making their grand entrance.

The prelude had become the cue for the Signaldahls to parade down the aisle and take seats in the front pews. On the right, men elbowed each other and tried not to smile, while on the left, whispers followed the latecomers as they passed like a carpet being unrolled. Hanna smiled and nodded as she proceeded toward the front, much like a queen entering her court. The only thing missing was the royal wave.

The whispers mostly concerned Hanna's dress. The color and fabric of the dress were unusual, even for Hanna. The high-necked, long-sleeved dress was a deep forest green and made of silk. Without a doubt, a person could count on one hand the number of silk dresses in Story County, and Hanna had two of them.

Helena tried not to look as Hanna swished by, but could not resist a quick peek. The peek became a stare. The dress was beautifully made and draped elegantly over Hanna's tall, slender frame. It was complemented by a matching green bonnet, high-top leather shoes, and a cameo brooch. Despite her best efforts, envy as green as the dress crept into Helena's soul. It was a feeling shared by every woman in the church. In fact, if envy had had actual weight and the church had been a ship, the vessel would have listed badly to port.

However, the ship was brought back to a nearly even keel when Hanna turned back and smiled at the women. Her expensive apparel could not offset the narrow-set, pale blue eyes, angular face, and long nose. Hanna was in calling distance of being homely.

Elsa quickly followed her mother into the pew and sat. She was a stoop-shouldered girl of twelve, with long blond hair and lovely deep brown eyes. While not a beauty, she would never face the taunts of "Horse-Face" her mother had experienced as a child. In cattier moments, women of the community had been known to say Elsa was lucky she did not resemble either parent. The girl was wearing a pastel pink dress with a bow in back and a matching bow in her hair. Unlike every other child in the church, she had on black leather shoes.

Emil sat stiffly in the front pew across from his wife and daughter. He was two inches shorter than Hanna, so he wore double-heeled boots to make up some of the difference. His black suit was new and pressed, his thinning blond hair was neatly cut, and his mutton-chop whiskers were carefully trimmed.

The Signaldahls were the wealthiest members of Saint Petri Church, and Hanna made a point of never allowing anyone to forget it. They owned over two hundred acres several miles north of Fairview, most of it under cultivation. The farm was considered a showplace. It had the latest in farm implements and required two full-time hired men. A hired girl was usually employed as well, but, due to Hanna's temper and demands, never stayed long.

Why Emil and Hanna had emigrated to the United States was a mystery and a popular subject of conversation. They came from the same area of northern Norway as Ole and Helena, but had arrived two years before the Branjords. What was known (because Hanna constantly spoke of it) was that Hanna was the daughter of a wealthy banker and Emil had been employed in the bank. This made them prominent people in Norway, and prominent people seldom sold everything and moved to the prairies of Iowa. But come they had, and were obviously highly successful.

Ole looked over at his wife and was relieved to see the clenched fists had become folded hands. The enmity between the two women had begun back in Norway, where Helena had been employed as a cook's helper and dairymaid by Hanna's aunt. Ole did not know much more than that, as Helena refused to talk about the experience. But he had gleaned that Hanna had hated his wife at first sight and caused her endless trouble. He knew the reason why. Helena was beautiful. In Hanna's well-ordered world of privilege, servant girls were plain and the daughters of the rich were beautiful. Unable to take the abuse any longer, Helena quit and went to work for the Lessing family, who, as luck would have it, also employed one Ole Branjord.

The prelude ended and Reverend Amlund rose from his chair. He was a tall, elegant man with wavy black hair, deep-set blue eyes, and a perfectly proportioned nose. A full beard, still without a hint of gray, added to his formidability. In 1860, before his marriage and Call, he had visited the settlement, causing numerous fantasies and unchaste thoughts to be born behind the pious eyes of certain left-side congregant members. Not all of these fantasies had died, and there was no doubt unchaste thoughts could still arise, often at the most awkward times, such as the opening of worship.

Reverend Amlund stood before the congregation wearing the vestments of the Norwegian Lutheran Church: a long black robe and a pleated white ruff around his neck that every woman, with the exception of Mrs. Amlund, was happy she did not have to iron. Mrs. Amlund was not thrilled with the job, either. Reverend Amlund was well aware his clerical garb was one reason for the tension now permeating each Sunday service like a constant toothache. But he was not about to give in to those who believed the vestments to be a "high church affectation."

Reverend Amlund raised his arms. The congregation stood. "In the name of the Father, Son, and Holy Ghost," he intoned in his rich baritone.

"Amen," came the response.

"Let us confess our sins," Reverend Amlund said, then turned to face the altar. "Most merciful God, we confess that we are by nature sinful and unclean. We have sinned against you in thought, word, and deed, by what we have done and by what we have left undone. We have not loved you with our whole heart; we have not loved our neighbors as ourselves. We justly deserve your present and eternal punishment. For the sake of your Son, Jesus Christ, have mercy on us. Forgive us, renew us, and lead us, so that we may delight in your will and walk in yours ways in the glory of your holy name. Amen."

Reverend Amlund turned to the congregation, which held its collective breath. It was time for the absolution. Nothing, not even the vestments, had become as controversial as the absolution. Ole noted the strong farmer hands gripping the back of the pew. Some were white-knuckled.

"Almighty God in his mercy has given his Son to die for you, and for his sake forgives you all your sins. As a called and ordained servant of the Word, I therefore forgive you all your sins in the name of the Father and the Son and the Holy Spirit."

There was a second or two of silence, then about three-fourths of the people said, "Amen."

Reverend Amlund again faced the altar and the liturgy continued. The white-knuckled hands relaxed. The moment of crisis had passed for another Sunday. Ole slowly shook his head. He did not understand this uproar over the absolution. The same words had been uttered for centuries, but only recently had become a lightning rod. Ole wished the controversy would just go away.

A hymn was sung, after which Reverend Amlund approached the pulpit. Tension again filled the church like an invisible fog. Feet shuffled. Mothers shushed small children. Would Reverend Amlund address the growing rift or ignore it? Most hoped for the latter. Open conflict would force hard decisions, decisions that only a few wanted to make. Most, like Ole, wanted the whole mess to disappear.

"The text for today's sermon is taken from the Gospel of John, chapter ten, verses eleven to fourteen," Reverend Amlund began. "I am the good shepherd. The good shepherd lays down his life for his sheep. He who is a hireling and not a shepherd, whose own the sheep are not, sees the wolf coming and leaves the sheep and flees; and the wolf snatches them and scatters them. He flees because he cares nothing for the sheep. I am the good shepherd. I know my own and mine own know me."

Reverend Amlund looked up from the Bible. "Christ as the Good Shepherd is one of our most cherished images. This image is especially vivid for those of us who raise livestock. We have seen firsthand what happens to a stray, unprotected animal. We have witnessed what wolves can do when a lamb or calf is separated from the group. Once the separation has taken place, the animal cannot be saved.

"What is Jesus telling us in these verses? He is saying he is our shepherd. We are his sheep. He loves us. He will lay down his life for us. He will die on the cross so that we will be saved from our sins. He is gathering us all together at the foot of the cross so that he can protect us from the devil. His love for us is incomprehensible to our mortal minds.

"When Jesus compared himself to the good shepherd, he knew his days on this earth were short. He knew his road led to Calvary. He knew he would die and on the third day rise again. Why then did he say these words? He was preparing his disciples to be shepherds, preparing them to spread the Gospel, to proclaim the good news, to gather the faithful together into congregations of believers where they could grow in their service to him."

Reverend Amlund smiled, spreading his arms. "And they succeeded! Christianity spread like a prairie fire across the Mediterranean world. But from the beginning there were problems. False prophets arose. They twisted the gospel. Some said Jesus was not God. Others said Jesus not a true man. Fierce arguments raged as to what being a Christian really meant. Theological battles were fought, and out of these battles came the creeds we say each Sunday. Out of these battles came the canon, the books we collectively call the Holy Bible. And out of these battles came the church.

"Christ ordained men to lead his church; to preach the good news; to protect the church from false prophets. These men were to be shepherds, not dictators. Have those called into the ministry always been faithful? Sadly, no. Our own Lutheran denomination was born because of the failures of popes and bishops. But, Martin Luther did not throw out the clergy. Instead, he demanded the clergy turn its back on worldly power and return to being shepherds.

"The Lutheran clergy has struggled with this order from Luther's time to our own. We, the clergy, must be shepherds; yet we also must protect the faith from false prophets. And make no mistake: there are false prophets today just as there were back in the early church. Protecting the church requires authority. Just as Christ gave authority to his disciples, the church gives authority to the clergy. To lead, whether in the military, or business, or the church, or even running our own farms, requires the use of power. It is the misuse of power that causes all the problems.

"I am sure that every adult in this congregation can tell stories about ministers in Norway who were seduced by power and went from being shepherds to being judges and dictators. Great harm and distress has been caused by these men. But we must not allow the good done by many to overshadow the evil done by a few.

"Reverend Rasmussen came to you in 1857 from Lisbon, Illinois. You asked for a pastor. He went back to Norway, and I accepted the call to serve this congregation. Together we have grown. Together we have built the edifice in which we now worship. Together we will continue to prosper and spread the good news in this new land.

"We must not allow wolves in sheep's clothing to scatter us. We must not allow disagreements to separate us. What we must do is huddle close to the Good Shepherd, who loves and cares for each and every one of us. Amen."

Reverend Amlund left the pulpit and sat. The congregation was stunned. Usually, the sermon lasted at least an hour, often longer. Mrs. Lyngen hurried from her chair to the organ. Pumping furiously, she began to play the after-sermon hymn.

The rest of the service went quickly, after which the members of Saint Petri stepped out into the warm noonday sun. Children broke free of their mothers, screaming with delight and generally acting like young colts that had been too long in a stall. The segregation of the sexes continued. Women gathered in groups, laughing and catching up on the week's happenings. For most, it was the only time they had to talk with other adult females.

Helena and Julia were joined by Martha Karina Tjernagel, who was carrying one-year-old Nehemise and holding the hand of four-year-old Peder Gustav.

"I want to play with Berent and Joseph," Peder cried.

"All right," Martha said, releasing the boy. "Don't get dirty," she added as the boy raced away.

"You're wasting your breath, Martha." Julia laughed.

Helena nodded. "Telling a four-year-old boy to stay clean is hopeless."

"I know," Martha sighed. She was a tall woman who looked older than her twenty-three years. Her brown hair was parted in the middle and pulled back in a severe bun, which accented the hard lines of an angular face. Although plain, she would have been more attractive with a softer hairdo. However, soft was not a word used to describe Martha Tjernagel. She could do a man's work in the field and spoke her mind in no uncertain terms. A person learned never to ask Martha's opinion unless she really wanted it. There was little sugarcoating. Yet Helena knew her to be kind, loving, and a true friend. "Did you two have a good week?" Martha asked.

"The usual," Julia answered. "Cooked, cleaned, washed, scrubbed, and chased after little ones."

"The same," Helena said.

"My, we do lead exciting lives," Martha said. All three women laughed.

Julia said, "I did get to Nevada on Thursday."

"You did!" Martha and Helena said together.

"Yes. My, how the town has grown. There is a new store going up that will sell nothing but women's clothes."

"No!" Helena said.

"That's what they said. Can you imagine just walking into a store and buying a dress?"

"No, I can't," Martha said. "Nor can I imagine having the money to do it."

The three women nodded. Having money to buy anything was an event. "Well," Helena said, "If I save my butter money, maybe I can buy one in, say … twenty years."

They laughed again. There would be no store-bought dresses for the three of them.

Chapter Seven

Their husbands were not laughing. Ole and Big Per were in a serious conversation with Hans Twedt, Ole Andreas Tjernagel, Saul Jaeran, Jacob Jacobson, and Jonas Duea.

"I'm telling you," Saul Jaeran snapped, his pale, narrow-set eyes bulging, "one day I'm going to challenge Amlund when he gives the absolution! What right does he have to forgive my sins?"

Ole Andreas shook his well-shaped head. He was a tall man of thirty-three, with blue eyes, broad shoulders, and thick brown hair. "He's an ordained minister."

"Does that make him God?" Saul asked, standing on his tiptoes, his voice rising. Even on his tiptoes, he was a good ten inches shorter than Ole Andreas. "Only Jesus can forgive my sins!"

"Reverend Amlund was just reading the liturgy," Ole Branjord said. "That's the way it has been for hundreds of years."

"And it's wrong! The liturgy just gives power to the clergy!"

"Now, Saul," Big Per said softly, "there's no need to shout."

"Per's right," Jacob Jacobson said in his low rumbling voice. His full, salt and pepper beard reached down to a broad chest and covered a thoughtful oval face. At forty-eight years old, he was one of the church's senior members. "We have more than enough shouting."

"Are you disagreeing with me, Jacob?" Saul asked, looking up at the taller man.

"No, I'm just saying we don't need to shout. What we have to do is convince Reverend Amlund to change the service."

Jonas Duea, a thin, slightly stooped man of forty-five with a thick mustache and drooping eyelids, kicked at a rock with his boot. "The chances of that are slim and none. Lars Sheldahl talked to him on Friday, and he wouldn't budge. He said he was an ordained minister of the Norwegian Lutheran Church, and he would continue to read the liturgy."

"That is just what I would expect." Saul snorted. "He's a young fool!"

Hans Twedt scowled, his blue eyes flashing. "Reverend Amlund is not a fool, Saul. He's a good man attempting to keep this congregation from tearing itself apart."

Saul pointed his finger at Hans, tapping him on the chest. "Then why won't he do what the congregation wants?"

Hans stepped back, his face flushed, his large hands clenched, his nearly six-foot frame coiled. Saul immediately took two steps back. Forty-two-year-old Hans Twedt was not a man to anger. The community knew him as a pious, hardworking, and caring man, but it also was well known that he had a quick temper and little patience. "Don't you point your finger at me, Saul Jaeran," Hans said, in a low voice coated with ice. He then took a deep breath and continued. "The answer to your question is that the congregation is split. Many want to keep the liturgy."

"And you are one of them," Saul accused.

"Yes, I am," Hans said, trying to stay calm. "I enjoy it. I don't know why. I … I find it comforting."

"Comforting?" Jonas asked with surprise.

"Yes."

Ole Branjord nodded. "That's a good word, Hans. It's the way I feel too."

"I don't understand," Jacob said. "To me, it's just high church mumbo jumbo."

"I agree," Jonas said.

"It is more than that!" Saul stated, again waving his finger. "The liturgy gives the clergy power. This is all about power and creating a state church!"

Ole Andreas folded his arms. "There can't be a state church in America. The Constitution says so."

Saul snorted. "That's just a piece of paper. Mark my words. The Norwegian Church is doing everything it can to control us here just like it did in Norway. Power! It is all about power!"

"I think you're wrong, Saul," Ole Branjord said. "Reverend Amlund isn't interested in power. He's too busy serving the north half of Story County."

"Oh, no?" Saul answered, waving his finger under Ole's nose. "Then why does he still use the liturgy? Why is he the only one who can give communion? Why won't he allow lay preaching? Why does he still wear that fancy high church robe and collar? Answer me that, Ole Branjord!"

Jacob placed his hand on Saul Jaeran's shoulder. "Lower your voice, Saul. You're shouting again."

"I'm sorry. I just feel so strongly."

"And so do the people who disagree with you." Ole Branjord said. "Reverend Amlund was ordained in the Norwegian Church. It stands to reason that he would follow the church's teachings."

"That I will agree with!" Saul said. "And that is why we don't need pastors from Norway. Elling Eielsen says every man is a minister. We need lay leadership, not clergy leadership."

"Elling Eielsen is a troublemaker," Ole Andreas muttered.

"Eielsen is a great preacher!" Saul responded.

"That he is," Hans said. "But he is also a troublemaker." Hans turned to Jacob and Jonas. "You two were here when Reverend Rasmussen came. Remember how we begged him to send us a full-time pastor? And do you remember how happy we were when Reverend Amlund accepted the call? We all wanted an ordained pastor from Norway to lead us."

"You're right, Hans." Jonas sighed. "I have nothing against Reverend Amlund. He's a fine young man. Jacob and I both want an ordained pastor. We just want more say in how the church is run and how the service is conducted."

Jacob added, "We don't think we need the trappings and liturgy of the old country."

"Amen!" Saul applauded. "We don't need to recite all those old creeds. I know what I believe. And I don't need a shepherd! I'm not a sheep."

Hans glared at Saul Jaeran. He did not like this little man and was having difficulty not showing it. "I think we all are sheep and need the Good Shepherd to lead us."

"Speak for yourself, Hans Twedt," Saul said sharply. "I agree I need Jesus, but I don't need any ordained minister to be my shepherd." Saul again poked Hans in the chest. "I am not a sheep!"

Before Hans could react, Big Per stepped between the two men. He looked down upon Saul much as a principal looks down on a misbehaving first grader. Big Per's voice was soft, but his eyes were hard. "I think that is about enough for today,"

Saul stepped back, growing slightly pale. He realized he had gone too far. "Yes. You are absolutely right, Per. I wish all of you a good week and God's blessing." He quickly walked to his wagon. The other men relaxed.

Big Per grinned. "Well now, that was exciting."

They all laughed, relieved that the tension had been broken. Hans Twedt shook his head. "This mess will end up destroying friendships."

"Let's hope not," Jacob said. "Maybe we can work things out."

Jonas changed the subject. "Are you all done plowing?"

Only Hans and Jacob shook their heads no. Jacob said, "I have about half a day left."

"I still have ten acres to go," Hans replied.

"Could you use some help?" Jonas asked.

Hans smiled. "Yes, I could. Thank you, Jonas."

Jonas nodded. "I'll be over after breakfast. We old-timers have to stick together."

"Yes, we do," Jacob agreed. "Well, have a good week."

As the men said their goodbyes and Jonas and Jacob left, Ole Andreas' seven-year-old son Lars and Martin walked up to the group. They were red-faced from running and hungry. Both had learned that standing around and fidgeting was a good way to get their fathers to stop talking and go home.

Ole Andreas turned to Big Per. "Well, Older Brother, you didn't have much to say."

"That is true," Big Per answered. "There was enough hot air without me adding to it."

The men laughed. Martin looked up at Big Per. "Mr. Larson, are you really Mr. Tjernagel's brother?"

"That I am. Although there are times I don't want to claim him."

"And that goes for me too." Ole Andreas grinned.

Lars poked Martin. "See? I told you."

Martin was confused. "If you are brothers, why don't you have the same last name?"

"Ah!" Ole Andreas said. "We were both Larson back in Illinois. But when I moved to Iowa, I did not want to claim this big fellow, so I changed my name to Tjernagel. That was the name of our village back in Norway."

"That's his story," Big Per said, his eyes twinkling. "I have the true story. The whole story."

Martin and Lars groaned. When Big Per started a story, they knew it would take a while.

Glancing over at her husband, Helena was relieved to see the men laughing. Three weeks ago, two men had come to blows. She and Martha and Julia had caught up on the community gossip, and it was time to go home and fix Sunday dinner. Turning back to the women, she saw that Julia and Martha were looking over her shoulder. Approaching them was Hanna Signaldahl and her retinue. Hanna gave a slight nod to Helena and Martha, accompanied by a minimal and completely phony smile, but directed her words to Julia. "Mrs. Twedt, I am having a few guests over to my home for a quilting party next Saturday. Would you like to join us?"

Julia smiled sweetly. "That is most kind of you, Mrs. Signaldahl. Are Mrs. Branjord and Mrs. Tjernagel invited too?"

Hanna's eyes widened as her face flushed. "Well … ah … no. My parlor won't hold everybody."

"I understand," Julia said, her smile remaining. "Your invitation is most kind, but I will be busy Saturday. Thank you anyway."

Hanna faked a smile, but her eyes were smoldering. "Perhaps some other time," she said and quickly walked away, her shadows following.

When the group was out of hearing range, Helena said, "I doubt you'll be getting any more invitations."

"That is fine with me," Julia answered. "I just don't understand her sudden interest in me. She usually is pained to say a simple hello."

"Maybe she learned Hans was one of the original founders of the East Settlement," Martha said. "That sort of thing is important to her."

"Oh, I don't think so. She must have known about that years ago. It's all very strange."

Helena tightened the bow on her bonnet. "I think the invitation was more of a snub to Martha and me than an invitation to you. What did you do to her, Martha?"

"Nothing. But Ole Andreas had some words with her husband over some cattle. Why does she hate you?"

"A number of reasons. First, I am Finnish. Second, I was a servant in her aunt's home in Norway. And third, she thought I should be her servant as well. I did not agree and told her so."

Julia, who was quite perceptive, said, "I think there might be more to it than that."

Helena gave her friend a rueful smile. "As usual, you are right, Julia. But I don't want to talk about it."

"That bad?" Martha asked.

"That bad," Helena replied.

The conversation ended with the arrival, on the run, of course, of Berent and Joseph. Both boys looked like they had been wrestling in the grass, which is exactly what they had been doing.

"I'm hungry, Mama," Berent said. "Can we go home?"

"Just look at your dress!" Helena cried.

"Joseph pushed me down!"

"You pushed me down first."

"Did not!"

"Did too!"

"It doesn't make any difference who pushed first." Julia sighed. "You're both filthy."

Joseph looked up at his mother. "I'm hungry too, Mama."

The three women looked at each other and laughed.

"Boys," Helena said. "God made them cute so we wouldn't kill them."

Martha agreed. "Amen. Where is Peder Gustav, Berent?"

"He went with some older boys down toward the river."

"Oh, dear!" Martha said. "I'd better go find him. I'll see you two next week."

Martha hurried off. Julia turned to Helena. "I had better be rounding up my brood too. Goodbye. Have a good week."

"You too!" Helena called as Julia and Joseph walked away. She then looked down at Berent. "Have you seen Oline?"

"No."

Helena gazed all around the churchyard. Her daughter was not in sight. "I wonder where she is?"

Chapter Eight

Oline was not in sight because she was alone inside the church, standing by the organ. She hesitantly reached out and touched it. A thrill went through her. Oh, how she would love to be able to play it! The wooden cover was over the keys. Did she have the nerve to push back the cover? She looked around the church; then, hands trembling, she lifted and pushed, revealing the gleaming white and black keys. They called to her. She responded. Touching the ivory and ebony keys was like feeling a cool stone made smooth by the river. Oline smiled and thought, "What a joy it must be to make music on such a magnificent instrument."

"I think it is beautiful too," a soft, feminine voice said, making Oline leap back from the organ. Inga Lyngen stood in the doorway of a small room behind and to the side of the pulpit. She was smiling.

"Oh, I'm so sorry!" Oline cried. "I didn't mean to hurt it. I … I just wanted to touch it."

Inga laughed as she walked to the organ. "You didn't hurt it. Touching it like you did makes it feel loved. Your name is Oline, correct? Helena Branjord's daughter."

Oline nodded, desperately wanting to run out the church door. "Yes, ma'am."

Inga gently patted the frightened girl's arm. "Relax, Oline. I'm not going to scold you. I've seen you watch me when I play. Would you like to learn?"

Oline gasped, her eyes wide. "Oh, yes!"

Inga could not help but smile at the girl's excitement. She remembered when she had felt exactly the same way. "Wonderful! But before you learn to play the organ, you must take piano lessons. I'll talk to your mother."

"Oline!" Helena stood in the doorway. "I've been looking all over for you! Is she bothering you, Mrs. Lyngen?"

"No, she is not, Mrs. Branjord."

Oline ran to Helena. "Mama! Mrs. Lyngen asked if I wanted to take piano lessons. Can I? Please! Can I?"

"Well, I … I don't know," Helena said, taken aback by the request. "We don't have a piano."

"That is not a problem," Inga said as she joined Helena and Oline. "Her school is only a mile from our house. She could come over after school one day a week for a lesson and perhaps two days to practice."

"Please, Mama!"

Helena looked at the joy and the heart-wrenching expectations on Oline's face and did not know how to say no. "Piano lessons would be wonderful, but I don't want her to be a bother."

"Having a student as excited about learning as Oline is not a bother. It is a pleasure," Inga said, then added, "and I'm sure we can work out the cost of lessons."

"I'll work, Mama! I'll work real hard!"

"We'll see, honey." Helena looked at Inga. "I'll have to talk this over with Ole."

"Of course. Just let me know."

As the Branjord wagon rolled home behind the stately walk of Doll and Lady, Ole and Helena were deep in conversation. The children slept on the straw.

"I would love to have her take piano lessons," Ole said. "You know that."

"Yes, I do," Helena replied. She added, "When the calves are born, there will be more milk than we need. Oline could churn butter and sell it at Turg's store in Fairview."

"It's not just the money. She'll be in the house with Karl Lyngen."

"He's not a bad person."

"No, he's not. But he's weird. And he drinks."

"He drinks to ease the pain from that terrible wound he got in the war."

"I know. I'm told he was a fine teacher before the war. But the fact is he drinks, and there's no telling what a drinking man might do."

Helena did not respond. She also had her qualms. They rode for nearly a minute in silence, then Helena sighed. "Life is a gamble, Ole. You should have seen her face."

Again the conversation died. The only sounds were the squeaking of the wagon wheels, the rubbing of the harnesses on the horses, the gurgling of the river, and the glorious murmurings of a beautiful spring day. Neither Ole nor Helena noticed. They were weighing the desires of their eldest child against the welfare of their only daughter. Finally, Ole said, "We'll give it a try." Helena smiled and gave her husband's arm a squeeze.

They drove in silence, now able to enjoy the sights, sounds, and smells surrounding them. Helena smiled as she gazed upon the blossoming prairie flowers. There were gray-headed coneflowers with drooping yellow petals; tall, red blazing stars; bunches of pink downy phlox; tall green weeds called Culver's root; and acres of a charming flower with six blue petals and yellow inner ring, for which she knew not the name. Had she been alone, she would have stopped and picked some. She loved the prairie flowers and promised herself that one day she would surround her real house with them.

There was no doubt the prairie had its own special beauty. It was not the majestic beauty of the Norwegian mountains or fjords, but rather a quiet, humble presence that projected lush fertility and endless possibilities. Helena was aware that some of the plant roots went down ten feet or more.

Ole read her thoughts. "It's a beautiful day."

"Yes," Helena answered. "It is a beautiful day the Lord hath made. Let us be glad and rejoice in it."

"Indeed. And that is what we will do, Reverend Branjord."

Both laughed. A woman in the pulpit was inconceivable. Helena looked back at the children. "They are so beautiful when they're sleeping."

Ole glanced over his shoulder. "Yes, they are. And quiet."

Helena said, "That too." She turned and faced Ole. "Saul Jaeran certainly wasn't quiet after church."

"You can say that again. And he almost got clobbered by Hans."

"No! Hans is such a sweet man."

"Hans has a temper, and Saul poked him in the chest. That man is a troublemaker."

"He's a radical, and I don't like him. But I do agree with much of what he says."

"Now, don't you start," Ole groaned. "It's too pretty a day to argue."

"I'm not going to argue," Helena replied, "but I do think there should be more lay preaching and lay control of the congregation. The clergy should not run everything."

"I agree they shouldn't," Ole snapped. "But I do think the clergy should be in charge, not some idiot like Saul Jaeran."

Helena opened her mouth to answer, but thought better of it. It was obvious that any more words would renew an old argument. Ole was right. It was too nice a day to argue. The rest of the drive home was in silence.

Helena

Out of the corner of my eye, I glance at Ole. He is staring straight ahead, his face stern, his jaw set. I agree with him about Saul Jaeran. Saul is a troublemaker and reminds me of a small, yapping dog.

My problem is that I agree with most of what he says. Ole enjoys the liturgy. Not me. I don't hate it. I could just do without it. I would like a simpler service with more hymns. The sermons could be shorter too. Preachers should be made to sit over an hour with squirming children while someone drones on and on. Today's sermon was about right.

And I don't see why the clergy has to wear robes and those ridiculous ruffs. A black suit would be just fine. Ole says the robe is a symbol of reverence. I think it's a sign of power. It makes the clergy feel important, above everybody else, the "holier than thou" sort of thing. In Norway, some people actually bow when the clergy walk by. What a joke! I've seen the way many pastors have looked at me. Their thoughts were anything but holy!

That's not the case with Reverend Amlund. I like him. And I really like his wife. They are good people. Reverend Amlund works hard. He does his best to be a good shepherd, unlike so many in Norway and Finland. They are not even bad shepherds. They are fat, uncaring owners who live off the sheep and even punish them.

Christina. I will never forget her face. Never. She was forced to sit on a high stool in front of the congregation. I was fifteen. She was a year older. She was also five months pregnant. The pastor stood over her like an angry, crazed animal, his face red and snot dripping from his long, pointed nose. He pointed at her with his bony finger and called her "wanton," "whore," and a disgrace to her church and community. He banned her from the church and told the congregation to shun the entire family. He ordered her father's employer to fire him as a warning to other fathers of young girls. Her family was forced to sit in the front pew and witness the tongue-lashing. Christina did not make a sound, but tears rolled down her cheeks.

And for what? For being raped, that's what! She had been employed as a cook's helper for the town's richest landowner. His son raped her. Everyone knew it was rape. The boy had done it before. She made the mistake of going to the pastor. Within hours, the landowner claimed the act was consensual and had been initiated by Christina, who was hoping for a marriage proposal. The story was supported by the pastor. Both men said it was all Christina's fault! And when she became pregnant, it was God's retribution for her sin.

All her fault. Yes, that's the way it always is, especially if the girl is a servant and the boy's father is rich. Three days later, Christina's mother found her hanging dead in the barn. Did the pastor feel any guilt? Oh my, no! He condemned her to hell for killing herself and her unborn baby. He refused to officiate at her funeral or allow her body to be buried in the church cemetery. From the pulpit he called her a polluted vessel and a daughter of the devil.

What a vicious hypocrite! He used to leer at all the pretty girls. He asked my mother if I could work as a maid for his wife. Maid! Ha! Thankfully, his wife knew what he wanted and hired a fat older woman to help her. If I had gone to work in that house, it could have been me sitting on that stool.

And that is what Hanna Signaldahl wanted to happen. What she planned to happen! But the Lord was with me. She failed. And then I met Ole. Dear, sweet Ole. I look over at him. His face has relaxed. His eyes are soft. I put my arm through his and lay my head on his shoulder. Although I cannot see it, I know he is smiling. Oh, Ole. I love you so.

Chapter Nine

Oline approached the Lyngen farm, located just south of Fairview, with a mixture of excitement and fear. Her first piano lesson. She had insisted on wearing her Sunday dress to school, even though it meant confining herself to jumping rope at recess. School had seemed to last forever, but now she could see the Lyngen house. The two-story frame home looked huge to Oline and very imposing. It had three gables, a large front porch, and was painted white. The house had been built by Inga's parents, both of whom had died of the flu during the Civil War.

Oline was glad it was dry and sunny. It would be awful to track mud into such a grand house. She went around to the back door. No Norwegian child would think of knocking on the front door.

Inga Lyngen opened the door and smiled her welcome. "Oline, how good to see you." She was wearing a simple cotton house dress, and with her long hair tied back with a bow, she looked almost girlish. "Come in. Are you ready for your lesson?"

"Yes, ma'am," Oline answered shyly as she followed Inga into the small entryway that led to the kitchen. Her eyes grew large. This was just the third real house she had ever entered.

The kitchen was nearly as big as the Branjord cabin. It had built-in cupboards, a large cook range, a tin sink with a drain, a red water pump, and a round oak table with six matching chairs. Two doors led from the kitchen into the main part of the house. The right door led to the dining room, which in turn opened into the parlor; the left door revealed a hallway leading to the front door. If one entered from the front, there were stairs leading to the second floor. To the left at the foot of the stairs was the parlor and to the right was the music room/library. Farther down the hallway on the right was the Lyngen bedroom.

Oline followed Inga past the closed bedroom door to the second door. "We call this our library and music room, "Inga said, opening the door. "We spend much of our time in here."

The room had two large, heavily draped windows, one opening on to the front porch, the other set in the north wall. On either side of the windows were floor to ceiling bookshelves, sagging with more books than Oline had ever seen. In front of the west wall was a potbellied stove. Matching wingback chairs and footstools were on either side of the stove. A landscape oil painting hung on the wall over each of the chairs. Against the inner wall was a black upright piano, in front of which were a stool and a straight-back chair.

Oline gasped as she entered the room. "Are all these books yours?"

"Some. Most of them are Karl's."

"Martin would love this room."

"Is Martin your brother?"

"Yes. He loves to read."

"Well, you tell him he can borrow any book he wants." Inga sat in the straight-back chair. "Come, sit on the stool."

Oline hesitantly did as she was told. Inga laughed. "The stool won't break. You look like a bird about to fly away. There is nothing to be afraid of."

Oline relaxed slightly, then stiffened again when she saw sheet music covered with notes. Her heart sank. Inga looked from Oline's horror-stricken face to the music. She smiled. "This is the music I play. Yours will be much simpler. Now, I'm going to show you a scale. But first, you must know each of your fingers has a number. Your thumb is one; forefinger, two; middle finger, three; ring finger, four; and little finger, five. Understand?"

Oline nodded. Inga smiled at the girl's intense concentration before placing the thumb of her right hand on middle C and slowly playing the scale. "We'll start with the right hand with middle C. One … two … three … thumb goes under and then it is one, two, three, four, five. When you come down, it is five, four, three, two, one, then three, two, one. Want to try?"

Oline nodded again. Her thumb hovered over middle C like a frightened butterfly before slowly lowering and softly striking the key.

There was no sound. Terror came into Oline's eyes. "Did I break it?" she cried.

"No, silly." Inga laughed. "You did not strike it hard enough. Try again."

Oline did so, and her triumphant smile spread from ear to ear as the sound of middle C filled the room.

"Good!" Inga responded. "Now, go up the scale."

For the next ten minutes, Oline struggled but improved. Inga was pleased. She loved the girl's determination and was impressed with her dexterity and coordination. Maybe, just maybe, she thought, Oline might be what all teachers dream of—a talented student, willing to work hard.

"Well done, Oline," Inga said. "Rest a little."

Oline took a deep breath. A worried frown crossed her face. "I don't know any notes."

"Of course not," Inga replied. "But you will learn them, and learn to play them."

"I hope so," Oline said, with little assurance. "When do you think I can play a song?"

"How about right now?"

"Really?"

"Yes. Do you know 'Twinkle, Twinkle Little Star'?"

"I do."

"We'll play it together. Give me your hand."

Inga placed her hand over Oline's and played the simple tune. She repeated the process and then said, "You do it by yourself."

Oline haltingly played the song, hitting only one sour note.

"Very good! You played your first song."

Oline was so excited she bounced on the stool. "I did! I really did!" she said, then blushed with embarrassment. "But it was pretty simple."

Inga patted her arm. "Everyone starts with a simple piece. Well, maybe not Mozart. But he was a genius. Would you like to hear what he did with that simple tune?"

Oline nodded and Inga opened a thick songbook. She began to play. The simple melody quickly became a complicated series of variations. When she was finished, Oline was stunned. "That is beautiful," she whispered.

"Yes, it is. And, if you work hard, someday you'll play it."

"Did you know Mozart?"

Inga laughed and clapped her hands. "Oh my, no! He died over seventy years ago. But his music will live forever. Wouldn't it be wonderful to write music like that?"

Oline was overwhelmed. Tears came to her eyes. "Yes, it would be wonderful."

The momentary silence was broken by the shattering of glass and a crashing thud from the Lyngen bedroom. Inga jumped to her feet, knocking over her chair as she fled the room. Without thinking, Oline followed. When she reached the open bedroom door, Inga was kneeling on the floor beside her husband Karl. The man's body shook and his arms flailed, almost hitting Inga. His eyes were rolled back into his head. Inga was forcing the handle of a large wooden spoon between Karl's teeth.

Oline stared in horror. She wanted to run but could not move. It was as if giant hands had reached through the floor, grabbing her feet. Inga looked up, her eyes filled with fear and concern. "Oline, I need your help! Take the ice bucket next to the dresser and go the log icehouse behind the kitchen and get some ice. Hurry!"

Oline heard the request, but just stared. She had never seen anything so frightening.

"Oline, Please! Get the ice!"

Without quite knowing how she freed herself from the paralyzing fear, Oline found herself running, ice bucket in hand, out of the kitchen door to the log icehouse. She pulled open the heavy door and was greeted with a wave of cold air. She shivered as she entered the icehouse, grabbed a large pick, and began chipping chunks of ice into the bucket. Tears were turning cold on her cheeks when she slammed the door shut and ran to the Lyngen bedroom.

Inga was wiping Karl's brow. The man's shaking had diminished but was still evident. "Thank you, dear," Inga said, taking the bucket from Oline. She quickly wrapped ice into a towel and placed it over the oozing scar tissue that made up the right side of Karl's face. Immediately, he began to relax. Inga removed the spoon handle from Karl's mouth. She too relaxed. "Thank you again, Oline. The ice relieves the pain and calms his nerves."

"What happened?" Oline whispered.

"He had a seizure," Inga answered, with a sad smile. "It was caused by his wound."

Oline studied the face of the man who now seemed to be sleeping.

The difference between the two sides was horrifying, yet fascinating. What she could see of the left side was quite handsome. The right side, however, was nothing but red blotches and angry scar tissue, interspersed with small patches of beard which looked like tiny islands in a sea of scabs and open sores. Her stomach began to churn. She looked away, fearing she might vomit.

It was then she noticed there were heavy drapes over the room's window. The only light came from the hallway and a lamp that sat on a round table in the corner by a large leather chair.

"Why does he sit in the dark?" Oline asked.

"Because bright light causes terrible headaches," Inga replied. "He used to love the sun. We would take long walks out onto the prairie … before the war." Inga paused, wiping some drool from the corner of Karl's mouth, then looked up at Oline with tears in her eyes. "He was quite handsome before the war. All the girls thought so. How they envied me … before the war." Her gaze drifted back to Karl. The sad smile returned.

Oline did not know how or what to reply, so she remained silent. Inga sighed and gathered herself. "Oline, will you hold the ice on his head so I can clean up?"

The girl hesitated a moment, then knelt beside Inga. "Just hold the ice right where it is," Inga said. Oline nodded, taking hold of the cold, ice-filled cloth. Karl moaned and moved. Oline lifted the ice, looking questioningly at Inga. "Just keep the ice on his head," Inga said. "He won't wake up." Oline lowered the towel. Karl did not move.

Inga crawled to the overturned bottle and broken glass. She placed the mostly empty bottle on the table. As she began picking up the glass, she said, "I know people say Karl is a drunk, but he's not. He doesn't even like whisky. He drinks to relieve the pain."

"Does he hurt a lot?"

"Yes. And it never stops."

Oline lifted the ice and looked at Karl's face. This time she did not see just the ugly scars and webbed flesh. This time she saw the sad, wounded soldier. She was about to put the ice back when she saw something metallic close to Karl's mangled ear. "Mrs. Lyngen, there is a piece of metal on his head."

Inga put the shards of glass on the table, picked up a pair of tweezers and a small, round dish, then crawled back to Karl. She barely glanced at the fragment before plucking it from the skin and putting it in the dish, where it joined others of the same type. "This is what soldiers call shrapnel. Cannonballs explode, sending metal flying in every direction. Tiny pieces keep oozing out of his head. They cause the pain."

Karl moaned as he opened his eyes. Oline removed the ice. His gazed focused on the girl. The intensity of the look frightened Oline. He pushed himself into a half-sitting position, lightly touching Oline's arm. The girl drew back. "You are real," he whispered, smiling as he lay back down. "Thank you for the water."

Inga and Oline looked with bewilderment at each other. Inga said, "She did not give you water, Karl. Her name is Oline Branjord."

"Oline," Karl said slowly, as if savoring the taste of her name. "How pretty. I never knew her name. She saved my life."

Oline stared at Karl's deformed features. She was so frightened, she trembled. She wanted to cry. She wanted to run home where all the people were whole. But she did neither. Instead, she gently placed the towel filled with ice back on Karl's wound. The man smiled, closed his eyes, and slept. His wife wept.

When her sobbing stopped, Inga said, "I am sorry you had to see this. His seizures don't come that often anymore."

"Why did he say I saved his life?"

"I don't know, dear. Don't concern yourself. He says strange things when he is ill. You had better go now."

Inga took the towel from Oline and dropped the ice into a washbasin. Oline unsteadily got to her feet. "Are you just going to leave him on the floor"

"Yes," Inga answered as she stood up. "He'll sleep for several hours, then I'll help him into bed." Inga took Oline's hand and led her into the hallway. "Thank you for your help. And you did very well for your first lesson. I think you have talent, Oline. I'll ask Mrs. Amlund if she will give you lessons."

Tears came to Oline's eyes. "Did I do something wrong? Don't you want to give me lessons?"

"You did nothing wrong. You were wonderful. But, after what has happened … it is probably better if you don't come again."

"Why? I want you to teach me," Oline said, tears now rolling down her cheeks.

"Oline, if your parents find out what happened, they won't let you come."

"Then I won't tell them!" Oline cried. "It will be our secret. Please let me come!"

Inga hugged the girl. "You can come anytime you want, Oline. Anytime you want."

Oline

Martin and Berent are asleep. So are Mama and Papa. I can hear both of them snoring. Mama doesn't think she snores, but she does, just not as loud as Papa.

This was the most exciting day of my life. I can still feel the smoothness of the keys. Touching them was like feeling melting ice, only dry. And when I played the first note—what was it called? Oh yes, middle C—it was as if some sort of charge went through my body. Playing the scale is hard, but Mrs. Lyngen said I did fine. Let's see, it was one, two, three, then one, two, three, four, five. Getting that thumb under was what I had trouble with. Mrs. Lyngen doesn't have any trouble. When she played what that man Mozart wrote, her fingers flew over the keys. And the sound! I think the piano makes the most beautiful sound in the whole world! Someday, I'm going to play like that.

I told Mama and Papa all about the lesson, and I told Martin about the books. He became really excited, but Papa said he couldn't go with me. I thought he was going to cry. Mama gave him a hug. I think she will find a way for him to see the library. I don't understand why he likes books so much.

I didn't tell Mama and Papa about Mr. Lyngen's fit. I might someday when I'm old. Like, maybe when I'm twenty. I've never seen a big person cry like Mrs. Lyngen did. It made me want to cry too. She said he was handsome before the war. He is ugly now. I don't think I could live with anyone that ugly.

Why did he thank me for giving him water? I had never seen him before today. All the children are afraid of him. Some big people are too. That's because he walks all over during the night. Christina went to the outhouse one night and saw him walking out on the prairie. She knew it was him because he wore a soldier's hat. Now I know why he does it. The sunlight hurts his eyes. He has a nice voice and a nice smile. Mrs. Lyngen would never marry anyone mean. I don't think I'm afraid of him anymore. I just think he is very sad.

Chapter Ten

"I think we're lost," seven-year-old Heinrik Hindberg said, his lower lip quivering.

Ernst, his older brother by five years, grunted dismissively. "We're not lost. Stop whining. Martin isn't whining. Neither is Oline, and she's a girl."

The four children were walking west, deep into the waist-high prairie grass, in search of their cows. The Hindberg boys, both with sandy-colored hair and freckles, lived on the farm nearest the Branjords. Their father, Albert, was German. Bertha, their mother, was Norwegian. Because of this union, both of the boys would eventually be able to speak three languages, Norwegian being the dominant one. Like Martin, both boys wore bleached homespun shirts and dark pants. Oline was wearing her gingham school dress, which was faded and becoming too small. All the clothes had been made by their mothers.

"I hate cows!" Heinrik stated.

"Me too," Martin agreed.

Ernst looked scornfully at his brother. "You sure don't hate their milk. You drink enough of it."

"That goes for you too," Oline said to Martin. "Look at all the butter you eat. Butter I have to churn."

Neither of the younger boys could respond, as they were guilty as charged. So they just put their heads down and walked. But in their hearts, they still hated cows.

"Do you suppose your cows dropped their calves?" Ernst asked.

Martin's pout turned to concern. He knew how important these new calves were to the family's well-being. "It's possible. Papa said they could come anytime."

"I sure hope not," Ernst said. "We've been hearing a lot of wolf and coyote howls at night."

Oline suddenly became worried. "So have we. The wolves might have eaten the calves and the cows."

"They could eat us too," Heinrik muttered.

"Oh, hush up!" Ernst said, shoving his little brother hard enough that the younger boy almost fell. "Wolves and coyotes mostly hunt at night."

Heinrik glared at Ernst. "Well, mostly isn't always. Look around us! I don't even know what direction we're going."

"We're walking west," Ernst answered, with a bravado he did not feel. He realized they were farther out onto the prairie than he had ever been before. "Just look at the sun."

"What happens when the sun goes down?" Martin asked.

Ernst had no answer. All the children had been warned hundreds of times never to be out on the prairie after dark.

At a casual glance, the Iowa prairie was a rolling sea of wildflowers and grass, a tranquil scene of nature's abundance and beauty. But lurking beneath the gently waving stems lay harsh and deadly dangers: snakes, half-buried rocks, gopher holes, sloughs, and quicksand that could swallow a team of horses and a wagon. The prairie could show a benign or savage face, changing from one to the other in seconds. It could be a garden that fed and housed you, or a feckless wasteland in which you could wander lost for days. Skeletal remains were its "beware" signs.

Oline broke the silence by changing the subject. "When is the new baby coming?"

Ernst shrugged. "Mama said in about six weeks."

"Does she want a boy or a girl?"

"She said the two of us are enough boys."

Oline laughed. "She's right. Two brothers are enough."

Martin responded by sticking out his tongue at his big sister.

"I don't understand why she doesn't know," Heinrik said. "She ordered it."

"What do you mean, 'ordered' it?" Oline asked.

"From the factory," Heinrik said. "The baby factory in Norway."

Ernst burst out laughing. "Do you still believe that?"

Heinrik's face turned red. Like all younger brothers, he hated being laughed at by his older brother. "That's what Pa said!" Ernst continued to laugh. "Well, he did!" Heinrik yelled, swinging his right fist at Ernst.

The older boy easily sidestepped the blow. "Don't get mad. He told me the same thing. It's just a story adults tell kids."

Heinrik was not convinced. "If there is no factory, where do babies come from?"

"From their mama's stomach, stupid! Why do you think Mama is so fat?"

Heinrik had no answer. He had been wondering about that himself. There also were his mother's complaints about the baby kicking. He turned to Martin. "Is that right?"

Martin shrugged. He was as astounded as Heinrik. Ole had told him almost the same story, the only difference being the baby factory was in Wisconsin.

"What I can't figure out is how the baby gets out," Ernst said. "Do you know, Oline?"

The girl shook her head. This was a problem she had mulled over a number of times since learning the baby factory was not in Wisconsin, in fact was nonexistent.

"I thought girls knew," Ernst continued. "Mama said it is something only girls had to know."

"I don't," Oline said, but after a moment's hesitation added, "I've seen the sows have little pigs. Maybe it's like that."

The boys were horrified. They had all seen animals give birth. "No!" Ernst said. "It can't be like that!" The other boys nodded their agreement. That was far too messy. Oline was not so sure, but hoped the boys were right.

The children walked along in silence for some time, each pondering the mysteries of life's beginnings. Finally, Martin put into words what they all were thinking. "I wonder how the baby gets in there in the first place." No one could answer the question, but all realized the answer was of monumental importance, and one adults were reluctant to give.

They reached the summit of a small hill and saw three Holstein cows ambling toward them in single file.

"There are our cows!" Heinrik yelled.

The Branjord children shared his excitement until they realized Maud and Mabel were nowhere in sight. "Where are ours?" Oline asked.

"They can't be far behind," Ernst said.

The children waited, searching the horizon. No cows. The three Holsteins paraded within arm's reach and, without so much as a side glance, continued east.

"What are we going to do?" Oline asked.

"Me and Ernst have to get our cows home," Heinrik answered.

"What about our cows?" Martin asked.

Heinrik looked down at his dirty toes. "I don't know. Let them find their own way home."

Oline turned to Ernst. "Papa is going to be really mad if we don't bring home Maud and Mabel."

Ernst frowned. "I know. Mine would be mad too." He looked back at the departing cows, then to the west. "Heinrik, you and Martin take our cows home. Martin, tell your pa that me and Oline are looking for yours."

"But we might get lost!" Heinrik said.

"Oh, don't be such a coward! Just keep the sun to your backs and follow the cows. They know the way home."

"Go on, Martin," Oline said, relieved Ernst was staying with her. "Tell Papa."

The two younger boys also were relieved. They had no desire to be lost on the prairie in the dark. They chased after the three Holsteins.

Oline and Ernst watched them go, then looked at each other and began walking west. There was no conversation. Both became tense. Nothing had changed, yet everything had changed. They were alone … together. For the first time in their lives, they were alone with someone of the opposite sex who was their own age. Oline's heart was pounding. She dared not look at Ernst. She knew she was blushing.

They walked on for nearly thirty minutes, looking every which way but at each other, then Ernst stopped. Oline glanced at him and saw the worried look on his face. "Oline, we're a long way out and the sun is setting."

"Do you think we should start back?"

Ernst nodded. "Your cows will just have to find their own way home."

The children began the long trek east. But like the hiker who walks too far into the wilderness or the day sailor who ventures too far into the open sea, they soon found themselves lost in the unforgiving darkness. Ernst led the way. Oline followed, hoping the boy knew the direction they were going in. Suddenly, Ernst stumbled and fell.

"Are you all right?" Oline asked.

Ernst slowly climbed to his feet. "I think so. I stubbed my toe on a rock."

"Do you know where we are?"

"No. Do you?"

Tears welled in Oline's eyes. "No," she whispered.

Ernst fought back his own tears. He looked around, then pointed. "Oline, isn't that red?"

Oline studied the horizon. Ernst was right. There was a tinge of red. "That's west!"

Ernst smiled. "I thought so. At least we're walking in the right direction. Come on!"

The children walked single file, Ernst in the lead, to the east. They had gone less than a hundred yards when Ernst tumbled down an embankment into a slough.

"Ernst!" Oline screamed.

Ernst was on his hands and knees in the water. "I'm fine, just wet. Help me out."

Oline held out her hand. Ernst grabbed it and scrambled up to solid ground. Oline did not let go of his hand. He did not release hers. They stared at each other through their tears. "We're lost," Ernst said.

Oline bit her lip to keep from crying. "I know. But we can't stay here."

Ernst took a deep breath, swallowed hard, and, still holding Oline's hand, began searching for a way around the slough. They walked slowly, making sure that each step was on firm ground. Holding hands helped lessen the terror both felt.

They finally reached the edge of the slough. Which direction to go? They searched the horizon. The red was gone. Ernst pointed. "I think east is that way." Oline agreed and they started off, silently praying they were right. A cool evening breeze, which should have been welcome, only added to their fear. It made the tall grass sway around their legs like clutching fingers, and better carried the sound of wolf howls, coyote barks, and challenging bellows of wild bulls.

Ernst felt the pressure of Oline's hand increase. He attempted a smile of reassurance. He failed, but received a slight smile from Oline for the effort. "Don't worry, Oline," he said. "Our fathers are out looking for us."

Saying the right thing at the right time is a gift. Young Ernst was so blessed. His reward was a charming, relieved smile he would remember the rest of his life. "That's true!" Oline answered. "And they'll find us too!"

Ernst had another good idea. He began singing a familiar childhood hymn. Oline quickly joined in. Their clear soprano voices rang out across the prairie, overriding the more scary noises. At once, the darkness seemed to lighten and their fears to lessen. They continued to sing until there were no more songs they both knew.

"How far do you think we've come?" Oline asked.

"A long way." Ernst replied. "We should be getting close."

They walked a few steps in silence, then Oline stopped. "Did you hear that?"

"What?"

"Listen!"

Something was approaching the children from the rear. Something large! Without thinking, they fell into a fierce hug. The noise grew louder. They were too petrified to move. Whatever was coming was only yards away. Oline wanted to scream, but no sound came. Then out of the darkness came the two missing cows.

"It's Maud and Mabel!" Oline shouted.

Ernst burst out laughing, then abruptly became silent. He looked at Oline. With wide eyes, she returned his gaze. Their arms became like lead. They stepped back and, for the first time since sunset, were thankful for the darkness. The two cows ignored them and disappeared into the night.

Oline recovered first. "Don't lose sight of them! They know the way home."

The children caught up with the cows. They did not sing. They did not speak. They could hardly breathe. Walking side by side, their hands occasionally brushed. Oline felt a jolt each time it happened. She wanted him to hold her hand. Should she take his? There were explosions in her brain that were new and very frightening. She was trying to sort out what was happening when Ernst grabbed her hand. She smiled. The explosions subsided, but did not go away. His hand was comforting and … something more. She could not explain what it was.

The cows did not walk in a straight line. They meandered about, avoiding the large rocks and sloughs. Ernst and Oline soon lost any sense of direction. They just followed the cows, praying that Maud and Mabel knew the way home.

They did. Faint voices could be heard calling in the distance. "Oline!" "Ernst!"

"That's my pa!" Ernst yelled.

"Mine too!" Oline cried.

The two children replied so loudly that the cows were frightened into a short trot. "Here! Over here!"

Within minutes, Ole and Albert appeared on horseback. Oline squealed with delight and ran to her father, who scooped her up and placed her on Lady's back in front of him. "Are you all right?" Ole asked, squeezing Oline in his arms.

"Yes. But I was so scared."

Ole kissed her cheek. "So were we. Don't ever do this again! If it is getting dark, come home. Forget the blasted cows. Let them find their own way home."

"Yes, Papa," Oline said, snuggling back against her father. "You're not mad at me?"

"No. Not at you. But I am mad at those rotten cows! I see you found them."

"No, they found us. We were just following them."

"Then I suppose I should thank the miserable beasts."

Albert, with Ernst riding behind him, came up alongside Ole. "I've got a wet one. He says he fell into a slough. Let's get these *kinder* home before their mothers have heart attacks."

"Amen to that," Ole answered. "The cows can find their way to my place."

The two thankful fathers turned their horses for home, relieved the prairie had claimed no lives this night.

"I love you, Papa," Oline whispered.

Ole answered by kissing her hair and squeezing her so hard it hurt.

Chapter Eleven

Ole lined up the marking square, a tired smile joining the dirty smudges on his face. The last one! When this square was marked, the field would be ready for planting. Weeks of hard work finished,

First had come the plowing, then the breaking up of large clumps of soil. Until this year, the breaking process had required days of back-wrenching work with a hand rake. However, during the past winter, Ole had created a device that eliminated some of the drudgery. He split a seven-foot-long log, and on the flat side of one of the slabs, he bolted two widths of short boards on either end. Onto the short boards, he nailed twenty-four inches of the curved end of a pair of old skis. He then drilled holes in the slab and inserted a series of metal rods. To complete what he called a "drag," he attached leather straps, to which he could hook the harness tugs. Hans Twedt and Big Per thought he had come up with something ingenious, but in the field, the heavy soil had clogged the rods rather than breaking up and passing through them. On the lighter sandy tops, the drag had worked reasonably well and had saved him some rake time. But Ole had learned that what was needed was some sort of machine that would dig into the plowed ground and grind up the clods. He hoped that some smart inventor was working on the problem.

With a heavy stick, Ole drew a line in the dirt around the perimeter of the marking square and down the middle. The square was a seven feet by seven feet frame made up of slats. There was also a vertical slat running down the middle and a horizontal slat across the middle. It looked like a large window frame with openings for four panes. When the marking was completed, the field looked like a large checker board, and wherever the vertical and horizontal lines intersected, a hill of corn was planted. This allowed for forty-two inch rows that could be cultivated lengthwise and crosswise with a horse-drawn cultivator.

The marking completed, Ole removed his slouch hat, wiped the sweat from his face with an old towel he had tucked into his pants, and looked up into the May sky. He estimated the time at two o'clock. Four hours to supper meant four hours for planting corn. It was time to call Oline and Martin.

He pulled out a sailor's hornpipe from a pouch he carried attached to his rope belt, and blew three short blasts. The hornpipe had been given to him by Ole Andreas Tjernagel, who in his younger days had been a sailor.

The signal had been agreed upon at the noon meal. Within minutes, Oline and Martin, each carrying a water jar, were walking toward the field, which lay to north of the cabin. Ole smiled. Behind them, also with a water jar, marched Berent. His presence had not been requested, but Ole knew there was no way to keep the boy from follow the other two.

While he waited, Ole poured shelled corn from a large bucket into two smaller pails. He then closely examined his planting stick. The stick was an old broom handle with a pointed end. Wedged three inches up from the pointed end was a wooden disk. Above the disk was wound homespun that had been soaked in water and shrunk tightly onto the handle. The depth of the hole was critical: too shallow and the birds would eat the corn; too deep and the corn would fail to germinate.

The children arrived. Only Berent was happy to be there. "Hi, Papa!" He smiled.

"Hello, Berent. Are all of you ready to plant?"

Martin looked down at his bare feet. Oline sighed. "Yes, Papa."

"Well, that's what I like," Ole said sarcastically, "Enthusiasm!"

"It's boring, Papa," Martin mumbled.

"Yes, it is," Ole replied. "It's boring for me too. But remember, if we don't plant, we don't harvest. And if we don't harvest, we don't eat. Understand?"

Martin continued to examine his feet. "Yes, Papa."

"All right, then. Pick up your pails. I'll be making holes in two rows. Oline takes one, Martin takes the other. Drop three kernels into each hole, and make sure the hole is covered. Let's get started."

Ole made his first two holes, but before he could continue, Berent said, "What about me, Papa?"

Ole smiled at his four-year-old. "Well now, that is a problem. I just have two pails." He then spied a small stick, which he handed to Berent. "Here, take this stick and chase away the crows and blackbirds that come to steal the corn."

Berent grinned. "I'll chase them, Papa!"

"You do that," Ole said, but before he could resume his work, he again was stopped by Berent.

"Papa, if I'm helping plant corn, shouldn't I be wearing pants?"

Ole took a deep breath. He was sick and tired of this pants business, but there was nothing he could do. Actually, he agreed with Berent. Keeping boys in dresses until they were five was a carryover from the old country. However, he was not about to go against Helena's wishes. "Oline is wearing a dress and she's planting."

Berent put his hands on his hips. "But she's a girl!"

Martin looked scornfully at his little brother. "I had to wear a dress until I was five. So can you."

"Did you like it?" Berent shot back.

Martin was surprised by the quick retort. "No, but that's just the way it is."

Ole put an end to the conversation. "Martin's right. You will get pants when your mother makes them for you. If you don't like it, go back to the cabin. We have work to do."

Berent looked as if he were about to cry. Ole made holes, and Oline and Martin dropped in the kernels and covered the hills. Then Berent saw a crow swoop down near the first hill. The boy loudly ordered the bird away, but the bird just hopped a few feet and looked disdainfully at the little boy in a dress. Berent charged, swinging his stick. The crow retreated into the air. Berent grinned in triumph.

By the completion of four rows, Berent was no longer chasing birds or yelling at them. Rather, he was dragging his stick and walking listlessly behind his brother and sister. "Are you tired, Berent?" Ole asked as he began rows five and six.

"Sort of," Berent answered, rubbing his eyes, which added to the dirt on his face.

Ole paused and wiped his own face. "Do you think Mama could use some help in the cabin?"

Berent's face brightened. "Yes, Papa."

"Well then, why don't you go home and help her?"

Martin grumbled, "What about the birds?"

"Oh, I think we can shoo them away," Ole answered. "Berent,

you go back to the cabin and don't stop to play in the prairie grass. Understand?"

"Yes, Papa."

Oline and Martin watched with envy as their little brother ran for home. They knew a kiss from Mama and a nap awaited him … after she washed his face.

The planting parade continued for nearly three hours. Ole had to pause periodically because the children could not keep up. He knew they were tired, but the planting had to be done. He thought, "Work is not play, and it usually is not much fun. They might as well learn that now."

The three had stopped to drink the last of their water when Ole saw Helena and a rejuvenated Berent walking toward them. Ole saw she was carrying neither food nor water, which meant something was wrong. When Helena was within shouting distance, she stopped. "Maud is having her calf."

Ole waved to her, relieved she was announcing an anticipated event rather than bringing him a problem. Helena and Berent waved back before beginning to retrace their steps.

"Well, that's all the planting for today," Ole said.

"Good!" the two children said in unison.

Ole laughed. "Don't be too happy. Stopping early just means more work tomorrow. You did well. I'm proud of you. Pick up your water jars and pails, and let's go home."

There was no moon, yet Ole, who was sitting on a milk stool near the open end of the barn, could see all the way to the Skunk River. The sky was alive with countless stars. To Ole, it was as if God had taken a piece of black velvet and, with a mighty heave, had sprinkled it with millions of diamonds. He marveled at the immensity of God 's handiwork. There was no doubt that nothing could make a man feel smaller than a cloudless prairie sky at night.

Ole looked over his shoulder at Maud. She was resting comfortably on fresh straw. Her calf could come anytime. He picked up an ear of corn from the small pile at his feet and began shelling the kernels into the planting bucket. The sheep inched closer. "Go to sleep. You're not getting any of this," Ole said. The sheep took a few steps back, but did not take their eyes off the corn.

Ole gazed out at the pasture. The horses, heads down, knees locked, appeared to be frozen silhouettes. Mabel's four-day-old calf lay sleeping a few yards from the barn. The cow stood protectively over the calf, but her focus was on the birthing process. Her empathy for Maud was evident.

A gentle breeze, which kept the mosquitoes at bay, grew cooler, forcing Ole to slip on a sweater Helena had insisted he take. Ole smiled and thought of the wedding-day advice given by his father. "Always listen to your wife," he had said seriously, Then, with a smile, had added, "Of course, that doesn't mean you always do what she says."

Ole was picking up another ear of corn when he heard a noise to his left. He looked to see Martin climbing over the gate into the pasture. "Shouldn't you be in bed?" he asked.

"Mama said I could check on Maud."

"I thought you hated cows."

Martin gave his father a sheepish grin. "I don't hate them. I just don't like to milk them."

Ole chuckled. "Well, pull up a stool and help me shell corn. Maud is doing fine."

Martin joined his father. "When do you think the calf will come?"

"Only God and Maud know that. And I'm not so sure about Maud. It could be five minutes or five hours."

Martin studied the dilated cow. "Is that where the calf comes out?"

"Yes, it is."

Martin paused, then asked, "Is that where babies come out too?"

Ole stopped shelling. He looked down at Martin's serious expression and decided the boy deserved a serious answer. "Yes. Yes, they do."

"You told me babies come from a factory in Wisconsin."

Ole nodded. "You're right. I did."

"Heinrik's father told him the factory was in Norway."

"Did he now?" Ole smiled. "That's what my father told me too."

Martin worked on an ear of corn for nearly thirty seconds before asking, "If you knew it was a lie, why did you tell me that?"

Ole sighed. Leave it to Martin to ask the tough questions. "I suppose because it is an easy answer for a difficult subject. It is something a small child can understand. I was also told babies are delivered by a stork."

"What's a stork?"

"A big bird."

Martin was shocked. "A big bird? Papa, that doesn't make any sense at all!"

71

"I know. But the man said it was true." Ole tousled Martin's hair, deciding it was time to change the subject. "Look at the sky. I don't think I've ever seen so many stars."

"How many are there, Papa?"

"I don't know. I doubt if there is anyone who knows."

"God knows. He knows everything."

Ole smiled at Martin. "You're right. God does know."

Father and son stared into the infinity of space. The enormity of it all awed them both into a long silence, after which Martin said, "Is God up there?"

"God is everywhere, Martin."

"Reverend Amlund says God sees everything we do. How can he see what I'm doing and what some boy in Norway is doing at the same time?"

Ole paused in his shelling. "I don't know. You'll have to ask Reverend Amlund that." What he did not add was that he had wondered the same thing many times.

Again there was silence. Kernels of corn fell into the bucket as man and boy contemplated the unfathomable mystery of God. A stern female voice interrupted their thoughts.

"Martin, I said you could check on Maud, not stay up half the night," Helena said, opening the pasture gate. "Get to bed right now!"

Martin sighed. These few minutes alone with his father had been far more important to him than either Ole or Helena realized. "Yes, Mama," he answered as he dropped his ear of corn and started for the gate.

"And wash your hands and face before going up to the loft," Helena continued.

"Yes, Mama."

"And close the gate."

"Yes, Mama."

Helena gave Martin a quick peck on the cheek as she passed him on the way to Ole. Martin closed the gate and walked to the cabin. Helena took his place on the stool, picked up the half-finished ear of corn, and began shelling.

"Have you and Martin had a good talk?" Helena asked.

"Yes, Mama," Ole deadpanned.

Helena gave Ole a sharp look, then punched him in the arm. Both laughed.

"That boy asks difficult questions," Ole said.

"I know. He's so smart, he scares me."

"Me too. There are many times I've wished he was just average."

"Well, he's not," Helena replied. "Someday that could be a problem."

They finished shelling their ears of corn in silence, thinking about what the future might hold for the little boy now washing his hands and face in the cabin.

Ole began another ear. "It's a beautiful night."

Helena took a deep breath of the cool evening air. "I can't remember one quite like it."

"I can. Our wedding night was like this."

Helena smiled, putting her hand on Ole's arm. "It was like this," she whispered, then giggled. "I was so scared."

"So was I," Ole said, putting his hand over hers. They leaned toward each other, but the kiss was interrupted by a low moan from Maud. Two small hooves were visible.

"It's time," Ole said, rising from the stool. He placed the remaining ears in the bucket and hung it on a nail far above the drooling sheep.

Helena knelt beside Maud's head and stroked her neck. "It will be over soon. Just a few more pushes."

And she was right.

First came a pink nose, next a head, then the entire calf slipped out onto the straw. Ole immediately pulled the afterbirth away from the calf's nose. This was all he had time to do before Maud was on her feet. The two humans stepped aside to let nature take over. Maud began licking the calf, cleaning it of the placenta. "Oh, what a pretty little calf," Helena cooed.

"A perfect birth." Ole grinned. "And it is a heifer. Two births, two heifers. We have the start of our dairy herd."

Helena laughed. "That will make Martin happy."

"Oline too." Ole chuckled. "You know how she hates to churn."

Maud began nudging the calf with her nose. The newborn gathered herself and struggled to her feet. Straw clung to her left side as she stood stiff-legged. She looked around as if to say, now what? Maud moved so her udder was close to the calf's head. Instinct answered the calf's question. She teetered forward and was soon gobbling down her first meal.

As Helena watched the calf nurse, Ole dug a hole and buried the afterbirth. When he was finished, he put his arm around Helena. "I think we can go to bed."

Helena agreed. "Yes, Maud is a good mother."

Ole lifted the bucket of corn from the nail, and the two left the barn. On the way to the cabin, Helena took Ole's free hand in hers and looked up at him. Ole finished the kiss that Maud had interrupted.

Two yellow eyes followed Ole and Helena until they closed the cabin door. Doggie then trotted down to the pasture fence, where he could see the cow and nursing calf. What normally would have been an easy kill was now an added responsibility.

Helena

What a pretty little calf! Ole is so excited. He hopes someday to have a herd of twenty cows. That seems like a lot of milking to me. One thing is for sure, I'm not milking any of them. I'll never milk another cow as long as I live!

Don't think about it. Bad memory. Think about tonight. It was lovely. Concentrate on that. Think about new life, not old wrongs. Pray the nightmares will someday go away.

Enough! No more sad thoughts. We're having a good year. Good rain. Good hog litters. Good health. Good friends. And now, two perfect little heifers. Perhaps Ole is right. It may be that 1869 will be a year to remember. I hope so.

Maud did well. No problems. She made it look easy. It's not. Especially the first time. I thought Oline would never come. Fourteen hours! I was sure I was going to die. Then she came, all wrinkly and red. I thought I had given birth to an ugly child. After I had slept, Ole brought her to me. Oh, she was so pretty!

Nettie was much easier. I was in labor for only … no, I'm not going to think about Nettie.

Martin … he arrived right on schedule, the very day I had predicted. But he scared me. He didn't cry. He just looked at me with those big, solemn eyes. Old eyes. How can a baby be born with old eyes? Martin was. I think he was trying to figure things out from the very start.

Then Berent came. I had barely gotten settled. Ole says Berent came out running and has never stopped. He is so maddening and so adorable. The little stinker asked for pants again today. I suppose I'll have to give in. No! The custom is to keep boys in dresses until they are five. I know most Yankees don't do it, but some of the old ways are good and should be kept. He can just wait. Martin did.

Custom … is that the real reason, Helena? Be honest. Why do I have to be honest? I'm just lying here thinking. Oh, all right! It's not the reason. When he starts wearing pants, he will no longer be my baby. I won't have a baby. If I had one, would I keep Berent in a dress? Probably not. Why haven't we had another child? It's been four years. Maybe there is something wrong with me. Maybe I'm done. I don't want to be done! I'm too young.

We haven't really tried to have another baby. On the other hand, we certainly have enjoyed each other. Like tonight. I wonder if the children heard us? When I checked them, they seemed to be sleeping. Then again, they could have been faking. I know I did when I was little. Oh, it would be so nice to have a room of our own, to have some privacy, to make all the noise we want.

Shame on you, Helena. You should be blushing. Well, I'm not. Maybe Finnish girls are fast. They certainly think so in Norway. However, I have had no complaints from Ole.

Ole is sleeping so well. Why am I not? I usually fall to sleep right after … we're finished. Did we make a baby tonight? It is possible. I hope so, but it won't help Berent. He'll be five before the baby arrives. I love you, Berent, but you might as well learn now that we don't always get what we want.

Chapter Twelve

The afternoon clouds were threatening as Oline and Martin paused at the back door of the Lyngen home. Both were dressed in "summer" clothes, which meant Oline's calico dress was faded and a size too small, and Martin's dark pants had a hole in one knee and were too short.

"Now, you promised," Oline said in a whisper. "You'll look at the books and then go home." Martin nodded. "And you'll pick eggs for me and feed the chickens for a week." Martin sighed and again nodded. "And you'll tiptoe by Mr. Lyngen's room. We don't want to disturb him."

Martin put his hands on his hips. ""For the hundredth time, *yes*."

"Shhh! You don't need to shout," Oline hissed. "Come on, and wipe your feet."

Oline did not knock. She opened the door and walked into the kitchen, followed by Martin. "It's me!" she called.

Inga answered from upstairs. "Hello, Oline. Practice for as long as you want."

"Thank you," Oline replied as she looked at Martin. His eyes were huge and his mouth hung open. She smiled and remembered her first time in this house. "Come on," she whispered. "And be quiet."

The children walked carefully out of the kitchen, past Mr. Lyngen's bedroom, and into the library. Martin's eyes nearly popped from his head. He deeply inhaled and forgot to exhale. The sight of all the books literally took his breath away.

"You've seen them," Oline said. "Now, go home. I have to practice."

Martin did not respond. He also did not move. He just stared.

"Martin, you promised!"

The boy continued to stare. "There is so much to learn," he said in a soft voice filled with awe.

"Oh, you'll never learn all that's in those books in a million years."

Martin turned to Oline with tears in his eyes. "I can try."

"Don't be silly. You're just eight years old. Go home!"

That was impossible. The books pulled at Martin like a magnet draws iron. He reached out to touch them.

"No, Martin! You promised!"

Martin's hand froze inches from the shelves when a deep voice said, "I think someone loves books."

Both children whirled to see Karl standing in the doorway. He was dressed in tan cotton pants and a white shirt with no collar, open at the neck. Because she was looking at his profile from the good side, Oline was struck with how handsome he was.

"And you would be?" Karl asked Martin.

The boy could not answer. The face he saw was scarred, ugly, and frightening. His mouth opened, but there was no sound.

Oline looked from Karl to Martin and back. "This is Martin, my brother. He wanted to see your books. He promised not to touch them."

The left side of Karl's face smiled. "Books are meant to be touched, aren't they, Martin?"

Martin nodded. Karl walked into the room. "Do you love books, Martin?"

Martin replied in a tiny voice, "Yes, sir."

"So do I," Karl said. "Books teach you things you never imagined, and take you places you've never dreamed of going."

"Can I touch one?"

Karl chuckled. "You can touch them all. When you're older, would you like to read them?"

"Can I read them now?" Martin pleaded.

"Do you think you can?" Karl asked with surprise.

"Maybe some of them."

Oline stepped forward. "He's read all the books at home."

Karl looked at Martin with keen interest. "Have you, now? How old are you?"

"Eight."

"Is that all? Well, I am impressed." Karl turned to the bookshelves. "Let's see what we have here that you might like."

Martin held his breath as Karl's eyes roamed over the volumes. "Ah, I have an idea. Do you read English?"

"I'm learning," Martin said eagerly, then made a face. "Or I was before Mr. Amenson got sick and Mr. Tuleffson took his place."

"Yes, I heard the Tuleffson boy was hired to finish out the year," Karl said. "I also heard he was so bad he couldn't teach a thirsty horse how to drink water."

Because the joke was so unexpected, there was a moment of silence before the two children burst into gales of laughter. The left side of Karl's face grinned.

When Oline had caught her breath, she said, "Mr. Tuleffson hated my brother. Martin kept pointing out his mistakes."

Karl gave Martin a pretend scowl. "Did you do that, Martin?"

Martin did not know if the scowl was serious or not, so he said defensively, "The answers were all in the book, if he had ever bothered to read it."

Karl laughed. It was a deep, musical laugh, perhaps a little rusty from lack of use. "Yes, a fundamental part of teaching is reading the book and keeping at least one chapter ahead of the students."

Inga came bustling into the room carrying a dust cloth. Oline noticed the woman was wearing a dress Oline had never seen. It was a faded yellow in color, but much too nice for a work dress. She wondered how many dresses Inga had; certainly more than the four or five most women possessed. Oline knew her mother had two old house dresses, a go-to-town dress, and two church dresses—one for winter, the other for summer. "What is all the laughing about?" Inga asked.

Oline answered, "Mr. Lyngen said Mr. Tuleffson couldn't teach a thirsty horse to drink water."

"That wasn't very nice," Inga said with a disapproving glance at her husband.

"But true," Karl said.

Inga decided it was time to change the subject. She knew Karl's joke would spread through north Story County by Sunday. "Martin, it is good to see you. Did you come to see Mr. Lyngen's books?"

"Yes, ma'am. He sure has a lot of them."

"Aha!" Karl said, pulling two books from the top shelf. "There you are!" He then turned to Martin and held up the top book. "This book is called *A Tale of Two Cities*. It was written in English by a famous author named Charles Dickens. This other book is a Norwegian translation. Do you understand?"

The confusion on Martin's face provided the answer. "Why did he write the same book in two languages?"

The left side of Karl's face grinned. Inga attempted to smother a laugh. "He didn't," Karl answered. "Mr. Dickens wrote the book in English. Another man translated it into Norwegian. What I want you to do is read a chapter in Norwegian, then read the same chapter in English."

Inga shook her head. "Karl, that's too hard."

"No!" Martin shouted so loudly that Inga jumped. "I want to try."

Karl handed the books to Martin and patted his shoulder. "Good for you. When you're finished, come back and we'll talk about what Mr. Dickens has to say."

"I'd like that," Martin responded.

Karl gave Martin's shoulder a squeeze. "So would I."

No one spoke, but all sensed that a mundane day had given birth to a special moment. Inga wiped tears of joy from her eyes. The look on Karl's face was one she had not seen since before the war.

Martin hugged the volumes to his chest as if they were priceless. He looked from one adult to the other, not knowing quite what to do. In true big sisterly fashion, Oline solved the problem. "You had better go home now, Martin."

"Thank you!" Martin said with a huge smile, and dashed from the room with his treasure. Inga and Karl laughed, then Inga turned to Oline. "I think it's time you started practicing."

"Yes, ma'am," Oline answered.

As Oline walked to the piano, Karl said, "Do you mind if I sit and listen? You really have improved remarkably."

"Hasn't she, though?" Inga smiled proudly. "She is my star pupil."

Oline blushed. "I don't mind," she said as she sat down at the piano.

"Well," Inga said, "if you two are all cozy, I'm going over to Ione and borrow some eggs."

"Go right ahead," Karl said, sitting in one of the stuffed chairs. "We'll be fine."

Inga gave them both a smile. "I won't be five minutes."

Karl watched his wife hurry out the door and chuckled. "Not likely.

She and Ione will get to talking and she won't be back for half an hour. Go on and practice."

Oline's hands lowered to the inviting keys, and she experienced the tingling sensation of the first touch. She wondered if this excitement would in time go away. Hopefully not. She began by playing scales.

Karl laid his head back, closing his eyes. He knew he should go back into the darkness of his bedroom. A headache was forming. He compared it to the development of a prairie thunder storm; at the moment, it was in the roiling black cloud stage. Next would come the flashes of lightning and the crashing thunder. Pain would explode behind his eyes, and his only recourse would be whisky and oblivion.

But the headaches and their aftermath were old hat. They were like old, unwanted companions. What was new was the lovely girl at the piano. Karl opened his eyes. "Inga believes she has real talent," he thought. "I agree. She also is so much like my angel. Maybe she is my angel, come to save me again. Save me from what? From myself, of course."

The pain struck as Karl had predicted. He gripped his chair but could not suppress a cry. Oline whirled around on the piano stool, her eyes large with fright. "Should I run and get Mrs. Lyngen?"

"No. This is not a seizure. It's just a headache." Karl struggled to his feet, swaying slightly. "I stayed in the light too long. We moles have to live in the dark."

Oline did not understand what Karl meant, but saw the tears in his eyes. "Do you need some ice?"

"No. It will not help," he answered, stumbling to the door. There, he paused. "Continue to practice, my angel. I enjoy hearing you play."

Oline sat frozen on the piano stool as Karl entered the bedroom next door. Soon, there was the sound of glass against bottle, then silence. Oline wondered if she should leave, but remembered he had asked her to practice. She slowly turned back to the comfort of the ivory keys.

Oline

Why does he call me "his angel"? Mrs. Lyngen said it was because he was out of his head. But he wasn't out of his head today. And he looks at me funny. Sort of like he doesn't quite believe I'm me. I'm not afraid of him, though. I used to be, but not anymore. He's really very nice. I just wish Mrs. Lyngen wouldn't leave me alone with him. It's not that I'm afraid he will hurt me. It's that I don't want to be alone with him if he has a bad attack. I'm glad he just had a headache today. How awful it must be to never be out in the sun. I would hate that! Papa said Mr. Lyngen often walks miles out on the prairie at night. How does he keep from getting lost? Me and Ernst were lost as soon as it got dark.

I think Ernst is mad at me. Anytime I try and talk to him, he just turns red and mumbles and walks away. Yet whenever I look at him, he's looking at me. Maybe he is mad because I grabbed his hand when we were lost. I liked it when he grabbed mine. Maybe boys don't like to hold hands. Boys are strange.

Martin wanted to take a candle up here to the loft tonight so he could read. Papa said if he ever caught him doing that, he would take the books back to Mr. Lyngen. Papa didn't want him to keep the books in the first place. Martin begged and cried and Mama gave Papa that look she gives him when she thinks he's wrong, so Martin got to keep the books.

When Martin was milking, I opened them to the first page. I could read some of the Norwegian, but the words were hard. I couldn't read anything in the English book. Papa said the books are too hard for Martin, but Martin kept studying them until it was dark. He's so smart he will probably read them both. I wish I were that smart. I wish I was pretty like Mama. I wish I could play the piano like Mrs. Lyngen. Will I ever be special?

Martin

All those books! I haven't read any of them. I don't know anything!

Chapter Thirteen

"Whoa, Doll!" Ole called as he reached the end of the corn row. The horse willingly stopped, and Ole leaned on the wooden handles of the cultivator. It had a single steel wheel, behind which were three arrow-shaped shovels that plowed up the weeds growing in the rows. Ole was tired. Guiding the horse and keeping the cultivator in the middle of the row, so that it was plowing weeds and not corn, was exacting work. His legs and backed ached, but the height of the sun in the afternoon sky informed him he had at least two hours to work.

Doll looked back at Ole as if to say, why are we stopping? Ole mopped his brow and said, ""Don't look at me like that. You work only a half a day." Doll snorted in reply. When cultivating, Ole had Lady pull in the morning and Doll in the afternoon. Doll required less driving, in fact little driving at all, which made the work easier.

A light breeze cooled Ole as he straightened up. He smiled and looked over at his fields of oats and wheat. Both were lush. If the rains came when needed, and if there was no wind or hail, and if the grasshoppers stayed away, the crops would be excellent. Ole chuckled and shook his head. There were too many "ifs" in farming; yet there was no other work he would rather do.

"All right, Doll. If you are so anxious to work, let's get going."

Ole pulled up on the handles, which took the shovels from the ground, and Doll did the required turn to get the cultivator lined up for the next middle. However, before Ole could start, he saw Martin running toward him. "Papa! Papa!" the boy called.

"Now what?" Ole muttered, knowing something serious had happened.

Martin reached his father red faced and out of breath. "Papa, Maud is stuck in a slough and can't get out!"

Ole groaned. Getting a large animal out of a slough was next to impossible. The harder they struggled, the deeper into the slough they sank. "What about Mabel?"

"She's fine. She should be home by now."

Ole unhitched Doll from the cultivator and jumped on the surprised horse's back. "Come on," he said to Martin, pulling the boy up behind him. "Let's see what we can do."

Maud was a forlorn-looking sight. Her sides heaved and head drooped from the effort to free herself. She swayed drunkenly as her eyes pleaded for assistance. Ole could only shake his head. Maude was ten feet from solid ground, buried up to her belly in the stinking, moss-covered marsh. She looked like a legless creature floating on the slough muck. This was worse than Ole expected.

"How did she get in so far?" Martin asked.

"I don't know, son," Ole replied. "Probably just by thrashing around trying to get out."

"Can we pull her out with a rope?"

Ole and Martin had stopped by the barn to get a length of rope and left behind a tearful Berent screaming that he should be allowed to come along.

"We can't," Ole answered. "But maybe Doll can if we can get a rope around Maud."

"You can lasso her, Papa." Martin grinned. "Like the cowboys do!"

Ole squatted down and spat. "Getting a rope around her neck won't do any good. We would just choke her to death. We need to get the rope under her neck and tied around her body."

Martin imitated his father by squatting down. "I'm light. Maybe I could get the rope around her."

"No!" Ole snapped. "You're not strong enough. That muck would suck you right down. Don't you ever go into a slough for any reason, understand?"

"Yes, Papa."

Neither moved for nearly a minute. All that could be heard were frogs and crickets; then Maud bellowed her pain.

Ole stood up. "I hear you, girl. I hear you."

Martin stood beside his father. "Are you going to shoot her, Papa?"

"Well, I can't let her suffer. But we're going to try something first. We'll hook Doll's tugs to the outer rings of the singletree and the rope to the center ring. I'll try and get the other end wrapped around Maud, then you and Doll can pull her out."

"What if you get stuck?"

"Then you'll pull me out."

Ole did what he had said and picked up the free end of the rope. There was no need to remove his boots, as he had been cultivating barefoot. He grinned at Martin. "Well, here we go," he said, stepping into the slough.

His left foot sank to the ankle. His right leg sank into the slimy muck up to his knee. Pausing a moment to make sure he did not fall, Ole brought his left leg forward. It sank above the knee.

"You're doing it, Papa!" Martin called.

"Maybe," Ole grunted, as he attempted to bring his right leg forward. It would not budge. He took a deep breath and tried again. The ooze grudgingly allowed a partial release. Ole again gathered himself and pulled. His leg broke free with a deep sucking sound that made Martin think the slough was angry. Ole leaped forward, almost falling. When he righted himself, his right leg was buried up to his thigh.

Martin clapped his hands. "You're almost there, Papa!"

As usual, almost was not good enough. Ole was about four feet from Maud, but the distance might as well have been a mile. He could not move. It felt like two giant suction cups had been attached to both feet. Although he knew it was hopeless, he made an effort to take one more step. It was not to be. He was as stuck as Maud.

"You have to pull me out, Martin. I can't reach her."

Martin ran to Doll, grabbing her bridle as Ole tied the rope around his waist. "I'm ready," Ole said. "Take it slow."

Martin led the horse forward, but as the rope grew taut, Doll stopped, surprised at the load.

"Come on, Doll!" the boy urged.

Doll responded by lunging forward. Ole popped free of the muck like a float on a fishing pole when the line breaks, and landed face down in the slough. Doll pulled the sputtering man onto dry land.

"Are you all right, Papa?" Martin asked.

Ole sat up, wiped off his face, and untied the rope from around his waist. "Outside of being filthy and soaked, I'm fine. Bring me the rifle, Martin."

"You can't just shoot her!"

Ole struggle to his feet. "Yes, I can. There's no way to get her out, and I'm not going to let her suffer."

Martin picked up the heavy, single-shot, black powder weapon and reluctantly carried it to his father. Ole said, "You don't need to watch, son. Take Doll up to the high ground and hold on to her. The noise is likely to make her jump."

Tears welled in Martin's eyes. He hated milking but did not want to see Maud shot. He also was aware of what an economic loss her death would mean to the family. The boy wiped his eyes and turned to Doll, just as a booming voice shouted, "Don't shoot that cow, Ole!"

Ole smiled. There was no mistaking that voice or the man striding toward them. Big Per.

When Big Per Larson reached the slough, he looked at Ole, scratched his beard, and shook his head. "You know, Ole, swimming in the river is much more fun than in a slough."

Ole laughed. "You won't get an argument from me, Per. I tried to get a rope around her, but got stuck. Doll had to pull me out."

Big Per put his hands on his hips and stared at the cow. "You've been a bad girl, Maud. But I don't think you deserve to be shot."

The mournful-looking cow nodded her head as if she understood.

Ole said, "I don't have a choice, Per. I can't get to her, and I can't leave her there to die."

"I understand that. Maybe I can get to her."

"You'll get stuck just like I did."

"Nah! I've got strong legs. Hand me the rope."

Ole did as he was asked. "The muck just sucks you down, Per."

"I know," Per said, removing the wooden shoes he always wore. Ole could not help noticing that both of Per's big toes were peeking out of his wool socks. "I had to do this once before and forgot to take off my shoes. Lost both of them." Per took a step into the slough.

"If you get stuck," Martin said, "Doll can pull you out."

Big Per paused. "Do you think so, Martin? I don't know. I'm pretty big. Maybe your pa will have to go get my oxen."

"I think Doll is up to it." Ole grinned.

"Probably, but you never know. She's just a horse."

Big Per laughed as he took a large step into the slough. Then a second, followed by a third. With a fourth step, he was standing beside Maud. "Told you!"

Ole could only marvel at Big Per's strength. The big man had made it look easy, but Ole was aware of how difficult each step had been. "Per, you are amazing."

"It's about time you recognized that." Big Per grinned as he tied the rope around Maud.

Ole took Doll by the bridle and waited for Big Per to finish. The big man checked the knot and said, "Get the rope taut. Then, when I say three, I'll lift and you pull."

Ole led Doll forward until the rope was out of the water. Big Per crouched and put his arms beneath the cow. "One, two, THREE!"

There again was the sucking sound as Maud's legs appeared. The surprised cow bellowed, her eyes wide, and her legs began to thrash. Big Per used every ounce of his strength to toss the cow away from him. She landed with a splash on her right side, her head briefly going under the green slime, but Doll quickly pulled her to onto solid ground, where she lay exhausted but safe.

Martin jumped up and down. ""You did it, Mr. Larson! You did it!"

"So I did," Big Per answered between pants. "Ole, untie the rope. I'm going to need it."

Ole quickly led Doll back, untied the rope, and threw it to Big Per. "Tie it around your waist. I don't think even you can hold on."

Big Per tied the rope, then grabbed it with both hands. "Ready," he called.

For the third time, Doll pulled, and with a sucking sound almost as loud as Maud had made, Big Per broke free. His attempt to keep his feet failed, which resulted in a perfect belly flop. Doll pulled him to the edge, where he lay gasping beside Maud.

Ole led Doll back to the slough. "I think that is the most incredible thing I have ever seen."

Big Per said nothing for a moment, then pushed himself to his hands and knees and looked at the cow. "Maud, if you ever do this again, I'll shoot you."

"Amen!" Ole said as he reached down and helped Big Per to his feet. It was then that Martin witnessed a sight few have seen. The two Norwegian men gave each other bear hugs and collapsed, laughing, into each other's arms.

As this was going on, Maud struggled to her feet and began wobbling to the farm.

Ole and Big Per sat on milk stools in the pasture behind the barn, smoking their pipes as the day ended with a glorious sunset, accented by fluffy, orange and purple clouds. The horses grazed nearby, their noses almost touching. The yearling calves slept in the barn. Mabel was at the water trough and the sheep had settled down for the night in a tight grouping near the center of the pasture. Maud lay as if dead only a few feet from where the men sat. After being milked, she had stumbled to her current location and collapsed. She hadn't moved in nearly two hours.

Big Per, clad only in his long underwear, pulled the blanket tighter around his waist and over his legs. "Did we really stink that bad?"

"Berent sure ran away in a hurry."

"Bah! What does a four-year-old know?"

Ole laughed. "Enough to run away from two men who have been playing in a slough."

"I wouldn't call it playing."

"No, you are right there."

Upon their arrival at the homestead, Helena had greeted the men with a bar of homemade soap and orders to go to the river, bathe, and wash their clothes. Big Per had protested, but to no avail. If he wanted supper, he had to do as told. Both men had refused to strip further than their underwear, just in case someone came along the stage road, but they had found waist-deep water in which to scrub themselves and their smelly clothes.

Big Per had been out at such a depth when Helena arrived with fresh clothes for Ole and an old blanket for Per. The big man actually blushed. Helena laughed, picked up the wet clothes, and informed him that she had built a fire to aid in drying the clothes. Even with the blanket, Big Per had refused to come to the cabin for supper, so he and Ole had eaten behind the barn.

"Don't you think my clothes should be dry by now?" Big Per fumed.

"Helena said she would bring them to you when they were."

"Well, it's taking too long! And I think that wife of yours is enjoying this situation a little too much. Both she and Oline were laughing when they brought out supper."

"You're right. But if you stop to think about it, we were quite a sight … and smell. Let her have her fun. There is not much to laugh at out here on the prairie."

Big Per snorted and gave Ole a sorrowful look. "Norwegians aren't supposed to laugh. It weakens the constitution."

"Who said that?"

"My father. I don't think I ever saw him laugh."

"Then why do you laugh more than anyone I know"

"I want to make my father mad," Big Per answered with a grin, causing both men to laugh.

Ole banged the ashes from his pipe and became serious. "Per, I don't know how to thank you. Maud should be dead, not sleeping."

Big Per waved his hand dismissively. "Ah, I just did what I could. Nobody can afford to lose a good milk cow ... even if she is dumb as a post."

"Well, I sure can't." Ole smiled at the big man, then reached out and gave Per's arm a pat. "Anyhow, thank you again for today ... and for everything ... especially for being my friend."

Big Per stared down at his massive hands. Slowly he turned to face Ole. There were tears in his eyes. "No, it is me who should thank you. You're a good man, Ole Branjord. Allowing me to be part of your family means more than you will ever know."

Ole did not respond. Both intensively studied their hands, embarrassed by this unplanned and unguarded moment of intimacy. Neither knew what to say or do. Expressing deep feelings, especially to another man, was foreign and a second thing seldom done by Norwegians.

The almost painful silence was broken by Martin as he climbed over the pasture gate. "Here are your clothes, Mr. Larson. The shirt is dry, but the pants are still a little wet."

"Well, it's about time," Big Per said in mock anger, relieved the intimate moment had been nudged into the safety of the past. "I thought for awhile I was going to have to pay cash money to get them back."

"What a good idea!" Ole said. "I'll remember that for the next time."

Big Per took the clothes from Martin. "I already told you, there will be no next time."

"Mama said to get dressed and she'll bring your violin down here."

"Oh, she did, did she?" Big Per said as he put on his pants. "I see she still won't let me in the cabin. That's what she thinks of me!"

Helena's voice came from the side of the barn. "You know what I think of you, Per Larson. Just put on your pants."

Per laughed and pulled the shirt over his head and shoulders. "Ole, that wife of yours is a pistol."

"Don't I know it."

Per tucked the shirt into his pants. "All right, you can come now! I'm decent."

Helena, carrying the violin case and followed by Oline and Berent, opened the gate and entered the pasture. "From the stories I've heard about you, Per, you've never been decent."

Big Per's roar of laughter sent a jolt of fear through the animals. Even Maud raised her head. "Well, I'm as decent as I can be."

"That you are, dear friend. That you are." Helena smiled as she approached.

The smile turned Big Per's knees to the consistency of bread pudding. The simple truth was that he had fallen in love with his best friend's wife. Not that he would ever touch her. He would die first. To hide his feelings, he gruffly asked, "Where are my socks?"

"In the cabin. They need darning."

"Oh, you don't have to do that."

"I know," Helena replied, handing him his violin case. "I want to."

Another awkward moment was avoided by Berent. "Mr. Larson, you still stink a little."

"Berent!" Helena cried.

Everyone but Berent laughed. "Well, he does!"

Big Per made a face at the little boy. "Oh, you think so, do you, Mr. Branjord?"

"I'm not Mr. Branjord. Papa is!"

"I keep forgetting that," Big Per said, bending down to Berent. "I'll tell you a secret, Berent. It is good for a man to stink a little. That smell keeps the pretty girls from attacking him."

Helena rolled her eyes. Ole laughed, and Oline and Martin giggled. Berent did not understand what was funny. Big Per's statement made perfect sense to him.

Big Per removed the violin from the case, tuned it, and played some scales. The caramel-colored instrument glowed in the remaining twilight. Unlike the case, which was battered and scuffed, the violin was without blemish. In Big Per's hands, the instrument looked tiny and fragile, as if it were about to be crushed. Many had been amazed that such heavy, long fingers could caress the strings with such agility and produce music worthy of a concert hall.

"Play 'The Old Woman With A Cane,'" Oline cried.

Per laughed as he put the violin under his chin. Oline's request was not a surprise. All Branjord concerts began with this old folk tune. "Only if you sing along."

"We will!" Oline and Martin said in unison.

Per played an introduction, then Ole's rich tenor and the children's soprano voices joined nature's evening chorus.

> The old woman with a cane,
> Way up in Haka Valley,
> Jumped over the creek,
> And, of course, fell in.
> But when she came up again,
> She was just as crazy,
> The old woman with a cane
> Jumped over the creek.

They all laughed, as they always did, and then continued with the further misadventures of the poor old woman with a cane. Helena swayed with the music and quietly hummed along, well aware she could not carry a tune in a bushel basket. But she loved music and was pleased the children had inherited Ole's ability to sing.

The song ended with a flourish of violin runs. Helena walked over to Ole, holding out her hands. "Play a dance tune, Per."

"With pleasure," he replied.

Ole grinned and deeply bowed to Helena. She responded with a deep curtsey. The music began and the two took the first steps of a familiar Norwegian folk dance. Oline clapped in time with the music. Berent attempted the same, with mixed results. Martin sat on one of the milk stools, his hands resting quietly on his lap. Suddenly, the music stopped.

"What's the matter with you, Martin?" Big Per asked.

"Nothing," came the embarrassed reply.

"Why aren't you clapping time?"

Martin blushed, seeing that everyone was looking at him. He looked down at his bare feet.

Helena became concerned. "Are you sick, Martin?"

"No, Mama," the boy stammered. "It's … it's just some people at church say dancing is sinful."

Beg Per groaned. "That's hogwash!"

"Well, they do," Martin said.

"I know they do," Big Per bellowed. "But don't listen to them. They think anything fun is sinful! Why, do you know when pants came out with fly fronts, some preachers thought they were sinful."

Martin was surprised. "Didn't pants always have fly fronts?"

"No. There used to be sort of a flap in front with a lot of buttons. It just shows you how silly some people can be. Don't be a sourpuss! Clap your hands and have some fun!"

"I'd have fun if I had pants!" Berent said.

Helena sighed, looking up at the heavens. "Oh, not the pants again."

Big Per pointed his bow at Berent. "It looked to me like you were having fun in that dress."

"I'd have more fun in pants!"

Big Per bopped Berent on the head with his bow. "I had to wear a dress until I was five. If I could live through it, so can you."

The music and dancing began again. Martin joined Oline in keeping time, and Berent, after five seconds of pouting, did the same.

Sweat beaded on Big Per's face. Helena threw back her head, her feet in perfect rhythm. She dance forward and back, then linked arms with Ole, who spun her around so fast she would have fallen if he had released her. But she knew he would never let her fall, never let any harm come to her. That was one reason she loved him so much.

Oline grabbed Martin's hands. The boy resisted at first, but was soon joining his sister in make-believe dance steps, which consisted mostly of jumping up and down and turning circles. Berent attempted to join them, but was pushed away by Oline. "Dancing is for two!" she said, sticking out her tongue.

Berent returned the favor, then spied Doggie, who as usual had materialized as quietly as ground fog, and lay about twenty feet from the action. The boy ran to the wolf-dog, giving him a huge hug. Doggie licked Berent's face. He then grabbed Doggie's front paws. "You can dance with me!" Doggie declined the invitation by backing away. Again Berent grabbed the wolf-dog's front paws. This was too much for Doggie. His lips curled back, revealing chipped yellow fangs, and a threatening growl informed the boy that enough was enough. Berent stepped back, crossing his arms. "Nobody wants to dance with me!" Doggie wagged his tail, but the boy had turned and was running for the center of the pasture.

For reasons known only to a four-year-old mind, Berent decided to take his hostility out on the sheep. He ran to the kneeling ram, jumping squarely on his back. The sheep jumped to his feet and raced toward the dancing humans. Since the sheep had been sheared in the spring, there was little wool to hold on to. Berent's ride lasted only seconds. He was dusting himself off and deciding whether or not to cry when the ram turned and lived up to his name. The angry animal charged full tilt at Berent and butted him in the rear end.

Berent's howls of pain brought an abrupt end to the music and dancing. Helena was soon cradling the boy in her arms. "What happened?"

"The sheep butted me!"

"Serves you right," Big Per said, having witnessed the whole episode. "You picked the wrong sheep to ride."

"What have I told you about riding the sheep?" Ole asked, doing his best to keep from laughing.

"Not to."

"Then Mr. Larson is right. You deserve a butting."

Helena carried Berent to the pasture gate. "It is time you were in bed. In fact, it's bedtime for all of us."

Big Per laughed. "I suppose that means I should go home."

"Well, it is dark," Helena called over her shoulder. "You are welcome to stay."

Big Per picked up his violin case, but did not put the instrument away. "No thanks. Buck and Pride will get me home."

While Helena put the children to bed, Ole helped hitch the oxen to Big Per's wagon. "How is your cultivating going?"

"Almost done crossing," Big Per answered. "I see you're almost finished too."

"Yah. I was thinking we might cut some hay before laying the corn by."

"Good idea. How about starting Monday?"

"Fine with me. Your place or mine?"

"Yours. The food is better."

Big Per climbed into his wagon. Ole handed him his violin and case. "Are you planning to play all the way home?"

"That I am. Buck and Pride know the way." Big Per eased his way onto the seat. "Buck! Pride! Home!"

The oxen leaned into their yokes, pulling the wagon toward the river.

"Thank you again!" Ole called.

Big Per made a wave with his bow. "I've had enough thank yous for a month! Good night, Ole."

"Good night, Per."

A beautiful but mournful melody drifted from the wagon back to Ole. He recognized it as an old folk song that praised the magnificent Norwegian mountains and fjords. A lump developed in Ole's throat. He knew he would never see either again. That was his old life. He turned to the cabin and walked toward his new one.

Standing unseen under a large cottonwood near the river, a man watched Ole disappear into the cabin. He had been standing there for some time, long enough to witness the dancing and laughter. This, he thought, is what a family should be. And then said aloud, "It is something I will never have."

He fingered the butt of the Navy Colt in his army-issued holster. "Tonight?" he silently asked himself. "No, not tonight," he answered. This was not the time or the place. He looked up at the beauty of the sky and felt the soft breeze soothe his scarred face. It would have to be another night; a night when there was less warmth, less laughter, and less love.

Berent

It's not fair! Nobody would dance with me. Oline stuck out her tongue at me. I was going to tell Mama, but I forgot. Even Doggie wouldn't dance! Nobody likes me. And everybody laughed when that mean sheep butted me. It hurt! Dumb sheep! But riding it was fun. I betcha I wouldn't have fallen off if I had been wearing pants!

Chapter Fourteen

Oline made a face as Helena poured milk into the churn. She hated churning like Martin hated milking. "Don't give me that look," Helena said, putting the lid back on the churn. "This butter helps pay for your piano lessons."

"I know," Oline sighed, pulling the churn to her. She sat on a stool by the table. "It's just that there is so much milk to churn."

"Be thankful. Having too much is far better than having too little," Helena replied as she sat on a stool by her spinning wheel and opened a bag of carded wool.

Spinning was usually a winter activity, but, wonder of wonders, Helena had some free time. Ole and Martin were down by the river chopping wood, and Berent was asleep in the loft. Helena hoped he wasn't coming down with something. He never napped.

A light but steady breeze was a welcome guest, and made the cabin quite comfortable. "Something else to be thankful for," Helena thought. "Enjoy it." The dog days of July and August lay ahead.

Oline scowled as she worked the plunger up and down. "Martin is old enough to churn."

"Yes, he is. But churning is women's work."

"So is milking."

"In Norway. Be thankful you don't have to milk."

Oline banged down the plunger. "Milking has to be easier than churning. I wish Maud had never gotten out of that slough!"

"What a terrible thing to say!" Helena cried. "That cow gives us milk and butter. She helps keep your belly full! When I was your age, there were people in Finland who would have killed to own that cow. Shame on you!"

Oline's eyes were wide with surprise and fear. She had never seen her mother so angry. "I'm sorry, Mama."

"You should be! My baby brother died because Mother ate so little, her milk dried up. I watched my grandmother starve to death so that there would be more food for my sister and me."

Tears flowed down Helena's cheeks. The suppressed memories of her Finnish childhood escaped their mental prison and destroyed her carefully constructed defenses like a rogue wave swamps a small boat. The wool dropped from her trembling hands. Horror filled her eyes. Spasms wracked her body. Her color became that of an alabaster sepulcher.

Oline stared in disbelief, fearing her mother was dying. "I'm sorry, Mama! I didn't mean it. I'm so sorry!" She leaped to her feet, almost knocking over the churn, and ran to her mother, throwing her arms around Helena's neck and sobbing.

Slowly, Helena put her arms around Oline. Her trembling stopped. Her tears ended. She gently stroked her daughter's hair.

"I'm sorry, Mama. I'm sorry."

"I'm sorry too," Helena whispered. "You didn't need to hear that. It just came out."

Nothing was said for several minutes, each content to hold the other. Then Helena pushed Oline from her embrace. "You need to get back to churning."

Oline reluctantly did as she was told. There was another prolonged silence, after which Oline asked, "Did your brother really starve?"

Helena picked up the wool. "Yes. And Grandma too. Many people died. Mama made birch bark soup so that we would have something in our stomachs. I thought I would die."

"What saved you?"

"God sent an early spring and a stray sheep. But it was too late for Grandma and the baby."

"Why was there no food?"

Helena sadly shook her head. "Because there was one crop failure after another. The year was too wet or too dry, too cold or too hot. The preachers said it was because we had turned away from God. He was punishing us for our sins." A rueful smile played at Helena's lips. "We must have been terrible sinners."

Again, except for the thumping of the churn, there was silence. Oline looked at her mother and shivered. The warm, beautiful eyes she so loved were distant and cold. It was obvious that, although Helena sat only steps from her, she was far away, in a different time, a different place. Oline brought her back by asking, "Is that why you went to Norway?"

"Mostly," Helena answered after a pause. "I turned sixteen and my father told me he could no longer feed me. I had to marry or get some kind of work. Either way, I had to leave."

"Grandpa must have been mean."

"No, Oline. He wasn't a mean man. He was a beaten man."

"Why didn't you get married? Weren't there any boys you liked?"

"There was one young man, but he was as poor as we were. Marrying him would have meant moving from one starving home to another. So I looked for work, but there wasn't any."

Helena began to spin the wool into thread. She did not tell her daughter there was one type of work open to her. Well-paid work. Work that had been offered to pretty girls since man first lusted after woman.

"How did you get to Norway?"

"Walked. My father had a cousin who was taking his entire family to Norway. I traveled with them and two peddlers."

"Where did you sleep?"

"Anyplace we could get shelter: post stations, homes, barns, huts. We almost died in a blizzard."

The churn plunger froze in the up position. Oline gasped. "You traveled in the winter?"

"Yes, that was the best time. The rivers froze. They were like roads."

"What happened?"

Helena stopped the wheel. "The snow began falling in the late afternoon. It was on our fourth day out of Tornio. The peddlers, who had traveled the route before, knew we were quite a distance from the next resting station and made us walk as fast as possible. The small children had trouble keeping up. The peddlers threatened to leave us behind if we couldn't keep up. I ended up carrying the five-year-old girl on my back. The parents carried the seven- and nine-year-olds. The wind picked up and soon we couldn't see six feet in front of us. Remember the blizzard last winter when we couldn't see the barn" Oline nodded her head. "It was much worse than that. We formed a single line, the men in front, and made sure we did not lose sight of the person in front of us. We heard the wolves howling, but we were more afraid of the wolverines. Wolverines are nasty, mean animals, like badgers, and they creep up on you with no warning. I was sure I was going to die. But God took mercy on us and led us to an abandoned Lapp hut. Thankfully, there was firewood. It was a small hut, so the fire and our body heat kept us from freezing. The next morning, we replaced the firewood and moved on."

Helena again began her spinning. Oline stared at her mother with awe. She knew that Helena had come from Finland to Norway, but her mother never spoke of it. In fact, Oline realized Helena had never talked about her life in either Finland or Norway.

"Why did you replace the wood?"

"It is a way of life in the North. You replace what you use. The wood in the hut saved our lives. The wood we left might have saved other travelers, or at least was there when the Lapps returned."

"Did you meet any Lapps?"

"Yes." Helena smiled. "When we reached Karesuando, there was a whole gathering of Lapps. That was the only fun part of the trip."

"Were the Lapps ugly and dirty?"

Helena looked at her daughter with surprise and touch of anger. "No! Who told you Lapps were ugly and dirty?"

"Elsa Signaldahl."

"Umph!" Helena snorted. "I'm sure she heard that from her mother. Well, it is not true. The Lapps were kind and hospitable. They shared everything they had. They even let us ride on their sleds. All the way to Lyngenfjord."

"Were the sleds pulled by reindeer?"

"Of course! That's how the Lapps travel. And oh! The reindeer run so fast. It was almost like flying! At times I closed my eyes. I was sure we would tip over."

"It sounds so exciting!"

"It was." Helena's eyes sparkled and a delighted smile enlivened her beautiful face as she remembered one of the few joyous episodes of her early years. "What made it even more exciting was that the travel was done at night under a moonlit, star-saturated sky."

"You traveled at night?" Oline asked in disbelief.

Helena laughed. "During the winter in Lapland, there is nothing but night. The sun doesn't shine."

"I don't think I'd like that."

"You would if you were riding on a sled pulled by reindeer. It was ... Oh, I can't really describe it, Oline. The stars seemed so close you could pick one from the sky and put it in your pocket. And the Northern Lights were so incredible, they were frightening. I truly felt the awesomeness of God."

Helena paused, her soft, upturned lips slowly turning into a hard, thin line. "Then we got to Norway. We arrived in Skibotn market. It was a big trading center for furs. We were fortunate to get a ship that took us to the Norland area of Norway. I worked as a maid for several families. It was an unhappy time."

Helena pretended to concentrate on her spinning. She was finished with this conversation; however, Oline was hungry for more. "Were they mean to you?"

Helena looked at Oline's sweet, innocent face. How much was she ready to know? Certainly not all of it. Hopefully, she would never know all of it. She sighed. "Yes. No servant should ever be treated the way I was. In my first home, I didn't even have a bed. I slept on a mat by the kitchen fireplace. I worked six days a week from sunup to sundown. I didn't understand Norwegian, so I was often yelled at and beaten by my mistress. As for the master and his sons, I did understand what they wanted."

Helena's eyes grew hard and again there was a long silence. Oline worked the plunger of the churn. She did not understand. What did her mother mean? She took a deep breath and asked, "What did they want?"

Helena did not look up. "I'll explain when you're older. Just pray to God you never have to be a servant girl in a foreign country."

"When did you meet Papa?"

Helena's face relaxed. She smiled at Oline. "That was when I went to work for Mrs. Lessing in Jasvar. Ole worked as a clerk for Mr. Lessing, who was a merchant trader. The Lessings were proper, but kind. Mrs. Lessing taught me how to rosemal. She was very good. Our big chest was a wedding present she painted."

Now Oline was excited. "Did you fall in love with Papa the first time you saw him?"

"Oh my, no." Helena laughed. "He was so shy, I thought he didn't like me."

"Then, how did you and Papa ..."

"Get together?" Helena asked, her blue eyes sparkling. "That was due to a broken fence. After he finished work at the store, Ole came over to the house and began fixing the fence in the backyard. I thought Mr. Lessing had told him to fix it, but after we were married, Ole admitted he had offered to repair it."

Oline giggled. "So that he could be near you. What did you do?"

"Oh, I found excuses to be in the backyard. I especially developed an interest in the garden, which just happened to be next to the fence."

Oline clapped her hands. "Did he kiss you?"

"Aren't you the nosy one! The answer is no, but we did have long conversations and get to know each other. After that, one thing led to another." Now it was Helena's turn to giggle. "I think Ole set a world's record for the length of time it takes to fix a fence."

"Did I see the fence?"

"Yes, you did. In the summer, Mrs. Lessing and I would work in the garden while you played in the yard and Nettie ..." The sparkle in Helena's eyes was replaced by pain. "Nettie lay on a blanket."

Fittingly, a cloud drifted over the sun, darkening the cabin. The mention of Nettie's name always brought gloom to the Branjord household. Neither parent talked much of their early years. Questions asked were, until today, either answered briefly or ignored. It was as if the memories were too painful to recall.

"If you like Mrs. Lessing so much, why did you leave?"

"You are just full of questions today, aren't you?"

Oline lowered her eyes, anticipating a scolding. But to her surprise, Helena answered. "The possibility of a better life. Neither Ole nor I believed the silly stories about America being a garden of Eden. We knew life would be hard. But if we had stayed in Norway, I would always have been a maid and Ole a clerk. We wanted more, not only for us, but for you and Nettie. Ole loved farming, but his family farm had been inherited by his older brother, and there was no way he could afford to buy one. So we decided to join the throngs of Norwegians who had already sailed for America."

"Weren't you scared?"

"Of course. But not as frightened as when I left Finland. Ole was far worse than me. The night before we were set to sail, he tried to talk me out of going. Do you remember the voyage?"

Oline rested on the plunger and thought for several seconds before answering. "I think a little. I remember all sorts of strange noises and clouds ... huge clouds that you could almost touch."

Helena smiled. "What you remember were not clouds. They were sails. We were at sea for seven weeks and three days."

"Was it fun?"

"Heavens no! It was cold and wet. Water constantly leaked down to what our captain called our cabins. Cabins! They were nothing but small areas divided by old sails. Even on sunny days it was damp. And the stink! I'll never forget the smell! Most of the passengers were seasick. Including me."

"Was I seasick?"

"No. You and Ole were good sailors. You two were even hungry. Oh, that was another thing. The food! We had to bring our own and prepare it ourselves. After a week, almost everything was either rotting or moldy or chewed by rats."

Oline's hands flew to her mouth. "There were rats?"

"Hundreds! Every sailing ship has rats. We made a hammock for you and Nettie to sleep in so the rats wouldn't crawl on you."

Color drained from Oline's face. She hated rats. She had nightmares about rats. Now she knew why. "Did they ever bite us? Maybe the rats are what made Nettie sick."

Helena sighed and shook her head. "No, I think it was the wet and the cold. She got better when we reached Quebec, and by the time we reached Chicago, I thought she was well."

"Was Chicago big?"

"Yes. Big, dirty, and noisy. We couldn't get out of there fast enough. A farmer gave us a ride to Lisbon. He and his wife were quite taken with you. They wanted to hire both Ole and me, but Ole had worked with a man who lived in Clinton, Iowa, so we bought a team and wagon and off we went." The sadness deepened on Helena's face. "If we had stayed, maybe Nettie would still be alive."

"Did she die in Clinton?"

"No. She got sick again on the way to Clinton. I thought we were going to lose her. But she was a fighter and rallied again. We stayed six weeks in Clinton. When we started for Hardin County, she seemed perfectly healthy." Helena's voice trailed off. She blinked back tears. "We buried her on the prairie."

A nearly forgotten memory formed in Oline's mind. "I think I remember that. It was night. Papa dug a deep hole. He was crying."

Helena stood up and crossed to the big chest, where she took out her box and returned to the stool. "We were all crying," she said, opening the box and removing the wispy, blond lock of hair. "You asked us not to throw dirt on her."

Helena caressed the hair. Her hands trembled slightly, and as had happened countless times before, tears dampened all that remained of her second child. "She was such a sweet baby," Helena whispered. "Even when she was sick, she smiled at me."

There were no more questions. The only sound in the cabin was the thumping of the churn.

Helena

"Don't throw dirt on Nettie." That's what Oline said as I held her in my arms. "Don't throw dirt on Nettie." But we did. Out on the prairie, we wrapped her in a small quilt I had made for her and threw dirt on her. No marker. Only God knows where she is buried.

I should not have told Oline about the dirt. She had forgotten. Now she will remember it as long as she lives. Some things are best for children not to know, even if they ask. Someday she'll ask me what it was like being a serving girl. I'll never tell her the truth. She has no need to know about wives beating you because their husbands want you, or about avoiding buildings where grown sons hide, waiting to pull you inside.

Oris … I wonder what happened to him. He was the only one who was nice. His smile was sweet. I think he was in love with me. I liked him too. Perhaps I could have loved him. But marriage was impossible. His mother would never have allowed him to marry a poor Finnish serving girl. I hope he is doing well. He did save me from Inar.

Inar was as mean as Oris was nice. Never have two brothers been more different. Inar had me pinned against the wall in the barn. I can still smell his bad breath and see the animal lust in his eyes. Oris yelled at him to stop. That surprised Inar. I got away and hit him with a milk bucket. Oh, that felt good. He was out cold for ten minutes.

Oris told his mother what happened, but Inar claimed I had flirted with him and wanted the attention. The mother believed Inar. It was all my fault. All the fault of the sluttish Finnish serving girl. I was fired and never paid a month's wages. I see now that God was looking out for me. If I had stayed, I'm sure I would have been raped. And then I would never have met Ole.

Dear, sweet Ole. You were so shy. I though you would never speak to me. But you did. And not only did you speak, you listened. You were the only man who ever listened to me. And when you took me in your arms, I felt safe. For the first since leaving Finland, I felt safe.

But being safe wasn't enough. I wanted more. I did not want to be a serving girl all my life. I wanted my own house. My own family. Ole wanted to farm, not be a clerk in a store. So we booked passage, the cheapest we could find.

I had very romantic notions about sailing on tall ships: the sails full, the ship slicing through moonlit waves. Silly me! There is nothing romantic about howling winds and huge waves crashing over the bow, drenching everything and everybody. Seven weeks and three days. There were times I thought I would never again set foot on dry land. Some did not. How many died? Six ... no, seven.

Then Nettie got sick. I was terrified she would be number eight, wrapped in canvas and thrown into the endless sea. She survived the voyage, but for what? To be wrapped in a quilt and buried in an endless sea of grass.

Would Nettie be alive if we had stayed in Norway? Probably. She would be almost ten. Oh, Nettie, forgive me. You died for my ambition.

Chapter Fifteen

Doll and Lady stepped without hesitation into the placid, shallow Skunk River. The water reached only to their knees. Ole looked back to the east from the wagon seat and saw Buck and Pride ambling along about two hundred yards from the ford. Ole grinned. When they reached Fairview, he would have to mention to Big Per how slow his oxen were,

As the horses climbed the opposite bank, Ole noticed a large bank of black clouds to the west. Good, the crops needed rain and the haying was done. Ole and Big Per had spent a week cutting prairie grass, first at his place, then at Big Per's. The hay was now stacked and drying. Too bad it was outside and not in the haymow of a real barn. Someday, Ole promised himself. Someday.

Ole drove to Fairview, where he tied Doll and Lady to the hitching post in front of the general store. It wasn't much of a store; then again, Fairview wasn't much of a town. Looking up what in later years would be Broad Street in the town of Story City, Ole saw a random conglomeration of frame and log buildings interspersed with fenced pastures and acres of virgin prairie. Fairview was still very much a settlement.

The store was an unsubstantial frame building that, although just a few years old, was battered and patched. Two upright support beams on either side of a small porch stood as mute evidence of a porch roof that had been blown into the Skunk River. The roof on the building itself appeared to be only a strong wind away from suffering the same fate. Despite its ramshackle looks and the fact that it stocked only a few staples hauled in from Nevada at the whim of the eccentric owner, the store was important. It gave the surrounding farmers hope that Fairview would one day be a real town.

Ole was relieved to see the front door was open. Too often, it was locked. The owner, Turg Thorson, liked to fish. No, he loved to fish. When the urge struck him, he would close up and head for the river. To his would-be customers, this was an annoying but not insurmountable problem. Everyone knew his favorite fishing hole and, if the purchase was absolutely necessary, a short walk and a polite request would get Turg to reopen. However, if the fish were really biting, he had been known to say, "Come back tomorrow."

Turg's ability to stay in business despite his suspect business attitude was based on three facts: his was the only store in Fairview; he was single and had simple needs; and he sold cold beer. Behind the store was a sturdy log icehouse. In it, behind a locked, heavy, iron-reinforced door and surrounded by ice, were two large kegs of beer. When the beer ceased to flow in one, it was time to go to Nevada for a new keg and to replenish other necessary items.

Two men stepped out of the store, each carrying a tin mug of beer. It was obvious from their unsteady gait that these beverages were not the first of the day. Ole recognized them as Emil Signaldahl's hired men. The first, nicknamed Rooster because he reminded everyone of a bantam chicken, was short, thin, and had the narrow face of a badger with a personality to match. The second was younger, taller, and much better-looking; however, his vacant eyes informed you there was not much between the ears. It was said he fancied himself a ladies' man. Ole remembered his name was Ingvald.

The hired men sat on empty nail kegs and took long swigs of their beer. Directly in front of them was tied a matched pair of black horses hitched to a forest-green wagon with "River Bend Farm" written in red block letters on the side. Ole was not envious of the team, but the wagon was something else. He wondered if he ever would own enough land to justify a name on his wagon. And if by chance he did, what name would he choose? He would have to think about that.

Out of the corner of his eye, Ole saw Rooster poke Ingvald and whisper something in his ear, which resulted in dirty, suggestive laughs. Ole felt his temper rise. He did not need to hear the words to know the whispered remarks concerned Helena. It was common knowledge that Hanna Signaldahl's ceaseless insults concerning the "Finnish Branjord woman" were aired to anyone who would listen.

With angry eyes and set jaw, Ole stepped onto the porch. He glared down at the men, who returned his look with smirks and feigned innocence. "Something bothering you, Branjord?" Rooster asked.

Ole stared at the two for several seconds before answering. "No, but I am wondering why Emil is paying you fellows to sit here and drink beer."

The smirk disappeared from Rooster's face. His scraggly beard exposed thin lips and yellowed, rotting teeth. "What we do is no concern of yours."

"That's true, Rooster. But it is a concern of Emil's. I'll have to ask him about it next Sunday."

Rooster half-rose from the keg. He hated being called Rooster. His eyes became burning black holes. But as he was about to respond, Buck and Pride pulled alongside of Ole's horses. Rooster sat. He wanted no part of Big Per.

"Is there a problem?" Big Per asked as he climbed down from his wagon.

"No," Ole answered. "Emil is paying these fellows to drink beer."

Ingvald growled, "We're picking up two kegs of rock salt."

"Well, you fooled us," Big Per said, stepping onto the porch. "I will admit, though, that drinking beer on a hot day like this is a good idea. Shall we, Ole?"

"After you," Ole answered, waving his right arm at the door.

The two men entered, leaving Ingvald and Rooster red-faced and steaming.

The store was a simple room just slightly larger than Ole's log cabin, with an uneven plank floor and haphazardly constructed shelves that offered for sale everything from harness parts to vegetables from local gardens. A tired, faded curtain separated the back left corner from the rest of the store. Behind it was a bed that was never made and clothes that were seldom washed. To the right of the door, attached to the front wall and running most of the way to the back, was an undressed slab of lumber that served as a counter and bar. Seated in a rocking chair by a cold potbellied stove, dressed in the male uniform of the time, black pants and an unbleached homespun shirt, was Turg Thorson.

"Afternoon, gents. Hot enough for you?"

"Yes, indeed," Ole replied.

Big Per scratched his beard. "Well, I don't think there is any danger of the river freezing over."

Turg laughed. "Could I interest you two in a beer?"

"That's what we stopped for," said Ole.

Turg rocked forward, pushing himself out of the chair. It took effort because he was pushing sixty and carrying over three hundred pounds. Turg stood over six feet tall and, according to those who had known him when he was young, had been slender. That, however, was years ago. Too much fishing, sitting, and beer had led to his current condition. He slowly walked to a large wooden tub containing about six inches of water and chunks of ice. Cooling in the tub were tins of butter—some from Ole's cows—fresh milk, cream, four fish, and a large pitcher of beer.

"I think there's enough for two," Turg said as he poured the dark liquid into tin cups that may or may not have been washed since the last imbibers. "Those loafers out front have drunk most of it. But as long as they're paying, I can't complain."

Ole and Big Per raised their cups. "Skål!" they said in unison and drank nearly a third of the brew.

"My, that's good," Big Per said, wiping his mouth with his sleeve.

Turg drained the last of the beer into his own cup and settled back into his chair. "Looks like you fellows have been working."

"Cutting prairie grass," Ole said, taking another sip of beer. "It makes good hay."

Turg nodded. "Better enjoy it. The way Story County is filling up, you'll soon be seeding red clover like they do in Illinois."

"Don't doubt it at all," Big Per said, after a man-size belch. "I hear talk there are plans to plat the whole state in six hundred and forty acre sections. We'll look like a big checkerboard."

"Yup. Things are changing fast. When I set up this store, I could drive to Nevada straight as an arrow. Now I have to swing around one farm after the other."

"That's the truth," Ole said. "Another twenty years and there won't be any prairie left."

Turg scratched his bushy gray beard, then picked up a damp towel and wiped his bald head. "Make that ten."

"Well, at least then we won't have to worry about prairie fires," said Big Per.

"Speaking of fire," Turg said as he finished his beer and picked up his battle-scarred pipe, "did you fellows hear about what happened up in north Hamilton County?" Ole and Per shook their heads. "The folks up there had a swarm of locust fly in."

"Locust!" Big Per bellowed. "Are they headed this way?"

"No, lightning started a prairie fire and every last grasshopper got burned to a crisp. How's that for luck?"

Ole drained his beer. "Luck, maybe. I see the hand of the Lord in that."

"Amen," Big Per said, placing his tin cup on the slab.

"You fellows want a refill? I got more in the icehouse."

The two men glanced at each other and reluctantly shook their heads. Ole said, "There's a storm building. We need to get to my place before it breaks."

They turned to go just as Rooster and Ingvald entered the store. "Where's that rock salt?" Rooster called.

"Right there by the door," Turg answered. "Be careful. They're heavy."

Ingvald snorted, giving Turg an "I'll show you" look. He rubbed his hands and attempted to lift one of the kegs. With great effort, he raised the salt a foot off the floor before it slipped from his grasp.

Turg chuckled. "I warned you. It takes two men to lift one of those. And by the way, if you break one, you clean up the mess."

Ingvald was embarrassed and angry. He looked up to see Rooster grinning. "What are you laughing at? Pick up an end!"

Rooster did so, and the two carried the keg out the door.

Turg lit his pipe. "I don't understand why Emil keeps those two around. They don't have half a brain between them, and they're lazy."

"Maybe Hanna likes the tall one," Big Per said.

Ole shook his head. "No, Ingvald's far beneath snobbish Hanna."

"Don't be too sure, Ole," Turg said, blowing a smoke ring. "I've seen Hanna look at him like he's stick of peppermint candy."

"Are you serious? I can't believe it."

Big Per grunted. "I can believe anything about that woman."

Ole plunked a dime down on the slab. "Thanks for the beer, Turg. I still can't believe it. I think Emil's afraid to fire them."

"Why would he be afraid of those two?" Big Per asked.

"Because," Ole replied, "Rooster is just plain mean."

"Now I agree with that." Turg nodded, taking another puff on his pipe.

Ingvald and Rooster returned and, without a word, picked up the other keg. Ole and Big Per followed them out the door. They watched as the keg was lifted onto the wagon. Sweat ran down the faces of both hired men.

Big Per smiled. "It looks like you boys could use some muscle."

Rooster's eyes narrowed. "I suppose you could do better."

"Probably,"

"Then prove it!" Rooster sneered. "I've heard a lot of stories about how strong you are, but I've never seen you do nothing."

Big Per stood for a few moments on the porch. Then, with thumbs in the waistband of his pants, he walked toward the hired men. Both hurriedly stepped back, fear replacing bravado. Big Per ignored them. He placed himself in front of the two kegs, wrapped his right arm around one and the left around the other, and lifted them off of the wagon. Then, like he was carrying pillows, he walked about ten yards up the road, turned, walked back, and placed the salt on the wagon. His lips smiled at Rooster while his eyes drilled holes in him. "That's the way we did it in the old country," he said softly to the two slack-jawed men. "Now why don't you get your scrawny asses into that wagon and go earn the money Emil pays you?"

Rooster turned beet red. He hated big men. He especially hated strong big men who made him feel impotent. He wanted to kill Big Per but was too frightened to move.

Ole called to his friend, "Come on, Per. We have rabbit stew waiting for us."

Big Per turned away from Rooster. Had he been sober, the little man would not have said, "Oh, so your Finnish whore is feeding him again. What else does she do for him?" But he was drunk ... and stupid, a combination that always means trouble.

Quick as a cat, Big Per whirled, and with one hand picked Rooster up by the throat.

"Per, no!" Ole cried.

Rooster kicked and squirmed like a pig about to be slaughtered. Ingvald's eyes bulged from their sockets.

"Per, let him go! He's not worth killing."

Rooster was turning blue, his eyes filled with terror. Big Per did not let him go. Instead, he jammed his free hand into Rooster's crotch and threw him into the wagon, where he lay crumpled and writhing in pain. Big Peer then calmly untied the hitching strap, freeing the team. "Ingvald," he said softly, "get this piece of shit out of here before I drown him in the river."

Ingvald leaped onto the wagon seat, backed the team out, and started for home at a fast trot.

Ole stared at the departing wagon. "That was my fight, Per."

"I know," Per answered. "But I was closer."

Ole

That miserable little weasel! I hope Per broke every bone in his damn body! But I should have been the one to do it, not Per. He was closer, but I just stood there. Had I been quicker off the mark, I could have gotten to Rooster first. Why didn't I? Am I afraid? I don't like to fight. Never have. Usually, fighting doesn't solve anything, just makes more problems. Or am I just making excuses? Yes, that's what I'm doing. Just making excuses. I should have fought today. I should have broken Rooster's scrawny neck! Instead, I waited for Per. What kind of man am I?

Helena is *my* wife! It is my responsibility to protect her good name, not Per's. Oh, I know how he feels about her. I've got eyes. If something happened to me, he'd marry her in a minute. But then so would half the men in Story County. They probably wonder what the prettiest woman in the county sees in me. I wonder that myself. Yet I know she loves me. Only God knows why. Am I a coward? She certainly deserves better than I gave her today. Damn! Why didn't I move?

What was it Rooster said? "What else does she do for him?" Is that what people think? Is that what they are saying behind my back? No, I don't think so. There is just one person who makes up these rotten lies: the witch of River Bend Farm. Why does she hate Helena so? What happened between those two when Helena worked for Hanna's aunt? Helena won't talk about it. She says what happened in the past should stay in the past. Not anymore. What happened then is affecting the present. I'll ask her again.

There is no way to keep this quiet. I'm sure Turg saw everything. By Sunday everyone in north Story County will know. And they will all wonder why it wasn't me who threw Rooster into the wagon. Per will tell them he was closer. But they will still wonder. So will I.

Chapter Sixteen

Beneath a blue sky populated with fluffy, pillow-like clouds, the Saint Petri congregation filed out of church, relieved to walk and stretch after a nearly two-hour service. The mood of the members, however, did not reflect the tranquil beauty of the day. Smiles were rare, furtive glances abundant. Speaking to or even smiling at the wrong person could cause disagreements among friends or family. The children raced out as usual, but they too were careful who they played with and who they avoided. The only thing the two sides could agree upon was that the tension was becoming unbearable. Worshiping God had become the most stressful act of the week.

Knots of people quickly formed, separated by sex and an ever-increasing distance. Ole Andreas observed drily, "If this continues, we'll have to expand the churchyard."

The others nodded.

"It's a crying shame," Jonas Duea muttered. "We've worked so hard to build this church."

Hans Twedt sighed. "I don't understand all the fuss over a ruffled collar."

Jonas stiffened. "It's more than the vestments—it's what they represent. Why can't Reverend Amlund lead the service in a plain suit?"

"Because that's what the synod wants him to wear," Ole Branjord replied.

"Who is the synod to tell us what to do?" Jonas shot back, his neck reddening. "This is our church."

Big Per crossed his arms. "If we are going to argue religion, I'm going home."

"I agree," Hans said, then turned to Jonas. "How's Jacob doing?"

"Much better," Jonas answered, relieved the subject had been changed. "He should be good as new in a week or so. It just proves how careful you have to be around the rear end of a horse."

"And the front end too," Big Per added. "I keep warning you fellows about horses, but you won't listen."

Ole Andreas crossed his arms in imitation of his brother. "As I recall, about a year ago, old Buck kicked you into the middle of next week."

The men laughed. "That," Per replied, "was because I did not speak kindly to him. Oxen have sensitive souls."

"Oh, sure they do!" Ole Andreas snorted. "About as sensitive as a basket of cockleburs."

The resulting laughter made other groups look with envy at the men's lack of tension and obvious pleasure in each other's company. However, the good feelings evaporated when Saul Jaeran strutted up to the group. "Jonas, I see you are enjoying yourself."

"Yes, I am, Saul. Do you want to join us?"

"No. I don't talk to papists."

"Papists!" Ole said with surprise. "No one here is a papist."

Saul glared at Ole. "You're high church. You love the liturgy. You want the preacher to wear fancy robes. That makes you a papist in my book!" Saul whirled to face Jonas. "Are you a traitor?"

"Why would you say something like that?" Jonas answered. "I'm just talking to my friends."

"Then I suggest you find new friends!"

Hans Twedt, his jaw set, took a step toward Saul. "And I suggest you leave before you get hurt."

Big Per casually stepped between the two men. He smiled down at Saul and gave him a pat on the arm that sent the smaller man skipping to the right. "I think Hans has made a good point."

Saul, his face as red as a newly painted barn, stepped back, and before marching away said to Jonas, "You're either with us or against us."

Jonas called after him, "I'm certainly not with you, Saul!"

The jovial mood departed with the annoying, angry man. Ole Andreas spat. "He sure does know how to turn a beautiful day gloomy."

"Yah," his brother agreed. "What a crape-hanger."

"I swear, "Jonas said, "I'm tempted to go back to having Sunday services at home and not come to church at all."

Hans nodded. "If you do, I'll join you."

"Speaking of crape-hangers," Ole said, "here comes Emil Signaldahl."

The men watched Emil approach. It was obvious from his angry expression that he was not joining them for a friendly visit.

"Per Larson, I want to talk with you," Emil said with bravado he did not feel.

"What about?"

"I have a hired man with a broken shoulder."

"Is that all? I must be getting weak in my old age."

"He and Ingvald said you attacked him for no reason."

The pretend smile vanished from Big Per's face. "That's a lie. He insulted me. He should be thankful he escaped with just a broken shoulder."

Ole took a step forward. "He was drunk, Emil."

"Stay out of this, Branjord!"

"I can't. He insulted Helena too."

Emil sneered at Ole. "Then why didn't you do something?"

Per hitched up his pants, a sure sign he was becoming angry. "Because I was closer. They were both drunk as skunks."

Emil stepped back. He had not wanted to confront Big Per at all. Hanna had shamed him into it. His voice cracked. "They told me they each had one beer."

Big Per laughed. "The two had been at the store for two hours. Ask Turg. Do you pay them to drink, Emil?"

"Certainly not! They're good workers."

It was Hans Twedt's turn to laugh. "Since when? Everyone but you knows they are worthless as teats on a boar hog."

Emil clenched his fists as the other men laughed. "This is no concern of yours, Twedt!"

"You're right, Signaldahl," Hans snapped. "Just stating a fact."

"I've told you the truth, *Mr.* Signaldahl," Big Per said so softly he was hardly audible, a sign that he was now very angry. "Are you calling me a liar?"

Ole Andreas lightly tapped Emil on the shoulder. "I know my brother pretty well. I advise you to walk back to your fancy buggy and go home."

Emil shrank under the hard, cold eyes of these Norwegian farmers. He knew his attempt at intimidation, ordered by his wife, had failed. He sputtered, "This isn't over, Per. I'm thinking of seeing the sheriff."

"Do that," Big Per answered, crossing his massive arms. "And see what happens."

Emil quickly turned and fled. The men watched him scurry away, then Jonas said sarcastically, "This has been a real pleasant Sunday. I think it's time to go home."

The others agreed, said their goodbyes, and gathered up their families.

Doll and Lady plodded home, the children asleep in the back of the wagon. Helena looked back to make sure no little ears were listening before asking, "What did Emil have to say?"

"Just what you would think. Per set him straight."

"Hanna put him up to it. I saw her watching."

"I'm sure she did. I think she enjoys embarrassing Emil."

"I know she does. Hanna is an evil woman." She paused and then asked, "Why did Reverend Amlund take you aside after church?"

"Oh, I almost forgot. He asked if he and Mrs. Amlund could stop by this afternoon."

Helena's mouth dropped open. Her eyes became blue ports of disbelief. She turned the color of bleached sheets. "Today! What did you tell him?"

"Of course. He wants to talk about ways to bring the church back together."

"Today! And Mrs. Amlund is coming too?"

Ole looked at his wife with bewilderment. "Yes, what's wrong? They're not coming for dinner."

"I don't care! I have to serve something! I don't have a cake. I don't have a pie. I don't even have cookies! And the cabin is a mess!"

"It is not," Ole said, attempting to calm Helena. "Besides, he said not to make a fuss."

"Not to make a fuss! Not to make a fuss! Ole, how dense can you be? The pastor is coming!" Helena screamed so loudly the horses broke into a trot and the children awakened. "Hurry, Ole! We have to get home!"

Ole slapped the reins. He did not quite know what he had done wrong, but he was aware he had made a grievous error.

"What's the matter?" Oline asked.

Her mother replied, "The pastor is coming!"

When the lathered horses stopped at the cabin door, Helena leaped from the wagon seat. "Hurry, children! Put on your work clothes. Ole, put the horses away and then wash the floor!"

"You washed it yesterday."

"I don't care! The pastor is coming. Wash it again!"

Helena turned to run into the cabin. Berent called to her, "What about dinner? I'm hungry."

Helena became rigid, as if frozen in place. Not a muscle moved. Then she looked up at Ole with the frightened eyes of a cornered deer. "I don't have time to fix dinner."

Ole knew whatever he said would be wrong, but he also was hungry. "Reverend Amlund said not to make a fuss."

In an instant, frightened doe eyes became those of an angry tiger, "Oh, that's just stupid men talk! I have to fix a dessert! There is johnnycake left over from last night. When you're done with the horses, feed the children!" With that said, she ran into the cabin.

Three small, questioning faces looked up at Ole. What had turned their mother into this crazy woman? Ole slumped on the seat and shook his head. "Go help your mother," he said. The children crawled out of the wagon and approached the cabin with trepidation.

Helena had her church dress off and was half into her work one when the children walked through the doorway. "Don't just stand there!" she cried, "Get your clothes changed! Then, Oline, get out my cake pan and the flour; Martin, get wood for the stove. Hurry!"

"What do you want me to do?" Berent asked.

"Stay out of the way!"

The boy's lower lip quivered and tears came to his eyes. Under normal circumstances, Helena would not have snapped at her youngest and, certainly, if she had, would have noticed the tears and comforted the boy. Not today. She did not notice. The pastor was coming!

Oline quickly changed, grabbed the cake pan from the shelf, and opened the flour box. "Mama! There's no flour. You used it up yesterday when you made bread."

Helena again turned pale. Tears blurred her vision. She hugged herself and sank into her rocking chair. "What am I going to do?" she whispered.

The children hardly breathed as they watched their mother. This was something new, something frightening. Mother always knew what to do. She could answer every question, confront any situation. She never asked them what to do.

Oline said hesitantly, "We have fresh bread."

"I know that, sweetie," Helena answered. "But I need more than bread."

"You could make hagletta, Mama," Martin said.

Helena stopped rocking. "I could. I have everything. But hagletta needs to be served cold."

"We could get some ice,"

"Where? Turg is closed on Sunday."

Oline grinned as she clapped her hands. "I know! Mrs. Lyngen has ice. She would let me have some."

Helena jumped out of her chair. "I'm sure she would! But it would melt before we get it home."

"Not if I ride Lady!" Martin said. "I could wrap a big chunk in a sack and get most of it home."

"Yes! Yes, you can!" Helena grabbed the two children, hugging and kissing them both. "Bless you! I love you! Martin, get Lady before your father puts her in the pasture, then ride as fast as you can to the Lyngen house."

"Yes, Mama!" Martin cried, running out of the cabin.

"Oline, get the milk and buttermilk from the cooling tank. We're going to make hagletta!"

Oline followed her brother out of the cabin. Helena watched her go with a smile that was broad and filled with relief. She would have something special to serve to the pastor and his wife.

Her smiled faded when she looked down at Berent. Tears were rolling down his cheeks. She quickly knelt beside him. "Berent, what's wrong?"

Tears dropped on the boy's bare feet. "You didn't bless me. You don't love me."

Helena drew Berent to her, bathing his wet cheeks with kisses. "Oh, yes, I do love you! I love you lots and lots! And I do bless you." Helena then proceeded to tickle her youngest until he shrieked with laughter.

Ole slapped Lady on the rump, sending the horse off toward Fairview. He watched as Martin urged the reluctant horse into a trot, feeling more than a little sorry for the animal but happy the crisis had been solved. Why had Helena acted as if the world was coming to an end? Reverend Amlund said not to make a fuss.

When Ole entered the cabin, mop and pail in hand, Helena was at the stove stirring a pot full of milk while Oline was at the table beating a bowl of eggs. Helena gave Ole her sweetest smile. "You don't need to mop the floor. I did that yesterday."

"But you said …"

"I know what I said, but it's not necessary. Just go smoke your pipe."

Ole could not believe it. Was this the same woman who minutes before had been a raving maniac? He had a basketful of questions but was wise enough not to ask them. Instead, he went out on the porch, sat on the bench, and filled his pipe. As he lit the tobacco, he looked up at the beautiful sky and said softly, "You made them. Maybe you can understand them."

She who could not be understood was happily preparing the hagletta, which resembled a curdled custard. Helena's recipe called for two quarts of milk, five beaten eggs, one cup of sugar, a pinch of salt, and four cups of buttermilk. To prepare it, she first took the whipped eggs and blended them with the buttermilk, sugar, and salt. She then brought the fresh milk to a boil, stirring frequently. When the milk boiled and turned a little brown, she added the blended ingredients and let it boil until curdled. At that point. she put the pot on the back of the stove and allowed it to simmer for fifteen minutes. The hagletta was then done. All that was left to do was pour it in a serving dish and allow it to cool.

Later, with everyone back in their Sunday clothes and the hagletta dish sitting in the sink surrounded by chunks of ice, Helena looked anxiously around the spotless cabin, wondering if she had missed anything. "What time did the pastor say he was coming?"

"He didn't. He just said afternoon."

Helena frowned. "Well, I think that is a little inconsiderate. He could at least have set a time."

"What difference would it have made, Helena?" Ole said. "We don't have a clock."

"I don't care," Helena snapped, unwilling to admit that without a clock, what she said made no sense. "He still could have set a time. And that reminds me, you promised to buy us a clock."

"Yes, I did. And I will when we sell the hogs."

"Humph!" Helena said. "You also promised to put a door on the outhouse."

A red blush began creeping above Ole's shirt collar. He had had enough of what he considered unreasonable behavior. He glared, gritted his teeth, but said nothing. Berent, however, who was sitting on the bed swinging his bare legs, did. "Mama, why are you so grumpy?"

Helena was brought up short by the question. "I am not grumpy."

Ole muttered, "You could have fooled me."

"What did you say, Ole?"

Before Ole was forced to answer, Oline and Martin raced into the cabin. "They're coming!" both cried.

Helena clutched her throat. Anguish replaced anger. "Oh, dear!" she said, then addressed the children. "You three be good! Do you hear me?"

"Yes, Mama," the children replied.

"And when the adults want to have a serious conversation, you three go out and play and don't come back until I call you. Understand?"

"Yes, Mama," came the reply in triplicate.

Berent jumped from the bed. "Can we have hagletta first?"

Helena could not help but laugh. "Yes, we will eat first."

Chapter Seventeen

Reverend Nils Amlund and his wife, Mathea, arrived in a buckboard pulled by a matching pair of strawberry roans named Bonnie and Max. Reverend Amlund was dressed in his usual black suit and white shirt. Mathea wore a long-sleeved white blouse, a black skirt with matching vest, and a straw bonnet decorated with a bright red ribbon. Helena immediately fell in love with the bonnet, but thought it quite daring for a pastor's wife.

Ole and family greeted them from the porch. "Welcome Pastor, Mrs. Amlund." Ole said.

"Whoa there!" Reverend Amlund called to the horses, who promptly obeyed. "Thank you, Mr. Branjord. It is nice of you to have us."

Mrs. Amlund smiled. "I hope you haven't gone to a lot of trouble."

"Oh, no trouble at all," Helena replied, returning the smile.

Berent, who was hugging Ole's right leg, looked wide-eyed up at his father. Ole sensed what was about to be said, so gently put his hand over the boy's mouth.

"Do you want to unhitch the horses, Pastor?" Ole asked.

"No, we can't stay that long. But I'm sure they can use some water."

Ole pointed to two buckets sitting on the porch. "I thought they might. There's a bucket there for each of them."

"That does not surprise me, Mr. Branjord," Reverend Amlund said as he stepped down from the buckboard. "A good farmer takes care of his stock."

Mrs. Amlund also stood, and Ole helped her to the ground. "Thank you, Mr. Branjord," she said, and then turned to Helena. "I didn't get to talk to you after church today. How are you feeling?"

"I'm fine, thank you. I love your bonnet."

"Thank you, so do I. Nils gave it to me. Do you think it's too daring for a pastor's wife?"

"No, it's perfect," Helena replied, crossing her fingers behind her back.

Ole and Reverend Amlund placed the buckets in front of the horses, who gratefully emptied the contents. "That should hold them nicely," Reverend Amlund said.

Berent stared hard at Reverend Amlund. "Where is your dress?"

"My what?" Reverend Amlund said with surprise.

"Berent!" Helena said, "Reverend Amlund doesn't wear a dress."

"Yes, he does. I see him wear it."

The adults looked at each other, then Reverend Amlund laughed. "My robe! He's talking about the vestments. Berent, I wear the robe only during the church service."

"Oh," Berent said, then added, "why?"

Reverend Amlund smiled and pointed his finger at the boy. "People much older than you are asking the same question."

There was a moment of awkward silence before Helena said, "Well, let's not stand here. Come inside."

Mrs. Amlund had no more than stepped in the cabin when she said, "Oh, you have a rosemal chest. Did you paint it?"

"No," Helena answered. "The lady I worked for in Norway gave it to me as a wedding present."

"She must have thought highly of you. It is beautiful," Mrs. Amlund said, examining the chest more closely.

"I think so too." Helena smiled, pleased that the pastor's wife admired her favorite piece of furniture. "Although some people think rosemaling is old country."

"Pooh! What do they know? I have one and wouldn't trade it for anything!"

Berent had no interest in painted chests. "Let's eat!"

Reverend and Mrs. Amlund laughed, then Reverend Amlund said, "Let's not. I'm full."

"Really," Mrs. Amlund added. "We just got up from the table."

"Well, at least you can have a cup of coffee," Helena replied. She knew this old Norwegian dance well. No one was ever hungry, yet everyone knew it was an insult to the lady of the house if you did not eat something. "Sit down at the table. I'll get the coffee. Oline, pour the water."

The boys slid onto the bench. Reverend and Mrs. Amlund sat opposite them on chairs usually reserved for Ole and Helena. Ole took his place at the head of the table, sitting on one of the stools. Oline poured each a glass of fresh water, and Helena followed with a pot of steaming coffee for the adults.

"Now please tell me you didn't go to any trouble," Mrs. Amlund said.

Ole closed his eyes. Berent was out of reach. But he was relieved when the boy said, "Mama made hagletta!"

"And it's cold!" Martin added.

"Cold hagletta?" Reverend Amlund said with genuine surprise. "How did you manage that?"

Oline slid onto the bench beside her brothers. "Mrs. Lyngen gave us some ice."

"Cold hagletta in the summer," Mrs. Amlund said with admiration. "Now that's something."

Helena blushed as she brought the dessert to the table and dished it into serving bowls.

Reverend Amlund rubbed his hands together. "My, that looks good."

"I thought you were full," his wife chided him.

"Never too full for hagletta!" Reverend Amlund replied with a grin.

Everyone laughed. Helena finished dishing the hagletta, placed butter and a freshly cut loaf of bread on the table, and then sat on her stool. "Pastor, would you say a prayer before we begin?"

"Certainly," Reverend Amlund answered. All bowed their heads. "We thank you, Lord, for this beautiful day, this wonderful family, and for your bountiful blessings. Especially we thank you for cold hagletta. Amen."

The children giggled. The adults smiled. Mrs. Amlund poked her husband. "Shame on you, Nils."

"I meant every word of it," Reverend Amlund answered.

"Can we eat now?" Berent asked.

"Yes, we can!" Reverend Amlund laughed.

As the hagletta and the bread were enjoyed, the conversation was as light as the soft breeze that fluttered the curtains of the open window above the table. But when the food was gone and the coffee drunk, the words began to falter until there was an uncomfortable silence. Ole realized the reason for the visit was now at hand. "Children, go out and play until I call."

"Yes, Papa," Oline said as she and her brothers scooted off the bench and ran outside.

Mrs. Amlund watched them go with a sad smile on her lips and a deep sadness in her lovely eyes. For reasons unknown, she could have no children of her own. She turned to Helena. "You have a lovely family, Mrs. Branjord."

"Thank you," Helena replied. "Most of the time they are a joy."

"But then there are the other times," Ole added.

After they all laughed, Reverend Amlund became serious. "Ole, why don't you and I take a walk?"

Helena interrupted Ole's answer. "If the discussion is about the church, I would like to be a part of it." Reverend Amlund looked at Helena with surprise. She took a deep breath and continued, "We women also are members of the church."

"I quite agree," Mrs. Amlund said. "I was hoping that is what you would say."

Reverend Amlund smiled. "I too agree, so let's get started. I am trying to keep Saint Petri from splitting apart. To do that, I need your honest thoughts. What do you consider the problems to be, and how do we solve them?"

Ole glanced at Helena, then cleared his throat. "What people seem most upset about is the robe and collar you wear and the liturgy."

"What are your feelings?"

"I have no problem with either."

"And you, Mrs. Branjord?"

Helena swallowed hard. He had said to be honest. "I don't see why you couldn't conduct the service without the vestments."

"I could. But the Lutheran Church wants its clergy to wear the vestments."

"Why?"

"Because the vestments represent the call to ministry. We put on the robes of Christ, not to set us above, but apart. The robe is a symbol that we are called and ordained ministers, whose sole purpose is to preach the saving gospel of Jesus Christ."

Helena looked directly at Reverend Amlund, challenge in her eyes. "Forgive me, Pastor, but I have seen much more *above* than *apart*."

Reverend Amlund accepted her challenge. Holding her gaze, he asked quietly, "Is that what you saw this morning in church?"

Helena blushed and quickly answered, "No. I can honestly say I do not see that when you stand before the congregation. You are a wonderful, caring minister. But in Finland and Norway, I saw far too many Lutheran pastors who believed themselves to be above everybody else. They acted as if they could walk on water! I saw a minister stand before the congregation and condemn and ridicule pregnant women who had been raped. I saw men fired from their jobs because they had offended the minister. I saw families forced to leave their villages because the minister ordered the father shunned. I left Finland at sixteen because our pastor was pressuring my parents to have me work in the parsonage. We all knew that girls who worked in the parsonage were in danger of becoming pregnant and being sent away to who knows where!"

There was a shocked silence in the cabin. Reverend and Mrs. Amlund stared down at their hands. Perhaps Ole was more shocked than anyone. This was a story he had not heard.

Mrs. Amlund spoke in a whisper. "That is an ugly story, Mrs. Branjord."

"Yes, it is," Helena replied. "But a true one."

Reverend Amlund sighed. "There is no doubt some of clergy have brought shame on themselves and the church. But you cannot tar all ministers because of the actions of a few."

"I do not!" Helena cried. "When Ole and I moved here from Hardin County, we were so happy to be near a real church with an ordained minister. You are an example of what a minister should be." Helena bit her lip. "You say you put on the robe of Christ. Many see you putting on the robe of power! There are people in Saint Petri who have had bad experiences with Lutheran ministers in Norway. These people love the Lord Jesus, but fear the church."

Reverend Amlund was taken aback, not only by the words, but by the fact they were spoken so well and so passionately by a woman. For the first time, he realized the controversy over vestments was not a minor issue brought about by a few petty minds.

Ole leaned forward. "Helena is right about the fear. Men like Jonas and Jacob have nothing against you. They fear the power of the

Norwegian church. They are afraid ministers here will have the same power as in Norway."

"That can't happen, Ole," Reverend Amlund said. "The American Constitution forbids it. There cannot be a state church."

"I know. But some fear the Constitution can be changed. I do not. In Illinois there are all sorts of churches. In a few years, the same will be true here."

"You are so right!" Reverend Amlund exclaimed. "How can we convince the fearful that this will happen? How can we convince them that the Norwegian church cannot run their lives?"

Ole folded his hands on the table and shrugged. "I don't know if we can."

"Perhaps," Helena said after a lengthy silence, "a start would be not wearing the robe."

Reverend Amlund sighed as he sat back in his chair. "You are probably right, Mrs. Branjord, but I can't do it. I just can't. Wearing the vestments during the service brings me closer to my Lord. Putting on the robe inspires me to preach the good news. Can you understand that?" Ole and Helena nodded. "Wearing the robe is part of the Lutheran service. It is like the liturgy. The church has decided what to include and say. Not me. I know the absolution is a problem, but it is part of the liturgy. And the liturgy is central to the Lutheran faith. The liturgy was adapted from the Roman Mass by Martin Luther himself."

"For some, that is the problem," Ole said. "They think the liturgy is too Catholic."

"Does that mean we should do away with it? Are you against the liturgy, Mr. Branjord?"

"No, no, not at all," Ole replied. "I enjoy the liturgy. I think it is the most important part of the service."

Reverend Amlund excitedly pounded the table with an open hand. "Yes! You are right again, Mr. Branjord. It is the core of the service. It is where we say our prayers and confess our sins and ask for forgiveness. That is why the liturgy is so important! Do you agree, Mrs. Branjord?"

Helena bit her lip and blushed. She looked at Ole, whose eyes were twinkling. "Helena and I have our differences over the liturgy," he said.

"Oh?" Reverend Amlund said with a smile and a raised eyebrow. "Is there some dissention in the Branjord household?"

Helena laughed. "Not really. I've come to the conclusion that Ole is right."

"This is news to me," Ole said.

"What changed your mind?" Reverend Amlund asked.

"Oline and Martin," Helena answered. "I've noticed they are joining in the responses. They are quite proud of themselves. After watching them, I remembered how proud I was when I could take part. Maybe the liturgy joins the generations."

"Not just the generations," Reverend Amlund said. "The centuries. The liturgy joins us with all the Christians who have worshipped before us." Reverend Amlund grinned as he sat back in his chairs. "Bravo, Mr. Branjord! We have a convert. Now all we have to do is convince the doubters and enlighten them about the vestments. I know you are friends with Jonas and Jacob. Will you talk to them?"

"Yes. But I don't know if it will do any good."

Reverend Amlund reached over and patted Ole's hands. "All any of us can do is try."

All nodded, and there was silence as Reverend Amlund removed his hand. Then an impish smile played at Helena's lips. "Pastor, is the white ruff you wear around your neck part of the robe of Christ?"

Reverend Amlund was surprised by the question. "Well, technically, no. It is just part of the vestments. Why do you ask?"

"I was thinking, a small compromise would be to leave on the robe and take off the ruff."

"Why? Don't you like it?"

"Well, you asked us to be honest," Helena said, the smile widening. "I think it is sort of womanish. When I look at it, all I can think of is how hard it must be to iron."

Mrs. Amlund clapped her hands, bursting with laughter. "It is a horror to iron, Mrs. Branjord! An absolute horror!"

Again Reverend Amlund looked surprised. "I didn't know that."

"Of course not," his wife answered. "You don't have to iron it."

Reverend Amlund scratched his beard. "Well now, that is an interesting thought. I'll tell you what. We have a meeting up at Luther College in a few weeks. I will put the question of the ruff before the other pastors. And, just between the four of us, it does itch."

Laughter filled the cabin. Outside by the barn, the children heard it and looked expectantly at each other. Martin asked, "Do you think they're done talking?"

"No," Oline answered. "Adults sit and talk a long time."

Berent disgustedly plopped himself down on the ground. "I'm hungry."

"So are we," Martin said.

"Get up, Berent," Oline ordered. "You're getting your good dress dirty."

Berent pouted but got to his feet. "I can't do anything."

"Neither can we," Oline grumbled.

Few things are as confining for children as being forced to stay dressed in church clothes for an entire afternoon. The fun part of childhood is running, jumping, climbing, rolling on the ground, and wrestling, all of which are prohibited by the parental admonition of "don't get your clothes dirty." All the Branjord children could do was wander around the farmyard, stealing glances at the cabin doorway.

Much to their delight and relief, the doorway filled with Reverend and Mrs. Amlund, who stepped out onto the porch followed by Ole and Helena. The children raced to the porch. The visit was over!

Reverend Amlund and Ole walked to the front of the horses. As Ole untied the hitch rein, Reverend Amlund said, "Do talk to Jonas and Jacob. Maybe we can still calm the waters."

"I'll do that," Ole answered. "I would hate to see the congregation break up."

"Amen to that."

Mrs. Amlund smiled at Helena. "Thank you so much for a wonderful visit, and especially for speaking your mind. We need to hear more from the women of the church."

"I agree," Reverend Amlund called as he stepped up into the buckboard. "And thank you for the hagletta. It was delicious."

"It was!" Mrs. Amlund said. "Please write down the recipe for me. But you went to too much trouble."

"I told Ole to tell her not to," Reverend Amlund said defensively.

"And I told her that," Ole said.

Mrs. Amlund gave Helena a knowing look. "They don't understand, do they?"

Helena smiled. "No, they don't."

"Don't understand what?" Reverend Amlund asked.

"I'll explain on the way home," Mrs. Amlund said. "And, Mrs.

Branjord, I want you to know I scolded Nils for giving you such short notice."

Reverend Amlund picked up the reins. "Mr. Branjord, I do believe I'm in for a lecture."

"I've had mine," Ole said as he prepared to help Mrs. Amlund into the buckboard.

"Please, do come again." Helena said.

"We would love to," Mrs. Amlund replied, stepping up into the buckboard. As she settled herself, she noticed Berent shaking his head. "Why, Berent, don't you want us to come?"

All eyes turned to the four-year-old. The boy knew he was in trouble but stood his ground. "No."

"Berent!" Helena and Ole cried.

"Why not?" Reverend Amlund asked.

"Because when you come, we don't eat dinner."

Mrs. Amlund giggled and Reverend Amlund burst out laughing. Helena blushed. Ole closed his eyes, wanting to sink into a hole.

"I'm so sorry," Helena said.

"There's no need to be." Reverend Amlund chuckled. "If I were Berent, I wouldn't want us to come either. Goodbye and thank you."

Mrs. Amlund waved and the Branjord family responded with waves of their own as they called their goodbyes. When the buckboard was out of sight, Helena heaved a sigh and sank to the bench. Ole and the children said nothing until Berent broke the silence. "Can we eat now?"

Helena looked at her youngest and realized, not for the first time, why God made small children so adorable. If they weren't, they would never live to grow up.

Ole motioned for the children to get into the cabin. "Change your clothes. I'll fix you something to eat."

The three dashed into the cabin. Ole turned to Helena. "I'm sorry. I told you not to make a fuss."

Helena's eyes blazed. "Don't you ever again say those words to me, Ole Branjord! Ever!"

Berent

They laughed at me! That wasn't nice. Mama says it isn't nice to laugh at people. Maybe it's all right for big people to laugh at little people, but

I don't think so. I don't think what I said was funny. Being hungry isn't funny!

I hope the pastor never comes again ... even if we eat first. Him coming makes Mama upset. It makes her yell at Papa. I don't like it when Mama and Papa yell. It makes me scared. Pastors should never visit! Pastors should stay in church where they give long talks. I don't mind that. I can put my head in Mama's lap and go to sleep.

I'm going to tell Mama that Reverend Amlund is not very smart. Every Sunday he puts a dress on over his pants. That's dumb! If I had pants, I'd never put on a dress!

Helena

I am such a ninny! Why did I act like that? I almost gave myself a heart attack. All because the pastor and his wife came. Why? I'm the one who doesn't bow down to the clergy. If it weren't for Ole, I might be siding with that awful Saul Jaeran. Yet when Reverend Amlund and his wife came to call, I went completely to pieces!

But I think the visit went well, thanks to Oline and Martin. I would never have thought of the hagletta. I could tell Reverend Amlund enjoyed it; Mrs. Amlund too. I'll have to remember to give her the recipe next Sunday. I like her. For a woman so talented and well educated, she is very down to earth. I like the way she laughed about ironing that silly ruff. Maybe Reverend Amlund will even stop wearing it. Wouldn't that be something?

I probably shouldn't have said anything. It's not a woman's place to speak out. I'll most likely be the talk of the church for sticking my nose into "men's concerns." Well, I don't care! Half of the congregation is women, even if we can't vote. What happens is our concern too.

I think Mrs. Amlund agrees with me. Someday I'm going to talk to her about families sitting together. Then again, maybe not. The poor woman can't have children. I know she wants them. I can see by the way she looks at mine. Not being able to have children must be horrible. I can't imagine what my life would be like without them. I don't want to imagine it! What would my life be without Oline, Martin, and Berent?

Berent! That scamp. Telling Reverend Amlund he didn't want him to come again. I thought I was going to faint! Thank heavens the pastor thought it was funny. I thought about spanking Berent, but for what?

Being hungry? Having a mother who goes half crazy because the pastor is coming? He's only four years old and doesn't understand. Ole doesn't understand either. He's still a little angry about the way I carried on. He didn't even kiss me good night. I say he should understand. But then, why should he? I don't understand the way I acted myself.

Chapter Eighteen

Ole stepped out of Rutchen's Hotel, a contented smile on his face. A full stomach will do that for a man. He had splurged for a meal consisting of pot roast, cooked carrots, mashed potatoes and gravy, and topped off with a cup of coffee and a piece of freshly baked rhubarb pie. It had cost him almost twenty-five cents. Ole was well aware he should feel guilty for spending that much on just one meal, but he did not. He felt good. He felt like a man who had fifty-two dollars and fifty cents in his pocket.

That morning, with the help of Big Per and Martin, Ole had loaded the wagon with five of the seven fall pigs. Of the other two, one was for butchering and the second would pay Albert Hindberg for the use of his reaper and threshing machine. The hogs had averaged two hundred and ten pounds, and had paid out at a handsome five cents per pound. The usual price was three to four cents.

Ole was surprised at the number of wagons and buggies on Main Street. Since the railroad had arrived in 1864, the population of Nevada (pronounced Na-VEY-da, and the county seat of Story County) had exploded. There were somewhere between eight and nine hundred full-time residents. Nevada had become a real town. It had a hotel, Alderman's General Store, a newspaper called *Aegis*, Mead Produce Plant, a blacksmith shop, a railroad station, and a brand-new courthouse. In sixteen years, Nevada had grown from one log cabin into a substantial community.

For a time, it had been the only town in Story County. But now the railroad had reached the town of Ames, five miles to the west, which had grown to nearly six hundred people. There were some who thought Ames might someday be larger and more important than Nevada. Ole agreed with them because Ames was where the new Iowa State Agricultural College had just opened its doors.

Two large covered wagons with "Quincy Boynton Dray Service" written on the side, pulled by four horses each, rumbled down the street. Two young boys dodged between the wagons, causing the second driver to pull up sharply. He yelled at the boys, who just laughed and ran across a low depression called "the slough." This depression ran east and west through the business district and was the source of much conversation and controversy. During a heavy rain, the slough became a small river, which could only be crossed by using a footbridge on Main Street. Some thought the slough should be tiled and filled; others argued that would be a waste of money.

Ole watched the wagons drive through the dry depression with little strain on the horses, and was about to turn away when he saw an adolescent boy staring at him from across the street. The boy was shabbily dressed. Dirty black twill pants with holes in both knees were held up by a rope belt. An equally dirty homespun shirt, torn at the left shoulder, hung from his bony frame.

As soon as the boy realized he had been noticed, he ducked behind a pile of lumber. Ole recognized the young man as the same person who had been hanging around the stock pens when he had sold his hogs. The hair on the back of Ole's neck stiffened. His eyes narrowed as he watched the lumber pile to see if the boy would reappear. Under normal circumstances, he might not have noticed the strange behavior, but having fifty-two dollars and change in his pocket was far from normal. No one emerged from behind the stacked lumber, so Ole stepped onto the street and began walking to Alderman's store.

Theodore Alderman had purchased the first two lots in Nevada in 1853, built a two-room cabin (one for the family, the other for a store), and prospered as Story County filled with immigrants. His store was now housed in a new frame building with a false front and a large glass display window.

Ole entered the store. A small bell hung on the door announced his arrival. Mr. Alderman, a large man with a long, pleasant face, most of which was covered by a salt and pepper beard, looked up from a ledger book. He wore a white shirt, no collar, and black dress pants. Ole could not remember him wearing anything else.

"Good day, Mr. Branjord," Alderman said in passable Norwegian.

Like any good businessman, Theodore Alderman remembered names and faces.

"Good day, Mr. Alderman," Ole replied in heavily accented English.

Both men smiled, having exhausted their respective knowledge of each other's native language. Mr. Alderman switched to English and called, "Anna! We have a customer."

Anna Hammerdahl, a short, round woman wearing a black dress protected by a long gray apron, came bustling from the back of the store. She brushed a strand of gray hair from her face and smiled as she approached the men. "Good day, Mr. Branjord," she said in Norwegian. "It's good to see you again."

"Thank you, Mrs. Hammerdahl," Ole replied. "How are you?"

"Oh, for an old woman, I'm doing fine."

"Old? Not you!" Ole smiled. "Why, over at the hotel, they said you had been dancing on the tables again."

"Oh, you!" Mrs. Hammerdahl laughed, slapping Ole lightly on the arm. "I only wish I could. How is that lovely wife of yours?"

"She's well. And the children too. Helena gave me a list of the things she needs."

"Of course she did. Give me the list and I'll fill it."

Ole handed her the list, which she studied briefly, then scurried off.

Mr. Alderman watched her with pride. One of his best decisions had been hiring Mrs. Hammerdahl. Although diminutive, she was quite strong and not one to be taken lightly. She could be very friendly, as she was at this moment, or, if required, be stern and feisty. Her ability to speak both English and Norwegian was invaluable. Knowing his customer was in good hands, he returned to his desk behind the counter.

Ole looked about the store. On the left wall were shelves of food. On the right was hardware, ranging from sledgehammers to washtubs. The back of the store was devoted to harnesses, horse collars, saddles, yokes for oxen, and wagon parts. The middle of the store consisted of tables piled with bolts of cloth, dishes, and pots and pans. There was one table devoted to shoes and boots, on which were even a few pairs of children's shoes. Ole thought, "What a waste. Before you can get the shoes home, the child has outgrown them."

He looked down at his own scuffed boots. A new pair would be nice.

Shiny, polished boots were something he noticed and secretly coveted. Maybe someday. Not now. The ones he wore could be half-soled again and made to last another two or three years.

A bolt of black velvet cloth caught his attention. Ole strolled to the table piled three high with different colors of cotton, wool, silk, and velvet. "Helena would look gorgeous in a dress made from any of these," he thought, fingering the bolt of black velvet. In this one, she would be stunning.

Ole sighed and let the cloth drop. "Not now. No, that's wrong. Not ever." Only horse-faced Hanna Signaldahl could afford a dress made of velvet.

Mrs. Hammerdahl paused by the table. "Does Mrs. Branjord need a new dress?"

"Doesn't every woman?"

Mrs. Hammerdahl laughed. "No. Every woman wants a new dress. That is not the same as needing one."

It was Ole's turn to laugh. "You're right. The fact is, Helena does need one, but I am not about to pick out the material. That she can do the next time she's in town."

"You are a wise man, Ole Branjord. Do you need pants? We have some black twill."

"No. My youngest, on the other hand, wants pants more than anything in the world."

"Is he five yet?"

Ole shook his head. "No. And he has a mother who is determined to keep him in a dress until then."

"I can understand that. Once you put a boy in pants, he ceases to be your baby," Mrs. Hammerdahl said as she crossed behind Ole and walked to the end of the next table. "However, we do have a black twill remnant here that is not enough for a pair of men's pants, but is more than enough for a little boy. Mr. Alderman might give you a good price."

Ole scratched his beard, wondering if he dared take the material home. One thing was for sure, he would have to hide it from Berent. "Well, put it with the rest. I'll think about it."

Within minutes, Mrs. Hammerdahl was finished and behind the counter. "Should I put this on your bill, Mr. Branjord?" Ole hated saying yes to this question, so it was with a broad smile that he answered, "No. I would like to settle the account."

Mr. Alderman almost jumped from his chair, smiling just as broadly as Ole. He did not know much Norwegian, but had learned the words for "settling accounts." Mr. Alderman grabbed the ledger book, found the proper page, and said, "Twenty-one dollars and forty cents."

Ole nodded. "Add that to what I bought today."

Mrs. Hammerdahl quickly did the math. "The total is twenty-four dollars and fifty cents."

"Does that include the material?" Ole asked. "Oh, and I want a bag of hard candy."

A few words were exchanged in English between owner and clerk. Mr. Alderman waved his hand and said one of the few English words Ole understood, "Free."

Money was presented, producing more smiles from Mr. Alderman and Mrs. Hammerdahl, both of whom then helped Ole carry his purchases out to the wagon. Cash was hard to come by on the prairie, so the settling of accounts that did not include some form of barter was an event.

"*Mange takk*," Mr. Alderman said in Norwegian.

"You are welcome," Ole replied in English.

The three laughed, the men shook hands, and Mr. Alderman and Mrs. Hammerdahl returned to the store.

Ole removed the black twill, which had been wrapped in brown paper, from the other items and placed it in the tool box that also served as a footrest. He had to make sure that Berent did not see the material. Ole tucked it carefully in a corner, away from the container of axle grease and over the box of matches. These were just two of the necessities no prairie farmer left home without, the others being a spade, a heavy hammer, a spare wheel spoke for the front and back wheels, and a twenty-foot length of rope or, better yet, a log chain.

From the box, Ole removed what he called his equalizer, a half-inch thick iron rod eighteen inches long, and stuck it in his boot. There was no telling what a man might run into on the prairie, especially if he was carrying hard cash.

Ole drove his team out of town, past the cemetery to the well-worn trail leading to the East Settlement and then on to Fairview. He had to travel almost a mile before getting to open prairie. All the land around Nevada had been turned into working farms. There was no doubt in his mind that in ten to fifteen years, virgin prairie would exist only in the memories of early settlers.

A smile spread across Ole's face as he passed the tilled, fertile fields. So far, knock on wood, 1869 had been a good year. Warm sun and adequate rain had produced knee-high corn and golden wheat and oats. Harvesting was just around the corner.

"Oh, damn!" Ole said out loud. He had forgotten to buy a clock. He looked back over his shoulder. Nevada was still in sight, but going back would delay his getting home by at least an hour. He decided not to go back. He would just have to explain to Helena that he forgot. Had he forgotten on purpose? No, not really. Although he did not think they needed a clock and, he was forced to admit, buying something he did not feel they needed was difficult for Ole Branjord. The clock would have to wait until next time.

Doll and Lady's ears perked up when they reached the open prairie. They now knew their destination was home. Ole quickly forgot about the clock as he admired the lushness and beauty of the ocean of grass; however, as he had learned, there was much more than just grass. The prairie was vibrant with colors, as if God had crumpled a rainbow and allowed the scattered pieces to gently fall from the sky. The drooping yellow petals of gray-headed coneflowers swayed in unison with tall, red blazing stars. Pink downy phlox grew in protective bunches, surrounded by blue pasque and green Culver's root. Butterfly milkweed stood over all, much like a watchful sentinel. Adding earth tones and vertical accents were stands of burr oak and an occasional cottonwood tree, both of which could survive the frequent prairie fires.

Yes, Ole thought, there was beauty on the prairie; not the magnificent grandeur of Norway, but beauty just the same. It was a shame that it wouldn't be appreciated until it was gone. He had once asked Hans Twedt if he had ever found the prairie beautiful. Hans had laughed and answered he was once deeply moved by the beauty of a sunrise, but that the feeling had not lasted long. Later that same day, Hans and Jonas had broken sod with four teams of oxen, and he had found himself thinking words that sailors use when the lines get fouled.

Ole smiled at the memory, but the smile faded when he topped a rise and saw a figure walking slowly to the north, about one hundred yards ahead of him. Someone walking on the trail was not unusual, and under normal circumstances—no money in his pocket—Ole would have welcomed the company, for it was expected that a driver would stop and offer the man a ride. (It was always a man. No woman would ever be walking alone on the trail.)

But there was money in Ole's pocket, and money changed everything. Also, there was something familiar about the person. Ole loosened the equalizer in his boot. Then the person stopped and turned. Ole was relieved to see it was just the boy who had acted so strangely in Nevada.

"Whoa!" Ole called as the team came alongside the barefoot boy. "Hello. Do you want a ride?"

"Yes, sir," the boy replied with a nervous smile and without meeting Ole's gaze.

The fact that the boy had answered in Norwegian made Ole feel better. "Well, climb in."

The boy started for the rear of the wagon. "No!" Ole said. "Sit up here with me."

The boy stopped. The confusion on his face was that of a person whose carefully prepared plans had been disrupted. "I c-can sit in the back," he stammered.

Ole shook his head. "No. If you want a ride, you ride up here on the seat." Ole was not about to let the boy sit anywhere he could not watch him. There was no sign the boy had a gun, but Ole was convinced a knife was hidden beneath the oversized shirt.

After hesitating a moment, the boy climbed up on the seat. He smelled as if he hadn't bathed in months. Doll and Lady moved forward without command, disgusted that their trip home had been interrupted.

The boy stared straight ahead. Ole saw the tension in his slight body. The tension matched his own. His relief that the person was just a boy had turned to wariness. Something was not right. He casually placed the reins in his right hand and let the fingers of his left encircle the equalizer. Out of the corner of his eye, he studied the boy.

A mass of dirty, uncut, blond hair partially covered light blue, frightened eyes set in a narrow, handsome, beardless face. He was skinny to the point of being gaunt. Ole estimated his age at no more than fifteen.

"My name is Ole Branjord. What's yours?"

There was no answer. Ole felt the boy's body become rigid. His hand tightened around the iron rod. The boy's right hand twitched, but before Ole could free the equalizer from his boot, the boy's shoulders slumped.

"Amos," he mumbled.

Ole took a deep breath. Maybe his fears were groundless; however, he kept his left hand on the iron rod. "Is there a last name?"

"No."

Ole glanced at Amos, who remained staring straight ahead. "Suit yourself." Ole shrugged. They drove in silence for some distance, their faces expressionless, their minds in turmoil. Each had a decision to make. Amos nervously tugged at a strand of hair. Ole fingered the equalizer.

"How old are you?" Ole asked.

"Eighteen."

Ole almost laughed. "Are you looking for work?"

Amos nodded.

"Good. It's almost time to cut the oats and wheat. I'm sure some farmer will need help."

"I hate farmwork," Amos muttered.

Ole snorted. "Then you're headed in the wrong direction. There's nothing but farms and prairie in north Story County. If you want a town job, you had better go back to Nevada."

"Nobody's hiring." Amos replied. "At least they're not hiring me. They tell me to go home. What a joke!"

"Are you running away from home?"

The reply was not what Ole expected. Amos laughed. Actually, it was closer to a howl: loud, bitter, angry, and saturated with pain. "Run away! You can't run away if you've been thrown out! My father told me I ate too much. He said my food was cutting into his whisky."

The boy's mask was off. He gripped the seat and glared at Ole, his suffering and anger twisting his soft features into a mask of hate.

Ole was shocked by the transformation, but kept his voice calm. "Was he drunk when he threw you out?"

"What do you think?" Amos snorted.

"I think when he sobered up, he was sorry and wanted you back."

"Oh, I'm sure he's sorry! He no longer has anyone to beat up! 'I'm doing you a favor,' he'd say. 'The world is a nasty place. I'm toughening you up for your own good!'"

"I'm sorry."

"Don't say that! It's a lie! That's what he'd say when he was sober. He'd even cry. But then he'd do it all over again!"

"Didn't your mother try and protect you?"

"When I was little. Then he would beat her up. That hurt worse than him beating me." Tears rolled down Amos's cheeks.

Ole sensed the boy's anger lessening. Perhaps his mother was the key. "It sounds like your mother needs you," he said softly.

Amos erupted. He stood up on the tool box, his teeth bared like a cornered animal. Ole had guessed wrong. "Do you think I'd leave her alone with him? What do you take me for? My mother loved me! She cared! But she had the good sense to die last year. Now, nobody cares! Nobody gives a shit about me!"

The boy's movement to his shirt was amazingly fast. Suddenly a hunting knife was in his hand. "I know you have money, Branjord! Give it to me!"

Ole's answer was a swift uppercut with the equalizer, aimed at the knife. He missed the knife, but struck the soft underside of the boy's hand. The knife flew and Amos screamed with pain, frightening the horses into a trot. The boy tumbled off the wagon, missing being run over by inches.

Ole's first reaction was to whip the horses into a run, but then he heard a sound that tore at his heart—the sound of a child sobbing. He stopped the horses, turned in his seat, and saw Amos sprawled on the ground like a discarded rag doll. Ole knew the smart thing to do would be to leave the boy to die or find his way back to Nevada. But the smart thing to do was something Ole Branjord could not do. He was a man of conscience, a man who hated to hear children cry. He turned the horses around and drove back to the weeping boy.

Amos hid his face. "Go away," he blurted in between sobs. "Leave me alone. Let me die."

"I wish I could, but I can't do that."

"Why not?"

"The Lord said, 'Help thy neighbor.'"

"Even if he tries to rob you?"

Ole couldn't help but smile. "No, but he does say turn the other cheek. Amos, if you were as old as you say you are, I'd haul you back to the sheriff in Nevada. But you're just a boy, and if what you told me about your pa is true, you've had a rough row to hoe. Things can change, boy. Get in the wagon."

The sobs ended. Amos looked up at the man who was gazing down at him with gentle blue eyes, and knew, somehow, this was a turning point in his life. He unsteadily climbed to his feet, wiped his tears on his shirtsleeve, and crawled up to the seat. Ole turned the horses for home.

"How old are you really?" Ole asked after several minutes of silence.

"Fifteen," Amos answered. After a pause, he continued, "On my next birthday."

"That I believe," Ole said. "When did you eat last?"

"I don't remember."

"Didn't you try and find work in Nevada?"

"I just got there this morning. I was lost on the prairie for three days."

"It's easy to get lost," Ole said. What he thought but did not say was, "I think you have been lost since your mother died." He reached over and patted the boy's bare left knee. "Well, I'm sure you are hungry. My wife is a good cook. You'll eat tonight."

Ole saw a smile spread across Amos's face. Then the smile turned down, and a flood of tears was released, accompanied by sobs. The boy did not regain control of himself until they had passed the East Settlement.

The Branjord children raced from the cabin shouting "Papa! Papa!" as the wagon approached. They skidded to a stop when they saw Amos. Ole pulled the horses to a halt. "Are the chores done?"

Martin answered. "I milked the cows."

"And I helped!" Berent added.

"You did not!"

"Did too! I held the cows' tails so they wouldn't swish you in the face."

Martin made a face at his younger brother. "That's not really helping."

Ole laughed. "Did you feed the calves their milk?"

"I did that," Oline said.

"Good!" Ole said. "Thank you for helping."

There was a pause as the children looked up at the stranger. Berent broke the silence. "Who's that?"

"This is Amos. I picked him up out on the prairie. Amos, these are my children: Oline, Martin, and Berent."

There were muttered "hellos," after which Berent asked, "Can we ride in the wagon, Papa?"

"Sure. Climb in, but don't step on the groceries."

The children scrambled into the wagon like squirrels running up a tree. Doll and Lady had been through this routine many times, so as soon as the young ones were safely in the wagon, they started up on their own, anxious to complete the journey.

"Did you bring us candy? Berent asked.

"Candy!" Ole answered with mock surprise. "Why would I bring you candy?"

"Because you always do." Oline giggled.

"Well, maybe I forgot this time."

"No, you didn't!" Martin shouted, holding up the bag. "I found it!"

"Just one piece!" Ole ordered. "And give one to Amos."

Martin passed out the candy, then handed the bag to his father. Four pairs of eyes lit up. "Oh, this is good!" Oline cried. "Thank you, Papa."

"You're welcome." Ole smiled, enjoying the pleasure the candy produced.

Helena was standing on the porch, a questioning look on her face, when Ole halted the team. Before Ole could speak, Berent blurted out, "Papa found him on the prairie. I forgot his name."

"His name is Amos," Ole said.

Helena smiled. "Hello, Amos. Are you staying with us?"

"Just for tonight," Ole stated. "He's looking for work."

"Well, good," Helena said. "Welcome to our home."

Amos blushed. He had never seen a woman as pretty as Helena Branjord. "Thank you," he mumbled.

Ole turned to the children. "Oline and Martin, unload the groceries. Berent, get a washcloth, soap, and towel for our guest. Amos, you are in bad need of a bath, but we don't have time for that. Go down to the well by the barn and wash yourself all over. And I mean *all over*. Understand?"

Amos blushed more deeply. "Yes, sir."

"All right, let's get at it. I'm hungry."

Before Ole could stretch and climb down from the wagon, Berent was back with the washcloth, soap, and towel. "Come on, Amos!" he called. "I'll show you where the well is."

Amos jumped down from the seat and allowed Berent to take his hand and lead him to the barn. Helena moved closer to Ole and whispered, "Runaway?"

"Worse. Throwaway," Ole answered softly. "I'll explain later. You had better add to supper. He hasn't eaten for several days."

"Oh, dear Lord! The poor boy," Helena said, hurrying into the cabin.

An hour later, the Branjords sat in awed silence as Amos finished his third plateful of food. He also had devoured half a loaf of bread. As he wiped his plate clean with a piece of bread, he realized everyone was staring at him. He swallowed the last morsel, blushed, and apologized for eating so much.

Helena smiled at him, which only made him blush more. "There's nothing to be sorry about. I've just never seen anyone so skinny eat so much." Her smile faded quickly when she noticed the bruise on his hand. "Oh! Let me see your hand, Amos."

Amos hesitated, then allowed Helena to take his hand in hers. "Oh my! This is deep. Does it hurt?"

"A little."

"I should think so!" Helena said, getting up from the table and crossing to the sink, where she took a tin of liniment from the shelf. "I have some salve that should make it feel better."

Helena returned to the table and gently applied the liniment to the injured hand. "How did you do this?"

Amos glanced at Ole and then said, "I fell on a rock."

"That must have been one nasty fall," Helena said. "You're lucky you didn't break it."

"Are you going to kiss it and make it better, Mama?" Berent asked.

The others at the table laughed. Berent did not understand why. To him it was a serious question.

"No, Berent. A mother's kisses only work on her own children." Helena released the wounded hand. "Now, Amos, I want you to give me your pants and shirt. I don't have time to wash them, but I can mend the shirt and put patches on the pants."

The boy's eyes widened and again he blushed. "I … I can't do that."

"Sure you can." Helena smiled as she patted his leg. "I'll give you a quilt. Go down to the barn with Martin. He can bring the shirt and pants back to me. When I am done, he can bring them back to you. It won't take me long."

Amos fought back tears. Acts of kindness had been as rare as hen's teeth since his mother died. "You don't have to do that."

"I know. But I want to. So, shoo! Get down to the barn. I want to finish before dark."

Ole got up from the table. "Get up, Amos. You too, Martin. Do as she says. I need to check the stock."

Ole and Martin exited the cabin. Amos paused at the door. "Thank you, Mrs. Branjord. I think that is the best meal I've ever had."

"Why, thank you, Amos." Helena smiled. "That is a wonderful compliment."

Amos returned the smile, and with it came a fresh blush. He felt a strange tingling when he looked at Helena. It frightened him, so he fled to the barn. Years later, Amos realized Helena Branjord was his first crush.

Five minutes later, Ole and Amos sat on milk stools in the barn. Amos sat wrapped in the old quilt Helena had provided. Ole smoked his pipe. "Thank you for not telling Helena how you really hurt your hand," Ole said.

"The whole thing was stupid," Amos replied.

"Yes, it was. You're only fourteen, but you are being forced to make the most important decision of your life. I don't think you're cut out to be an outlaw. You're too nice a person. But if you continue down the path you took this afternoon, I can predict your life will be miserable and short."

Amos tucked the quilt more tightly around him and, even though it was warm, shivered. "I know."

"Is there any chance your pa will take you back?"

"Sure." Amos snorted. "If he's sober. But he'll just get drunk and do it all over again. I'm not going back there, Mr. Branjord."

Ole knocked the ashes from his pipe. "Then you are going to have to find a job. You say you hate farmwork. That means you had better head for Ames. It is about ten miles south."

"I know where it is," Amos mumbled, staring down at his dirty, bare feet.

Ole refilled his pipe. He didn't say anything until the tobacco glowed and he had taken several puffs. "Amos, what would you like to do? What are your dreams?"

There was a long silence before the boy answered. "If I tell you, you'll just laugh at me. Pa did."

"I never laugh at dreams, Amos. Mine was to own land. To make the dream happen, I had to cross an ocean. But here I am, living on my own forty acres."

Amos looked up at the kind, gentle man gazing at him and thought, "Why couldn't you have been my father?" He took a deep breath. "I would like to be a railroad man and drive one of the locomotives."

"Oh!" Ole said. "Those things are monsters!"

"No, they're not!" The boy's eyes were suddenly alive. They sparkled with desire and fascination. "They're wonderful! All that power! All that steam! The bell! And the whistle is the most beautiful sound in the world. The locomotives are … are … I can't explain it, like they are alive!"

"Well now." Ole laughed. "If you feel that way, you should be in Des Moines. They are laying track every which way from there."

The life faded from Amos' eyes as quickly as it had arrived. "Ah, Pa's most likely right. It's just a pipe dream. I'll never be an engineer."

"He's right only if you don't try. Look at me, Amos." The boy raised his eyes. Ole continued with intensity, "Go to Des Moines. Get a job in the yards. Any job! Be a runner. Carry water. Load wood. Do whatever is needed. Then hang around the engineers and firemen. Ask questions. Men love to show boys the secrets of their trade."

Amos could hardly breathe. It was the first time he had been encouraged to do anything except slop hogs and hoe corn. "Do you really think I can?"

"I see no reason you can't."

The two grinned at each other. Amos wanted to throw his arms around Ole's neck, but instead bounced on the stool like there were springs in his bottom. Ole Branjord had given him the greatest gifts a man can give a boy: confidence and hope.

"When you get to be an engineer," Ole said, "you'll have to wave to me at the railroad crossing."

"I will!" Amos said excitedly. "I promise."

"Hello in there!" Helena called from the gate. "Your clothes are ready, Amos."

"I'll get them," Ole said, getting up from the stool and walking to the gate.

Helena handed Ole the pants and shirt. "Is he all right?" she whispered.

"Yes, he's fine."

"When he's dressed, bring him to the cabin. He can sleep in the loft."

"No," Ole answered firmly. "He'll sleep in the barn. I'll explain later."

Helena gave Ole a puzzled look, then equally firmly said, "You'll explain as soon as you get to the porch."

Helena returned to the cabin, and Ole gave the clothes to Amos. The boy smiled as he saw the neatly done patches on his pants. "Your wife sews as good as she cooks."

"Yes, she does," Ole answered. "Amos, I'm almost certain you are a good boy who will grow into a good man. But I can't forget what you did this afternoon. You'll sleep in the barn tonight. And I want you gone in the morning. Understand?"

Amos nodded as he bit his lower lip. "I understand. I'm really sorry about … what happened."

"Good." Ole reached into his pocket and pulled out two greenbacks. "Here are two dollars. If you're careful, that will feed you for several weeks." He dropped the money by the stunned boy's feet. "I know you have been treated badly. But remember, there are good people in this world, and God loves you. Good luck."

Ole left the barn. Helena was waiting on the bench by the cabin door. "Talk to me," she said as Ole sat beside her.

Ole talked. Helena listened without interruption. When he was finished, her eyes were wide and her hands covered her lips. "And you brought him home?"

"He's just a boy, Helena. I couldn't leave him out on the prairie."

"Oh my," she answered and walked into the cabin.

Ole followed and bolted the door, something he had never done since moving in. Helena did not comment, but it was obvious she approved.

As Helena prepared for bed, Ole took down the old muzzle-loading rifle from over the fireplace, sat in the rocking chair, and loaded the weapon. "I think I'll stay up a while," he said.

Helena bent down and kissed her husband. "You are a good man, Ole Branjord."

"Either that or a damn fool," Ole replied.

The sun was an orange ball in the eastern sky when Ole awakened, stiff and sore from spending the night in the rocking chair. Everyone else was still asleep. He stretched and put the rifle back in its place, reminding himself to fire off the ball later. He carefully opened the door, stepped out onto the porch, and welcomed what looked to be another beautiful day.

He walked to the barn. Ole expected to find a sleeping boy. He did not. What he found was a dollar bill resting on a milk stool, held down by a small rock. The boy and the quilt were gone. Ole gave a sigh of relief and smiled. "I wish you well, Amos," he whispered.

Chapter Nineteen

Karl Lyngen peeked through the heavy drapes covering his bedroom window and watched Oline and Martin approach the house. He smiled. Oline's visits to practice and have lessons had become important to him. She gave a sparkle to a childless home. Karl had not seen Martin since giving him the two copies of *A Tale of Two Cities*. He saw that the boy was bringing back the books. Not surprising. Martin was only eight years old. The books had proven to be too advanced.

Karl was able to look out of the window because low, dark clouds threatened rain. The farmers were of two minds concerning the precipitation: the corn needed it, but the oats and wheat were ready to harvest, and a heavy rain, especially if accompanied by wind, could cause great damage. The ideal would be an inch or two of soft, gentle showers; however, there was nothing gentle about the fast-moving, angry clouds streaming above the house.

Karl turned from the window, his smile fading like a winter twilight. Crops were not his concern. His land was rented out. A man who feared the light like some evil vampire could not expect to work his own land. Oh, no! Such a man was a cripple who could only sit on his ass and wander the prairie during the late-night blackness.

Karl slumped into his chair. He listened as Inga greeted the children. He heard the joy in her voice. He could imagine the delight in her eyes and the warmth of her smile. She loved children. She wanted children of her own. But children were not possible. Just another of his failures.

As Oline began her scales, there was a timid knock on his door. "Come in," Karl said, more gruffly than he intended.

There was a moment of hesitation, then the door opened and Martin peeked in, his eyes wide, his voice soft. "It's me."

This entrance brought back Karl's smile. "Come in, Martin," he said in a much kindlier tone. "It's good to see you. Have a seat."

Martin closed the door and sat in a cane-back chair next to Karl. He looked down at his dangling feet. "I brought back your books."

"Are you finished with them?"

"No. I've just read seven chapters. The Norwegian goes pretty fast, but the English takes forever."

"If you've just started, why are you bringing them back?"

"Papa says I've had them too long," Martin answered, turning to face Karl. "Will you tell me what happens?"

"Do you like the story?"

"Yes! It's interesting. Was there really a French Revolution?"

"Indeed there was. It began in July of 1789."

"Did they really cut off people's heads?"

"Yes. What began as a revolution ended in a bloodbath."

"Wow!" Martin said. "I thought it might just be a story."

"The book is a novel, but it is based on actual events."

"What happens to Lucie Manette?"

"Ah, that you have to find out for yourself. Tell your father I want you to keep the books until you have read every last word. I don't care if takes you a year. Or two years!"

A huge smile lit up Martin's face. "That's wonderful! Thank you."

"You're welcome," Karl said, loving the boy's enthusiasm. "What do you think of Paris?"

"Dirty!" Martin answered. "And smelly! Did they really dump chamber pots out of windows?"

"That's what I've read."

"It must have been an awful place to live," Martin said, wrinkling up his nose. "And the people were starving."

"Yes, they were. Hunger was a major cause of the revolution."

"Why didn't the rich people help feed them?"

"Good question. Probably because they had plenty to eat and felt the poor's problems were none of their concern. They soon found out how wrong they were."

"Did only the rich get their heads chopped off?"

"To begin with." Karl scratched the scar tissue on his face. For some reason, it had begun to itch. "But the leaders of the revolution turned on each other, and many innocent people were put to death."

Martin stared unblinkingly at the damaged face, which glowed like a dying ember in the semi-darkness. Karl's initial reaction was anger. He was not used to unflinching looks. Most gave him quick glances, then turned away in horror or pity. But Martin's eyes were filled with neither horror nor pity, just simple curiosity.

"How could one mini ball do so much damage to your face?" Martin asked.

Karl said nothing. He just stared at the boy's unblemished face until Martin dropped his eyes and bit his lip with embarrassment. Karl never talked about the wound; he never talked about the war, not even to Inga. But he felt obliged to answer Martin's question. "It was shrapnel fired from a cannon. I had turned to encourage my men to charge faster when I was hit. Had I not turned, I probably would be dead."

"You're lucky you turned," Martin whispered.

Karl gave the boy a rueful smile. "Am I? Would you like to live in the dark and have a face like mine?"

The answer came in a small voice. "No. But you are alive."

"That is debatable, Martin. There is a difference between living and existing." Karl saw the confusion on Martin's face. "You don't understand, do you?"

"No, sir."

"Good. I hope you never do," Karl said, lightly touching Martin's arm. "Take my advice. Never join the army."

"Why did you join?"

Karl sat back in his chair. "Why did I join? I suppose for the same reason most young men do. Excitement, adventure, finding out what it's like to be a soldier."

"What was it like?" Martin's eyes were shining.

"Not what you think. It is not parades and glory. A friend of mine put it best. He said, 'Being a soldier is like rowing a boat in a sea of boredom interspersed with whirlpools of terror.' Now I know you don't understand that. What it means is soldiering is mostly boring. But when the shooting starts, it becomes very frightening."

"Were you scared?"

"Every soldier is scared, Martin. Don't let anyone tell you different. A battlefield is a horrible place. It is filled with smoke and noise and confusion and crying and cursing and praying and dying. I pray you never experience it."

There was silence: Karl remembering, Martin imagining. It was a question as to whose images were the more vivid. There was no question as to whose eyes were filled with tears.

Karl sighed. "Martin, I'm getting tired. We'll have to continue this conversation some other time. Keep reading. When you have read a few more chapters, come again and we'll talk about them."

Martin hugged the two books as he got up from the chair. He shifted awkwardly from one foot to the other before saying, "I'm sorry I made you cry."

Karl clasped the boy's arms, perhaps a little too hard. "You didn't make me cry, Martin. You brought light into this dark room. Thank you."

Martin did not know how to respond, so he simply said what he had been taught. "You're welcome."

Karl released the boy's arms, and Martin left the room, quietly closing the door behind him.

Inga smiled as she watched Martin dash out the kitchen door and race for home. He still had the books. That meant he would be back. She hoped this visit with Karl had gone as well as the first. Her husband had talked about Martin for days. His mood had been lighter, his demeanor more pleasant. He had even laughed! She had been shocked. It was a sound she had not heard since before the war. Inga wished the boy could stay with them. Oline too, for that matter. She wished … well, there was no use wishing for that. It would never happen.

She sighed and crossed to the music room and opened the door. Oline immediately stopped playing. "It sounds good, Oline. You're making wonderful progress."

"I'm having trouble with the A scale."

"Three sharps are hard, but you'll master it," Inga said. She added, "Wait until you get to B. It has five sharps."

Oline made a face and Inga laughed. "Don't worry. You'll master that one too. I'm going to run to Turg's store. I'll be back before you go home. Does your mother need anything?"

Oline shook her head. "I don't think so, but thank you for asking."

For some reason she did not understand, this polite response brought tears to Inga's eyes. She suddenly had a desperate need to hug this child and hold her close. Of course, she did no such thing. After all, she was

Norwegian, and Norwegians did not go about hugging other women's children. She just smiled, closed the door, and left for the store.

Oline returned to her scales, willing her hands to move faster over the keyboard. There was no doubt that practicing the scales was boring, but she did not hate doing it. She could see the progress she had made in less than three months. But she longed to play the beautiful melodies residing silently on the staves of Inga's composition books.

A cry from Karl's bedroom followed by a loud thump ended the practice session. Oline knocked over the piano stool as she leaped to her feet and ran to Karl's aid. He lay on his back between the chair and the bed, his body in convulsions, his eyes rolled back. Drool flowed from his mouth. Oline's heartbeat raced. She was frightened, but knew there was no one else to help. What had Inga done first?

The spoon!

Oline grabbed the large wooden spoon from off the dresser and forced it between Karl's teeth, dodging his flailing hands as she did so. She then picked up the pan and ran to the icehouse, where she chipped off several chunks. On the way back to the house, she looked in vain for any passing adult.

When Oline reached Karl's room, she saw the convulsions were worse and that the spoon had slipped from his mouth. Blood now colored the drool. The girl was shaking as she knelt behind Karl's head. The man moaned, half rose, then fell back to the floor. His arms continued to flail, while his legs bounced as if attached to springs. Karl cried out, allowing Oline to force the handle of the spoon back between his teeth. Then, without wrapping the ice in a towel, she placed a chunk against the flaming wound.

The effect was immediate. Karl's body began to relax. The convulsions degenerated into occasional spasms. The ice was so cold it began to burn Oline's hand. She held it as long as she could, but it hurt so much, she allowed it to slip from her grasp. Karl moaned. Oline quickly grabbed a towel from the dresser, wrapped it around the ice, and placed the towel against the scar tissue. The moaning ceased. Karl's breathing returned to normal. The seizure was over. It was only then that Oline realized she was crying.

Minutes passed. Slow minutes. Oline prayed that Inga would return. Her tears dried. She removed the towel to add more ice. In doing so, she saw three tiny pieces of metal oozing from Karl's head. She knew Inga would take tweezers and pluck them out. She could not. It was impossible for her to actually touch the wound. She covered it with the towel and stared down at the man. Again she felt like crying—not out of fear, but out of compassion for this good man who endured so much suffering and pain.

Karl's eye lids fluttered. He slowly opened his eyes. At first they were filled with confusion, then they focused on Oline. "My angel," he whispered. "Why do you keep saving me?"

Oline removed the ice. "I'm not your angel, Mr. Lyngen," Oline replied, a slight tremor in her voice. "I'm Oline."

Karl stared at the pretty, young face a long while before saying, "Yes, you are Oline. Oline Branjord. I had another seizure, didn't I?"

"Yes, sir."

"I'm sorry you had to see this again. Help me sit up."

Oline assisted Karl into a sitting position, his back against the bed footboard. "Would you like more ice?" she asked.

Karl replied, "Yes. That would be good."

Oline handed Karl the towel-wrapped ice. He put it on the wound. "Where is Inga?"

"She went to Turg's store. She should be back soon. Can I get you something?"

"No. You've done quite enough, my angel."

Oline sat back on her heels. "Why do you call me that?"

"Because you remind me of her."

"Who was she?"

Karl laid his head back against the footboard. He closed his eyes. "I was running across a field, leading my men, then everything went black. When I woke up, it was night. All around me were the dead and the wounded. Those who were alive were crying and begging for help. I was very thirsty. I heard myself calling for water. No one came. As the night wore on, the cries became fewer and fewer. I looked up at the stars. I thought I was going to die."

Karl paused, reliving what he had so desperately tried to forget. Oline asked, "What happened next?"

"They came," Karl continued. "A mother and daughter, each carrying a bucket of water and a dipper. The daughter, who looked so much like you, approached me. She was silhouetted against a full moon. I was sure she was an angel sent by God to take me to heaven. She knelt beside me and put a dipper of water to my lips. Never have I tasted anything so delicious. I drank it all and asked for more. 'Just one,' she said. 'Please,'

I begged. She hesitated, then gave me a second dipperful. I thanked her. She smiled and went on to the next soldier."

Karl opened his eyes. "I must have fainted after she left. The next thing I remember is being in a hospital tent. I found out later that a truce had been called so the wounded could be picked up. Without that water, I am sure I would have died." Karl took a long breath and whispered, "Which is what should have happened."

"Don't say that." Oline frowned. "God sent her to care for you. She was an angel of mercy."

Karl turned to Oline with a sad smile. "Perhaps he made a mistake. Perhaps he should have sent the other angel."

"I don't understand."

"Of course you don't. Don't even try."

Karl struggled to get to his feet. "Help me to the bed, Oline. I need to sleep."

Oline jumped up and did as she was asked. Karl slumped onto the bed when Inga burst into the room. She saw the spoon and melting ice. Her hands flew to her face. "Oh, dear God!"

"It's all right, Inga. My angel helped me." There were not more words. He was asleep.

"Was it a bad one?" Inga asked.

Oline nodded. Inga took the girl in her arms and hugged her. "Thank you. I am so sorry. So sorry. I shouldn't have left you. He hasn't had a bad one in months. I thought … it doesn't matter what I thought."

Oline felt tears fall on her hair. "I know why he calls me his angel."

"Why?"

"When he was hurt, a girl who looked like me came in the night and gave him water."

"He told you that?" Inga asked, releasing Oline. "He never talks to me about the war. He never says anything."

Oline looked up at Inga. She was surprised by the anger in Inga's voice. She also saw anger in her eyes. "I … I'd better go."

Inga stared at her sleeping husband. "Yes, go home."

Oline quickly slipped from the room. Inga walked to the bed. Her lips began to tremble. "Why couldn't you have told me about the girl?" she whispered. "Why can't you talk to me about the war? Why can't you tell me what you're feeling? Why do you shut me out?"

Tears began to flow. She loved him so much; yet she felt that love slowly dying and being replaced by anger and resentment. She stood a long while by the bed, weeping for herself, her husband, her marriage.

Martin

Mr. Lyngen had another seizure. Oline told me what to do if I'm ever alone with him and he has another one. I hope it never happens. I don't think I'll go there unless Oline is with me. She also told me not to tell Mama or Papa. She's right. They wouldn't let us go there if they knew. I want to go back. Mr. Lyngen is real smart. He's fun to talk to. But I wish he didn't have to sit in the dark. It's spooky.

You know what? His face doesn't bother me anymore. I forgot all about it until he asked me if I'd want to have a face like his. That would be awful. I'm never going to war. Never!

I wonder what the difference is between living and existing? I think it is important to know the difference. Mama and Papa know, but I can't ask them. They would want to know why I'm asking. And then Mama would start asking me a bunch of questions. She's real good at finding out what I've been doing. No, I'll just have to find out for myself. But he said he hoped I'd never find out. Why is it that there are things big people want us to learn and other things they don't want us to learn? It is confusing. Being an adult must be complicated.

Mr. Lyngen is very sad. I think he wants to die. Maybe if I had to sit in the dark and have a face like his, I would want to die too. Maybe, but I don't think so. There are all those books to read! I never want to die.

Chapter Twenty

Ole held the sack beneath the grain spout. Sweat soaked his shirt. Perspiration dripped from his floppy hat, ran down his nose, and saturated his beard. Every pore seemed to be in a race to see which could release the most liquid. Ole glanced up at the merciless sun, painted high on an endless canvas of blue. "Thank God it is almost noon," he thought. "Thank God the harvest has been bountiful and almost trouble free. And thank God it is almost over!"

The process had begun two weeks and three days before, when Ole and Big Per helped Albert Hindberg pull the reaper and threshing machine from Albert's makeshift machine shed, which resembled Ole's barn. Albert had purchased the two machines from a farmer near Randall who had upgraded his equipment.

The reaper was the old style, which required a man to walk behind and rake the cut grain off the platform. A later version had a sweep attached to the platform, which was controlled by the driver, thus eliminating the need for the trailing man. The latest model, purchased by the farmer near Randall, had a system of canvas rollers that fed the grain up to an upper platform, where two men tied the grain into bundles. That machine was much too expensive for most Story County farmers.

The cutting of the grain had required a parade of laborers following the reaper. Ole raked the platform while Albert drove the team of horses. Behind the reaper came Big Per, swinging a scythe with a cradle attached. The blade slashed through the golden grain with what appeared to be effortless ease. It fell onto the cradle, and was then deposited in neat piles. Big Per could not keep up with the reaper, but no man in Story County could match his ability with a scythe.

Keeping a safe distance behind Big Per were the bundlers. Bertha Hindberg, Helena, and their older children raked the grain into small piles, grain heads facing the same way, and then took a couple of long straws and tied each pile into a bundle. Bertha's new baby girl was tied papoose-style to her back. Berent and three-year-old Sarah raced around chasing butterflies, grasshoppers, and each other. The work was not hard, but required stooping, bending, and a watchful eye. One had to be careful not to include a snake in the bundle.

When the cutting and bundling were completed, the bundles were stacked, grain end up, into shocks. Each shock consisted of six to eight bundles and a cap. There the grain would sit until it was time to thresh.

Depending on whose farm was being worked, Bertha or Helena would leave the field to prepare the noon and evening meals. At Big Per's farm, Helena did the cooking.

The threshing was all done at the Hindberg farm. Albert's machine was on skids, not wheels, so the grain had to be brought to his farm. Sideboards were placed on the farm wagons, and the wagons were then piled high with bundles.

The threshing machine was mostly made of wood. It stood about six feet high, three feet wide, and ten feet long. The grain was fed into rotating blades that cut up the bundles. The grain and straw then fell into a series of shakers which separated the two. The straw was blown out the far end of the machine by a large fan, while the grain was augured into a spout, from which it could be loaded into burlap bags. Power for the machine was provided by a team of horses walking on a tilted treadmill. The machine was connected to the treadmill by a long belt that ran from the flywheel on the treadmill to the flywheel on the threshing machine.

Ole's sack was nearly full. He gave a nod of his head, and Big Per came quickly to his side with an empty sack. With a minimum of spillage, the transfer was made. Ole carried the full sack to near his wagon, where the other full sacks stood like sagging pillars. Oline waited with a large needle and heavy yarn. Her job was to sew the sack shut. Ole gave her a proud smile as he plopped the sack down. This was her second year of closing sacks, and her needle darted quickly and confidently through the rough material. Not one of her sacks had broken open when being loaded into the wagons or being unloaded from them. Oline wore a large bonnet and a long-sleeved dress to protect her face and arms from the sun, but neither could protect her hands and bare feet, which had become quite dark. She hated the difference between the tan and light skin. Her mother and Bertha had the same problem, but they could wear gloves and shoes to cover it. She could not, and last Sunday at church a girl had called her two-tone. Strangely enough, Elsa Signaldahl had not laughed, and had told the girl she was not nice.

Ole was about to pick up another empty sack when Albert gave a loud yell. He was grinning and holding up the last bundle. It was good to see the man smile. Since the past Sunday, he had been grim of face and foul of mood. Albert had become a true believer in the Saul Jaeran camp, which resulted in tension between himself and Ole and Big Per. At every meal he attempted to bring Ole and Big Per into the fold. When they resisted, he became sullen and angry. Ole waved and grinned back at Albert. Maybe today would be different.

Big Per gave a wave as the last of the grain trickled into bag, and Ernst halted the team on the treadmill. The harvest was over. Neither the oats nor the wheat had been bumper crops, but both had been good. There was sufficient wheat to grind into flour and more than enough oats for the winter feed.

"Well now," Big Per said, carrying the half-filled bag to Oline. "That is a good job done."

"Amen!" Albert responded in his deep, gravelly voice as he took off his straw hat and wiped his nearly bald head with a towel. He was a tall whippet of a man, thin-faced and long of limbs. His beard was somewhat scraggily and his eyes were bloodhound-mournful; however, he was a good man who possessed a pleasant smile and a wonderful laugh, both of which were rationed out with miserly precision. To Albert Hindberg, frivolity was a first cousin to sin. "The Lord is good."

"Indeed he is," Ole agreed. Then, attempting to head off another harangue about the church's problems, he quickly added, "Now if he only would give us some rain."

It worked. Albert said, "We sure need it. If we don't get rain by next week, I'm going to have to start carrying water to the corn."

Ole nodded. "Me too."

Big Per watched as Oline sewed the last bag closed. "I must say, Oline, you are getting good at that."

Oline blushed. "Thank you," she replied, stealing a glance at Ernst, who was backing the horses down from the treadmill. Ole smiled. The two had spent the entire harvest pretending not to look at each other.

"Ernst!" Albert called. "Bring the team over and tie them to the wagon." He then turned to Oline. "When you finish that sack, go tell Mrs. Hindberg that we can eat anytime."

"Yes, sir," Oline answered. She quickly tied off the sack, slipped the needle into the cuff of her sleeve, and ran to the house.

"Stop!" Albert shouted. Oline came to skidding halt and looked back. "Not you, Oline. Ernst! He almost drove the horses into the threshing machine. What is the matter with you, boy?"

Now it was Ernst's turn to blush. Big Per folded his arms and attempted a stern look. "Ernst, there is one thing a man must learn. Driving horses and staring at pretty girls don't mix."

The three men laughed as the boy turned scarlet and Oline fled to the house. For a moment, the men shared a single thought: "How fast they grow up."

Twenty minutes later, they were washing up for dinner under the shade of a large cottonwood, whose broad lower branches reached out like green, protective fingers over the Hindberg two-room cabin. Ole was envious of the great old tree; but he was more envious of the new barn that dominated the farmyard. It was a *real* barn with cow stanchions, horse stalls, an area for calves and beef cattle, and above, a large haymow. The barn raising had taken place the previous September. It had been hard work and great fun. Families from all around had come to take part. Like most raisings, when the framing was up, the partying began. Albert had Turg bring a keg of beer, and Big Per played his violin.

Everyone was having a wonderful time until Big Per noticed that an end section of the barn appeared to sway. He dropped his violin, ran to the barn, grabbed a center brace, and called out, "I've got it, boys! I've got it!" And he did have it. He held the structure in place until more bracing was added. Big Per had saved a day's work and added to his legendary status.

Ole watched Oline carry a bowlful of greens grown in Bertha's garden from the cabin to a makeshift table consisting of planks and two sawhorses set up under the cottonwood tree. It was far too hot to eat in the cabin. Even the cook range had been moved outside.

The three men sat at the table and were soon joined by Ernst, Heinrik, and Martin. Oline and Helena brought creamed potatoes, creamed peas, flatbread, and a platter of fried rabbit to the hungry males. Bertha carried a basket containing her sleeping baby. The faces of both Helena and Bertha glistened, and sweat spots marked their cotton dresses. A quick glance told them two children were missing.

"Where are Sarah and Berent?" Bertha asked. She was a tall, stately woman, who, as she said, "was in the process of becoming more stately." At age thirty-eight, her skin was amazingly supple, and her long, blond hair, which she wore in two braids, still had a youthful sheen. Her deep-set blue eyes focused accusingly on her youngest son. "Heinrik, you were supposed to watch them."

Heinrik shot a guilty look at Martin, who stared down at his plate.

"Well?" Helena said. "You were to watch them too, Martin."

"We did," Martin mumbled.

"We played hide-n-seek," Heinrik added.

Bertha crossed her arms. "I see. They hid, and you forgot to seek."

Heinrik could not meet his mother's gaze as he said, "You called us for dinner."

"Oh! I ought to take a switch to both of you!" Bertha snapped, then turned to the barn and used what she called her outdoor voice. "Sarah! Berent! Come and eat! Now!"

Within seconds, two small bodies, both in faded dresses, ran from the inside of the machine shed and raced to the table. Their eyes were shining and both were grinning. "You couldn't find us!" Berent yelled.

"You couldn't find us," Sarah repeated.

The adults smiled at the unadulterated joy running toward them.

"We won!" Berent cried.

"We won!" shouted the echo.

"Yes, you did," Bertha said as the children reached the table.

"Did you wash your hands like I told you?" Helena asked.

Berent stopped grinning. "Sort of."

Bertha failed at hiding a smile as she asked, "And what does 'sort of' mean?"

"It means they did not," Helena answered.

Each woman grabbed her child and wiped tiny hands on their aprons. "There, that will have to do," Helena said. "Go sit down."

"I want to sit by Berent," Sarah said, her brown eyes demanding. The color of her eyes came from her father, but, thankfully, her sweet oval face was from Bertha's family tree.

"All right," Bertha said. "But no playing with your food."

"Ernst wants to sit next to Oline." Heinrik smirked as the two small children sat beside Helena.

"That can be arranged," Big Per said, sliding one place down the bench.

Blushing furiously, Oline sat in the vacated spot, as far from Ernst as she could get.

Grace was said by Albert, and the serious task of eating began. There was almost no conversation. What little there was consisted mostly of "pass this" or "pass that." Halfway through the meal, Berent announced he did not like peas. Of course, this meant that Sarah, who had eaten most of her peas, proclaimed the same sentiment. Both mothers commanded them to clean their plates and to be thankful for all they had to eat because there were children starving in Norway. Berent and Sarah made faces, but obeyed.

After the food had disappeared, the women and Oline cleared the bowls and platters and replaced them with two freshly baked apple pies. The two apple trees the Hindbergs had planted in 1860 were now producing.

The pieces were cut to a chorus of "ooohs" and "ahhhs." The coffee was poured. Now was the time for conversation.

Big Per gave a contented sigh. "That was a wonderful meal, Mrs. Hindberg."

"Indeed it was," Ole added.

Bertha beamed. "Helena made half of it."

"Oh, all I did was peel some potatoes and apples, and cut up the rabbits," Helena said.

"Well, you are both great cooks." Big Per belched. "I'm sorry to see harvest end. Now I have to go back to eating my own cooking."

They all laughed, although Berent and Sarah did not know why.

"Ernst is to be thanked for the rabbits," Bertha said proudly. "He shot them last evening."

"Well done, Ernst," Ole said. "I hear you are a good shot."

"Pretty good," Ernst mumbled, not quite knowing how to handle being the center of attention.

"There's no need to be modest," Bertha said. "You are a very good shot. Isn't that right, Albert?"

Albert nodded. "Yes, but don't you be giving him the big head."

"Oh, bosh!" Bertha replied. "You brag about how good a shot he is to anyone who will listen."

"Well, I can't deny that," Albert said with one of his rare laughs. "The boy has a gift."

Big Per gave Ernst a long, thoughtful look. "A gift to be proud of. The girl who marries you can consider herself lucky. She'll always have meat on the table."

Oline and Ernst stared down at their empty plates. It was a contest as to who was blushing most.

"Stop teasing, Per," Helena said, smothering a laugh.

"Oh, is that what I'm doing?"

"Yes, it is," Bertha answered. "Ernst, you and Oline take the others and go and play."

Ernst did not have to be told twice. Within seconds, he and Oline were racing for the barn, the younger children on their heels.

Big Per grinned. "I think it is the big ones who need the watching."

"Oh, Per, stop it!" Helena said. "They're only eleven and twelve. You're turning into a dirty old man."

Ole pulled his pipe and tobacco from his pocket. "What do you mean, turning?"

The men laughed. The women pretended to be offended. "Come on, Helena," Bertha said. "Let's clean up and leave these three old goats to smoke their pipes."

"That's a good idea."

Helena and Bertha cleared the table and carried the dishes into the house, which consisted of the original cabin and a wood-framed room added the previous summer. (Bertha had demanded the extra room if Albert was going to build his barn.)

The men lit their pipes, enjoying a contentment that only farmers experience when a crop is safely harvested.

Big Per blew a perfect O of smoke into the air. "Well, Albert, now that you have your barn, what's next?"

"A corncrib you can drive through, with bins for oats on top."

"How soon?" Ole asked.

"Oh, I'd say three or four years. I'll need more land before I build. Probably around forty acres."

Big Per raised an eyebrow. "You already have eighty acres."

"True. But Ernst will soon be able to do a man's work."

Ole shook his head. ""You'll need more than Ernst to farm that much land."

"I'm not so sure," Albert said. "The way the implement companies are inventing new machinery, one man will soon be able to do the work of three." He leaned forward in his chair. "I had to go to Turg's store last evening, and ran into a fellow who had been to a farm implement fair in Marshalltown. You won't believe the things those companies are working on."

"Like what?" Ole asked.

"All sorts of things. There's what they call a gang plow. It has two bottoms and you ride on it. The contraption needs four horses to pull it. Then there is something called a disk that takes the clods out of a plowed field. And a drag, sort of like that thing you built, Ole, only made of steel. It's supposed to make a field smooth as a carpet."

"Ah!" Big Per snorted. "You don't need all that stuff."

"You do if you're going to plant by wire," Albert said, sitting back in his chair.

Ole leaned forward. "What in the Sam Hill is planting by wire?"

Albert laughed for the second time in five minutes, an almost unheard-of occurrence. "You won't believe this. You unspool a wire with knots every forty inches from one end of the field to the other and stake both ends down. Then you put the wire into a fork on the planter."

"Whoa! Whoa!" Big Per said. "What are you talking about?"

"The corn planter. It's a two-wheel affair pulled by two horses. In front of the wheels are sharp blades that sort of look like the curved runners on a sled. They cut three inches deep into the soil. On top of the runners are gallon buckets that hold the seed corn. The corn drops down through pipes to the runners."

"How does the corn get out?" Ole asked.

"That's where the wire comes in," Albert continued, getting more and more excited. "There's this fork attached to a spring that opens a little door in the bottom of the blades. You put the wire in the fork, and as you drive down the row, the fork is pushed back by the knots in the wire. When the fork is pushed back, the doors open, releasing three kernels of corn. The spring pulls the fork upright again when you pass the knot, closing the doors. You plant two rows at a time!"

Big Per and Ole stared at Albert, their pipes cold and forgotten. Finally, Big Per shook his head. "I don't believe it."

"The fellow said he saw a drawing of it. The salesman told him that they hope to have it on the market in four or five years."

Ole pounded the ashes from his pipe. "Can you imagine how much corn a man could plant with one of those in a day?"

"That's why I'm looking to buy more land," Albert said, relighting his pipe.

A sad look settled on Big Per's face. "If what you say is true, it means the end of my oxen."

Ole put fresh tobacco in his pipe. "Oh, I think you could find some use for them." He turned his attention back to Albert. "Were there any other new machines?"

"You bet. There will be new types of cultivators, better mowing machines, and threshing machines on wheels that can be pulled from one farm to another, powered by steam tractors."

"That, I've heard of," Ole inserted. "Farmers back east are forming what they call threshing runs. What a wonderful idea!"

"Oh! The fellow told me about a new reaper that McCormick is working on. This one I don't believe. They are trying to come up with a machine that not only cuts the grain, but ties it into bundles. No men needed except the driver."

The three men laughed. Big Per said, "I think that fellow was pulling your leg."

"Without a doubt!" Ole agreed. "That's about as wild an idea as I've ever heard."

"The fellow told me he didn't believe it either," Albert said, blowing a smoke ring of his own. "But who knows? A few weeks ago, it took months to get to California. Now, it just takes days."

Ole scratched his beard and nodded. "You make a good point, Albert. We live in amazing times."

"The Lord has been good to us," Big Per said, but immediately regretted saying it.

Ole inwardly groaned, hoping Albert would let the comment pass. No such luck. The man's body stiffened. His face grew dark. His friendly demeanor disappeared faster than food set before a hungry boy.

"That's right!" Albert said. "It is the Lord who provides. Not the pastor. Not the church!"

Big Per threw up his hands, sending pipe ashes flying onto his shirt and into his hair. "Don't start, Albert! I get enough of this on Sunday."

"Oh?" Albert answered in a strained voice. "I noticed you were not in church Sunday."

"That's right. And do you know why? I'm tired of walking on eggs. If I talk to Ole or Hans Twedt, I'm high church. If I talk to you or Saul

Jaeran, I'm low church. Well, I decided to stay home and read my Bible and be no church!"

"Humph! Maybe that's what we all should do until Reverend Amlund sees the light," Albert growled. "I don't need some young preacher from Norway telling me what to do and what to believe. And I sure don't need him forgiving my sins."

"He's not forgiving your sins, Albert." Ole sighed. "God is forgiving your sins."

"Oh, no!" Albert yelled, sitting on the edge of his chair. "He says, 'as a called and ordained servant of the word, *I forgive you all your sins*'!"

"That's not all of it." Ole felt his own temper rising. "He forgives our sins in the name of the Father, Son, and Holy Ghost."

"I don't care in whose name he forgives! He's still doing the forgiving! And he can no more forgive my sins than I can forgive yours."

"Lower your voice, Albert," Big Per said. "We're not deaf."

"I think you are. Both of you! You don't understand what is happening!" Albert's eyes were filled with the fire of the true believer. "If only the clergy can forgive sins, then we are all under their power. The Norwegian church is sending over pastors to control us, make us servants. The bishops want America to be just like Europe, where everything is controlled by the nobility, the rich, and the church!"

Ole was becoming more and more exasperated. "Albert, the Norwegian church can't do that in America. There is no state church."

"Not now! But that's what the clergy wants. And that's what we're fighting against!"

Big Per banged his pipe against the table, breaking the stem. "Now look what you made me do."

"You blame me for breaking your pipe?"

"Yes! Albert, there is something I don't understand. If you are so against the clergy, why did you help build Saint Petri and call Reverend Amlund?"

"Because I want to go to church. I want a pastor to preach the gospel. But I want the congregation to be in control. If the congregation doesn't want the pastor to wear a robe, he shouldn't wear one. And if the congregation doesn't want him to use the liturgy, he shouldn't use it."

"What if most of the congregation wants the service to stay the way it is?" Ole asked.

"Then most of the congregation is blind! Saul is right! The liturgy was conceived by the devil!"

Ole groaned. "Albert, Martin Luther, the founder of our church, created our liturgy."

"No! He did not! Saul told me Luther only adapted the Roman Mass!"

Ole stared at Albert in disbelief. "Are you calling Martin Luther a papist?"

Albert jumped to his feet. "He was a monk, wasn't he? The liturgy is nothing but a way for the Norwegian church to bring us back under the control of the pope!"

"That is ridiculous!" Big Per said, rising like a menacing bear from his chair. "Saul is no expert on religion. He's just a damn troublemaker."

Albert's face became the color of dark wine. "Shame! Shame on you, Per Larson! Saul is like an Old Testament prophet. He sees the truth! And the truth is that all of you who agree with Reverend Amlund are being led like blind sheep back to the Roman church. You all are becoming papists! And everyone knows that papists are going to hell!"

"That's enough!" Big Per roared. "I will not be called a papist! I'm going home."

As Big Per strode to his oxen, Bertha and Helena came running from the house. "What's wrong?" Bertha cried.

"Ask your husband," Big Per said without stopping.

"Per!" Albert called. "Your soul is at stake!"

Per whirled to face Albert, but walked backward as he said, "Maybe so! But if you call me a papist again, your face will be at stake!" He whirled again, muttering words that made both women blush.

Ole walked to his wife. "Get the children, Helena. We're going home."

Helena took one look at her husband's face and almost ran to the barn. Ole turned back to Albert. "I'll be over in the morning to get my straw."

"Do it this afternoon," Albert yelled. "I don't want papist straw on my place."

"As you wish!" Ole replied, stomping toward his wagon.

Bertha hurried to Albert, who was literally shaking with rage. "Albert, you promised. The Branjords are our neighbors and friends."

"They are no longer our friends! They've become papists!"

Albert stormed into the house, leaving Bertha to watch in dismay as Big Per and Ole hitched up their teams and drove from the yard. The Branjord children sat on the sacks of grain, confused and frightened, looking back at their equally confused Hindberg friends. Sarah and Heinrik gave little waves. Berent and Martin returned them. Oline and Ernst just stared at each other.

Bertha's heart ached as she watched the children. She sank into a chair and wept. What she did not know was that scenes such as this were becoming common in north Story County. Friendships forged in the holds of leaky sailing ships and nurtured by the efforts to build a new life in a new land were being hammered to splinters on the anvil of religious certainty.

Ole

Papist! That's what he called me. Papist! And Big Per too! Ridiculous! I saw Bertha crying. Helena is all upset. The children don't understand what is going on. When I went back to load the straw, Ernst tried to help, but Albert called him back into the house. It was like I had the plague or something. What has come over the man? All of a sudden it is like God is going to send another flood because Reverend Amlund wears a robe and gives the absolution.

A year ago, Albert could not have cared less about either one. This is all because of Saul Jaeran. Albert thinks he's a prophet. If he is, he's the prophet of the devil. Per's right. The man is nothing but a troublemaker. Talk about making a mountain out of a molehill! He has made a disagreement into a war!

I don't understand it. I don't understand why some people feel the absolution and the robe are so important. I know they do. I just don't understand it. All I know is I've lost a good friend and a neighbor.

DAMN!

Chapter Twenty-One

Helena heard the scraping sound as part of dream in which she was sailing a boat on a fjord, a cool breeze drifting over her, filling the sail. The sound annoyed her. She wanted it to stop. She sleepily reached for Ole. He would make it go away.

He was not beside her.

Helena instantly was awake. She snapped into a sitting position so quickly she was momentarily dizzy. Her face was moist. Her long, blond hair, which hung loose and unbraided, was damp. Her nightgown clung to her like a frightened child.

When the blur caused by the dizziness cleared, Helena looked out the windows for the soft yellow of dawn. She saw only the heavy blackness of night. Where was Ole? What was the scraping sound?

Helena swung her legs to the floor, careful not to disturb the sleeping children. It was far too hot to sleep in the loft, so they lay like tousle-haired angels on quilts she had made for them. She momentarily forgot the scraping sound and smiled, maternal love overpowering all other emotions. Watching one's children sleep was truly a blessing of motherhood.

Her reverie was shattered by the crack of a hammer on metal. She sidestepped the children and walked to the porch. What she saw in the dying light of a quarter moon made her shiver despite the heat. She sharply inhaled the dry, stagnant air.

Hoops. Ole was putting hoops on the wagon. Three were in place. He was working on the fourth. Helena hated hoops. A covered wagon meant travel: endless days on the prairie; fear of what lay hidden over the horizon; the excruciating pain of loss; a tiny grave in a vast land.

Helena hurried to the wagon. "Ole, why are you putting hoops on the wagon?"

"We're going to Nevada. All of us," was the reply, as Ole inserted the final hoop into its iron sheath.

"We don't need the tarpaulin to go to Nevada. It's not going to rain."

Ole jumped down from the wagon box. "I wish it would. Then I wouldn't have to go at all. The cover is to protect us from the sun."

Helena was relieved they were just going to Nevada, but was mystified as to the reason. "Ole Branjord, you are talking in circles."

Ole wiped his brow. "If the corn doesn't get water in the next two or three days, there will be no crop. Carrying buckets of water from the well or river would be like trying to save a thirsty man with a thimble. I need something to haul water to the field. Remember that big, fancy tin bathtub you liked in Alderman's store?"

"The one you could stretch out in?"

"Yes. You're going to get it. Tomorrow I will put it, the washtub, and the big, black, lard-rendering kettle in the wagon, fill them with water from the river, and drive the wagon to the field. From there we can carry buckets of water to the corn."

"That's a wonderful idea, Ole," Helena said, again impressed by Ole's ingenuity.

"You may not think so tomorrow. It will be back-breaking work."

Helena softly touched Ole's cheek. "We're strong. We can do it."

Ole drew her close and kissed her hair and neck. "I know. Thank you."

Helena pulled back. "For what?"

"For being you." Ole smiled. "Now make a list of what you need. And I want you to buy material for the children and yourself. Martin's good pants are too short. Oline needs a new dress. You need a new dress. I don't know what Berent needs. Certainly not a new dress!"

Helena laughed. "No, he doesn't need a new dress, and neither do I."

"Yes, you do," Ole stated firmly. "I would have bought the material when I sold the hogs, but I didn't know what you wanted. Look, we have had a good harvest. You have all worked hard. Let's give ourselves a little treat."

Helena kissed her husband on the lips. "I love you, Ole Branjord. What are you getting for yourself?"

"The tub." Ole laughed. "After watering the corn, I'll need to soak in it for a week. While I put on the tarpaulin, get the children up and have breakfast ready. I want to get started at first light."

Helena did not bother to reply. She almost danced to the cabin. She was going to town!

Ole was pleased. The family had traveled nearly two miles before the sun was completely visible. Barring trouble, they would be in Nevada well before noon. Doll and Lady actually seemed to be enjoying themselves. Ole knew this would end within an hour. It was going to be a long, hot, difficult day for the horses. Thank heavens there was a breeze. It was from the southwest and, at the moment, was quite pleasant. There was no doubt that too would change. By noon, the wind would feel more like a blast of hot air from a furnace, but at least it would keep the mosquitoes away and the horseflies off the team.

The excitement of the trip to Nevada was subsiding for the Branjord children. The jumping, pushing, pointing, and laughing had stopped. At Helena's suggestion, they had settled into a game of "Yitts." In this game, the first child to see a wild animal and yell yitts was awarded points; one point for a rabbit, two for a deer, three for a fox, five for a coyote, six for a wolf, ten for a badger, and twenty for a buffalo. Nobody had seen a buffalo for years, but Helena told the children to look hard.

Helena sat beside Ole wearing her second-best summer dress and a large sunbonnet. Her eyes sparkled. Going to Nevada was as big an event for her as for the children. Other than going to church and her walks to Fairview, she had not been off the farm for nearly nine months. "Maybe it won't be so hot today," she said, smiling.

"Don't let the morning fool you. It will be hot, especially on the way home."

After a short pause, Helena's smile turned to an impish grin. "If it gets too hot, we can put water in the new tub and all sit in it."

Ole laughed. "Now that would be a sight."

Helena joined in the laughter but became serious when she glanced to the north. "There's more smoke."

"I know," Ole replied, not bothering to look. "There was a lot of heat lightening up that way last night."

"I hate prairie fires."

"You're not alone. But don't worry. If the fire comes from the east, we have the river for protection. If it comes from the west … well, that's why I plowed a fresh firebreak yesterday."

Both were silent for some time. They were no strangers to prairie fires. In Hardin County, the farm had been saved only because of a change in wind direction.

Helena sighed. "I don't think I've ever seen the prairie so dry."

Ole answered, "I know I haven't. If we don't get rain soon, there not only won't be a corn crop, there won't be any grass to cut for hay."

Ole could hardly believe how the prairie had changed since his trip to Nevada in June. The lushness was gone. Butterfly milkweed drooped like a tired old man after a day of heavy work. Spiderwort, a flower that opened in the morning and closed by noon, was firmly shut, as if trying to hide from the burning sun. The tall yellow stems of the compass plants bowed as if suffering from osteoporosis. It made no difference that roots went down nearly ten feet. Large cracks in the parched earth told the story. The prairie was in survival mode.

The Branjords traveled in silence, with the exception of an occasional "yitts" from Oline and Martin after spotting small animals. Each grew excited when Oline spied a badger sunning himself on a mound and Martin saw a red fox dash across the trail behind the wagon. Berent, who was always late seeing anything, stomped his foot.

"It's not fair! I never see anything first!"

Helena turned and smiled at the frustrated boy. "You will. Just look harder."

"I am looking hard! It's not fair! Oline and Martin have older eyes than me!"

Ole laughed. "Your eyes are old enough. Pay closer attention."

Berent pouted for several seconds, then shouted, "Yitts!"

"What did you see?" Martin asked.

"A buffalo!"

"Oh, you did not!" Oline said.

"Did too!"

"Did not!"

"You're lying, Berent!" Martin accused.

"Am not!"

"You are too. There are no more buffalo in Story County."

"How do you know?"

"Papa said so!"

This brought Berent up short. Papa knew everything. "Is that true, Papa?"

"Yes, it is, Berent," Ole answered.

Berent returned to his pout. The two older children looked at him with disgust. After nearly a minute, he said, "I saw something."

"I'm sure you did," Helena said with motherly kindness. "But it wasn't a buffalo. Keep looking."

"Phooey!" Berent muttered, flopping down on the bags of wheat that were about to be ground into flour. Before another minute had passed, he was asleep.

It was almost eleven o'clock when the Branjords approached Nevada. The sun was brutal. Even with the tarpaulin giving shade, Ole's shirt was soaked, Helena's dress clung, foam dripped from under the harness of the plodding team, and sweat glistened on the faces of the sleeping children. Neither Helena nor Ole could remember it being so hot.

Ole talked to the horses. "Not much farther, girls. There will be feed and water waiting." Doll and Lady could see the destination and increased their pace without being asked.

"I suppose I should wake the children." Helena sighed.

"Do you have to? I'm enjoying the quiet."

"They won't want to miss driving into town."

Ole looked down at Helena's pale legs that were beginning to acquire a red tinge. He grinned. "Not that I mind the view, but if we drive into Nevada with your skirt up, we'll cause quite a scandal."

Helena reluctantly flipped down her skirt. "Wouldn't Hanna Signaldahl love that?"

"Yes, old Horse-Face would be as happy as a hog in slop."

"Ole!" Helena scolded. "Not in front of the children."

"They're sleeping."

"Not for long."

Helena reached back and gently patted her eldest on the shoulder. "Oline, we're almost there."

Oline was immediately awake. She looked out and saw they were only a quarter of a mile from town. She shook her brothers. "Wake up! I can see Nevada."

The boys, especially Berent, who had slept most of the way, were still groggy. They yawned and rubbed their eyes.

"Do you see?" Oline asked.

Both nodded, not quite as excited as their big sister.

Ole glanced back. "Who won the Yitts contest?"

"I did!" Oline cried. "I had eighteen points."

Martin frowned. "You're just lucky you saw that badger before I did."

"I didn't have any points," Berent mumbled, sticking out his lower lip.

Sensing there were about to be tears, Helena quickly said, "But you had a good long sleep."

"Humph," Berent said, undecided whether or not tears were in order. Before he could make the decision, the wagon rolled into Nevada and the game was forgotten.

The children's eyes became wide and filled with wonder. To them this community of close to nine hundred souls was huge. Oline could not remember and the boys had never seen a larger town. Everywhere they looked there were buildings, some two stories high, and wagons and buggies and people—more people than were in Saint Petri on Sundays. And there was noise! To young ears used to the silence of the prairie, the combination of squeaky wagon wheels, neighing horses, barking dogs, shouting children, and the steady drone of human voices was awesome and a little frightening.

Ole stopped the horses in front of Alderman's store. "Take the children and start shopping. I'll drop off the wheat at Tolbert's mill."

"Can I come with you, Papa?" Martin asked.

"Well, I suppose so. Climb up here by me."

"Me too!" Berent cried.

"No!" Ole replied. "I don't want you anywhere near the mill."

The boy's lower lip extended in preparation for a world-class wail, but Oline deftly squashed it by saying, "The store has candy. Come on!" Berent's momentary pout became a grin as he followed Oline over the end gate of the wagon. Martin scooted onto the seat vacated by Helena, who had gracefully stepped from the wheel hub to the ground.

"Should I wait for you to buy the tub?" Helena asked.

"No. I just hope Alderman has one left," Ole answered, slapping the reins. The wagon moved on down the street, Martin sitting proudly by his father.

"Ouch!" Oline yelled as she leaped from the wooden sidewalk to the dirt street. "Mama, the boards are hot!"

Berent also gave a yell, and did a little dance before jumping off the scorching wood.

"I'm sure they are," Helena said. "You'll have to run quickly into the store."

Neither child hesitated. They dashed to the door, reaching it just as a tall, thin woman, carrying a bag of groceries, stepped out. Helena watched in horror, her mind conjuring up a vision of food flying one way and the woman the other. But the children rushed by, barely touching the startled patron.

"Watch where you are running!" the woman snapped.

Helena stepped up onto the sidewalk, grateful the remark was in Norwegian and not English. "I'm sorry. The boards are hot on their bare feet. They had to run."

"That's no excuse for almost knocking me down!" the woman replied with a disgusted look. "I suggest you teach your children some manners!" With that, the woman stomped off. Helena bit her lip to keep from responding. She wanted to say, "If you had no shoes, you'd run too."

When Helena entered the store, Mrs. Hammerdahl was waiting with a big smile. "It is so good to see you again, Mrs. Branjord."

Helena returned the smile. "Thank you, Mrs. Hammerdahl. But I don't think the woman who just left would agree with you."

"Aw! Don't pay any attention to her. She's been complaining about something since the day she was born."

Berent pulled at Helena's skirt. "Can we get candy now?"

"No," Helena replied, tousling his blond curls. "When we are done shopping. But only if you are good."

"That's right," Mrs. Hammerdahl said with mock seriousness. "Only if you are good."

Berent quickly ran behind his mother's skirt. Mrs. Hammerdahl laughed. "Don't hide. I won't bite." She turned to Helena. "Do you have a list for me?"

"Of course. And I'll need some dress material and some black twill for pants."

"For me, Mama?" Berent asked, darting from behind her skirt.

"No. For Martin and your papa. And don't start about the pants."

Berent plopped himself on the floor in a man-sized pout. Both women, having seen many pouts, ignored him.

"We've just gotten in a bolt of fine black wool," Mrs. Hammerdahl said. "It will make up into a wonderful winter dress."

"The material isn't for me. It's for Oline. She is growing like a weed."

Mrs. Hammerdahl glanced over at the material table, where Oline was already examining the different bolts of cloth. "I see that. They grow up so fast, don't they? But look at the black wool. It is beautiful."

"I don't need another dress."

"Every woman needs another dress," replied Mrs. Hammerdahl, patting Helena on the arm and taking the list from her hand. "You look at the material. I'll start your order."

She turned to go, but was stopped by Helena asking, "Do you still have any of those long bathtubs?"

"Yes. There are two in the back."

"Good. We'll take one."

Mrs. Hammerdahl laughed. "You'll enjoy a good soak in that."

"Someday, I hope. But now Ole is going to use it to haul water to the corn."

"YITTS!"

Berent's scream startled everyone in the store. Mr. Alderman jumped up from his chair behind the counter. All stared at Berent, who had leaped to his feet and was pointing to the back wall. "A buffalo! I win! I win!"

"What is with that child?" Mr. Alderman called out in English. Mrs. Hammerdahl translated the question into Norwegian. Helena blushed a deep red. Hanging on the back wall was a mounted buffalo head.

"Do you see it, Mama? Do you see it?" Berent was jumping up and down.

"Yes, I see it! Now be quiet!" Helena said, before turning to Mrs. Hammerdahl. "It's the buffalo head. The children were playing the Yitts game on the way to town. Seeing a buffalo is worth twenty points."

Mrs. Hammerdahl laughed. She was familiar with the game. In English, she explained the situation to Mr. Alderman, who shook his head and returned to his chair.

"I'm so sorry," Helena said.

"Don't be," Mrs. Hammerdahl replied. "I think it's funny."

Oline had returned to her mother's side. "That doesn't count, Mama."

"Does too!" Berent said.

"Does not!"

"Does too!"

"Stop it!" Helena barked.

Oline whined, "Mama, that's just a head."

"It still counts!" Berent yelled.

Helena grabbed both children by their arms. "I said stop it! One more word out of either of you and there will be no candy! We'll let your father decide."

"Good thinking," Mrs. Hammerdahl said. "I'll get your order together."

Helena glared at the children as Mrs. Hammerdahl scurried away. "You heard me! Not another word!" She gave each arm a pinch before walking to the material table. Berent stuck out his tongue at Oline, who returned the favor.

The bolt of black wool was on the top. Mrs. Hammerdahl had not exaggerated. The material was beautiful. Helena fingered the softness, imagining how it would feel next to her skin. She sighed. Imagining was possible; buying was not. It was far too expensive. She would have to settle for coarser wool or perhaps velveteen.

Oline had followed her mother. "I like this," she said, holding up a bolt of blue calico.

"It is pretty, but you need something for winter."

Oline next picked wine-colored brocade. Helena shook her head. "Too expensive. You are growing. Whatever I make won't fit next year."

The black wool was Oline's next choice. "Oh, this is nice."

"It is," Helena said, taking the bolt from Oline and placing it back on the table. "Too nice. Besides, you're too young for black."

"Excuse me."

Helena looked up from the table to see a pretty young woman in a faded, travel-worn, yellow calico dress and a green bonnet smiling at her.

"Yes," Helena said, returning the smile, immediately liking the stranger, who had a small boy peeking out from behind her skirt.

"I couldn't help hearing your son yell 'Yitts.' What is this yitts?

Helena giggled. "It's just a silly game the children play when we are going places." She went on to explain the game. "A buffalo is worth twenty points. That's why my son yelled so loud."

"Dead animals don't count," Oline inserted.

Helena rolled her eyes. "We'll let your father decide that."

"It sounds like fun," the young woman said.

"It is. And it keeps the children occupied." Helena added, "You'll have to teach it to yours."

"Oh, I just have my three-year-old. His name is Elmer. My name is Sonja Halverson."

"Hello. My name is Helena Branjord. This is my daughter Oline. And somewhere in the store is my loud son, Berent. Do you live near Nevada?"

Sonja sighed. "I wish. I am so tired of traveling. We stopped to get supplies and fix a wagon wheel."

"Where are you settling?"

"In Hamilton County. How much farther is it?"

"About two days. Do you have land there?"

"Yes. My sister lives close by, so we'll be staying with her family until we can build a house."

"Good," Helena said. "Getting situated is so much easier when you have family to help."

"I hope so. This land is so different from Norway. I don't quite know what to expect."

Helena smiled. "Hard work and a sore back. But there is one thing we didn't have in the old country ... hope. This is a land of promise."

Sonja took a handkerchief from the sleeve of her dress and wiped her brow. "Is it always this hot?"

"No. This is unusual. I've never seen it so hot or so dry. We are in terrible need of rain."

"I hope the heat breaks soon. Last night I dreamed of the fjords back home."

"Those dreams won't go away. I still dream of cool, dark forests."

At that moment, Berent decided to appear. Helena drew him to her. "This is Berent. He's four."

"Hello, Berent." Sonja smiled. "This is my son, Elmer."

Berent's eyes became wide. He stared at Elmer, then asked, "How old are you?"

Elmer said nothing, but held up three fingers.

"Mama!" Berent exploded. "He's three fingers and he's wearing pants! I'm four fingers!"

It was true. Elmer was dressed in a gray, store-bought shirt and black twill pants.

"It's not fair, Mama! It's not fair!"

Helena knelt beside Berent. "You hush! I told you I didn't want to hear another word about pants. Do you understand?"

Tears welled in the boy's eyes. "It's not fair."

"Berent is consumed by wearing pants," Helena said, rising. "I told him he will get them when he is five."

"I know what you're going through," Sonja said. "Elmer started in on me when he turned three. I just caved in."

This might have ended the encounter had Elmer not looked up at his mother and asked, "Is that a boy or a girl?"

Berent flew at the younger boy as if catapulted. Before either mother could react, the two boys were on the floor, the one in the dress on top. "I'm not a girl!" Berent screamed. Elmer wailed in terror.

"Oh, my! Oh, my!" Sonja cried.

It took all of Helena's strength to pull her furious son off of the terrified three-year-old. "Berent! You stop! Do you hear me? Stop! I'm ashamed of you!" She emphasized her words with a firm swat on Berent's rear end.

The commotion brought both Mrs. Hammerdahl and Mr. Alderman running. "What is going on?" Mrs. Hammerdahl demanded.

Helena held tightly to Berent, who was now crying as loudly as Elmer. "I'm so sorry. It's Berent's fault. He jumped on Elmer because the boy is wearing pants." She turned to Sonja. "Please forgive him. He is usually a sweet boy."

Mrs. Hammerdahl understood. Mr. Alderman did not. He just wanted the noise to stop. "Can you stop this crying?" he asked Mrs. Hammerdahl.

As a matter of fact, she could. Having dealt many times with angry and weeping children, she pulled two pieces of hard candy from her apron pocket. "Anyone who wants candy has to be quiet."

The boys became as silent as Trappist monks, their tear-filled eyes staring at the candy. "That's better," Mrs. Hammerdahl said, popping a piece of candy into each boy's mouth. "Here's one for you too, honey," she added, handing a piece to Oline.

"Thank you," Oline said.

Mrs. Hammerdahl put her hands on her ample hips. "What about you two? Can you say thank you?"

Both boys nodded.

"Well, I'm waiting."

A low decibel "Thank you" came from each.

"Good! No more crying." She turned and continued filling the Branjord order.

Mr. Alderman walked back to his desk, reminding himself to give Mrs. Hammerdahl a raise in pay.

"Say you're sorry, Berent," Helena ordered.

"But he ..."

"I don't care what he said! What you did was wrong. Say you're sorry!"

Berent glared at Elmer, who was now clinging to Sonja's leg, and mumbled, "I'm sorry."

"Thank you." Helena sighed, turning to Sonja. "I hope you will forgive him, Mrs. Halverson."

Sonja could not help but smile. Even after he attacked her son, she found the tear-streaked four-year-old to be adorable. "He is forgiven. And I guess Elmer found out that he is a boy."

Helena rolled her eyes. "Oh, he's a boy all right!"

Sonja glanced out the store window. "Oh, there is my husband. The wheel must be fixed."

Helena followed Sonja's gaze and saw a covered wagon, pulled by a black and white team of horses, obviously travel weary. Attached to the side of the wagon was a metal pole on which was flying a small American flag. Seeing that Helena was watching the wagon, Sonja said, "Sven is proud to be an American. It has been a pleasure meeting you, Mrs. Branjord. I hope we see each other again."

"It has been a pleasure meeting you, Mrs. Halverson." Helena smiled. "We live two miles south of Fairview. When you get settled, come and see us. I'm sure the boys will have more fun."

Sonja laughed. "I'm sure they will, and I would like that very much. Come, Elmer. Let's get in the wagon."

Elmer dashed to the front, followed by Sonja. She picked up her supplies, gave a wave to Helena, and left the store. Sonja's husband jumped down from the wagon. He loaded the supplies while Sonja and Elmer climbed up to the seat. Within seconds he had joined them and was urging the tired horses north to the open prairie.

"I'm ashamed of you!" Helena snapped at Berent. "I should tell your papa."

Berent produced his best pleading look, a look that melted Helena every time she saw it. "Please don't tell Papa."

Helena maintained a stern face, even though she had no intention of telling Ole. She did not want her son spanked on the main street of Nevada. "Well, I should tell, but I won't. And that goes for you too, Oline."

"Yes, Mama," Oline answered. She did not want the embarrassment of a spanking either. She would not tell Papa … at least not until they reached home.

Mrs. Hammerdahl came bustling up to Helena carrying several yards of royal blue velvet material. "I had this laid aside for another woman, but she decided not to buy it."

"Oh, Mama! It's beautiful!" Oline cried.

Helena fingered the plush cloth. "It is beautiful, but too expensive."

"No, it's not," Mrs. Hammerdahl whispered, taking a quick glance toward the front of the store where, to her relief, Mr. Alderman was walking out the front door. "It is half price. There is not enough material for a woman's dress, but more than enough for a young girl."

"Mama, please!"

"You say half price?"

"That's right."

There was a long pause. Oline could hardly breathe. Finally, Helena nodded her head. "We'll take it."

Oline gave her mother a hug, then jumped up and down. "Thank you! Thank you!"

Berent wrinkled up his nose. He could not understand why anyone would get so excited over material for a dumb old dress. But then, for no other reason than he was four and the thought popped into his head, he said to Mrs. Hammerdahl, "You have pretty hands."

"Why, you little darling, you!" Mrs. Hammerdahl said with a huge smile. She turned to Helena, who was rolling her eyes. "He is just adorable. Someday he's going to break a lot of hearts."

"Don't I know it," Helena said.

Oline frowned at Berent, who was smiling from ear to ear. He liked being called adorable.

"Now, Mrs. Branjord," Mrs. Hammerdahl continued. "How about the black wool? It will make a stunning dress."

"I'm sure it will, but I can't afford it." Helena sighed. "Wrap up the velvet and enough twill for Martin and Ole."

"Speaking of Ole, I want to show you something," Mrs. Hammerdahl said, leading Helena and the children to a side table. "We got these in a few weeks ago and have sold almost all of them. They are made of denim and are called overalls." She held one up for Helena to see.

Immediately, Berent went from bored to excited. "Look at all the pockets, Mama!"

Mrs. Hammerdahl laughed. "That's what all the men say. There are front pockets, back pockets, and pockets on the bib. They love the pockets."

"I don't think that would fit Ole," Helena said. "It's too big."

"Oh, this is a large. Ole would take a medium." Mrs. Hammerdahl flipped through the stack until she found the smaller size. "Here! This will fit him. And see? It has adjustable straps."

Oline tugged at Helena's hand. "Get it for him, Mama."

"Yes!" Berent agreed. "Buy one, Mama. And get one for me!"

"They don't make them for little boys." Mrs. Hammerdahl smiled.

"Shoot!"

Helena took the overalls from Mr. Hammerdahl. "Oh, they are heavy. How much?"

"Three dollars. But they wear forever. The salesman said many farmers call them iron pants."

Oline closed the deal by saying, "Please, Mama. Papa deserves some new clothes."

"You're right," Helena replied. "I'll take these overalls. I just hope Ole likes them."

She would soon find out. Ole and Martin walked into the store. Oline and Berent ran to their father, followed by Helena and Mrs. Hammerdahl, who did not run.

"Papa! Papa! Mama bought you some overalls!" Berent called.

"Bought me what?"

"Overalls," Oline replied. "It has lots of pockets."

"I haven't bought them yet," Helena said. "We can put them back."

Ole grinned. "No. Last week I saw a fellow wearing them. I was thinking about getting a pair."

"You'll like them," Mrs. Hammerdahl said as she began adding up the purchases.

Oline pointed out the blue velvet. "This is for my new dress. Isn't it pretty/"

"Yes, it is," Ole answered, then looked at his wife. "Where is the material for your dress?"

"I don't need one," came the reply.

Mrs. Hammerdahl did not look up from her work, but smiled. "We have some beautiful black wool that your wife loves."

"I told you, Mrs. Hammerdahl, that I don't need a new dress."

"Yes, you did."

Ole stuck his thumbs in the waist of his pants, unaware that he was being drawn into a clever female conspiracy. "Mrs. Hammerdahl, do you know how many yards of that wool would be needed for a dress?"

"Yes, I do."

"Would you please add that material to the list?"

"Yes, I will."

"Ole, I don't need …"

Mrs. Hammerdahl waggled her finger as she interrupted. "Now, Mrs. Branjord, you hush. The man of the house has spoken." She hurried away to get the black wool.

Helena gave her husband a disapproving look. She had never loved him more.

The buying of the material was not a surprise to Helena, nor was it completely calculated. But she knew her husband and Mrs. Hammerdahl. She already had a pattern in mind for the dress.

When the bill was presented, Ole swallowed hard. It was nearly fifteen dollars. "You'll have to put that on my account, Mrs. Hammerdahl."

"Already done. We thank you for your business."

"Thank you," Ole said. "Put everything in the tub. We'll pick it up on our way out."

The Branjords were about to leave when Berent yelled, "Wait!" He pointed to the buffalo head. "I saw the buffalo first and said yitts. Does it count?"

Mrs. Hammerdahl giggled. Helena bit her lip to keep from doing the same.

Martin realized what a positive answer would mean. "It's dead, Papa!"

"It's just a head!" Oline added.

Three upturned faces and two amused women awaited the answer. Ole frowned. Once again he was forced to play Solomon. He sighed. "Well, I know it is just a head, but it is a buffalo head. And I know it is dead, but remember, Martin, on the way to church last Sunday, you saw a dead skunk and I counted it. So, Berent, you win."

"I win! I win!" Berent cried as his siblings groaned.

Ole and Helena waved to Mrs. Hammerdahl as Ole opened the door.

Behind their backs, two tongues were sticking out at Berent, who just clapped his hands and grinned.

Outside, Helena noticed something missing. "Where is the wagon?"

"I left it under a tree to give the horses some shade," Ole replied.

Martin beamed. "I helped Papa feed and water Doll and Lady."

"Good for you," Helena said.

"Oh!" Oline moaned. "We forgot to bring any food."

"We didn't forget, Oline." Helena smiled. "Your father decided we would all eat dinner in the hotel."

Disbelief registered on three small faces. None of the children had ever eaten a meal in a restaurant. Martin spoke for the other two when he whispered, "Wow."

Chapter Twenty-Two

The Rutchen Hotel dining room was neither large nor fancy. Unmatched tables, some square, some round, all covered with different colored calico tablecloths, were scattered about on a wide plank floor. A cold potbellied stove squatted on clawed feet between sash windows on the street side. Opposite the windows was a door leading to the kitchen. The long north wall had no windows but was decorated with two Currier and Ives prints. The south wall was mostly dominated by a large, square archway that separated the hotel lobby from the dining room.

Ole and Helena entered from the hotel lobby, their children clinging close to them. Berent had decided it was best to hold Mother's hand. Nearly all the tables were taken. Helena gazed around the room and inwardly groaned when she saw Emil and Hanna Signaldahl and their daughter, Elsa, sitting near the windows. She wanted to turn around and leave, but Ole had already claimed a table near the lobby entrance. The children excitedly chose places to sit. Oline had no more than sat down when Helena asked her to move to the opposite side.

"Why?" Oline asked.

"Because I want to sit there," Helena snapped.

The harshness of the reply made Oline quickly move. She did not understand that Helena wanted to sit with her back to Hanna Signaldahl.

A young girl of about sixteen, with long, blond hair tied back with a frayed yellow ribbon, approached the table. A faded brown hand-me-down dress, two sizes too large, hung like a half-fallen tent from her thin frame. She did wear shoes, although there were holes in the toes of both. To make the holes less noticeable, she had put boot black on the toes of her socks. Her eyes were tired, her smile weak. "Do you speak Norwegian?" she asked.

Ole smiled. "That's all we speak."

The girl sighed. "Good. My English is poor."

"I'm sure it is better than mine," Ole said. "What is your name?"

"I'm Tina. What can I get for you?"

Helena asked, "What are you serving today?"

"We have pork roast with boiled potatoes and creamed peas, or pot roast with browned potatoes and carrots."

"Pot roast!" Oline said.

"Me too!" Martin agreed.

"What's pot roast?" Berent asked.

"You'll find out," Ole said to his youngest and then looked at Helena. "Five pot roasts?"

Helena nodded. "We get plenty of pork at home."

"Would you like coffee?"

"Yes," Ole answered. "Five waters and two coffees."

"Oh, Ole," Helena said. "It's too hot for coffee."

Ole laughed. "It's never too hot for coffee if you are Norwegian. Isn't that right, Tina?"

The girl smiled, showing a mouth filled with perfect teeth. "That's what my mama says."

"Does your family live here in Nevada?" Helena asked.

The smile faded. Her large blue eyes became sad. "No. They're about twenty miles southwest, out on the prairie."

Tina quickly fled to the kitchen. Helena's heart went out to her. She saw a girl much like herself, turned out into the world before she was ready, simply because she was a mouth to feed. Helena knew exactly how the girl felt.

"Is Tina a waitress?" Oline asked.

"Yes, she is," Ole answered.

"And I'm sure she works in the kitchen too," Helena added. "She's probably the one who peels all the potatoes."

"Does she get paid?"

"Yes, Oline," Helena said. "But not much."

"That's why she wears that ugly dress," Martin said matter-of-factly.

Helena looked at her middle child. "He notices everything," she thought. She said aloud, "Yes, that's right. Now hush. She's coming back."

Tina returned with five glasses of water on a tray. "I'll bring the coffee with the dinner," she said, placing the glasses on the table.

"That will be fine," Helena said. After a pause, she continued, ""Tina, you have lovely hair." She was rewarded with a dazzling smile. Helena thought, "This girl could be very pretty if she gained fifteen pounds and had some decent clothes."

"Well, look who is here."

Helena did not have to look to know who had spoken. The saccharine voice was as phony as the person to whom it belonged. Helena forced the smallest of smiles. "Mrs. Signaldahl."

Ole reluctantly pushed back his chair to stand, but Hanna stopped him with a queenly wave of her gloved hand. "Please don't get up. It is just too hot for formalities, isn't that right, Emil?"

"Yes, dear," Emil replied, giving a stiff nod to Ole. "Branjord."

Ole's nod was equally stiff. "Signaldahl."

"What brings you to town?" Hanna asked, leaning lightly on a lime green parasol that matched her fine cotton dress.

"We had some shopping to do," Helena replied.

"Us too! Elsa and I had new dresses to pick up. Emil didn't want to come because of the heat, but we just couldn't wait. Isn't that right, Elsa?"

"Yes, Mama." She twirled around. "Isn't it pretty?"

Oline bit her lip. It was pretty, one of the prettiest dresses she had ever seen. The material was a brightly colored cotton print, finely stitched. It was accented by a white lace ruffle on the skirt, a matching lace collar around the neck, and a large yellow bow in the back.

Helena attempted but failed to widen her smile. "Yes, Elsa. It is very nice."

"It's a half-birthday present," Elsa said, doing a second twirl. "I got new shoes too!"

The Branjords all gaped at the highly polished, black, high-top button shoes.

Hanna smiled and rolled her eyes. "They are somewhat expensive, but she had outgrown her other pairs. I suppose I should let her go barefoot like your children, but I'm so afraid that she will step on something sharp."

Helena grabbed her chair so hard her knuckles turned white. All the self-control she possessed was required not to stand up and slap the supercilious smile from Hanna's face.

"What's a half-birthday?" Martin asked.

"Oh, it's nothing more than an excuse to give a present," Hanna answered. "I know it sounds silly."

"So your birthday is in January," Ole said.

"Almost," Elsa replied. "December twenty-eighth."

Hanna turned to Emil. "Well, come along. Let's go up to our room and rest."

Helena was surprised. "You are staying in the hotel?"

"Oh my, yes. It is too hot to start back now. We'll leave early tomorrow morning. Isn't that right, Emil?"

"Yes, dear," Emil said in a tight, low voice that stated unmistakably what he really thought about staying the night.

Hanna gave him a sharp look and turned to go. Berent stopped her cold by asking, "Do you have ugly hands?"

Hanna whirled to face the boy. Her narrow-set eyes shot daggers. "Why in the world would you ask that?"

"It's hot and you are wearing gloves."

"Ladies wear gloves."

"Mama doesn't."

With a contemptuous smile, Hanna said, "I know," and led her husband and daughter into the lobby and up the stairs.

Ole half rose from his chair, his face as red as a ripe strawberry.

"No, Ole! Don't let her spoil our meal," Helena hissed.

Ole settled back into his chair. He looked from the disappearing trio to his youngest son. "She does have ugly hands, Berent. And they go well with her ugly face!"

"Ole!" Helena said.

"Well, it's true," Ole growled.

The children sat wide-eyed and silent. Hearing their father speak badly about anyone was so rare that his outburst was shocking.

Berent broke the silence. "I was right," he said proudly, "and so is Papa."

Oline and Martin looked at each other and giggled. Berent did not know what was funny, but he joined in. Ole snorted, attempting to keep from laughing. He failed. Soon the laughter was so loud it drew attention from others in the room.

"Now hush!" Helena scolded in a half-hearted manner. She could not hide the smile on her own face.

Thankfully, at that moment the food arrived. Grace was said and the meal devoured, no one enjoying it more than Helena. It had been years since she had eaten food that she had no part in preparing. Tina kept the water glasses full and poured second and third cups of coffee. All in all, it was a dinner to remember.

When the family prepared to leave, Helena whispered to Ole, "Leave Tina a tip."

"I intend to," he answered, putting a dime on the table.

"More than that," Helena said.

Ole looked at her with surprise. A dime was considered a good tip.

"She needs it."

Ole added a nickel. Hanna nodded as she led the children out into the lobby, leaving Ole to pay the bill. It was a dollar and ten cents. Ole shook his head. This was indeed an expensive day.

Helena and Oline waited in the lobby while "the men" retrieved the wagon and the newly ground flour. In front of Alderman's store, Mrs. Hammerdahl helped Ole and Helena lift the tub, which now contained their other items and a bag of hard candy, into the wagon.

"Do you need any water?" Mrs. Hammerdahl asked. "It is so hot!"

"No. I filled up the kegs at the pump."

Mrs. Hammerdahl wiped her face. "Have a good trip home. I'm getting out of the sun."

"Good thinking." Ole laughed.

Mrs. Hammerdahl went back into the store as Ole climbed up onto the wagon seat. Hanna and the children were already situated. Ole slapped the reins. Doll and Lady, heads down, knowing full well what lay before them, put the wagon into motion.

Helena looked back at the children, who were each sucking on a piece of hard candy. "We won't be home until suppertime. It is going to be hot. I want no complaining, arguing, or fighting. Cause any form of problem and you will walk behind the wagon. Understand?" The children nodded, and before Nevada faded from view, they were asleep.

The horses plodded mile after weary mile, sweat pooling into foam beneath the harness straps. More cracks appeared in the parched earth, spreading like a web spun by a monstrous spider. Prairie flowers wilted, bending as if praying for relief. No animals moved. Hunter and hunted lay within yards of each other, beneath whatever shade they could find, barely breathing. No birds flew, nor did they sing. It was as if any exertion would cause them to fall unconscious from their perches. There was not a cloud to be seen. God's window shades had been frightened away by the glaring sun. There was a breeze, a rather strong one in fact, but instead of bringing relief, it acted like a blower on a furnace, only adding to the misery.

Ole and Helena sat on the wagon seat more asleep than awake. Ole almost dropped the reins. His quick movement to catch them stirred Helena. "Are we halfway?" she asked.

"Just a little more than half," Ole answered. "We still have about three hours."

Helena groaned. "I don't think I've ever been so hot. How are Doll and Lady doing?"

"All right, I think. But I'm going to stop at that stand of burr oak ahead and give them some water. It also should give us a little shade."

The conversation ended. Talking was too much work. They stared at the burr oaks, which, thanks to swirling heat devils, appeared to be a mirage. Minutes passed. Helena was beginning to wonder if the burr oaks were imaginary when Ole pulled the team to a halt beneath their gnarled branches.

Ole grunted as he crawled down from the seat. His bones ached. He then helped Helena down, to the accompaniment of her moans. Both stretched before walking to the water kegs on the side of the wagon. While Ole removed a keg from the shelf, Helena untied two tin cups from a brace. The water was almost coffeepot hot, but their bodies welcomed it as if the liquid were from a cool mountain stream.

"Are we home yet?" a sleepy voice asked from inside the wagon.

"No, Oline," Helena replied. "Wake up Martin and Berent so you all can get drinks."

The children scrambled out of the wagon and took turns with the cups. Ole untied the second keg, divided the water into buckets, and watered the horses. Each gratefully buried her nose in the liquid, which disappeared as if sucked up by a small tornado.

"I'm sorry, girls," Ole said, scratching the horses' foreheads. "That's all until we get home."

He carried the empty buckets back to the wagon, and was retying the kegs to the wagon when Helena said, "Ole, do you smell smoke?"

He took a deep breath. "Yes, I do."

The horses raised their heads, suddenly alert. They too smelled it.

Ole looked, but could see nothing until he ran out onto the open prairie and saw a wall of smoke to the southwest.

Prairie fire! And it was coming fast.

"Fire!" Ole yelled, racing back to the family. "Berent, get in the wagon! Oline and Martin, hold the horses! Try and keep them calm. Helena, we have to set a backfire."

At first no one moved, then they all did as ordered. Ole grabbed a folded scythe and matches from the toolbox. He tossed the matches to Helena. "I'll cut some torches!"

Helena watched the approaching fire with fearful fascination. Clouds of smoke, ranging in color from light gray to the deepest black, billowed and swirled in a macabre dance above the flaring, devouring flames. The fire was coming straight at them, and there was no way they could outrun it.

Ole ran up to her with two bunches of prairie grass he had twisted into makeshift torches. "Light them!" he ordered. Helena struck a match. It broke. She grabbed another. It flickered, then died in the wind. A third did the same. Her hands began to shake. She looked at Ole, her eyes wide with fear. He smiled at her. "We have time. Cup the match with your hands." A fourth match was struck, then a fifth. Finally, on the sixth try, the flame held long enough to ignite the first torch. Ole quickly lit the second and handed it to Helena. "Fire in a line from northwest to southeast."

Ole and Helena chose a line and began running, trailing their torches in the dry grass. A snake of fire followed them, but it failed to move until a fresh gust of wind caught it and swept the flames forward. Helena's torch burned down to a point where she could no longer hold it. Without a second thought, she ripped off her petticoat, lit it, and continued the line. When the cloth had been consumed, she looked at the length of fire she and Ole had created. It was nearly fifty yards long and was roaring to the northeast.

"That's enough!" Ole called. "Back to the wagon!"

Helena ran to the family, her heart pounding and tears running down her cheeks. The approaching fire was now less than a quarter of mile away.

"Help us, Papa!" Oline screamed as she and Martin attempted to control the terrified horses. Doll and Lady reared, pulling the children off the ground, where they dangled like rag dolls swung by an angry child. Ole grabbed both bridles, bringing the horses back to having all four hooves on the ground. "Whoa, girls! Easy now ... you'll be fine."

The team settled under Ole's firm grip, but still snorted and pranced. Ole yelled to his two sons. "Martin! Berent! Take off your shirts!" Both boys quickly obeyed, and were handing the shirts to Ole when Helena reached the wagon. "Helena, tie the shirts over the horses' eyes!" Ole commanded.

Helena did so with trembling hands. The horses relaxed slightly but could still smell the fire. By now, smoke was enveloping the Branjord wagon. Frightened and nearly exhausted wildlife ran helter-skelter on either side. Rabbits, ground squirrels, gophers, foxes, raccoons, field mice, deer, and badgers—predators and prey—raced side by side, attempting to escape their common fate.

"Into the wagon!" Ole ordered. "Lie flat and cover your faces with something!"

Helena and the children scrambled into the wagon, where Helena lay like a mother hen, Oline under one arm and the boys snuggled together under the other. Ole stayed in front of the horses, using all of his strength to keep them from bolting. He knew he had to wait until the last minute to lead the horses into the burned area. The ground had to have time to cool.

The smoke became so thick, Ole was gasping for breath. He could barely see the horses. He could wait no longer. Ole prayed as he led his team forward.

The fire was now a hissing, devouring monster, sucking oxygen from the air, feeding itself on dead brush, dry grass, and wilted flowers, and sustaining its life by killing everything, flora and fauna, that lay in its path.

Ole choked and coughed as he desperately clung to the bridles. He knew it was his presence that kept Doll and Lady from blindly stampeding. His lungs felt like they were on fire. He gasped, growing weaker and weaker with each step. He had to stop. There was no more he could do. He buried his face in Lady's neck and prayed.

As if by magic, the smoke cleared and the sun blazed brightly in the clear blue sky. To Ole's right and left were roaring flames and impenetrable, billowing smoke. He sucked in clean air and threw up as he fell to his knees. Had the team moved, he would have been run over, but the horses stood still, coughing and wheezing.

Ole struggled to his feet. "Helena! Are you all right?"

He was answered by a stifled "I think so," and the sound of weeping children.

They all had survived. Helena appeared first in the front of the wagon. She was covered with black soot. Then came the children, equally black, but tears had created little rivulets of white on their faces, which lit up with smiles at the sight of their father.

Helena coughed. "I could hardly breathe."

"I know. Thank the Lord we are all safe," Ole said, removing the shirts from the horses' eyes.

What Doll and Lady saw was a smoldering prairie that resembled the top of a giant, steaming cook stove. The many hues and colors were gone, replaced by an endless expanse of grays and blacks which reflected in the frightened eyes of the horses. It was a world they had never seen, and had it not been for the soothing words and comforting touch of Ole, one they would have fled from in panic.

Ole gazed in disbelief at the devastation. What struck him most was the silence. With the exception of a pop or hiss from a hot spot, there were no sounds. He realized for the first time how noisy and filled with life the prairie was. What he had thought of as silence when he walked the land alone was not silence at all; rather, it was a chorus of plant and animal voices, conducted by the wind, singing the song of life. What he was experiencing now was true silence, the silence of the grave. Tears welled in Ole's eyes. Nothing could have survived this.

He was proven wrong by his irrepressible four-year-old. "Yitts!" Berent cried. Then again, "Yitts!" And for the third time, "Yitts!"

"What in the world?" Helena said. "Berent, what is the matter with you?"

"Look, Mama!" the boy said, pointing.

All the Branjords looked. There, not ten feet from the wagon, shivering with fear, was a mother fox and her two kits. Behind them were several cringing rabbits. And not three feet from the rabbits was a stunned group of prairie chickens. All were covered with soot, but all were alive.

The silence broken by the young boy was followed with relieved laughter, laughter so loud it frightened the wildlife, saved by the backfire, into motion. There was suddenly scurrying in every direction. The song had not been silenced, only interrupted.

"I win!" Berent cried. "I win!"

Ole could only shake his head. "No, Berent, we all won. Thank you, Lord."

After dividing the remaining water between the family and the horses, and using a damp towel to wash most of the soot off their faces, the Branjord family resumed the trip home. The children sat in the back, apart and silent. The game of Yitts was forgotten. Helena sat beside Ole, staring at the blackened earth. "It's hard to believe the grass will grow again."

"You're right," Ole answered. "But by next summer you will never know there was a fire."

"Do you think the fire will reach the East Settlement?"

"No. The creeks should stop it. And if it does, there shouldn't be much damage. Hans Twedt told me all the farmers have been plowing firebreaks."

Helena laid her head on Ole's shoulder. She whispered, "Thank you for saving us."

Ole kissed her hair. "You did just as much."

"No. I just did what you told me. Without you, I probably would have run."

Ole squeezed her hand. "Don't ever think you can outrun a prairie fire. And don't ever go out any distance on the prairie without matches."

"I won't," Helena replied with a smile, while thinking she would never venture far onto the prairie without Ole by her side.

They came to a small rise and Helena put her hands to her mouth. "Oh, dear Lord!"

Before them lay the charred remains of a wagon, resting precariously on three wheels. The canvas was gone. The bottom of the box had collapsed, leaving the contents of the wagon a pile of ash and blackened metal on the ground. Still attached to the left rear was a metal pole on which was a partially burned American flag. There were neither people nor horses.

"I know that wagon!" Helena cried. "It belongs to the Halversons!"

"Who are they?"

"A new couple. I met Mrs. Halverson and her three-year-old son in the store. They were on their way to Hamilton County."

Ole reined in the horses a few yards from what remained of the blackened wagon. "It looks like they broke a wheel."

Oline stuck her head between Ole and Helena. "Is that Mrs. Halverson's wagon?"

"Yes," Helena answered. "Now go sit down."

"Are they burned up?" Oline continued.

"No," Ole answered. "I think they broke a wheel and were trying to fix it when the fire came. They must have unhitched the horses and made a run for it."

Helena stared at the grim scene, knowing the fear the family must have felt. "Do you think they survived?"

"If they made it to a farm or a creek," Ole replied, slapping the reins and turning the team off the trail to the northeast. "Pray that they did."

Helena prayed.

Her prayers were not answered. After traveling less than a mile, she saw the remains of the horses. "Children! Don't look!" But, of course, they did.

The horses lay only feet apart, tangled in each other's harness. Their mouths were open in a silent cry of pain; their unseeing eyes reflected agony and terror. Huge sections of hide had been burned away, exposing flesh that was now covered with ants and flies which somehow had survived the flames. The smell of roasted meat filled the air.

Huddled together, a few yards from the horses, were what had been two young adults and a small child, who had been looking forward to a new life in a new land. The fire had consumed clothes, hair, skin, flesh, personality, and dreams. The remains were providing a feast for insects.

Martin and Oline vomited. Berent stared in horror, his face drained of all color, realizing, perhaps for the first time, the fragileness of life.

"I told you not to look!" Helena cried.

Ole turned the horses back to the trail. Helena whispered, "We can't just leave them."

"We can't do anything else," Ole replied. "We'll stop at the first farm. The man will have to get men from the East Settlement to take them to the cemetery."

Helena began to weep. A mindless force of nature had brought death. Her tears fell to the earth, providing traumatized feeder roots with life.

Helena

I don't see how Ole can sleep. After all that has happened, how can he lie there snoring? I can't sleep. Oline and Martin have had nightmares. Perhaps Berent is too young to understand. I hope so. The sight of the three of them will haunt me as long as I live. She was so young. So excited about her new life. Last night she slept in the arms of her husband; tonight she sleeps in the arms of the Lord.

At least, I hope so. That's what Reverend Amlund would say. Is she in heaven with her husband and son? Is there a heaven? We are taught there is. We are also taught God loves us. Did he not love the Halversons? If he loves us, why does he allow such terrible things to happen? Ole said you can't blame God for a prairie fire. But couldn't he have stopped it? Isn't he all powerful? With a big breath, couldn't he have blown out the fire? He did nothing. Can you blame God for a broken wheel? No, that's silly. It's not only silly, it's unchristian. I am a stupid woman! Forgive me, Lord Jesus.

I have to get to sleep. Tomorrow will be miserable. We will be carrying water to the corn. Why can't it rain? Why couldn't it have rained today? Had it rained, there would have been no fire. Sonja and her family would still be alive. Her son was so cute. Only three fingers old. What was his name? Oh, Lord! I have already forgotten his name. When I die, will I be forgotten so quickly? Will people say, do you remember what's her name?

We think we are so important. We're not. We're about as important as field mice. We think we control our lives. We don't. Something as simple as a broken wheel can kill us. I could have died today. My children could be wrapped in canvas waiting to be buried. Ole saved us. He said I did as much as he did. How sweet of him, but it is completely false. Without him, I would have run. Without him, I would have died.

I roll on my side and kiss Ole's shoulder. Dear Ole. I know at times you wonder why I married you. You have told me I am too beautiful for you. Such nonsense. It is because of how you handled today that I love you. I hope my beauty gives you pleasure. Your strength gives me security that I have never known.

I have to sleep.

I am afraid to sleep.

Chapter Twenty-Three

"Mama fell in! Mama fell in!" the Branjord children cried.

Helena had indeed fallen in … on purpose. The water of the shallow Skunk River, where she and the children were wading, felt so cool on her legs that she simply sat down. The water barely came to her waist, but provided a coolness she had not experienced in weeks. Within seconds, her offspring were feeling the same joy as they happily soaked each other. She watched them with a smile, wondering where they found the energy. She was exhausted. The past two days had been the longest and hardest she had experienced since coming to America.

The day after the trip to Nevada had begun with a streak of light in the east and ended with darkness swallowing the sun. The only plus was that Helena had been too tired to think about the family caught in the fire.

Ole was up well before dawn. He placed the washtub and the big, black kettle used for rendering lard and making soap into the wagon beside the new bathtub, hitched up the horses, and drove down to the river, where he used a bucket to fill the tubs and kettle. Breakfast was ready when he returned to the cabin. The children were sleepy-eyed but up and dressed. No one talked as they ate cornmeal mush, flatbread, and salt pork.

After breakfast, Helena and the children walked behind the wagon to the cornfield. Precious water sloshed from the containers, leaked through the floor boards, and left a trail of moisture which was quickly consumed by the parched earth. Ole stopped the horses at the edge of the field. The drooping stalks were now six feet high. He half-filled two buckets for Oline and Martin and filled two for Helena and himself. Lastly, he poured water into a toy bucket for Berent. He jumped down from the wagon and said, "Helena, we're going to try and water eight stalks per bucket. Oline, Martin, that means four stalks for you. Remember, don't get in a hurry. Pour the water slowly."

"What about me?" Berent asked.

Ole smiled. "Just one for you."

And so they began the tedious, mind-numbing work of pouring water on the base of each stalk. At first their steps were light, but after only a half an hour, when the tubs and kettle were empty, their arms were sore and their backs ached. All were relieved to sit in the wagon as Ole drove the team back to the river to refill the containers.

Fill the tubs and kettle. Dump the tubs and kettle. That is how the day went. By afternoon, the temperature was hovering around ninety-five degrees. Oline and Martin were near collapse. Berent was fine, having decided that sitting under the shade of the wagon, interspersed with chasing rabbits, was more enjoyable than carrying water. When Martin stumbled and spilled his bucket, Ole yelled at him. Helena screamed at Ole. The two adults, their clothes clinging like a second skin and sweat running down their faces, glared at each other until Ole apologized and sent the two children to join Berent under the wagon. Within seconds, they were asleep. Ole and Helena continue to work.

Helena emptied her bucket. She was deep in the field, surrounded by stalks. There was not even a hint of a breeze. The weight of the still air forced her to her knees. She struggled to breathe. Panic rose like an untapped gusher. Her mouth formed words, calling for Ole, but no sound came. She stared in blurred horror at the stalks, which had metamorphosed into rows of demented, angry fiends, marching forward to smother her.

Ole found her lying on the ground, moaning and crying. "Helena!" he screamed, kneeling beside her and cradling her in his arms. "Talk to me! Helena, talk to me!" He splashed water from his bucket onto her face. Her eyes fluttered. She opened them and clung to Ole. "They're going to get me," she whispered.

"No one is going to get you," Ole replied. With his free hand, he took the nearly empty bucket and poured water onto Helena's head and neck. She pushed away from him, a surprised look on her face.

"Ole, what are you doing?"

"Trying to cool you off. You came close to fainting."

Ole struggled to his feet and held out his hand. "Come on. You're going to rest under the wagon with the children."

Helena took her husband's hand. "I will if you will," she answered as she stood up.

"Helena, I can't. I …"

"If you won't, I won't," she interrupted. "Ole, we both need to rest."

Ole realized Helena was right. He just nodded his head and picked up both buckets, and the two stumbled out of the field and collapsed beneath the wagon. The children were still asleep. Their parents were soon in the same blissful state.

Helena was awakened by light pats on her shoulder. She opened her eyes to see a worried look on the face of her four-year-old. He had never seen his mother sleep during the day, so it was a little frightening to see her take a nap. He gave her an angelic smile, the kind that ensures a child's survival, and said, "I'm hungry, Mama."

At the sound of Berent's voice, Ole sat up, hitting his head on the front axle. "Oh! Ouch! What time is it?"

"I don't know," Helena answered, reluctantly pushing herself into a sitting position. Ole crawled out from beneath the wagon and looked at the sun. He pounded the ground with his fist. "It must be past four o'clock. I must have slept for two hours. Damn!"

"Ole!" Helena scolded. "Watch your language."

Martin and Oline were now awake and looking at their father.

"I'm sorry," Ole muttered, getting to his feet. He grimaced and shook his head as the family came out into the sun. "I've wasted half a day!"

"No, you haven't," Helena said, using the side of the wagon to help her stand. "We've been working since sunup. We needed a rest."

"Not two hours' worth," Ole growled. "Now we'll have to work until dark." He turned to the children. "Martin, milk the cows and feed the hogs. Oline, fix some supper."

Oline looked up at her mother. She had help fix many meals, but none by herself. Helena smiled. "There is smoked ham. Peel and boil some potatoes and pick some string beans from the garden. You know how to fix them."

"Yes, Mama," Oline said, then gratefully began walking to the cabin. Never had she been so happy to prepare a meal. The boys followed.

Ole untied the horses and climbed up to the seat. "And watch Berent!" he called as Helena joined him in the wagon. Ole turned the horses toward the river for another load of water.

The sun was nodding good-bye and the moon was stretching hello when Ole and Helena dragged themselves out of the field. They threw their empty buckets into the washtub. There was no need for words. Their blistered hands and dirty, tired faces said it all. Ole helped Helena up onto the wagon seat and then, with effort, climbed up himself. Ole slapped the reins. The horses started for home. Helena rested her head on Ole's shoulder. Neither had ever been so tired.

They were halfway to the cabin when they saw Oline and Martin running toward them. A surge of adrenaline raced through Helena's body. She was suddenly wide awake. Something was wrong. Something was very wrong. And as the children reached the wagon, she knew what it was. "Where's Berent?"

Oline and Berent looked up at their parents with frightened faces. "We don't know," Oline answered. "I thought he was with Martin."

"And I thought he was with Oline," Martin added.

Ole groaned. "He is probably just playing hide-n-seek."

"No," Oline said, biting her lip. "We checked all the places."

"Get in the wagon!" Helena ordered.

The children scrambled onto the running gear and into wagon. "Where did you last see him?" Helena continued.

"I was milking. He said he wanted to go into the cabin."

"He came in but said it was too hot."

Ole and Helena looked at each other. Too hot. "The river!" they said together.

Ole turned the horses, urging them into a run. Helena hung on to the seat with ever-increasing fear of falling off, but never considered telling Ole to slow down. Oline and Martin grabbed hold of the sideboards, keeping a wary eye on the bouncing tubs and kettle. The buckets banged in the washtub like out-of-tune bells.

Doll and Lady were wheezing when Ole halted them where the prairie ended and the river woods began. He leaped from the wagon and swung Helena down beside him. "Take Oline and go north. Martin and I will go south." He looked at his wife's stricken face and added, "Don't worry. The river is only two feet deep."

Ole took off running, followed by Martin. Helena started for the river, then froze as she glanced up the rise to the north. Her heart seemed to stop. The badger den was fifty yards up the slope. She began to run.

"Mama! Where are you going?" Oline cried.

Helena did not bother to answer. She raced through the waist-high grass, tears blurring her eyes. Only minutes before, she had been so tired that she had to be helped into the wagon. Now she ran like a rabbit escaping a fox. Fear and adrenaline gave her legs the freshness of a young colt.

Through luck or a mother's instinct, Helena ran straight to the den. There were tracks but no sign of the badger. Her breath came in gasps. She rested her hands on her knees, sweeping the prairie with her eyes.

There was movement!

Helena wiped her eyes and saw a furry gray shape move, then disappear about twenty yards to her left. She cried out, running to the spot with bared teeth. She had no weapons, not even a rock. She did not care. She ran!

Helena almost stepped on him. Berent lay in a fetal position, his cheeks stained with tears, his right thumb in his mouth. She fell on her knees. "Berent! Berent!"

The boy's eyes opened. Seeing his mother, he leaped into her arms. "Mama! I called and called, but you didn't come."

"I didn't hear you," Helena replied, holding him close.

"I got lost in the high grass. I couldn't find you."

Helena kissed him numerous times. "I know, but you're all right now."

Helena looked over the top of Berent's head and saw Doggie sitting on his haunches about ten feet away. The wolf-dog stared at her with his strange yellow eyes and appeared to smile. "Did Doggie find you?"

"Yes. I was crying and Doggie came and licked my face. He lay down, so I stayed with him."

Doggie rose to his feet as Oline approached. "Is he hurt, Mama?"

"No," Helena answered, hugging the boy closer. "He's fine."

"Good!" Oline sighed. Then, in true big sisterly fashion, she said to Berent, "Boy, are you going to get it!"

Berent clung to his mother. "Are you going to spank me, Mama?"

Helena closed her eyes and whispered a silent thank you to God. "No," she answered, "I'm not going to spank you."

"Why not?" Oline asked.

"Because he is safe," Helena answered, getting to her feet but still holding Berent. "Just because he is safe. Go find your father and Martin. We'll meet you at the wagon."

Oline made a face at her little brother before doing what she was told. But she too was relieved and happy he was safe.

There were bare spots around the area where Berent had slept. In these spots, Helena could see tracks. Not wolf tracks. Badger tracks. It was obvious the badger had circled Doggie and her son many times. She carried Berent to Doggie and knelt beside him. He did not move away. Helena buried her face in his ragged coat. "Thank you," she whispered.

The wolf-dog licked her face, something he had never before done. He then sniffed Berent as if to make sure he was all right, then soundlessly disappeared into the high grass.

The second day was a repeat of the first, except Berent did not get lost and Ole and Helena paced themselves better. After a light noon meal, the family rested for two hours. Even so, both adults were exhausted when the last corn stalk was watered. However, they could see the positive results of their hard work. The moisture had performed its magic. Corn irrigated the first day stood tall and free of wilt. Stalks done the second day were already starting to perk up.

"How soon do we have to do this again?" Helena asked as they drove home under the pale light of a full moon.

"Four, maybe five days."

Helena groaned. "Pray that it rains."

"Amen. There might be hope. At least we had clouds this afternoon."

Berent squirmed in Helena's lap, but remained asleep. She kissed the top of his head. He had been like a second shadow to Helena all day, even refusing to go with his siblings when they were sent home to do chores and fix supper. This was just fine with Helena. She squeezed him a little harder and again kissed his hair.

When they reached the cabin, Martin and Oline greeted them. "I milked the cows and fed the pigs and chickens," Martin said.

"Good," Ole replied, getting down from the wagon and taking Berent from Helena. He then helped her down. "I'm proud of both of you," he added, handing the sleeping boy back to his mother.

Oline frowned. "Supper has gotten cold."

Helena gave her daughter a tired smile. "I'm sure it will still taste good. Thank you for making it."

Ole climbed back up to the seat. "Go ahead and eat without me. I'll have something when I get back."

"Where are you going?" Helena asked.

"Down to the river to get some more water."

"Why?"

"You'll see."

Helena and Berent had eaten and the dishes had been washed when Ole returned with the two tubs filled with water. He parked the wagon by the crib, removed the harness, and turned the horses into the pasture. His family met him on the porch, wrapped in towels. He laughed. "I see you figured it out. Berent, you get in the washtub. You other two get into the big tub."

The children squealed as they ran to the wagon. By the time Ole and Helena reached them, they were splashing happily in the water. "Hey!" Ole said. "No splashing. Save some water for us."

Ten minutes later, the three children reluctantly climbed out of the tubs. They were wrapped in towels and told to go straight to bed. There were no arguments, only yawns. Oline took Berent by the hand, and the children returned to the cabin.

Helena and Ole removed their sweat-stained clothing. "You take the big one," Helena said.

"No, that's for you. Have a good soak. I'm sorry you had to work so hard."

Helena shrugged. "We didn't have any choice. Besides, hard work never killed anybody."

"Yesterday came close," Ole grunted.

"I won't argue with that," Helena answered, stepping out of her underclothes. Her skin, shining with perspiration, made her look like a Greek statue. Tired as he was, the sight took Ole's breath away. He smiled.

"Don't even think about it," Helena said.

Ole laughed as he lifted her into the wagon. She stepped into the long tub. "Ohoo! The water is a little chilly, but it feels wonderful." She then lowered herself into the tub until only her neck and head were clear of the water. "Oh, dear Lord. This is heaven!"

Ole climbed into the wagon. Picking up a bucket, he stepped into the washtub and began dumping pails of water on his head. Helena watched the water drip down her husband's lean, hard body and felt certain desires start in her toes and creep up to her loins. Perhaps she had been too quick to say don't even think about it. However, she could not help but notice that Ole was not "thinking about it." She smiled and closed her eyes. "It is just as well," she thought. "The children are still sleeping on the floor. There will be other nights."

Helena, still enjoying the cool water of the Skunk River, was brought back to the present by a sudden silence. She looked to see her children staring at something behind her. Turning, she saw Rooster leering at her from the opposite bank, his homespun shirt torn and his narrow, rat-like face dirty.

"Well now, ain't this a pretty picture," Rooster said, his words slurred. He was quite drunk.

Helena's heart began to pound. She was reliving a nightmare, but attempted to keep her voice calm. "What do you want, Rooster?"

"My name ain't Rooster!" he snarled, then gave a dirty laugh that made Helena's skin crawl. "And I think you know what I want."

Helena turned pale. She knew too well what he wanted. She started to get up, but Rooster stopped her by saying, "Stay where you are if you don't want those brats of yours hurt!"

"Don't you touch me! My husband …"

"Your husband and those other do-gooders are helping the preacher build a shed. I saw 'em, so don't try and bluff me." He then grinned, exposing broken and missing yellow teeth that reminded Helena of an old rotting picket fence. "I ain't never done it underwater before," he continued, wading into the river.

Rooster weaved with each step. His eyes were pinpricks of lust. His tongue hung out of the side of his mouth, allowing drool to drip down into his unkempt beard.

"Stay away from me!" Helena yelled, anger beginning to overcome her panic.

"Not likely. This is payback for your husband getting me fired!"

Rooster paused, his addled mind trying to remember something important. Then his hands clenched into fists and his face turned a red so deep it was almost purple. "Not Ingvald! Just me! Horse-Face Signaldahl would never let her henpecked husband fire dear old Ingvald! Oh, no! Who would she roll in the hay with if Ingvald wasn't there? Anytime Signaldahl leaves the place, Horse-Face finds some excuse to get Ingvald into the barn. The slut!"

The outburst took the edge off Rooster's anger. His focus returned to Helena. "She says you're a slut too. That's what she calls you, a Finnish slut." Rooster giggled like a teenaged girl. "She really hates you. She asked Ingvald to find someone to rape you. She told him that you like it rough. Well, let's find out."

Before Rooster could take a step, a rock whistled by his head. "Stay away from my Mama!" Martin yelled.

"Stay away!" Berent mimicked, as he threw a rock that splashed no more than three feet in front of him.

"Stop it, you brats!"

"No!" Oline cried as she threw a rock that made Rooster duck.

Rooster was furious. He screamed at Helena. "Tell them to stop throwing rocks or I'll kill 'em!"

Helena's fear for her children brought back the panic. "Don't! Stop throwing!"

Her words were too late. A well-aimed rock thrown by Martin struck Rooster in the chest.

"Ow!" Rooster bellowed. "I'll kill you!"

Rooster lunged toward the children, but Helena reached out and tripped him, sending him sprawling into the river.

Seeing Rooster was down, Helena struggled from a sitting position to her knees. Before she could stand, Rooster regained his feet and whirled on her. "Bitch! You're all going to die!"

Not this day.

As Rooster dove at her, Helena struck him between the eyes with a rock she had grasped during his tirade. The man fell on top of her, sending them both underwater. Helena pushed Rooster off of her and surfaced, gasping for air.

"Mama! Are you all right?" Oline screamed.

Helena coughed and nodded. "Yes, I'm all right." She struggled to her feet. The children rushed toward her. "Stay back!" she ordered, stopping them a few yards from her. They all stared down at the bloody face of the would-be rapist. His mouth was open, water flowing in.

"Are you going to let him drown, Mama?" Martin asked.

The children looked at Helena. She looked at them, then back to Rooster. There was no doubt that she wanted him to die. He was an evil, dirty man who had tried to rape her. Yes, she not only wanted him to drown, she wanted to take a large rock and smash in his head. Perhaps if the children had not been there, she would have done just that. Instead, she grabbed his hair and pulled his head out of the river.

"Oline, Martin, help me pull him to the bank."

Helena checked Rooster's pulse when they reached land. He was still alive. "Come," she said, "Let's go home, and promise me you will not tell your father about this." Helena did not want Ole chasing after Rooster. "Promise me!"

The children nodded.

As they started back to the cabin, Martin asked, "Will he follow us?"

"No," Helena answered. "Men like him don't have the courage to attack someone who is ready for them."

She was right. An hour later, Rooster crawled up the bank to the stage road. He was hurt and still drunk, but knew he had to get as far from Fairview as possible.

Helena

Of course, the children did tell. It was foolish of me to make them promise not to. Ole knew something was wrong by just looking at them. Berent couldn't wait to tell him how he had thrown a rock at the bad man. Ole listened to the whole story without saying a word. When they were done, the fury in his eyes frightened them. It also frightened me. He took down the old rifle and checked the river. Thankfully, Rooster was gone, leaving a blood trail. I think the reason Ole didn't go after him was because I had almost killed him. I'm so glad Big Per wasn't here. I know the two would have jumped on horses and chased Rooster down like the stinking dog he is.

I have never seen Ole so angry. He hasn't said ten words since he came home. The angrier he gets, the more silent he becomes. Martin told me that when they were milking, Ole pulled Mabel's teats so hard she tried to kick him.

The children are asleep. I know Ole is not. Like me, he is pretending. When he kissed me good night, he said I should have let Rooster drown. Maybe he's right. Probably Rooster will try to rape some other woman. I think I would have done the world a favor by letting him die. Reverend Amlund would consider me a sinful woman for thinking like this. But Reverend Amlund has not faced being raped three times. Dear Lord, forgive me my sin. Can you forgive Rooster his? Why do you allow such trash to live? Hanna put the idea in his head. Is she really sleeping with Ingvald? There have been rumors. He is good-looking. But Ole says he's dumber than

Big Per's oxen. I thought about riding up to her farm and telling her what Rooster said. That would be foolish. She would just deny everything. There would be a lot of talk, and who would they believe, the daughter of a Norwegian banker or a Finnish maid? No, it is better that no one knows about to today. Ole has promised not to tell a soul. He has ordered the children not to tell. Perhaps they won't. It is so unfair! Why must I always keep silent? Dear Lord, you say blessed are the poor. If so, why does Hanna always win?

I must sleep. I don't think I can. If I do, which rapist will attack?

Ole

I shouldn't be lying here. I should have gone after him. Helena begged me not to. She said killing Rooster would just call trouble, and people like Horse-Face Hanna would still blame her. She's right. The woman always gets the blame. What kind of stupid horseshit is that?

If I had ridden hard, I might have caught up with him. Helena says I am smart for not chasing him down. Am I smart? Or is that just an excuse for doing nothing? The rotten bastard is going to get away with no punishment at all. Helena should have let him drown.

Chapter Twenty-Four

The inside of Saint Petri Lutheran Church was stifling. Shirts were soaked. Dresses clung like wet newsprint. The smell of body odor permeated the suffocating stillness. Reverend Amlund had preached for less than half an hour, partially due to sweat dripping from his face onto his sermon notes, blurring the ink. The congregation was grateful.

Actually, the service went surprisingly well. The animosity, which had grown like mold on a damp wall, was, at least for this Sunday, smothered by silent and verbal prayers for rain. Bone-tired parishioners put aside their differences, folded blistered hands, and prayed for deliverance from disaster. Impending doom has a way of focusing priorities.

The benediction was given, the postlude played, and the members fled the building, gathering in the usual groups beneath promising steel-gray clouds. There was an even darker bank to the west. Everyone looked, but no one said a word about the weather. There had been clouds on Friday and Saturday, but the rain had fallen to the north and south.

A harried Julia Twedt, carrying one-year-old Carl and holding back two-year-old Sam, who wanted to run after Joseph, Berent, and Peder Gustav, joined Helena and Martha Tjernagel.

Helena smiled. "You have your hands full."

"Always! Samuel, stop pulling! You are too little to run after Joseph."

"Not too little!" Sam cried.

Helena reached out for the baby. "Let me take Carl."

The transfer was made, and Julia turned her attention to Sam. "Now you stop pulling or I'm going to give you a swat! Understand?"

Sam nodded, his lips turning down. Julia released him and he sat on the ground in a classic two-year-old pout. "Mama bad."

Julia pulled a stray strand of hair from her face. "No, Mama is hot and tired."

Helena snuggled Carl, enjoying the baby smell. "Maybe it will finally …"

"Don't say it!" Martha interrupted, switching her sleeping baby, Nehemias, from her right shoulder to her left.

"You're right," Helena said, giving Carl a kiss. "My, you are a sweet little boy."

Julia sighed. "Sometimes. Other times he is a stinker."

"Aren't they all?" Martha laughed. All three women nodded in unison. Martha continued, "Helena, you have the look of a woman who is ready to have another."

Helena rubbed noses with Carl. "Could be."

Julia took a step forward. "Are you?"

"Not sure."

"Have you told Ole?" Martha asked.

"No. And don't you two say anything. It could be a false alarm. I've been late before."

Just then Hanna and Elsa Signaldahl walked by. Elsa gave the women a shy smile. Hanna ignored them like they were invisible.

"Is that another new dress Elsa is wearing?" Martha whispered after the two had passed.

"Yes," Helena answered, turning her back to the departing pair. "She calls it her half-birthday present. She was born in December, so Hanna gave her a new dress in July."

Julia gave Helena a questioning look. "That can't be. I remember when Hanna and the baby arrived."

"Didn't Emil and Hanna come at the same time?" Helena asked.

"No. Emil came in the summer. He said his wife was pregnant and was staying in Chicago until he had built a house. Hanna and the baby came in April of the following year."

"I don't see the problem," Martha said.

"The problem is Elsa's birthday. When did she say it was?"

Helena thought for a moment. "I think she said December twenty-eighth."

Julia shook her head. "Not possible. I know the difference between a six-month-old baby and one that's three months."

The three women looked at each other, all busy calculating. Julia added, "A child knows her birthday because that's what she's been told."

"Well, certainly Hanna knows when Elsa was born," Martha said.

"Of course," said Julia. "But that doesn't mean Elsa and Emil know."

Helena had the answer. "They were married in April and immediately sailed for America."

"Really!" Julia said, covering her mouth. "That means … well, we know what that means."

Martha frowned. "Yes. It means they rushed it a little. But that's not unusual in Norway. There are areas where it is expected. Once the betrothal is announced, the couple begins sleeping together. The girl has to prove she can have children. Being pregnant before the wedding is no reason for Hanna to lie to Emil about when Elsa was born."

"Papa!" Sam cried as he ran to Hans, who was approaching the women with Ole, Big Per, and Ole Andreas.

Hans scooped the boy up in his arms. "Let's start for home, Julia." He nodded to the dark clouds in the west. "We just might get wet."

"That goes for us too, Martha," Ole Andreas said.

The question of Elsa's birthday was quickly forgotten. Children were gathered and good-byes were said, leaving Ole, Helena, and Big Per waving as the Twedt and Tjernagel wagons left the churchyard.

Ole grinned at Helena. "This big fellow here went fishing before church. He says he caught four big bass and can't eat them all."

"Oh, what a shame." Helena laughed. "I have a solution. If he wants to bring them to our place, I could fix a delicious Sunday dinner."

"Well," Big Per said, his eyes twinkling. "If you insist."

"I do."

The three laughed. A fish dinner was something they all would greatly enjoy.

Dark clouds allowed Ole and Big Per to sit out on the bench. Smoke from their pipes was twirled toward the river by a freshening breeze. It was the first time in weeks that sitting outside was comfortable. However, what should have been a time of contentment was one of concern. Both studied the western sky. What they saw was not the same bank of clouds that they had seen at church. Those clouds had drifted to the south, leaving Ole and Big Per shaking their heads while they glumly ate a wonderful bass dinner. These clouds were darker, larger, and more menacing.

"If this were May, I'd say we are looking at tornado clouds," Ole muttered.

"And I would agree with you."

Neither said anything more until Ole saw his two cows coming in off the prairie at an udder-swinging pace. "That does it, we're in for a storm," Ole said, knocking the ashes from his pipe. "I think we should get Buck and Pride into the barn."

Big Per stood, placing his pipe on the bench. "I agree again."

Helena stepped through the cabin doorway, dish towel in hand. She and Oline were cleaning up after the meal. "Should we take in the stove?"

Ole could see the worry on Helena's face. "Yes. It should be cool enough to carry."

Because of the heat, Helena had been cooking outside for the past three weeks. Ole cleaned the ashes from the stove before he and Big Per carried it into the cabin and hooked the stovepipe back up to the chimney. He then turned to Martin, who was sitting at the table reading *A Tale of Two Cities*. The boy was more than halfway through. "Martin, bring in the chairs and anything else that will blow around."

Martin marked his place in the book with a small piece of cloth. "Are we finally going to get some rain?"

"Yes. I hope that's all we get."

Big Per looked down at the book. "How is your reading in English coming?"

"Slow," Martin answered, as he got up from the table. "But I'm getting better."

"Well, you're way ahead of me," Big Per said with admiration.

"He's way ahead of all of us," Ole added, unmistakable pride in his voice.

Maud and Mabel were waiting placidly by the pasture gate when Ole and Big Per brought Buck and Pride to the gate. The cows suspiciously eyed the oxen. Buck and Pride showed no interest at all in the cows. Ole opened the gate and let the animals into the pasture. Maud and Mabel went directly to their milking stations. Buck and Pride were led next to Doll and Lady, who had already claimed their usual places. The other animals had found shelter in the far corner.

"The stock all agree a storm is coming," Big Per said.

"There is no doubt about that. I just pray it's not a tornado."

"Or hail."

"Amen. Let's get up to the cabin."

During the walk from the barn to the cabin, the temperature seemed to drop ten degrees. A gust of wind nearly knocked Ole into Big Per. Helena waited for them on the porch. "Is Berent with you?" she asked.

"No!"

"Oh, that boy!"

Before real panic could set in, Berent came running from behind the cabin with a box turtle. "Look, Mama! I have a new pet!"

"Berent, get in here!"

"See, Papa? He's my friend."

Ole reached the porch. "Put the turtle down, Berent, and get into the cabin."

"No! It's going to rain and he'll die!" Berent wailed, hugging the turtle to his chest. Wisely, the turtle drew his head back into his shell. "He's my pet!"

Big Per knelt beside Berent. "If he is your pet, what's his name?"

"Zacharias," Berent answered with no hesitation.

Big Per roared. Helena and Ole joined in the laughter.

Ole asked, "Where did you come up with that name?"

"It was a name I heard in church today." Berent grinned, thoroughly enjoying being the center of attention.

Big Per got to his feet. "Well, you can't say he doesn't listen to the sermon."

Helena, hands on hips, shook her head. "Oh, bring Zacharias in. Otherwise we're going to get soaked."

Berent dashed through the doorway, followed by the adults. Before entering, Ole looked to the west. Towering black clouds rolled and twisted as if in agony. The wall of advancing rain reminded him of the smoke and flames from the prairie fire. "Please," he silently prayed, "no hail."

Ole had no more than closed the door when the first bolt of lightning struck, followed by a reverberating clap of thunder. Zacharias was unceremoniously dropped as Berent jumped into Helena's waiting arms. Both knew the drill because of previous thunderstorms. Oline and Martin fled to their safe place beneath the table. Light fled as well, leaving the cabin in midnight darkness, intermittently pierced by flashes of lightning. The thunder was so loud, the children covered their ears. Berent whimpered, burying his face in his mother's breasts.

Then came the rain.

It was as if the cabin had been lifted up and deposited beneath a waterfall. Windows rattled and walls groaned as the torrents of rain attacked the roof. Helena, who was sitting in her rocker, glanced out the window and could not see the barn. She squeezed Berent tighter, feeling the same fear she had experienced on the ship when it fought rain and heavy seas. There, sitting in her cabin in the middle of the Iowa prairie, she had the overwhelming dread that she was going to drown.

After ten minutes, the cacophony lessened and light timidly tiptoed back into the cabin. The storm rumbled toward the East Settlement, leaving in its wake a steady, drenching downpour.

Ole crossed to the door and, with a silent prayer, opened it.

"Any damage?" Big Per asked.

Helena held her breath.

Ole did not answer until he had carefully studied the outbuildings. He then turned to Big Per, a smile on his face. "No damage. No hail."

"Thank the Lord!" Helena sighed.

Oline and Martin came out from under the table, clapping their hands. Berent did nothing. He was sound asleep in his mother's arms.

Oline asked, "Does this mean we don't have to carry any more water?"

"I sure hope so," Ole said. "Most of the hard rain probably ran off, but if this good rain keeps up, we should be fine."

It did continue. For three hours the parched earth drank its fill, while the residents of north Story County watched from the safety of their homes and thanked their God for his blessings.

Late in the afternoon, the clouds were wrung dry and rays of sunlight penetrated the gloom, making the thousands of rivulets glisten like silver serpents. Big Per rose from his chair. "Time for me to be getting home."

"Why don't you stay for supper?" asked Helena from the rocking chair where she was darning a hole in one of Ole's socks.

"I'm still full from dinner. Besides, I have cows to milk."

"So do I," Ole said, rising reluctantly from his chair. "Come on, Martin. We have chores to do."

Martin, who was back beneath the table with Oline and Berent, tormenting poor Zacharias, groaned but crawled out into the room. Berent followed, carrying Zacharias.

Ole looked at his youngest. "As for you, Berent, the storm is over. Put the turtle outside."

"Papa, no! Zacharias is my pet."

"Turtles make poor pets. Put him outside."

Berent hugged the turtle, widened his stance, and stuck out his lower lip. "No! He's my friend."

Ole was about to snatch the turtle from Berent when he was interrupted by Helena saying, "Berent, what if Zacharias is a mama and her babies are looking for her?"

The expression on the boy's face turned from defiance to concern. He held the turtle out at arm's length. "Zacharias doesn't look like a mama."

"But what if he is? Do you think his babies might be frightened?"

Berent blinked several times. Being in his mother's arms during the storm was fresh in his mind. After saying nothing for several seconds, he walked to the door and out onto the porch. Oline and Martin followed.

Big Per turned to Ole. "As I have said many times, we know where your children get their smarts from."

"You'll get no argument from me," Ole replied.

Helena smiled. "You just have to know how a four-year-old thinks. Thank you for the fish, Mr. Larson."

"And thank you for the meal, Mrs. Branjord," Big Per said with a slight bow. "As usual, it was delicious."

"Thank you. Don't be a stranger."

Big Per grinned broadly. "Well, if you insist."

They all laughed and the men walked out into the wonderful, delightful, beautiful mud.

Martin followed Ole and Big Per to the barn. After Buck and Pride were hitched to the wagon, Martin asked, "Papa, can I ride with Mr. Larson down to the river?"

"We have to milk."

"I know. But I can milk Mabel when I get back."

"All right. But why?"

"I just like to see Buck and Pride pull the wagon."

"Ole, your son is definitely a genius!" Big Per said, reaching down and pulling Martin up into the wagon. "Martin, I'll make an oxen man out of you yet!"

"Not likely." Ole laughed.

"We'll see," came the reply from the wagon. "Buck! Pride! Home!"

Ole waved as the oxen lumbered down the hill toward the river. He was somewhat surprised by Martin's request. But then Martin was full of surprises. He dumped rainwater from a bucket and went to get corn for the hogs.

Martin stood by Big Per, grinning from ear to ear. The big man looked down at the boy. "I thought you were a horse man, Martin."

"I am." The boy giggled. "I just wanted to tease Papa."

Big Per slapped his thigh and laughed. "Oh, I like that! I really like that!"

The two laughed all the way to the river.

"This as far as you go," Big Per said after stopping the oxen.

Martin looked at the rapidly flowing water. It had no resemblance to the placid stream of yesterday. He asked Big Per, "Aren't you going to the ford?"

Big Per snorted. "No need. Buck and Pride will get me across."

Martin looked hard at the river, remembering that awful day. Almost to himself, he mumbled, "The river is a lot higher than when Mama hit that man with a rock."

"What man?" Big Per demanded.

Martin put his hands over his mouth. "Oh, I wasn't supposed to tell. Mama made me promise."

"What happened to your mama, Martin?" Big Per's voice was an angry rumble, his usually friendly eyes narrow slits.

Martin told the story, including how he, Oline, and Berent had thrown rocks at the bad man. He finished by saying, "Mama didn't let him drown. Me and Oline helped her pull him to the bank."

"Does your papa know about this?"

"Yes. Mama begged him not to go after the bad man. She said it would just make matters worse."

Big Per ground his teeth. "She's probably right. Does this bad man have a name?"

"Mama called him Rooster."

"Rooster!" Big Per bellowed so loudly that Buck and Pride took two steps forward. More roughly than he intended, Big Per picked Martin up and lowered him to the ground. "Your mother should have let that bag of horseshit drown. If he ever shows his face around here again, he will wish she had!"

Big Per growled at the oxen, who stepped into the water without hesitation. Before the back wagon wheels reached the water, Buck and Pride were swimming, not walking, but it was too late to turn back. "Pull boys! Pull" Big Per shouted. "The boys" responded with an effort that matched their massive bodies. Even so, at the midpoint of the crossing, the current caught the wagon, turning it parallel to the bank. "Pull harder, boys! You can do it! Pull harder!"

Martin watched wide-eyed as the oxen struggled to reach the opposite side. Then Pride slipped beneath the surface. Seconds later, his nostrils and fear-filled eyes reappeared. A gargling sound came from deep within him before something again pulled him down.

Big Per jumped from the wagon, landing in the water by Pride's head. With one quick jerk he released the yoke from the frantic animal. It was not enough to free the ox. Whatever had hold of Pride's leg was not letting go. Big Per grabbed on to Pride's front leg and dove beneath the churning water. He immediately saw that the right front hoof was wedged into a V-shaped section of a rotting log. Big Per tugged at the leg, attempting to free it. He failed. He jerked it again with all of his strength. Again he failed.

Big Per, never much of a swimmer, had to surface for air. He gulped the life-saving oxygen, imagining what Pride was feeling. With a snarl, he dove again for the log. He was not going to lose Pride.

The struggles of the ox were becoming more and more feeble. Big Per tore at the log. It remained firm and solid. In desperation, Big Per put both feet on the log and yanked at the "V" section with his adrenaline-powered muscles. Rotting wood exploded, sending fragments streaking through the water like tiny torpedoes. Big Per ignored them as he reached for Pride's massive head and pushed it to the surface.

Martin stood frozen. He thought both Pride and Big Per had drowned until he saw them break water a few yards down from where Buck was still attempting to reach the opposite bank. Pride drifted downstream, sucking in air between coughs and wheezes.

Big Per swam to Buck, grabbed the yoke, and aided the animal to where he could get his footing. Gasping for breath, Buck and Big Per pulled the wagon out of the river and onto the bank. Ox and owner appeared to lean on each other.

"What about Pride?" Martin called.

Big Per looked down the river at the now strongly swimming animal. "He'll be fine, and he knows the way to my place." Having said that, Big Per took Pride's place under the yoke, and he and Buck trudged for home.

Not sure that Big Per was right about Pride, Martin raced south. He rounded a bend in time to see Pride struggle up the opposite bank. The big ox shook himself, then, as Big Per had predicted, began ambling east toward Big Per's farm.

Martin ran to the barn. He knew his father would scold him for taking so long, but what a story he had to tell!

Chapter Twenty-Five

A gentle breeze sweeping along lazy, fluffy clouds made picking vegetables from the garden a pleasant task. Had she been a child, Helena would have been lying on her back, imagining the clouds were exotic animals and birds. Instead, she pulled up several onions to add to her basket of carrots and potatoes. If Ole and the boys caught some fish, a tasty dinner would be had by all.

Helena brushed dirt off her dress and walked to the cabin. The rain had broken the terrible heat wave. The corn crop had been saved. It would most likely be just an average crop, but average would see them through the winter. Unlike in Finland, there would be no sunken cheeks and bloated stomachs, no need for birch bark soup, which was all that mattered.

When Helena entered the cabin, Oline was churning the morning milk. Helena smiled her approval. The smile was not returned. Rather, Oline looked up, opened her mouth as if to speak, thought better of it, and lowered her eyes to the churn. Helena frowned as she put the basket on the sink. Something was bothering her daughter. She had not been herself since Sunday.

"What is wrong, Oline?" Helena asked as she settled into her rocking chair.

"Nothing," came the meek reply.

"Did someone say mean things to you at church?"

Oline looked up, relief in her eyes. She wanted to talk. "No. Nothing mean. Anna told me she was … bleeding, and I asked her if she cut herself. She said no. She said she was bleeding from … from …" The words would not come. Oline looked at her mother with wide eyes, her mouth open.

"From where she pees," Helena said, completing what Oline could not.

"Yes! And her mother told her it would happen every month. Is that true?"

Helena closed her eyes. It was time for "the talk." She had dreaded this moment, but was grateful it had come about because of Anna. Helena shifted slightly as she remembered her own introduction to the menstrual cycle. No one had told her a thing. One day, a Tuesday, she began to bleed. She tried to stop it but could not. Her dress was being ruined. The more she bled, the more frightened and ashamed she became. She thought she was going to die.

When Helena had her own children, she promised herself that her daughters would be told what to expect. That moment had arrived. "Yes, it's true. Most women call it having their monthlies. It begins when a girl is about twelve or thirteen, sometimes earlier, sometimes later, and lasts four to five days."

"Do you …?"

"Yes."

"Anna's mother said it goes on forever,"

Helena laughed. "Not forever. It usually stops in your forties."

"That's forever!" Oline moaned. "Is it what Mrs. Twedt calls the curse?"

"Yes." Helena nodded. "Some women call it that because it seems to always come at the most inconvenient times."

"Does it hurt?"

"Sometimes. But don't worry. It just becomes a part of a woman's life."

"Do boys bleed?"

"No."

Oline slammed down the churn plunger. "That's not fair."

"I agree. But that's just the way it is."

There was silence for a moment as Oline digested the facts of life. Then she asked, "Why does it happen?"

"It happens so we can have babies. I don't know exactly how it works. I don't know anyone who does. What I know is that each month a woman produces an egg. If the egg is not fertilized, she bleeds. If the egg is fertilized, a baby begins to grow."

"How does the egg get fertilized?"

Helena squirmed in her chair. Now came the hard part. She took a deep breath and began to explain the sex act in a way that was honest but not too explicit. When she finished, the churn was quite literally rocking.

"It's like what the pigs and sheep do," Oline blurted.

"No! No! It's different. What happens between a man and a woman usually happens in bed."

Oline's eyes appeared to pop out of her head. Certain unexplained occurrences suddenly made sense. On several occasions she had awakened in the loft to hear her mother moaning and the bed squeaking. She and Papa were ... Oh my!

Helena read the expression perfectly. "I know this is a lot to take in. I remember how overwhelmed I felt. Believe me; the sex act with the man you love is beautiful. It is a wonderful part of marriage. But know this: sex without love can be brutal and ugly."

The churning abruptly stopped. Oline turned pale. "The bad man at the river, was he going to ...?"

"Yes. That is the ugly part. It is called rape."

Oline had trouble breathing. This was much more than she had expected. Once again there was silence. Helena realized enough information had been imparted for one day. After nearly a minute of sitting motionless, Oline returned to her churning. The cold, hard look in her lovely eyes expressed what she was thinking before her lips said, "You should have let him drown."

Helena sighed. Her heart went out to Oline. Growing up was hard. "Rooster is a foolish, stupid man, and he was drunk. He didn't deserve to die."

"What if he tries to do it again?"

Oline watched her mother's face turn to stone. "Then he deserves to die," Helena whispered.

The conversation was over. Both knew it. Helena got up from her chair, a smile returning to her face. "It looks to me like that plunger is getting heavy."

"Oh!" Oline said with surprise. "I think the butter is done."

Helena's smile turned to a laugh. "I think so too." She picked up the butter pail and began emptying the churn. "I do believe you might have set a world record for turning milk into butter."

Oline blushed and giggled. "I think you're right."

Once the churn was empty, Helena handed the pail to Oline. "Put the butter in the cooling tub and then wash up the churn."

Helena watched Oline walk to the artesian well, realizing her daughter was peeking into the world of women. Two tears flowed down her cheeks. It seemed like only yesterday when Oline was nursing at her breast.

Helena returned to her rocker, planning to finish darning one of Ole's socks; however, her hands would not cooperate. They lay quietly in her lap as the words she had spoken played over and over in her head. She prayed that Oline would never experience the ugly side of sex. She had. She remembered every moment of the attempted rape. Not the one in the river. The one Hanna had planned.

Helena

There was a light rain falling when I picked up the milk pail and began walking down the gravel path that connected the house to the log barn. Fog was rolling in from the sea, creating a mist that chilled to the bone. The weather perfectly matched my mood. I was going to lose. Servant girls always lose.

Regina Alving, a wealthy, middle-aged widow, had hired me to be a serving girl and milkmaid. I was so happy. Mrs. Alving was strict but fair. And best of all, there were no men in the house—just the cook, the housekeeper, and me. Oh, and such a house! The parlor was bigger than my father's cottage. I had a small room all to myself. With a door I could lock! I had never had a room before. It should have been so good. It would have been good, except for her.

Hanna's hatred of me began the first Sunday of my employment. Mrs. Alving had a tea at four o'clock every Sunday. Relatives and leading families of the town were invited. Present that Sunday were Mrs. Alving's brother, Jacob Goodman, a large man with a long, rectangular face, which was accentuated by a bushy, squared-off beard; his sixteen-year-old son, Georg, who in thirty years would look exactly like his father; Jacob's eighteen-year-old daughter, Hanna, who was openly flirting with a handsome young man named Johannas, whom she had insisted Aunt Regina invite; and several other neighbors and friends.

I was nervous when I pushed the tea cart into the parlor. Never had I been so close to wealthy and beautifully dressed people. The older women wore the latest fashions, set off by gold and silver jewelry. A diamond brooch sparkled at Mrs. Alving's throat. Hanna was dressed in a lavender brocade with a daring scooped neckline. All the men looked distinguished in black suits and white, starched shirts.

"Ah, here comes the tea," Mrs. Alving said.

As I pushed the tea cart to Mrs. Alving, all conversation stopped. I felt their eyes following me, but I pretended not to notice. Of course, I did notice. The women's eyes narrowed in judgment. The men's eyes widened with interest.

"Well, my dear sister," Jacob said. "I see you have hired a new serving girl."

"Yes, and a very competent one she is. Her name is Helena. She is from Finland."

Johannas, who was standing behind Hanna's chair and next to Georg, poked the boy lightly and said with a leer, "A Finnish girl and a pretty one!"

"I agree." Georg grinned.

Hanna's face became rigid, her mouth a narrow slit. "I don't think she's that pretty."

The grin on Georg's face widened. He recognized a chance to irritate his older sister. "That, Hanna, is because you are not looking at her through the eyes of a man."

Jacob snorted loudly. "And when did you become a man?"

The room filled with laughter. Georg blushed. Gratefully, I fled. Before closing the parlor doors, I glanced at Hanna. She glared back at me. Without saying a word to her, I knew I had made an enemy.

Mrs. Alving was one of those people who do the same thing at the same time on the same day. So it was not by accident that Hanna arrived at the house on the days she knew her aunt was out. I did my best to avoid her, but each time she would demand to see me, then order me to wait on her as if she were a queen. When we were alone, she purposely spilled tea that I handed to her, and then blamed me. She tripped over potted plants so that I would have to clean up the mess. Everything I did was stupid or wrong or both. When Mrs. Alving was present, Hanna was sickeningly sweet, but at the same time made one snide remark after another.

I thought if I worked hard and ignored her, she would tire of her game. She did not. The more I ignored her, the nastier she became. It all came to a head on a rainy, cold day when Mrs. Alving and Hanna came home from shopping. Mrs. Alving had bought Hanna a new dress. Hanna was modeling the dress as I brought in the tea.

"Oh, Auntie, I love it! I'm going to wear it home!"

"Do you think that wise?" Mrs. Alving said with a frown. "It is more of an evening dress."

"I don't care! I'm going to stop at the bank and see Papa. Do you think Johannas will like it?"

"I'm sure he will. And so will Emil Signaldahl."

Hanna danced around the room. "Who cares about Emil? He barely comes up to my shoulders."

"You should be nice to him, Hanna. Your father thinks highly of him, and he follows you around like a puppy."

Out of breath, Hanna plopped into a wingback chair. "I don't want a puppy! Have you noticed Johannas's eyes? They are almost black. I think he might be part Arab."

Mrs. Alving laughed. "That's silly. There are many Norwegians with dark eyes."

"Not like his!"

I was about to leave when Mrs. Alving said, "Wait, Helena. After I pour us each a cup, you can take the cart back to the kitchen."

"Yes, ma'am," I replied.

Hanna glared at me as her aunt poured the tea. "Have you noticed Johannas's eyes?"

"No, Miss," I answered without looking at her.

"Good." Hanna sniffed.

Mrs. Alving handed Hanna a cup, then sat in her chair. "After you remove the tea cart, Helena, bring back a bag for the dress Hanna was wearing."

I nodded and was about to leave when Hanna said, "That won't be necessary. I don't want the dress. It is all out of style."

"What should I do with it?" Mrs. Alving asked.

"I don't care. Give it to the poor."

At that moment, the housekeeper entered the parlor. "Pardon the intrusion, Mrs. Alving, but Cook needs to speak with you?"

"Oh, of course," Mrs. Alving said, placing her cup on the table and standing. "I forgot to give her the dinner menu. Excuse me, Hanna. I'll be right back."

Mrs. Alving and the housekeeper had no more than left when Hanna started in on me. "Do you like my dress, Helena?"

"Yes, Miss. It's very pretty."

"It is. I can see you wish it were yours."

"No, Miss. I could never afford such a dress."

Hanna's laugh was as nasty as the look on her face. "You are so right! This dress cost more than you make in a year. A dress like this is made for a woman of quality, not a serving girl."

I forced myself to stare at the tea cart. Anger was churning in me like a whirlpool in a storm. If I allowed it out, there was no doubt I'd be fired. I turned the cart to leave.

"Wait!" Hanna ordered. "Pour me another cup of tea before you go."

There was no way I could refuse. She held out her cup. I poured the tea, being especially careful not to spill a drop. As I stood up straight, I saw that she had extended her left leg. If I had turned normally, I would have tripped, fallen, and broken the teapot. So instead of turning, I swung my right foot sideways, striking her ankle.

"Ow!" she cried. "That hurt!"

"You tried to trip me," I said, stepping back and then returning to the tea cart.

"I did not! You kicked me on purpose!"

"No. I just ran into your leg that happened to be sticking out." I began pushing the cart out of the parlor.

"Stop! Don't you turn your back on me! I haven't dismissed you, serving girl!"

I closed my eyes, took a deep breath, then turned back to her. I had never seen anyone so angry. "Is there something you need, Miss?"

For a moment she could not speak, then she screamed, "Yes! My rain boots are muddy. Clean them!"

This I would not do, even if it meant getting fired. "No."

Surprise was added to her anger. "No? How dare you tell me no! You are a serving girl. You will do as I say!"

"No. I work for Mrs. Alving, not you."

"You forget your place! I am your better! You will do as I say."

My heart was pounding. Tears stung my eyes. But there was no turning back. My voice quivered. "I will clean your boots only if Mrs. Alving orders it."

Hanna jumped to her feet, spilling some of her tea. "How dare you talk to me in this manner? You are a servant! If I tell you to clean something, you will clean it!"

She then smiled viciously, held up her cup and saucer, and dropped them onto the floor. The china shattered. "There is a mess on the floor, serving girl. Clean it up!"

I was shocked. The china was beautiful and expensive. I stared at the broken pieces, not believing what she had done.

"Don't just stand there! Clean it up!"

I could hold back no longer. I shouted at Hanna, "No! You dropped the china on purpose. I won't clean it up!"

Now it was her turn to be shocked. "You ... you can't yell at me like that."

"I just did!"

"I will not stand ..."

Hanna suddenly stopped. I turned to see Mrs. Alving standing in the doorway. Hanna ran to her.

"Auntie! I accidentally dropped my tea, and this uppity serving girl refused to clean it up."

"She dropped it on purpose, Mrs. Alving," I blurted.

"She's lying!"

Mrs. Alving gazed down at the broken china, then looked up at Hanna with eyes as cold as her voice. "No, Hanna. You're lying. I saw you drop it."

Hanna turned pale. "Auntie! You're taking the side of a serving girl?"

"I am taking no one's side. I saw what happened. You clean it up."

"Never!" Hanna screamed, only inches from Mrs. Alving's face. "I'm not a servant! Never!"

Hanna stomped to the front entrance, where she grabbed her boots, cape, and bonnet. "I'll never come back here, Auntie! And I'll tell my father you insulted me!"

"I have done no such thing, Hanna," Mrs. Alving snapped. "When you tell your father, make sure you mention that you purposely broke one of my most prized tea cups."

Hanna slammed out of the house. Mrs. Alving stood rigid as an icicle, her face a mask of embarrassment and anger. "I am sorry, Helena. I have been informed that Hanna has treated you badly. I apologize for the family. I love my niece, but there are times she has a highly exaggerated opinion of her own importance."

I have never appreciated an apology more. For Mrs. Alving to say she was sorry to a serving girl was difficult and humbling. "Thank you," I whispered. "Do you want me to leave?"

Mrs. Alving looked surprised. "Of course not. You are an honest, hardworking young woman. I like you."

"And I like you," I thought, but did not say it. What I wanted to do was throw my arms around her neck and hug her, but that would have been improper. However, I could not hold back my tears. "Thank you. You are most kind," I sniffled. I then turned my attention to the floor. "I'll clean up the pieces."

"I will help by getting the broom and dustpan," Mrs. Alving said with a smile.

I had the large pieces picked up and placed on the tea cart when Mrs. Alving returned. She swept up what remained while I held the dustpan. When we finished, she leaned on the broom. "Helena, we make a good team." The statement was such a surprise, I laughed. She smiled and continued, "You have a lovely laugh. I would like to hear more of it."

I returned the smile as I got to my feet. Again tears came to my eyes. "Thank you. I don't want to cause you trouble. You have been so nice to me."

There was an awkward silence. Through my blurred vision, I saw tears in her eyes. We stood there, two women who wanted to hold each other but could not. That would not have been proper.

The silence was broken when Mrs. Alving looked away and saw Hanna's old dress lying on the floor. "A new problem," she said as she picked up the dress. "Who do I give this to?" She turned to me, a twinkle in her eyes. "You and Hanna are about the same size. Would you like it?" I heard myself gasp. She walked to me and held the dress against me. "Yes. I think it will fit nicely."

The dress was gray with a high neck and full skirt. It was beautifully made from soft, expensive wool. "I ... I would have no place to wear it."

Mrs. Alving laughed. "Oh, I think you will find somewhere appropriate. Try it on."

"Now?"

"Yes. Let's see how it looks."

In a daze, I took off my apron and slipped out of my dress. I was surprised that I felt no embarrassment. It was almost as if I were undressing in front of my mother. Mrs. Alving helped me into the dress and buttoned up the back.

"Turn around," she ordered.

I did so. She gazed at me with an approving nod. "Perfect. It fits like it was made for you."

"How do I look?"

"Stunning. You are a beautiful woman, Helena. Go to my room. There is a full-length mirror there. See for yourself."

I turned and had taken one step when the front door opened and Hanna burst in. "Auntie! I am so sorry! I was wrong. Please …"

That is when she saw me.

The color drained from her face, making her eyes huge as they filled with recognition. "My dress! You are wearing my dress!"

"You told me to give it away," Mrs. Alving said defensively.

Hanna screamed. "Not to her! Not to her!"

She flew at me like an angry hawk. I might have avoided her charge had I not stepped back into the tea cart, which went crashing to the floor. Her long fingernails caught the dress, shredding the soft wool fabric. My face would have been next if Mrs. Alving had not grabbed her by the arms and spun her around.

"Hanna, stop it! Do you hear me? Stop it!"

Hanna was panting like a rabid dog. "She's a slut, Auntie! You gave my dress to a Finnish slut!"

Mrs. Alving slapped Hanna in the face. "How dare you? What proof do you have?"

Hanna stepped back, tears rolling down her cheeks. "I don't need proof! She's a slut!"

"Get out of my house! Don't you ever call a woman that without proof!"

"I'll get you proof, Auntie! I'll prove to you she's a slut!"

Hanna then ran out of the house, leaving the front door wide open.

I started to cry. "Why … why does she hate me so?"

Mrs. Alving walked down the hall and closed the door. With her back to me, she said, "The answer to that, Helena, can be found in your own mirror."

It was three weeks later when I finished my walk to the barn and entered it for the evening milking. The three Holstein cows, which had entered through the open pasture door, were waiting for me. I put them in their stanchions, fed them some grain, and sat down to milk. I never enjoyed milking, but these cows were gentle and the barn was warm. As I squeezed the milk into the pail, I leaned my head against the cow's flank. There was no escape. No escape from the angry arguments between Mrs. Alving and her brother; no escape from the lies Hanna was spreading through the town about me; no escape from the loneliness of having no family or friends.

A male voice startled me. "The pretty milkmaid is at work. How nice."

I looked to see Georg Goodman leering at me. There was no doubt what he had in mind. I had seen that look before. But I also saw he was nervous, so I tried to make light of his being there. "Have you come to help me milk, Georg?"

"Not likely." He laughed. "I've never milked a cow in my life. But I would like to play with two smaller teats."

He took two steps closer, his mouth frozen in a crooked grin, his eyes gleaming with lust.

"Stay away from me, Georg!"

He took another step. "Not likely, again. Don't play hard to get with me, Helena. I've heard you love to make the two-backed monster."

I screamed at him. "That's a lie, a lie started by your sister! Get out of this barn!"

"You don't give orders to me, milkmaid! Come on, let's find some soft hay."

He was now standing so close he could reach out and touch me. I was between two cows. There was no way I could run. He reached out grab me. I pushed closer to the cow, turned a teat upward, and squirted him in the face.

Georg jumped back. "Ahhh! You bitch!"

"Stay away from me!"

Georg wiped the milk off his face, which was red with fury. He snarled, "Hanna said you liked it rough. Well, you're going to get it rough!"

He charged.

I jumped off the stool and flung half a pail of milk at him. He screamed but kept coming. The cows panicked. Both lashed out with their hind legs. The cow behind me missed. The cow I was milking did not. Her hoof smashed into his left leg just above the knee. I heard the bone crack.

Georg howled with pain as he grabbed on to the back of the cow. She kicked again as he was falling, catching him in the chest and sending him hurtling against the back wall. He lay there in a crumpled ball. I thought he was dead. The barn became silent, but a noise came from the back door. I glanced and saw a whirling skirt and a foot. Hanna!

Georg groaned and began to cry. "My leg! My leg! Oh, it hurts."

My fear turned to anger. I screamed at Georg. "Hanna put you up to this, didn't she? Didn't she?"

He whispered, "She said you wanted it. My leg! It hurts. Help me!"

I felt like kicking his other leg, but instead went up to the house for help.

Help came. There were shouts, accusations, demands, and denials. Naturally, it was all my fault. Hanna was nowhere to be found. The next morning, I was called into Mrs. Alving's sitting room. I knew what was coming. I had already packed my few belongings.

Mrs. Alving sat behind a small walnut desk. She looked tired and upset. "Sit down, Helena."

I stood.

Mrs. Alving sighed. "I don't know what really happened in the barn, but it doesn't matter. Jacob and Hanna demand that you leave."

"Hanna was there, Mrs. Alving. She was behind it all."

"That too doesn't matter," Mrs. Alving said sadly. "She is family. Right or wrong, family must come first. But I want you to know, I believe you."

I had sworn to myself that I would not cry, but I could not keep back the tears. "Thank you. You have always been fair to me."

Mrs. Alving smiled. "Don't cry, Helena. There is some good news. I have a friend who needs a maid. She is very nice. So is her husband." Mrs. Alving rose from the desk and handed me a piece of paper and two weeks' wages. "The address is on the paper. Her gain is my loss. Good luck, my dear."

It was raining when I left the house. That was fitting. Important things always happened to me when the weather was bad. Little did I know that I was taking my first steps to a new beginning in a new land.

Oline

It started with them whispering. No! That's not right. It started with Mama giggling. Then she climbed the ladder to see if we were sleeping.

I pretended I was. They've stopped whispering. I think they are kissing. Oh my!

Anna said you could get a baby in you by kissing a boy. Could that be true? It's not what Mama said. Cows don't kiss. Pigs don't kiss. No, that's only a stupid story like babies coming from a factory in Norway.

The bed is starting to make noise. Are they …? Oh my! I've heard the bed make noise before, but I never knew what it meant. Is Papa touching her? Is she touching Papa? When Ernst touched my hand, it felt nice. Does touching down there feel nice? The bed is making more noise. How do they do it? Are they lying down? Oh my! Shall I peek? There is a crack in the loft floor. No, I can't do that!

Mama is moaning. Does it hurt? Papa would never hurt Mama, but why is she moaning? I don't want to do that if it hurts! Oh, this is too complicated. Why aren't I asleep?

I pull the blanket up over my head. In doing so, I poke Berent with my elbow. He groans and wakes up.

"You hurt me," he says groggily.

I whisper, "I'm sorry. Go back to sleep."

"It hurts."

"Shhh! I said I was sorry. Go to sleep."

Berent rolls over and lies still.

The bed noise becomes louder. Papa is grunting.

"What's that noise?" Berent asks.

"Nothing. Go to sleep."

Berent pulls down the blanket. "That's the bed. Are Mama and Papa jumping on the bed?"

"No!"

"Yes, they are!" Berent sits up and crosses his arms. He says loudly, "That's not fair! Mama won't let me jump on the bed!"

I pull the blanket back over my head. The bed noise stops, replaced by muffled laughter.

Berent gently taps my head. "Oline, are you playing hide-n-seek?"

"No! Go to sleep."

Chapter Twenty-Six

Ole slapped the reins, urging Doll and Lady into the river. The Skunk was relatively high for August. The water came to within a few inches of the wagon floor, where the Branjord children sat in their Sunday best.

The morning sun shone benevolently. It was warm, not hot, making for the promise of a perfect day. Rain had fallen during the night, leaving everything in sight looking scrubbed and clean, much like the Branjord children.

Berent looked over the side of the wagon. "Are we going to get wet, Papa?"

"No. The water isn't that deep."

Berent made a face. "Shucks."

"Doesn't everything smell wonderful?" Helena said after taking a deep breath.

Before Ole could reply, Lady decided to relieve herself. Ole grinned. "Well, not everything."

Helena laughed as the horses pulled the wagon out of the river and onto the trail that lead to Saint Petri Church.

"Look, Mama!" Oline said, pointing to a wagon about forty yards behind. "Here come the Tjernagels." Helena and Ole both looked and waved.

"Ole!" Ole Andreas called. "Wait up."

When the wagons were side by side and the "hellos" and "good mornings" had been exchanged, Ole Andreas said, "I need to talk to you before church, Ole. How about if I ride with you and Helena and the children ride with Martha?"

"Well, if it's that serious, we had better talk," Ole answered.

"It's fine with me," Helena said. "I can talk with Martha."

Ole Andreas handed the reins to Martha, jumped down, and then helped Helena down from the Branjord wagon and up onto the seat by his wife. The children followed with the agility of spider monkeys. Martha started her team for the church, and Ole Andreas climbed up on the seat beside Ole.

"What's this all about?" Ole asked as he slapped the reins.

"More trouble. Saul Jaeran had his group meet last Thursday at the church. Reverend Amlund was supposed to be up north all day. Well, he came back early and caught them. I was told he was madder than a wet hen. He said there would be no more meetings in his church without him being there."

"What did the men say?"

"Not much. They just sort of left. I guess Saul was jumping up and down mad."

Ole shook his head in disgust. "Saul again! But, you know, it's not right to call them Saul's group. I know for a fact that Jonas, Lars, and Jacob can't stand him. He just thinks he is the leader."

"Well, he sure talks a lot," Ole Andreas grumbled.

"Truer words were never spoken. If it weren't for Saul, I think we could find a compromise for this mess."

Ole Andreas spat, hitting the wagon tongue. "Things have gone too far, Ole. I think we are headed for a breakup."

"I hope you're wrong, but fear you're right. It is such a shame. We have a nice-sized congregation." The men rode in silence for a distance, then Ole asked, "Do you think there could be a blowup in church today?"

"It's more than possible. That's why I wanted to warn you."

In the wagon ahead, the children sang while Helena and Martha talked in low tones. Martha asked, "Did Rooster really attack you like they say?"

Helena sighed. "I don't know what they are saying, and I don't know how this got out, but yes, it is true." She then told the story to Martha, whose eyes became larger and larger.

When Helena was finished, Martha said, "I would have let him drown."

"Maybe I would have if the children had not been there."

"No, you wouldn't do that. You're too tender-hearted. What did Ole say?"

"I can't repeat it. I've never seen him swear like that. He wanted to take the rifle and kill Rooster. I begged him not to. Nothing happened, and I did hit him with a rock. I was hoping no one would find out."

"There is no chance of that. It is already the talk of Fairview and the East Settlement."

Helena groaned and hit the side of her fist on her leg. "Just what I need!"

Martha patted Helena's hand but said nothing. They were almost to the church when Martha said, "Oh, I almost forgot. The man who bought your farm in Hardin County stopped by our place for water. He is moving his family west."

"I'm not surprised. That farm is just bad luck."

"He said there is an outbreak of diphtheria up that way."

Helena turned to face Martha, her eyes filled with concern. "Diphtheria!"

"That's what he said. A neighbor of his has been quarantined."

Helena clutched her throat. "Did he say a name? Was it Thornwald?"

"Yes, that's it. Ben Thornwald. Do you know the family?"

The color drained from Helena's face. "Emma Thornwald was my first friend in America. She probably saved my life."

"Saved your life! How?" Martha said, bringing the horses to a halt by the other wagons in the churchyard.

"It's a long story. I'll tell you after church."

The children piled out of the wagon as Ole and Ole Andreas pulled up beside them. Both women waited on the seat until the men tied the horses and came to assist them down. They, of course, were perfectly able to get down by themselves, but that would not have been proper in front of the church. Besides, they enjoyed the attention.

Inside, the men took seats in a pew with Hans Twedt and Jonas Duea. Martha, Helena, and the children found room in a pew behind Julia Twedt and her brood. Nods and smiles were exchanged. Inga Lyngen began to play the prelude. People were settling in for the service when Joseph Twedt stood up where Berent could see him.

The yell from Berent was so loud that Inga stopped playing. Everyone in the church stared at Berent, who was pointing at Joseph.

"Mama! Joseph has pants!"

Joseph grinned as he did a complete turn.

"Shh!" Helena hissed. "Sit down!"

"No! He's four fingers like me and he has pants!" Tears streamed down the boy's face.

Helena grabbed Berent, but in his frenzy he broke away and ran out into the aisle. He screamed at an astonished Ole, "Papa! Joseph has pants! It's not fair! It's not fair!"

Berent was having a full-blown tantrum. There were some stunned looks of disapproval, but most of the congregation was doing a poor job of smothering laughter. In one swift movement, Ole stood, grabbed Berent like a sack of feed, and strode out of church. All the while, Berent sobbed and cried, "Don't spank me, Papa! Don't spank me!"

The boy's pleas fell on red and deaf ears. Before Inga could recover and begin playing the organ, the sounds of hand hitting bottom, accompanied by the appropriate wails, were heard through the open windows of the now silent sanctuary.

Martin slid as far down in the pew as he could. Oline covered her face with her hands. Helena sat frozen, staring straight ahead, her face the color of Christmas ribbon.

Finally, Inga began to play the organ. Ole and Berent did not return. For Helena, it was the longest church service in the history of the world. When the congregation stood to sing the closing hymn, Helena took the hands of her children and walked out the door.

Ole was waiting with the horses untied and pointed for home. Helena and the children, without a word, jumped into the wagon. Ole had the horses going at a trot before Helena was settled onto the seat.

No one spoke for nearly a mile. After crossing the ford, Helena glanced at Ole. His jaw was set, his nostrils flared, and his eyes were as cold as a Norwegian glacier. Seeing his anger made her own temper flare. She crossed her arms. She didn't make the rules! It wasn't her fault boys did not wear pants until they were five! Martin waited. So could Berent!

Helena looked back at the children. All were asleep. Berent was curled up in a fetal position, his right thumb in his mouth. Her anger dissolved, leaving a pain in her chest. Tears came to her eyes. It was her fault. She had wanted to keep Berent a baby.

Ole noticed the tears. His face softened, but his voice was firm. "You will make the boy a pair of pants." It was a statement—not a question, not a request. Helena did not fight what she knew was inevitable. There was no way Berent would ever again go to Saint Petri in a dress. She nodded.

They continued in silence, but the anger was gone. The embarrassment remained. Helena clenched her teeth as she thought about how her family would be this week's major topic of conversation. Then she remembered what had so shocked her before church. "Ole, did Ole Andreas tell you about the Thornwalds?"

"No. What about them?"

"They are quarantined. Diphtheria. The man who bought our farm told Martha when he stopped for water. He's moving farther west."

"Good for him," Ole muttered. "Is the diphtheria widespread?"

"I don't know," Helena answered. She took a deep breath before continuing. "But I do know Emma needs help. I have to go to her."

Ole looked sharply at his wife. "No! There is nothing more contagious than diphtheria."

Helena stared straight ahead. "That makes no difference. When we had the fever, she saved both of us. She not only nursed us, she took care of Oline. And all without the help of that no-account husband of hers."

"Well, I'm sure he's there now."

Helena turned to Ole. "Why would you even think that? You remember how he would disappear for weeks at a time. He probably doesn't even know his family is sick."

"What about your family? What if you get diphtheria?"

"The Lord will protect me."

Ole's face became grim. "Then why do so many good people get sick and die? I think the Lord protects those who protect themselves."

"Don't you blaspheme, Ole Branjord! And don't make this harder than it already is." Helena's voice cracked and tears rolled down her cheeks. "She would come to me if I were sick. I must go to her."

"How do you know she's even alive?"

Helena wiped the tears from her eyes. "She is. I know it. Don't ask me how. I just know it."

Ole gripped the reins so hard his knuckles turned white. "Helena, please. This is foolish."

"No," Helena answered. "This is necessary."

"What if I forbid it?"

"You won't."

"What if I say you can't take a horse?"

"Then I'll walk."

Ole looked up at the sky in exasperation. "Lord in heaven! You are the most stubborn woman on earth!"

Helena folded her hands and said in a small voice, "She needs me, Ole."

Ole sighed. Some men could control their wives. He was not one of them. "Then we'll both go."

"No!" Helena said fiercely. "The children need at least one parent."

"Then I'll go and you stay."

"Now you are talking foolishness. You know nothing about nursing the sick. What good would you do? No, I'll go, and I'll leave right after dinner."

"Absolutely not! It's a six-hour ride. If you're going, you'll go as soon as we can get you ready."

Not another word was spoken for the rest of the way home.

Oline watched her mother put on her oldest dress, then gasped when Helena removed a torn pair of Ole's pants from the quilting material bag and put them on. Helena smiled at Oline's expression. "Did you think I was going to ride all that way in just a dress?" she said, securing the pants with a strip of cloth. "There are times when a woman needs to wear pants. This is one of them. Can you see Papa and the boys?"

Oline looked out of the door. "No. They are still in the barn."

"Good." Helena took a piece of muslin, folded it into a six-inch square, poked holes into the corners, and tied homespun through each.

"What are you doing?" Oline asked.

"Making a mask."

"Is diphtheria that bad?"

Helena gave her daughter a questioning look. "How do you know the family has diphtheria?"

Oline looked down at her toes. "I heard you and Papa talking in the wagon."

"Yes, it is." Helena sighed, reminding herself to be more careful what she said when her daughter was supposedly sleeping. "It closes your throat so you can't breathe."

Oline sank into a chair, watching with fear as Helena packed food in one sack and quinine, liniment, and a half bottle of whisky in a second. She felt her own throat constricting. "If it's so bad, why are you going?"

"Because I have to. Emma Thornwald saved us all."

"How? Were we attacked by Indians?"

Helena shook her head as she sat in her rocker. "Nothing so dramatic. Do you remember anything about Hardin County?"

"No, not really."

"You're lucky. They were bad years. We wouldn't have survived without Emma. She helped us put in the first crop, showed us what to plant in the garden, and explained how to live off the prairie."

"Did Mr. Thornwald help?"

"Ben?" Helena snorted. "He was mostly worthless. All he wanted to do was hunt, fish, and drink. But Emma always stood up for him. I have to admit he was a good hunter. When he was around, we had plenty of fresh meat."

Oline frowned. Her thoughts were going back to when she was younger than Berent. "Did he whistle? I sort of remember a tall, thin man who whistled. I was afraid of him."

"That was Ben. You would hide when you heard him coming. But you didn't hide from Emma. You loved her."

Forgotten memories suddenly came flowing back to Oline. "I remember her! She was big with wild hair. She would swing me up and then give me hugs! She had a loud laugh."

"Yes, she did." Helena smiled. "She really liked you … and almost took you away from me."

Oline's expression changed from happy to one of concern. "Why would she do that?"

"Because I was neglecting you," Helena replied, the memory embarrassing and difficult. "Ole and I worked harder that first summer than we ever have before or since. Both of us lost so much weight, we were skin and bones. In the fall, after the corn was picked, I gave out. I came down with nervous fever. I couldn't even get out of bed. I wanted to die."

"What is nervous fever?" Oline asked, shocked by her mother's words. "Does it hurt?"

"No. It doesn't really hurt. It's more in the mind than the body. I can't explain it." Helena searched for words. "Nervous fever is like being in a deep, dark hole. All I wanted to do was sleep. I couldn't stand the light. Then Ole came down with it. He just hid in the barn.

"Emma came most every day. I'm sure we all would have died without her. It all came to a head on a cold, raw day. When she came, you were hungry, dirty, crying, and covered with ant bites. She screamed at me, calling me awful names. Then she wrapped you in a blanket and said, 'If you won't take care of her, I will. Just lie there and die, Helena!' She stomped out of the cabin. The thought of losing you sent a bolt of lightning from my head to my toes. Emma had taken no more than ten steps from the door when I caught her and snatched you back. She just looked at me and said, 'Good,' and walked home."

Oline stared at her mother, slowly realizing there was so much about this woman she did not know. "What did you do?"

"I cleaned you up, put liniment on your bites, and made you a big bowl of cornmeal mush. When you had eaten it all, you crawled into my lap, gave me the most beautiful smile, and put your arms around my neck. Then I cried. I cried so much your hair was wet. But from that day on, I started to feel better."

"Did Papa get better too?"

"Yes. By Christmas we were looking forward to spring."

Martin stepped into the cabin. "Lady's ready."

Helena rose from the rocker and put on her oldest bonnet. She did not glance in the mirror, knowing that she looked like a refugee from the poorhouse. It was her hope, perhaps even prayer, that because it was Sunday, no one would see her. "You two be good now. Mind your father and watch Berent," she said, tying the two sacks of supplies together. "Oline, you can do most of the cooking. Martin, you help and don't argue. Understand?"

"Yes, Mama," they replied in unison.

Helena picked up the sacks and went out into the yard, where Ole waited with Lady. They did not own a saddle, so Ole had placed an old, folded blanket on the horse and secured it with a harness strap. His face was glum, his eyes worried. As Helena approached, he opened his mouth to speak, but Helena lightly put her gloved hand on his lips. "Please don't say anything, Ole. Just help me up."

Ole nodded, handed her a canteen of water, and placed his hands together. Helena used them as a stirrup and swung on to the horse's back. As she hung the two sacks on either side of Lady's neck and placed the canteen strap over her shoulder, she saw Berent standing by the side of the cabin, tears streaming down his face. "Berent, what is the matter?"

Berent wiped away the tears. "You're going away because I was bad in church."

"Oh, I am not," Helena replied, choking back her own tears. "Ole, lift Berent up to me."

Ole did so, and Helena hugged her four-year-old and kissed both cheeks. "I'm not going because you were bad. I'm going to help people who are very sick."

Berent's eyes became fearful. "Are you going to get sick too?"

Helena gave Berent another hug. "I'm not going to get sick. And you know what? When I get home, I'm going to make you a pair of pants."

"You promise?" Berent asked with a grin as wide as the Iowa prairie.

"I promise," Helena answered, handing the boy back to Ole. Then to her husband she said, "Don't worry if I'm not back in a day or two. I'll be fine."

Ole failed at an attempt to smile, but nodded his head. Helena gave Lady a soft kick in the ribs and started down to the river. She did not look back. Helena knew if she did, she would turn around.

Thankfully, the stage road was empty. Helena rode through Fairview, past the cemetery, and on to the ford without meeting a soul. She crossed the river and paused for a moment. Following the stage road is what Ole had told her to do, but if she struck out northeast across the prairie, she would still run into the east-west Randall Station road and would save time. She chose the prairie.

Lady was not happy and showed it by refusing to leave the road. Helena responded by kicking her in the ribs. Lady turned in a circle. "Come on, Lady! I don't like this any more than you do," Helena said, slapping the horse with the reins. Lady reluctantly stepped out into the belly-high grass.

As she had done on the trip to Nevada, Helena marveled at the new homesteads. The prairie had seemed so trackless when she and Ole had moved from Hardin County. Now, the emerging farms dotted the landscape and served as landmarks. Some of the cabins were log, but most were sod or dugouts. There were even a few frame houses. The homes were a comfort to Helena. No matter what the construction, they all meant families. She was not out in the middle of nowhere. There was little doubt in her mind that in ten to fifteen years, all of this would be cultivated land.

After what she judged to be two hours, Helena began to worry that she had missed the Randall Station road. It was not a road at all, just a wagon trail, so if you were not paying attention, you could cross the trail without being aware of it. Helena kicked Lady into a trot, searching the high grass for a break. Actually, she was kicking herself for not staying with the stage road. If she had missed the Randall Station road, her shortcut would become the long way around. Helena was on the verge of turning back when Lady stepped out of the high grass and, of her own accord, turned east onto the trail.

Helena was relieved and surprised. The wagon trail had become wider and much more defined than when she and Ole had moved to Story County. It was almost as broad as the stage road. She smiled and patted Lady's neck. "We did it, girl!" Lady tossed her head, happy to be out of the high grass.

Helena's smile faded when she saw a wagon approaching. There was no avoiding it. She was not about to go back into the grass. She just hoped it was not anyone she knew.

In this, Helena was lucky. The stranger in the wagon was a tall, thin man with red hair and a beard to match. He was wearing a homespun shirt and overalls. Helena would not have stopped, but as they came abreast, the man pulled his team to a halt.

"Are you lost, ma'am?" he asked in a concerned voice.

Helena reined in Lady. "No. I'm going to Hardin County."

The man's concern deepened. "That's not such a good idea. There is diphtheria over there."

"I know. A friend needs help."

"Well," the man said, "either you are a saint or a damn fool. Good luck."

Helena smiled. "Thank you. I can assure you I'm no saint."

The man laughed and slapped his reins. His wagon rumbled off.

Helena continued east. She too hoped for luck, but did not expect to find any. Luck was something the Branjord family had not found in Hardin County.

Helena

I was trying to be strong, trying to share the excitement I saw on Ole's face. We were almost there. Over the next small hill was our first home in America. But instead of being excited, I was numb. Two weeks before, we had buried Nettie out on the open prairie, her grave marked by a cross made of sticks. We put her in hole and drove away. Just … drove away.

It was a beautiful spring day. Sparse, pillow-like clouds accented a blue sky that seemed to have no end. A light breeze whispered through the tall prairie grass, which had drunk heavily from an overnight storm. The air smelled of fresh flowers, rich earth, and new beginnings. How inappropriate. For what we were about to find, the clouds should have been dark, the wind howling, and the prairie dying and stinking of decay.

We topped the hill. A thousand times we had imagined this moment, but never expected what we saw. I gasped. Ole looked stunned. The agent had told us the farm was forty acres, twenty-five of which had been cultivated. He also said there were a barn and a fine cabin. The part about the land was true, the rest a heart-shattering lie. The roof of the prairie grass and stake barn had collapsed. It looked like nothing more than an ugly, brownish hump which had burped out of the ground. The cabin was a badly constructed shack with two small windows and holes in the thatched roof. The caulking between the logs looked like it had been attacked by giant woodpeckers, and the door stood open, supported by one leather hinge.

We drove in silence to the cabin, where Ole pulled the horses to a halt. Oline stood in the wagon between us. "Is this our new house?" she asked. I bit my lip to keep from crying, then nodded. Her three-year-old innocence beamed a wonderful smile. "Good! I'm tired of riding in the wagon."

Ole and I sat as if made of marble, our faces drained of color. Neither of us attempted to stop Oline from jumping from the wagon and entering the cabin. Her screams jarred us from our stupor.

We both leaped from the wagon seat as Oline ran from the cabin. She was covered with black bugs. They were crawling over face and arms and falling from her dress. Because she was shrieking, bugs were crawling into her mouth. Ole reached her first. He cleaned out her mouth with one hand and wiped the ugly creatures from her face with the other.

"Take off her dress!" he yelled.

I grabbed the hem and ripped the dress over her head, sending the collar buttons flying. I threw the dress, but not quickly enough. Both of my hands were covered with the bugs. My screams joined Oline's. But I was able to brush off the insects before they could get under the sleeves of my dress.

"Get a brush and comb!" Ole ordered. "They are in her hair."

I rushed to the wagon. By the time I returned, Oline had stopped crying. Ole talked to her softly while I brushed the remaining bugs from her hair. When I was sure there were none left, Ole picked her up and held her close. She clung to him as if she would never let him go. I picked up the dress and beat it against the wagon box until it was bug free. Ole began walking to the door of the cabin.

"Don't go in there, Papa!" Oline pleaded, burying her face in Ole's neck.

"I won't, sweetheart. I just want to look." Without thinking, I followed. I nearly fainted at what I saw. The walls, the rafters, the, dirt floor all appeared to be moving. It was as if the cabin were alive. Bugs were crawling on bugs. Thousands of them. There were so many on the windows that they prevented light from entering. They dropped from the rafters and thatch like black raindrops.

I ran!

I ran back to the wagon.

I could pretend no longer.

I hung on to the side of the wagon and wept.

My dreams, my hopes, my plans were as black and broken as that bug-ridden cabin. Was it for this we had crossed the ocean and half a continent? Was this our reward for trying to better ourselves? Was this God laughing at us for our brazen confidence? For the first time in my life, I wanted to die.

I felt Ole's arm go around my shoulder. I turned and lay my head on his shoulder. He held and slowly rocked Oline and me. I felt his tears on my cheek as they mingled with mine. "I'm sorry," he whispered. "I'm so sorry."

It was then she arrived; there is no doubt in my mind that she was sent by God. He knew we were at the end of our rope and could not go on. So he sent an angel. A most unusual angel.

"Hello!" she called in a booming voice.

We all turned to see a tall figure striding toward us through the high prairie grass. She was wearing overalls and a man's worn, store-bought shirt. When she stepped out of the high grass into the farmyard, I could see she was barefoot and that the overalls were patched at the knees with cloth from an old dress. Had she not been wearing a faded bonnet and had breasts, I would have taken her for a man. She was carrying a small basket.

"My name is Emma Thornwald. Me and my husband Ben live a half a mile north."

Ole recovered first. He lowered Oline to the ground. "Good morning. I'm Ole Branjord. This is my wife Helena and our daughter Oline."

A broad, wonderful smile transformed her plain, lined face into a thing of beauty. "Oh, good! You speak Norwegian. The people who lived here before spoke Yankee. I couldn't understand a word they said. Not that they said much. Weren't friendly at all." She looked down with laughing blue eyes at Oline. "My, aren't you a cute one! Do you always run around naked?"

Oline ducked behind me. "No," I answered. "She ran into the cabin and came out covered with bugs." I then knelt beside Oline and slipped the dress over her head.

"Bugs! That's awful. What kind?"

Oline made a face. "Big, mean, black ones."

Emma Thornwald threw back her head and bellowed a most unladylike laugh. Her bonnet fell back, revealing a mass of unruly chestnut hair. "I love it! I'm sure they were mean and ugly!" She gently touched Oline's cheek with a long, calloused finger, then looked at me. "Is she the only one you've got?"

I sucked in my breath, tried to answer, and could not. Ole said, "We lost our baby daughter on the trip here."

Emma rolled her eyes and slapped her thighs. "I'm sorry. Ben says I talk too much. Of course, he doesn't hardly talk at all. Maybe that's why I talk so much. I'm real sorry. I have two: Aaron, thirteen, and David, eleven. I lost a third boy two years ago. He was almost five. I don't think I'll ever get a girl." The pain in her eyes was the same as I was feeling. There was no need for further words. She turned to Ole. "Well, let me see this home of yours."

"I wouldn't call it a home," I muttered as we walked to the cabin. "It's more like a shack."

"It's got windows," Emma said. "I wish my dugout had windows."

"What is a dugout?" Ole asked.

"Half cave, half soddy," she replied. "You dig a cave into the side of hill, then build a soddy in front of it. Ben keeps telling me he's going to build a cabin, but he never gets around to it."

Oline hung back as we approached the door. "Don't go in there!"

Emma smiled at her. "Don't you worry, Oline. I just want to take a peek."

Emma looked into the cabin, but quickly stepped back. "That's the worst I've ever seen."

"How do we get rid of them?" Ole asked.

"Scalding hot water. Do you have a big, black, lard-rendering kettle?"

"Yes."

"Good. We'll build a fire and bring water up from the creek. But first, I've got a little welcoming gift. Some biscuits!"

We returned to the wagon, where Ole pulled three chairs from beneath the canvas. Emma handed out the biscuits. "I'm not a great baker, but I thought you would be hungry."

She was right on both counts. The biscuits were hard and dry, but must have been a little magical. Not only did they provide energy, they also raised our spirits and gave us hope.

When we had finished the last biscuits, Emma said, "I suppose I should explain why I'm wearing men's clothes. The truth is, I don't have a decent dress anymore. I discovered dresses and field work don't mix."

I was surprised. "Doesn't your husband do the farming?"

Emma snorted. "No, not much. Ben is a sorry farmer. He's a great hunter and fisherman, though. I have to give him that. When he's around, we have plenty of meat and fish."

"He's not at home now?" Ole asked

"No. He's been gone several weeks. He should be getting home any day." Emma caught the disapproving look I gave Ole. She laughed. "Don't be too hard on old Ben. The man has a good heart and treats me fine. He just should have been one of those mountain men out west, not a farmer. Oh, speaking of farming, do you have your planting seed?"

"Yes," Ole answered. "I have corn, oats, and wheat."

"Then you're in good shape," Emma said. "You'll have to sow your oats and wheat as soon as possible. We plant corn in May. I'll lend a hand if you like."

Ole grinned. "I'll take all the help I can get. And if you need a strong back, you know where to come."

Emma slapped Ole's knee. "I thank you. There are plenty of times I need male muscle."

The two laughed. I did not. It was foolish, I know, but I felt more than a twinge of jealousy. I don't like other women, even if they are wearing pants, touching my husband. Emma must have seen the displeasure in my eyes, because she quickly retrieved her hand and apologized.

"But before we do anything else," Emma said as she stood up, "We have to get rid of those bugs."

For the next three days, with the help of Emma and her two boys, we did nothing else. Ole cut down an old cottonwood snag by the creek and chopped it into kindling. The boys carried the water from the creek to the kettle. Emma and I threw the water on the walls and rafters and then swept out piles of dead bugs. We never completely rid the cabin of the ugly things, but we did gain control and were able to move in.

Ben Thornwald returned, bringing fresh venison with him. He never said much, but he helped Ole fix up the cabin and barn and sow the oats and wheat before again disappearing out onto the prairie. Why Emma put up with him, I will never know. Love is a powerful and unexplainable emotion, and love was something Emma possessed and gave freely. It is because of her love that Ole and I survived the first year. I am alive because of Emma Thornwald.

Chapter Twenty-Seven

Helena began to worry. Had she gone too far? Everything seemed different. There were so many more farms. She knew she was close, but could not find her landmarks—the meandering creek that ran near their cabin, the pine tree which had been struck by lightning and stood alone and forlorn on a small hill, the large slough where Ole had shot a wild boar—nothing was quite the way she remembered. The only things familiar were the long shadows cast by Lady and herself. She glanced over her shoulder. The sun was still a round ball, but was preparing to splash its color across the western horizon and give the prairie over to twilight and then darkness.

Worry was quickly turning to panic when Lady perked her ears and turned south of her own volition. They were at the creek. With a sigh of relief, Helena patted the horse's neck. Emma's farm was less than a mile away.

Helena was now able to study the area she had once called home. To her surprise, it was lush and attractive. Her memories of Hardin County were so negative that she had come to think of this land as desolate, a place that bore bitter fruit. Instead, in the soft glow of sunset, she saw gently rolling hills that one day would be prosperous farms. Her spirits rose. She smiled and kicked Lady into a trot. Perhaps this was a sign she would find Emma well and happy and greeting her with a wave from the doorway of her home.

It was not to be.

From the moment she saw the dilapidated dugout, foreboding settled over Helena like a clinging fog. Emma was not waving in the doorway. There was no activity in the yard. There were no animals in the corral.

Save for a shirt flapping on a clothesline, there was no movement at all. The cornfield was brown, dead from the drought. The oats lay like a frozen wave, unharvested. Worst of all was the silence. The place had a look and feel of abandonment.

Helena tied Lady to the hitching rack in front of the open, sagging door. "Emma! Can you hear me?" Her question was answered by silence. She was about to call again when what she saw to the right of the dugout made the words die in her throat. Fresh graves. Three of them. All marked by crosses made of prairie driftwood, almost identical to the cross she and Ole had placed on Nettie's grave.

Helena turned pale. Was she too late? She hurried to the door. "Emma! It's Helena. Are you in there?"

A cough, followed by a weak but unmistakable order. "Stay out. Diphtheria."

The order was disobeyed. Helena quickly tied on her mask and entered the dugout. She paused a few feet inside to allow her eyes to adjust to the darkness.

What she saw shocked her. Emma had never been an especially neat housekeeper, but the home was in shambles. The table and two chairs were overturned. Shelves had collapsed. Broken dishes lay scattered on the dirt floor.

There was more coughing from the cave part of the dugout, followed by, "Helena, leave. There is nothing you can do."

"I'll decide that," Helena replied as she stepped around the stove that squatted cold and unused in the center of the room. Emma lay on a grass-filled mattress atop a rope bed at the back of the cave. Her face, glistening from the fever, was like a mask suspended in complete darkness and separated from her body, which was shivering beneath a soiled, sweat-soaked quilt. Helena knelt beside her.

"Don't get too close," Emma gasped.

Helena picked up a towel that lay next to the bed and wiped Emma's face. "I'll get as close as I have to get."

Emma attempted a smile. "You always were a stubborn one."

"Now that is case of the pot calling the kettle black. Are you thirsty?"

"Yes," Emma whispered before falling victim to a fit of coughing. Helena placed the towel over the sick woman's mouth. A minute passed, then another. Helena feared Emma was about to die, but the coughing finally subsided and Emma lay back, exhausted.

Helena stood up. "I'll get some water." She found the water pail and dipper in a corner. "What could have caused such a mess?" she wondered as she walked out of the door. On the way to the creek, she passed Lady, who whinnied softly. "I'll get you some water too," Helena said, scratching the horse's neck.

After finding a wooden bucket, Helena filled it and the water pail, left the bucket for Lady, and carried the pail into the dugout. She found a tin cup and wash pan, filled them with water, and again knelt by Emma, who appeared to be asleep. Helena began to wash her friend's face. Emma opened her eyes. "That feels so good."

"I'm glad. I'll do more after we get some water in you."

Helena raised Emma's head and put the cup to her lips. Helena poured slowly, but most of the water ran out of Emma's mouth. "I can hardly swallow."

Helena paused. "I know. But keep trying."

Emma did try. With Helena's patient help, she drank much of the cup. When she could take no more, Emma sank back onto the bed. "Enough," she sighed.

Helena resumed wiping Emma's face, a face she hardly recognized. The once ruddy complexion was now a dull yellow. Her skin had the texture of old parchment. Her dark, lush eyebrows had disappeared, and the tangle of unruly chestnut hair had turned gray. Helena shook her head. Was it possible this dear woman was just forty years old? She looked twice that.

Thinking Emma was asleep, Helena got to her feet and began to pick up the dugout. She righted the table and chairs and swept up pieces of china, dishes that had been Emma's most prized possessions.

"I'm sorry the place is such a mess."

Helena was startled by Emma's voice.

"A badger and her two babies came calling. I must smell real bad. They didn't come close to me."

Emma did smell. But it wasn't just body odor. She smelled of death. "Don't apologize, Emma. I'll clean it up."

"Don't bother. I won't need this place much longer."

Helena stopped sweeping. "Now don't you talk that way. You're going to get better."

"I don't want to get better. Everyone I loved is dead."

Emma's words were followed by another coughing spasm. Blood was mixed with mucus. Helena hurried to her side. "I have some quinine. It should help."

"No," Emma answered as the coughing eased. "I gave it to Ben and the boys. It doesn't help at all. Just come sit by me."

Helena hesitated, then put the bottle back in her sack and pulled up a chair beside the bed. Emma smiled. "Thank you for coming. I thought I would die alone."

"You're not going to die," Helena said, again wiping Emma's face with a damp towel.

"Yes, I am. Just like my boys. Ben brought it home. He died first. Then the boys on the same day. The man who bought your farm dug their graves. He and his family never had much to do with us. I think his wife was scared of me. I guess I did look pretty scary."

"You were never scary to me."

Emma closed her eyes and sighed. "I was to her. I think it bothered her that I wore men's clothes. The funny thing is I like wearing dresses, especially pretty ones with lace on the collar and cuffs. You won't believe this, but when I was young I looked pretty in a dress."

"I'm sure you were beautiful in a dress."

When there was no response, Helena looked closely at Emma. She was asleep. Helena sat back in her chair, staring at this once boisterous and powerful woman. She was astonished by Emma's words. Never had she seen the woman in anything but men's clothing. It had not occurred to her that Emma might have wanted to wear a dress with lace on the collar and cuffs. Helena felt ashamed. Emma had been her best friend, her only friend, yet Helena had not recognized the woman's basic femininity. Their conversations had not been about dresses, or lace, or pretty things; they had only talked of children, of food, of shelter, of survival.

Helena looked down at the pants she wore. What if she were faced with wearing them all the time? What if she could never again feel the softness of a dress, or the rustle of a dress when she walked, or experience the admiring glances of men when she was wearing a figure-hugging dress? Tears came to her eyes. Emma was dying, but Helena realized that much of what it meant to be a woman had died for her friend years ago.

While Helena cried for Emma's loss, night defeated the last rays of sunlight, causing the dugout to turn from gloomy to frightening. Helena sensed more than saw the change. She got up from the chair, angry that she had not thought of looking for a candle while there was still light. She carefully felt her way to the broken shelving, remembering it was there that Emma kept the candles and matches. Thankfully, that had not changed. Among the debris, Helena found both, plus a candleholder.

The flickering light created intimidating shadows, but the shadows were by far preferable to the darkness. Helena sat at the table and, not for the first time, wondered how Emma could have lived all these years in this … this hole. She placed her bag of food on the table and was about to open it when she looked closely at her gloves. To eat she would have to remove them, something she was not about to do. She did not want to touch anything with bare hands. Her food was useless. Why hadn't she thought of this when she packed it? Stupid!

Her dilemma was forgotten when Emma groaned and began coughing. Helena rushed to the bed, where she wiped Emma's face and cleaned the mucus from her mouth. The dying woman gasped for breath between coughs. Helena held her own breath, thinking these were her friend's last moments, but the spasm ended and Emma lay back on the pillow. "I'm cold," she whispered.

Helena felt the damp quilt. It was no wonder Emma was cold. Helena saw a blanket folded on the chest. She shook it out. The blanket was thin but would provide more warmth than the quilt. She pulled the quilt from the bed.

"Oh!" Helena gasped.

Lying next to Emma like a rumpled doll was a small girl with chestnut hair. Her unblinking, half-closed blue eyes stared up at Helena. Emma caressed the child's hair. "I finally got my little girl. She is eighteen months old. Her name is Jurina."

Helena fought back tears. "Emma, she's … she's …"

"I know. She died shortly before you came."

Helena dropped the blanket, reaching out for the girl.

"No!" Emma cried. "Leave her. Please, leave her. She's still warm."

Helena stepped back, horrified at what she saw. Emma continued to caress the baby's hair. "Isn't she pretty?"

There was nothing pretty about the poor dead child, but Helena answered, "Yes, she is pretty."

Emma looked up at Helena. "Bury her with me. Promise?"

Helena could no longer hold back the tears. "I promise."

"Thank you." Emma hugged Jurina closer to her. "Cover us. We're getting cold."

Emma was asleep before Helena could pick up the blanket and tuck it around her dying friend. She then sat in the chair and silently wept. She felt so helpless, so useless. All she could do was watch as the horrible disease slowly claimed Emma's ravaged body, and wait for the inevitable end.

For the next few hours, the silence of the dugout was disturbed only by Emma's labored breathing and occasional moans. Helena dozed in the chair, awakening to see Emma staring up her. "I've missed you so." Emma smiled.

"I've missed you too."

"I watched your wagon leave from the hill. I cried the rest of the day. Ben said it was the only time he saw me cry."

Helena felt fresh tears run down her cheeks. "I should have come to see you. I often thought about it."

"I thought the same about visiting you. But it's a long way, and we were both busy raising families." Emma coughed several times.

"Don't talk. Just rest."

"I want to talk. I have eternity to rest. How are Ole and the children?"

"Fine. We're all healthy. Oline is eleven, Martin eight, and Berent is four," Helena answered, her voice filling with pride. "Oline is taking piano lessons and doing quite well. Martin is reading a book in both Norwegian and English. The boy is so smart it scares me. And Berent ... well, Berent is just being Berent. He is a little dickens!"

Emma smiled. "He was such a cute baby."

"He still is cute. It's what keeps him alive. He is now obsessed with wearing pants." Helena then told Emma what had taken place in church that morning. When she finished, she said, "I have never been so embarrassed in my life."

Emma laughed. It was her old, boisterous belly laugh. Helena was somewhat taken aback. "I don't think it's funny."

"I do. And you will. I predict it will be one of your favorite Berent stories."

"Well," Helena said with a giggle, "It wasn't funny this morning."

"I'm sure it wasn't," Emma replied with a chuckle. "Most of the best stories aren't funny when the event happens."

"I haven't thought about that before, but you're right," Helena said, admiring Emma's wisdom. "Oh, I have a secret to tell you. I've told just one other woman."

Emma smiled. "Then it is no longer a secret. What is it?"

"I'm going to have another baby."

"Especially a secret like that!" Emma said. "Wonderful! When is it due?"

"In the spring."

Emma reached her left hand out from beneath the blanket and patted Helena's knee. "I'm so happy for you."

The two women shared the most feminine of moments with a love-filled silence. Then Helena whispered, "If it is a girl, her name will be Emma."

Emma wiped tears from her eyes. "Thank you. That is very special."

Again there was silence. Words were unnecessary.

The moment was shattered by a frightened, nervous whinny from Lady. Helena jumped to her feet. "There is something out there!"

"Probably those badgers. There's a rifle under the bed."

"I don't know how to shoot," Helena said, fear choking her voice.

"There's nothing to it. Just point and pull the trigger." Helena bent down and pulled out the weapon. "Be careful!" Emma ordered. "It's loaded and cocked."

The rifle was not like any Helena had seen. The barrel was relatively short and there was some sort of a lever underneath the trigger. Emma saw her surprised look. "It's a Henry repeating rifle. Some of the soldiers used them during the war. Ben won it in a poker game. He was real proud of it."

"If I have to shoot, how will I reload?"

"You won't have to. It holds seventeen shells. According to Ben, the soldiers used to say you could load it on Sunday and fire it all week."

"If you had this, why didn't you shoot the badgers?"

"She had babies." Emma answered. "Besides, I won't need this stuff much longer."

Lady whinnied again.

"You had better see what's out there," Emma said.

As Helena turned to the door, she kicked a pot that went rattling across the room and out the door. Helena followed the pot. The light from the moon allowed her to see Lady staring to the left, her ears pinned back against her head. Helena pointed the rifle in that direction, but nothing moved. After about a minute, Lady's ears came forward and she relaxed. Helena lowered the rifle. Whatever had frightened the horse had slipped away. She sighed in relief, turning back into the dugout. "I think it's gone."

"Good," Emma answered in a tired voice. "Put the rifle on the table. The badger might come back."

Helena did as she was told. Emma coughed, then said, "I want Ole to have the rifle. And don't argue. I certainly won't need it. I think I'll rest now."

Emma's eyes closed. She was asleep within seconds. Helena sat at the table, facing the door. She knew she should close it, but the moonlight filtering through the entrance made the dugout less oppressive, less like a tomb. She feared the darkness, even with a candle burning, more than any critter that might wander in.

Helena yawned. It had been a long day. She settled into her chair. There was little doubt it would be a longer night.

So it proved.

Emma's coughing spasms became longer and more frequent, and after each, she was weaker, her breathing more labored. When the rays of a new day replaced the fading moon, Helena sat bent over the table, her head resting on her folded arms. She was exhausted. From behind her, she heard Emma moan and then whisper, "Helena, are you sick?"

Helena raised her head. "No, just tired."

"I'm sorry for taking so long to die."

Helena blew out the candle, pushed herself away from table, and returned to her chair by the bed. "Now you hush. I don't want to hear talk like that."

Emma responded with a loving smile. "Nevertheless, it is true." She coughed and took several shallow breaths before continuing. "I'm being punished for leaving Norway."

"Oh, don't be silly," Helena replied.

"It's not silly. The pastor said God would punish us for abandoning Norway."

Anger flushed Helena's face. She had heard the same sermon. "God is not punishing you for anything. Many preachers said that. They didn't want to lose the cheap labor."

Emma said nothing. Helena looked down at her friend's closed eyes and thought she was asleep. But the eyelids fluttered open and, in a barely audible voice, Emma asked, "Do you remember when we talked about America being the land of promise?"

"Yes, I remember."

"We were wrong. It is the land of tears."

Helena made no attempt to answer. Platitudes would not change the fact that, for Emma and her family, this had been the land of tears.

Helena felt a sudden guilt. For her, things had been difficult at the start, but each year had been better and easier than the one before. Not for poor Emma. Through no fault of her own, she had lived, year after year, in this hole, and now had watched her family die. It wasn't fair! Emma had a heart as big as the prairie. She deserved so much better.

Helena sighed. What people deserved didn't seem to matter much. And as for fair, she had learned long ago that life was not fair. "Lord," she prayed, "if you are going to take your servant Emma, please do it now. She has suffered enough."

Apparently not. Emma convulsed into the worst coughing spasm yet.

Helena awoke disoriented. She raised her head and stared out the dugout door. It was dark. She did not remember sitting at the table. She did not remember falling asleep. But she had done both and slept for hours. The deathly silence of the dugout explained why. She did not have to look at the bed to see that her prayer had been answered.

Now what? The obvious answer was to dig a grave. Should she go to a neighbor for help? No. If they hadn't come before, they wouldn't come now. The burial party would be a party of one.

Helena lit the candle, then forced herself to the back of the dugout. Emma's left arm dangled, her hand resting on the floor. Helena stared down at her friend. There were no tears. Emma's agony was over. For that, Helena was grateful. Besides, as her mother had told her, don't waste tears on the dead. Tears are for the living. Helena shut her eyes, then picked up Emma's hand and tucked it beneath the blanket.

Washing the body was next. Under normal circumstances, the entire body would be washed, followed by putting Emma's best dress on the body. But these were not normal circumstances and there was no dress. Washing Emma's face and hands was all Helena could bring herself to do.

She had no more than dipped her towel in the pan of water when Lady trumpeted a loud whinny. Helena did not reach for the rifle. She smiled. The whinny was one of excitement and was answered by a similar whinny from not far away. She had told him not to, but Ole had come anyway. She was not surprised. She was, however, thankful and grateful—not only for his arrival but for Ole being her husband. She did so love this quiet and thoughtful man.

Helena reached the doorway as Ole came riding up on Doll. "Don't come any closer than the hitching rack," she ordered. "I don't want you to touch anything in the dugout."

Ole pulled Doll to a stop next to Lady. The two horses nuzzled each other. Ole asked, "How are you?"

"I'm fine. Emma died today. Her daughter died yesterday."

"Daughter?"

"I didn't know either. She was only eighteen months old. The others are buried about twenty yards to your right. I saw a shovel there. You need to dig a grave."

Ole dismounted and tied Doll to the hitching rack. "I'm sorry. But at least she didn't die alone."

"Did you leave the children with Bertha?"

"Yes. I thought you might need help."

"I do. Thank you for coming."

Ole grinned, relieved that Helena was not going to make a fuss about him not staying at home. "I'll get started on the grave."

Helena returned to the bed. She could not bring herself to wash the child's body, which was beginning to smell. The problem was how to get the bodies to the grave. Helena did not want Ole to carry them, and she was not strong enough to do so. She decided the only way was to put Emma on a blanket and drag her.

After moving her chair, Helena spread the quilt onto the floor by the bed. She then removed the blanket and placed it on top of the quilt. Emma's feet were now exposed. They were filthy. She stared at them, struck by how small and delicate they were. For some unknown reason, this made Helena cry for the dead. While she cried, she washed Emma's feet.

Helena dried her tears with the same towel she had used to dry Emma's feet. Her task now was to get the body onto the blanket. As gently as possible, she eased Emma from the bed onto the blanket. She was surprised at how little the large woman weighed. Helena positioned the body in the center of the blanket, then lay Jurina on top of her, the child's face turned to the side, her head resting on Emma's breasts. Helena arranged the girl's hair before taking one last look at Emma, and then covered both with the blanket.

Because there was no coffin, Helena was well aware this portrait in death she had created could not withstand being dragged to the grave. She looked around the dugout and discovered two lengths of rope about twelve feet long, and a ball of twine. The purpose of the ropes was immediately obvious to Helena. They would be needed one more time. She found a knife, cut lengths of twine from the ball, and tied the blanket tightly around the bodies, being especially careful to tie the girl to her mother. It was all Helena could do. The two were now ready for their eternal rest.

Ole dug, thankful there was a light breeze. He had expected this would be his task, and he was no stranger to it. In Norway, he had helped dig graves for his parents, and there was the hole he had dug in the prairie near Clinton. That was the grave which would forever haunt him.

As he dug, Ole thought of the loved ones in his own life, the living and the dead. There was nothing like digging a grave to make a man focus on the fragility of life. With the exception of Nettie, he and Helena had been lucky. He prayed that his luck would continue. The Lord giveth. The Lord taketh away. Blessed be the name of the Lord.

The moon was high above when Helena grabbed the end of the quilt and began dragging the bodies to the doorway. She again was surprised at the lightness of her load. Emma must have been mostly skin and bone. Carefully she exited the door and continued past the horses to the makeshift cemetery. Ole saw her coming. "I can help you," he called.

"No. Finish the grave. I can do this," Helena replied.

Helena reached the grave and saw that it was almost done. "I'll get the ropes to lower her down." She turned and walked back to the dugout.

Ole completed his work and was out of the hole when Helena returned. There were no words. Together they worked the ropes beneath Emma's back and thighs. Ole tied off the ropes. He was not about to save them. He stood up. "Ready?" Helena nodded. They each took a rope, lifted, and gently lowered Emma into the grave. To Helena's relief, Jurina remained securely attached to her mother's chest.

Ole dropped his rope. Helena did the same, then flipped the quilt into the air. It floated down as if guided by an unseen hand and covered the bodies. Neither spoke. They just stood there, both thinking: when will it be my turn?

Ole broke the silence. "She would want you to say a prayer."

Helena closed her eyes. "Dear God, take this wonderful woman and her child to your heavenly home. Give her peace and joy. She deserves it. I know your ways are not our ways, but why was life so difficult and so short for Emma? I don't understand. She was the salt of the earth. She was my angel of mercy. She saved me. Maybe you need another guardian angel. If so, I can think of no one better. But, why couldn't you help her? I don't understand. I … I … can't say anymore. I am too angry at you. Amen."

Helena quickly threw a handful of dirt into the grave. "Ashes to ashes, dust to dust," she said softly, then turned and stomped back to the dugout.

"Amen," Ole whispered, tossing in the first shovelful of dirt.

Helena gathered anything that would burn and placed it beneath the table. She did not know what caused diphtheria, but knew it lurked in this home like a wild beast waiting to pounce. *Burn everything. Kill the beast! Protect any innocent who might be curious enough to stop by.* These were her thoughts as she prepared to cremate Emma's meager possessions.

As the pile grew, so did her anger at the unfairness of life. "Why," she thought, "do some people have so much and others so little? Why does a bitch like Hanna live in a large house and a saint like Emma live in hovel? Why does God not reward the righteous and condemn the evildoers? The Bible says God loves us. If so, how did he show his love for Emma? It makes no sense! There are no answers."

This made Helena more angry. Perhaps her father was right. He said life was nothing more than a crapshoot, a losing game of dice. She did not want to believe that. But standing alone in Emma's miserable dugout, it was hard to believe anything else.

Ole's arms ached when he finished filling the grave. He stuck the shovel in the ground and looked for two sticks. It was foolish, he knew. The first strong wind would blow the cross away, but he tied two pieces of wood together with prairie grass despite that. He said a silent prayer as he placed the cross on the grave, then walked to the dugout.

Helena stood in the doorway. "There is a repeating rifle and a box of shells by the hitching post. Emma wanted you to have the rifle. Get the horses ready. I'm going to start the fire."

Ole picked up the rifle in disbelief. He had heard of such weapons, but never seen one. Never in his wildest dreams did he think he would own one. He wanted to take off his gloves and feel the metal and polished wood, but resisted. That would have to wait. From the corner of his eye, he saw flames in the dugout. Quickly, he picked up the box of shells and led the horses to a stump where it would be easier for Helena to mount Lady.

When she was sure the fire was burning well, Helena exited the dugout and, without a backward glance, mounted Lady and turned for home. Ole jumped on Doll, but before following his wife, he looked back at the hovel Emma had called home for over ten years. The true ugliness of the place was exposed by the flames. Ole shuddered. Emma had simply traded one hole for another.

Helena did not allow Ole to ride beside her. She desperately wanted him close, but asked that he ride at least five yards behind her. She did not want him to touch her, and she knew that if he were close, she could not resist touching him. They both wanted to get home as soon as possible, so they urged the horses into a ground-covering trot. Doll and Lady needed little encouragement. They knew where they were going.

The sun was rising above the eastern horizon and just beginning to generate warmth when Ole and Helena reached their farm. Ole called out, "The tub is in the crib alley. I filled it with water before I left. The water should be fairly warm."

Helena slid off of Lady. She was sore, but so happy to be home. "Thank you. I'll jump in the tub. You take care of the horses and start a fire."

Within minutes, Helena was standing naked by the tub. On a small stand by the tub were towels, a washcloth, and soap. Ole had thought of everything. Well, not quite everything. There were no fresh clothes. In spite of the ordeal of the last two days, Helena laughed as she stepped into the water. It was colder than she expected, but still inviting. Slowly she lowered herself until only her head and shoulders were not submerged. She moaned as her body relaxed. It was the first time in years that she did not have to hurry her bath for one reason or another. "I think I will stay in here forever," she said aloud, then giggled at her own foolishness.

From the crib she could see the cabin and part of the barn. A light ground fog was lifting, wrapping the buildings in a golden hue. Never had her home looked so beautiful. Tears came to her eyes, which blurred the scene and made it even more like a watercolor painting. She then closed her eyes, laid her head back against the tub, and asked God to forgive her anger. "I am truly blessed," she whispered.

Ole's eyes lit up as he entered the crib. "Now there is a lovely sight."

"It feels wonderful." Helena smiled, sinking lower into the tub.

"You have to wash your hair too."

"I know," Helena replied, a jolt of desire awakening her body. Ole was not looking at her hair. "I've just been soaking."

Ole swallowed hard. "Soak as long as you like. I have a fire going. I'll burn your clothes."

"Pick them up with sticks and burn your gloves too."

"Gloves are expensive," Ole argued. "I didn't touch anything."

"You might have. Please burn them. And when you are done, bring me the dress hanging behind the bed."

Ole gave a quick nod, found two sticks, and carried everything Helena had worn out to the fire. Helena began scrubbing herself with lye soap she had made. She was finishing her hair when Ole returned with her dress. He placed it on a sawhorse near the tub. "That's done, gloves and all."

"Thank you," Helena answered, before holding her nose and sinking completely under water. When she came up, Ole was laughing. She laughed too, then did it again. When she surfaced, Ole said, "Keep that up and you'll be swimming in no time."

Helena laughed as she pushed back her long hair. "I'll never be able to swim a stroke, and you know it."

There was a moment of charged silence as husband and wife read each other's thoughts.

"Wash my back." Helena was breathing heavily.

Ole knelt. Helena leaned forward. Ole took the soap and began washing her neck, shoulders, and back. To Helena, each touch of his hand was like a caress. She could not remember ever wanting him more. Her mind told her this made no sense. Hours before, she had buried her best friend. But her body was not listening.

She leaned back and pulled Ole's face to hers. The kiss was long and passionate. His hand found her breast. She moaned, then whispered, "Spread out the towels." Ole trembled as he spread the towels. Helena lifted herself out of the tub and stood proudly before her husband. Water trickled down her lovely body as rays of the morning sun caressed her skin.

"You are a water sprite," Ole said with awe.

Helena knelt before him and took his face in her hands. "I am whatever you want me to be." She kissed him several times, then pulled back, mischief in her luminous eyes. "We're going to have another baby, Ole."

Ole was startled. It was the last thing he expected to hear.

Helena giggled. "Are you happy?"

"Yes!" Ole grinned. "When?"

"In April, I think."

Ole drew her close and hugged her. "That's wonderful news." He paused for a moment, then whispered, "Does that mean we shouldn't …?"

Helena lay back on the towels, pulling Ole to her. "Definitely not." She smiled.

Chapter Twenty-Eight

Berent leaned over the table, his face inches from the scissors, his eyes wide with anticipation that was usually reserved for a birthday or Christmas Eve.

Helena smiled but said sternly, "Sit back, Berent, or I'll cut your nose."

The boy popped his head back so quickly it made Helena laugh. "Are these really my pants, Mama?" he asked for the fourth time.

"Yes."

"When will they be done?"

"By Sunday," Helena answered, finishing the cut. She did not say that there was no way on God's green earth she would ever again take him to church in a dress. "However, if you ever cause another scene in church, it's back into a dress for you!"

"I'll be good, Mama. I promise."

"You'd better be," Helena snapped, attempting to sound tough, but spoiling the desired effect by tousling the boy's curls. She added, "Do you know where the men are cutting hay?"

"Yes, Mama."

"I want you to take them some water. Can you do that?"

Berent jumped down from the chair on which he had been kneeling. "You know I can!" He grabbed the water jar, ran for the doorway, but came to a skidding stop. "What about Martin? Should I give him some too?"

"Well, of course! Why would you even ask such a thing?"

"He's not a man," Berent replied, his face stone-serious. "He's a boy like me."

Helena laughed. "Yes, he's a boy like you, but he is learning to do a man's work. By all means give him a drink."

Berent ran out the door, his skirt flying up around his hips, revealing a cute bare bottom. Helena watched him race to the well. "Yes," she thought, "it is time Berent was in pants." Smiling, she turned her attention back to cutting the material.

It was so good to have the children home. Bertha had kept them for two weeks while Helena and Ole isolated themselves on the farm. They allowed no visitors and did not leave their forty acres. Neither had gotten sick. Thank God!

Helena's smile turned into a frown. The day before yesterday, she had discovered her trip of mercy to Hardin County was being hotly debated in Fairview and the East Settlement. Some were praising her compassion; others condemned her actions as putting their health at risk. Helena hated being the topic of gossip, but she was not sorry about her decision to go. No one should die alone out on the prairie, especially Emma, who had deserved so much more from life than she had received. Helena sighed. If people were going to talk, there was nothing she could do about it. Better they argue about this than laugh at the Berent episode.

"Oh!"

Helena turned to Oline, who was at the sink peeling potatoes. "Did you cut yourself?"

"No, I just dropped a potato," Oline answered. "Is this enough?"

Without looking, Helena said, "A few more."

Oline groaned. "It sure takes a lot of potatoes to make kumla."

"Yes, it does. But just think of how good the kumla will taste."

Big Per had presented Helena with a ham shank which had large chunks of meat still on it, and mentioned that kumla was his favorite food. This came as no surprise to Helena. Ham shanks had arrived before, accompanied by the same words. And, as before, she had been more than happy to make the Norwegian dumplings. Everybody loved kumla.

Helena finished cutting the material, folded it, and put it on top of her sewing basket by the spinning wheel. She then checked the ham shank, which was boiling in a large kettle on the stove. Thankfully, the weather for late August was reasonable, so the fire was not unbearable. She inhaled deeply, breathing in the aroma. Helena dearly loved kumla.

"How about now?" Oline pleaded.

Helena glanced at the pan of water-covered potatoes. "That will do. Put them on the stove."

"Are you going to fix the dumplings after the potatoes are cooked?"

Helena sat in her rocking chair. "No, it's too early. And I am not going to fix the kumla. *We* are going to fix the kumla. It is time you learned how."

Oline's eyes lit up. Learning to cook made her feel very grown up. "Can I put the kumla in the kettle?"

"Yes, but you'll have to be careful. We don't want to lose any."

Oline clapped her hands. Helena laughed. She was well aware that she should enjoy these moments. In a few years, her requests for help would draw complaints, not applause.

Helena picked up the material for Berent's pants, then threaded a needle with black thread. It did not occur to Helena to sit in a chair and do nothing. To her, slothfulness was one of the deadly sins. Oline plopped down on the floor beside her.

"When are you going to start on my dress, Mama?"

"October."

"Not 'til then?"

Helena patted her daughter's head. "Don't worry. I'll have it ready in plenty of time. I don't want you to outgrow it before Christmas."

"What about your dress?"

"Well," Helena said with a smile, "I'm afraid it will have to wait a year. You are going to have a new brother or sister."

"Oh!" Oline said, her hands flying to her mouth. She immediately thought of the squeaking bed and blushed. Helena did not seem to notice. "When will it be born?"

"Late March or early April."

"I hope it's a girl. I have enough brothers."

"I hope so too." Helena laughed. "But I will be satisfied if she or he is healthy."

There was silence for a moment as each thought about the new addition to the family. Then, Oline brought the conversation back to what was really important ... her dress. "Mama, can I have a high, ruffled neckline like the one Mrs. Twedt has on her gray dress?"

Helena was puzzled. "I suppose so. Why?"

"Well, I was thinking," Oline said, biting her lower lip. "Your *solje* would look real nice on my blue dress."

"Why, you little plotter, you!" Helena said, lightly pulling Oline's hair.

"It would! Do you want to see?"

"Yes, I would," Helena answered, knowing full well what Oline said was true.

Oline jumped to her feet and ran to the big rosemal-decorated chest. Within seconds she was back with her dress material and Helena's box. She opened it, ignoring the lock of hair, took out the piece of jewelry, and placed it on the blue cloth. "See! I told you so. It's beautiful!"

Helena smiled. It was beautiful. The lacy, filigreed, sterling silver brooch sparkled against the dark material, reflecting light in every direction. She picked it up and lovingly examined it. The basic section was a delicately carved piece shaped like the number three with the open side down. Above the piece were three tiny crosses. Below were a series of teardrop disks and spoons that made a tinkling sound when moved. She had not worn it for years. "How did you remember this?"

"You showed it to Emma one time. I thought it was the most beautiful thing in the world."

"Oh, that's right. Emma loved it too," Helena said, making the spoons and disks dance. "This was my wedding present from your papa. He had to save a long time to buy it. This solje is real silver. I wore it for the first time on my wedding day."

"You must have been so beautiful."

Helena kissed the brooch. "Your papa thought so. I was very happy."

"Did you wear it with the red vest?"

Again Helena was surprised. "Oh, you have been snooping, haven't you?"

Oline responded with a sheepish grin. "I just thought it's pretty."

"You're right. It is pretty." Helena handed the solje to Oline as she got up from her chair. "Hold this. I'll show you what it all looked like."

Helena pulled the black skirt, white linen blouse, red vest, and matching red cap from the trunk. "I'll lay everything out on the table," she said.

"I didn't know there was a cap!" Oline squealed.

"Oh, yes. The cap matches the vest." Helena laid the cap and clothing on the table. "This outfit is called a *bunal*. It was traditional dress for Norwegian women."

"But you are Finnish."

"True enough. But your Grandmother Branjord made this for me. She was superb with a needle and thread. See these blue flowers embroidered on the hem of the skirt? That is very difficult. And see? She repeated the flowers on the vest and cap."

"What was Grandma Branjord like?"

Helena thought for a moment. "She was a small, pretty woman with a lovely laugh. She was sweet and gentle … like your papa."

Tears welled up in Oline's eyes. "I will never know her, will I?"

"No," Helena answered, giving Oline a hug. "That's the price we pay for moving an ocean away." She thought of her own mother, who had died the previous winter, and swallowed hard. Helena had not been much older than Oline when she had hugged her mother for the last time.

Oline buried her face in Helena's shoulder. Helena held her close, remembering when Oline's tears dampened her waist, not her shoulder. Her little girl was growing up.

"No more tears," Helena said, kissing Oline's hair. "I've shed enough tears for this month." She released her daughter, picked up the cap, and plunked it on her head. "How do I look?"

Oline wiped her eyes with her sleeve and laughed. "Nice. Put it all on?"

"Oh my, no! I am too hot and sweaty."

"Please, Mama! Please!"

"Not today. The skirt is heavy wool. Maybe in the fall."

Oline clapped her hands. "Wear it to church! And the solje too!"

"Oh, I don't know about that," Helena said. "Bunals are old country. Nobody wears them over here."

"Please! You would look so pretty."

Helena shook her head. "We'll see, but I don't think so. Now help me put all this away. We have to get started on the kumla."

Oline stared at the bunal as Helena carefully folded the blouse and skirt. "Can I wear that on my wedding day?"

Helena laughed. "Why? Have you picked out a husband?"

Oline blushed as red as the vest. "No, silly."

"Well, I'm glad to hear it. You're a little young to be thinking about getting married," Helena said as she touched Oline's cheek. "Of course you can wear it. But I doubt if you will want to. In America, girls wear fancy dresses."

"Oh, I will want to! I know I will."

"We'll see. This is a discussion for the future. Right now, we must clear off this table and make kumla."

After the bunal was carefully put away in the chest and the solje in the box, Helena placed a large mixing bowl and a chopping board onto the table. She next drained the potatoes and put the hot pan on a round wooden slab by the chopping board. "Oline, bring me the …" She did not have to finish. Oline had already gathered the flour, baking soda, and salt. "Good girl! Once I get the potatoes diced, you can do the mixing."

Helena chose a large, sharp knife and began chopping the potatoes. "When you make kumla, you have to slice the potatoes as finely as possible. Grinding would be even better, but I don't have a grinder."

Oline watched in awe at the speed with which each potato was chopped into fragments. She was certain she would cut off her fingers if she attempted to cut that fast.

"Whew! That is work," Helena said after finishing the last potato. She wiped her forehead with her sleeve. "Now it's your turn. Put four and half cups of flour into the bowl." Oline did so with great care, which made Helena smile. "That's good. Next, you need three pinches of salt." Oline followed directions. "You had better put in another. Your fingers are smaller than mine. Now, a pinch of baking soda." When Oline had put in the soda, Helena said, "Seven cups of potatoes is next." Performing this task took Oline three times as long as it would have taken Helena, but she nodded her approval. "Well done. Now take the big wooden spoon and mix it all up."

"How many kumlas will this make?" Oline asked as she began to stir.

"About twenty-five."

"That's more than we will need."

"I know. But tomorrow for breakfast we can fry up the leftovers in butter."

"Oooh! I like that best!"

Helena smiled. "Me too."

When the mixing was done, Helena and Oline dampened their hands and began forming the kumla into balls.

"How big?" Oline asked.

"About two and a half inches."

They worked mostly in silence. Every so often Helena would say

"A little bigger" or "A little smaller," until the last dumpling lay on the cutting board.

"Twenty-six! Mama, we made twenty-six."

"That we did, and they look perfect. Now comes the tricky part"

"Putting them in the water," Oline said.

"That's right. We don't want them to fall apart."

Helena crossed to the stove and examined the pork shank. It had been soaking for four hours. "Perfect!" she said as she removed the meatless bone. "The ham has boiled right off the bone."

"Are you going to give the bone to Doggie?"

"Of course. He'll be one happy wolf tonight." Helena put down the bone and picked up the cutting board. "Oline, I want you to put the kumla in the ham broth."

Oline's eyes became wide. "What if I drop one?"

"Then you drop one. It's time you learn. Put a kumla on the wooden spoon."

Oline was trembling as she placed the first kumla on the spoon. She looked up at her mother with eyes that begged for her to do it. Helena smiled her encouragement. "Just guide the point of the spoon down the side of the kettle. You can do it."

The wooden spoon shook as it was lowered, oh so slowly, down to the bottom of the broth. The kumla survived the perilous journey and Oline grinned in triumph. "Good work!" Helena laughed. "Now only twenty-five more to go!"

The immersing time lessened with each dumpling. When Oline was finished, there had been only one casualty. She was exhausted from the tension and gave a huge sigh as she asked, "How do you know when they are done?"

"They rise to the top. It takes about forty-five minutes," Helena said. "So tell your father supper will be ready in an hour."

Oline ran out the door, no longer tired. Eleven-year-olds recover quickly.

Ole and Big Per were already striding for home, scythes on their shoulders. Both were tired, but it was a good tired—the kind of tired one feels after a successful day of hard work.

"Do you need me tomorrow?" Big Per asked.

"No. You've got your own to do. The family and I will load and bring it home."

"You are a blessed man, Ole Branjord."

Ole did not argue. "That I am," he answered with a contented sigh. The season's work was almost done. The oat and wheat crops were safely in the crib; there would be more than enough hay to get through the winter; and, if there were no wind or hailstorms, the corn yield would be sufficient. No creature, two- or four-legged, would go hungry when the snow flew and the ground froze. "We are all blessed," he continued softly. "Look at the abundance here compared to what we had in Norway."

Big Per nodded. "There's no doubt about that. Every year was a struggle to keep hunger from the door."

"And sometimes we lost. I don't miss birch bark soup."

"Amen. The Lord has indeed provided."

The men walked briefly in silence, then Ole said, "Speaking of the Lord, have you been to church lately?"

"I went last Sunday. You were lucky not to be there." Big Per spat on the ground in disgust. "It's getting worse. Before church, some women were actually shouting at each other. And after the service, two of the older boys got into a fist fight. I'm telling you, Ole, it's like a boil about to burst."

"Is there any way to lance the boil?"

"No. Saint Petri is going to split. The problem is that both sides want the building."

"That's understandable. Both sides built it."

Big Per spat again. "What a mess. Are you going Sunday?"

"Yes. It looks like we didn't bring home diphtheria."

"Oh!" Big Per snorted. "That's another thing. Horse-Face Hanna is really stirring the pot on that one. She is saying you and Helena put the whole settlement at risk."

"That doesn't surprise me. Hanna wouldn't help a soul if he were headfirst in a slop barrel."

Big Per grinned. "You have that right." What he did not say was that Hanna also was ratcheting up the gossip concerning Rooster. He felt badly because it was his big mouth that had first spilled out the story. His grin turned into a hard line. He took a deep breath and was about to confess his stupidity to Ole when he saw Oline skipping toward them. "Oh, I wonder what's wrong?"

"I would say nothing," Ole replied. "Girls only skip when they're happy."

Oline waved and shouted, "Mama says kumla will be ready in less than an hour."

Big Per called back, "That's the best news I've heard in weeks!"

"We'll be ready," Ole said. "Have you seen Martin and Berent? I sent them to get the cows."

"They're in the barn," Oline answered as she stopped and waited for the men. "I helped make the kumla."

"Good for you," Ole said, giving her a hug.

"I even put the dumplings into the pot!"

"Whoa!" Big Per said. "I am impressed. Are you sure you won't marry me?"

Oline placed her hands on her hips and cocked her head to the side, a small replica of her mother. Her reply was a hint of the budding woman stirring within her. "Yes, I will marry you. But only if you sell your oxen and start driving horses."

Both men roared with laughter. Oline blushed with pleasure at the male attention.

"What do you say to that offer, big man?" Ole asked.

"I say she is her mother's daughter. Oline, I cannot give up Buck and Pride. Therefore, I must take back my proposal." Oline giggled like the girl she was. "However," Big Per continued, "If you were ten years older, the decision would be different."

"Thankfully, she's not," Ole said, giving Oline another hug. "Go tell Mama that we will be in as soon as the chores are done."

"Yes, Papa," Oline answered, with a smile that melted Ole's heart, and ran for home.

Both men watched. Big Per said, "In a couple of years, you're going to have to build a fence around that one to keep the boys away."

Ole nodded. "But at least I won't have you for a son-in-law."

Ole and Big Per trooped into the cabin just as Helena took the last kumla out of the kettle. The platter of ham was already on the table. "Perfect timing," she said. "Sit!"

"Well, if you insist, Mrs. Branjord."

"I do, Mr. Larson."

Ole sat in his chair and Big Per pulled up two stools across from where the children were scooting down the bench. Helena brought the kumla to her chair, surveying the table as she came. There was coffee and water for the adults, milk for the children, and a bowl of butter next to the ham. Satisfied, she sat, placing the kumla in front of her plate. "Children, say blessings."

The children bowed their heads, but before they could begin, Ole said, "No. Mr. Larson brought the ham shank. I think he should say the blessings."

"I quite agree." Helena smiled.

"All right," Big Per said, bowing his head. "Lord, we thank you for this bounty. We thank you for the loving hands that prepared it. And Lord, most of all, we thank you for the wonderful woman who invented kumla! Amen."

The Branjords erupted with laughter. Big Per grinned. Oh, how he enjoyed eating with this family.

"How do you know it was a woman who invented it?" Helena asked, passing the kumla to Big Per.

"It had to be a woman," he answered as he put three of the dumplings on his plate. "No man could have thought up anything this delicious."

All at the table, including Berent, nodded in agreement. Berent was not quite sure what he was agreeing with, but if had to do with kumla, he was for it.

The ham was transferred from platter to plates, kumla was properly buttered, conversation ceased, and serious eating began. In short order, plates were emptied and refilled. These second helpings were devoured more slowly, as stomachs became contentedly full. Sighs and groans were heard as forks were laid to rest on empty plates.

"You have done it again, Mrs. Branjord," Big Per said, patting his ample midsection. "That is the best kumla I have ever tasted."

"You say that every time." Helena laughed.

"And every time it is true! I thank you."

"You are most welcome. But I have no dessert."

"Of course not! Kumla is its own dessert."

"Amen," Ole said.

Helena got up and poured more coffee for the men and herself. "Oline did much of the work."

"So she told us," Big Per said, winking at Oline. "I asked her to marry me, but she turned me down."

"Well, I should hope so," Helena said with mock seriousness. "You are much too young for her."

Berent was the only one who did not laugh. When Helena sat down, he whispered, "That's not true, Mama. Mr. Larson is old."

Oline and Martin giggled. Big Per raised his bushy eyebrows. "What's that you say, Mr. Branjord? I'm old? Why, I'll have you know that I will be five on my next birthday and get my first pair of pants."

"Oh, you are not!" Berent yelled over the laughter.

Big Per leaned over the table toward Berent. "I'm told your mama is making you a pair of pants. Maybe they will fit me."

"No! Those pants are mine!"

Big Per leaned back on his stool, pouting. "Does that mean I'm going to have to continue wearing a dress?"

The thought of Big Per in a dress made all the Branjords laugh so hard that tears came to their eyes.

"You are so silly, Mr. Larson," Berent said.

Big Per grinned at the boy, then turned to Ole. "Speaking of silly, there was a fellow at Turg's store yesterday who was all upset about some Indians moving this way from the south."

"He must be new. It is probably just a wandering band coming back to Tama," Ole said.

"He said it was a war party."

"Well, if it is," Helena said, "you can play your violin for them."

Big Per laughed. "Well, it worked once. I suppose it could work again."

"Tell us that story, Mr. Larson," Oline said.

"Oh, I think you know my Indian story better than I do."

"I don't!" Martin said. "I've just heard it once. And Berent can't remember it at all, can you, Berent?

The four-year-old looked confused. "I don't know any story about Indians."

"Please, Mr. Larson!" Oline begged.

"Well, if you insist."

"We do!" Oline and Martin said together.

"Me too!" Berent added.

Big Per's grin was almost as wide as he was tall. He loved telling stories. "I can't tell it without my violin."

Oline slid off the bench. "I'll get it!" She picked up the violin case, which was by the door, and handed it to Big Per.

"Thank you, Oline," Big Per said, removing the instrument from the battered case. Oline hurried back to her seat.

The violin was soon tucked under Big Per's chin whiskers. His huge left hand seemed about to swallow the neck, but his fingers caressed the strings as lightly as a those of a delicate woman. He played a scale, adjusted two of the tuning pegs, then lowered the violin to his lap.

"It was late spring of 1851. We had made the big crossing from Stavanger, Norway, and had booked passage on a lake steamer to Green Bay, Wisconsin." Big Per paused and looked directly at Martin. "On which of the Great Lakes is Green Bay?"

"Lake Michigan," Martin replied without hesitation.

"Correct!" Big Per continued, "There were nearly thirty of us. From Green Bay, we wanted to get to Waupaca, where some in the group had relatives. We were told the best way to get there was by riverboat. So we scraped together what little money we had and hired this Yankee who owned a small sternwheeler. Bad decision. He was a shifty-eyed little varmint. Never stopped smiling. Sort of like a weasel. The kind of a fellow you know in your bones not to trust. But we were in a hurry, so down the Winnebago River we went.

"At first everything went fine. But then the river got narrower and filled with floating logs and underwater snags. That Yankee captain wanted to turn back, but I told him he had been paid hard money, and the only way he was turning back was if he wanted to swim!"

Berent clapped his hands and giggled. "Did you hit him, Mr. Larson?"

"No, Mr. Branjord, but I should have. That snake in the grass told us that he had to tie up on the bank for repairs and that we had to unload our baggage. He said the boat had to sit high in the water to fix the hole. I should have known there was something fishy. We had no sooner unloaded our stuff when that miserable Yankee backed off and headed back up the river to Green Bay. So there we were. Out in the middle of nowhere with no shelter and no food."

"What did you do?" Berent asked, his eyes wide with excitement.

Oline and Martin leaned forward. They knew what was coming next.

"Not much we could do. I threw a big rock at the boat and almost hit it, too. That sneaky captain shouted some words at me in English that I'm sure you won't hear in church. And I shouted some words back in Norwegian that my mother didn't teach me."

Ole and Helena laughed. They had heard the story several times, but were as caught up in it as the children. Also, with each telling, there was something new. Neither had known about the rock throwing.

Big Per leaned back on his stools. "Once we got over being angry, we became really worried. It was decided that I was to stay and protect the women and children and our meager belongings, while the rest of the men foraged for food and tried to find help. Well now, wouldn't you know, the men had not even been gone an hour when one of the boys spied a Winnebago war party paddling toward us in their canoes. I knew right away there was too many of them to fight. The children started crying and the women began wailing. Oh, such a noise! We all thought we were going to be scalped, just like the preachers back in Norway had predicted."

"Did they have bows and arrows?" Berent asked.

"Yes, and long knives and tomahawks too. Some even had rifles. I hoped they would paddle by, but they turned right to the shore. They jumped out of their canoes, their faces painted with different colored berries, and glared at us with angry black eyes."

This had become much too scary for Berent. He dove under the table and, within seconds, was crawling into his mother's lap. Helena wrapped her arms around him, kissing his blond curls as he pressed the back of his head against her breasts. Now that he was safe, he whispered, "What happened next?"

"Nothing," Big Per answered. "We just stared at each other. I think they were as surprised by us as we were by them. I knew I had to do something. But what? To this day, I don't know why I thought of my violin, but I went to my chest and pulled it out. I could see the Indians were curious, so I sat on the chest and began to play a hymn. I wanted the women and children to remember the Lord was with us."

Big Per began to play. After only two measures, Oline cried, "'A Mighty Fortress Is Our God'!"

"That's right," Big Per replied, continuing to play. "And it worked! The women and children stopped crying and the Winnebagos were impressed. They weren't glaring at us anymore. I then played a Norwegian folk dance. I told the women to clap in time." Dance music filled the cabin, bringing smiles and loud clapping in time from the Branjords.

"Well, the Indians loved it. A few even did some dance steps, which made the others laugh and point. I kept on playing and, before you knew it, the Indians were sitting on the ground listening. I played every song I knew." Big Per put down his violin. "When I stopped, their leader pointed at me to play more. So I started all over again.

"All at once, a young Indian jumped up and stood over me, demanding my violin. I pretended I didn't understand what he wanted, but he became angry and snatched the violin out of my hand. I wanted to hit him, but was afraid he would break the instrument, so I handed him the bow. He placed the violin under his chin and began to play. The sounds that he made were awful!"

Big Per scraped the bow over the strings, making screeches and shrieks that made the Branjords laugh. "That's exactly what the Indians did. And the more they laughed, the angrier the young man became. He then grabbed the violin by the neck, like he was going to bash someone over the head with it. So, I stood up and snatched both the instrument and the bow, gave him a swift kick in the britches, and yelled 'No!' as loud as I could.

"Well now, I've got to tell you, that got their attention. They all jumped up and grabbed their weapons. I looked the leader in the eye and hugged the violin like it was a baby. He understood, said some harsh words to the young man, and they all sat down again."

"What did you do then?" Berent asked.

"I played some more. I played until the leader stood up. He divided the men into two groups. One group went hunting and the other made lean-tos, not only for themselves but also for us. One was bigger than the rest. The leader let me know that one was for me."

Big Per grinned and played a little jig before continuing. "In no time at all, the hunters came back with a deer. They gutted it. The women got out their kettles and we all had a feast! Those Indians stayed with us for four days and nights. I have never played the violin so long or so often before or since. By the fourth day, I was getting worried. Some of the Indians had taken a real shine to some of the women. Others were teaching the boys how to shoot the bow and arrow. We were in real danger of being adopted! Two of the Indians got into a fight. I think it was over which of them was going to get a pretty sixteen-year-old girl.

"Well, the good Lord was looking out for us. We all heard shouts coming from the woods. The women shouted back. Our men had found a settlement and were returning with a kubberule pulled by oxen. The Indians jumped in their canoes and disappeared down the river. We were saved from being adopted!" Big Per played a short tune that ended with a flourish.

"Thanks to you and your violin," Helena said with admiration, fully aware of what could have happened to those women without his quick thinking.

"What's a kubberule?" Martin asked.

Big Per answered, "It's a wagon with wheels made from narrow disks cut from a log. There used to be some around here, but you never see them now." He opened his violin case, but Ole stopped him from putting the instrument away.

"Play us one more tune. Something slow and easy."

"Happy to." Big Per smiled, putting the instrument to his chin.

Soon the cabin was filled with an old folk melody that made Ole think of Norway's rugged mountains and magnificent fjords. Helena hugged her four-year-old, grateful for her family and snug little home.

Chapter Twenty-Nine

"Maybe nobody's home," Oline whispered.

"Knock again," Martin replied. "You said Mr. Lyngen asked to see me."

Oline rapped harder on the back door. "Mrs. Lyngen, it's me, Oline!"

There was a pause, then the children heard through the open window the sound of footsteps hurrying down the stairs. A disheveled Inga Lyngen opened the door. Both children were startled. Neither had ever seen Inga when she was not perfectly together. Bloodshot, tear-swollen eyes, partially covered by loose, unbraided hair, looked down on the children. The top of her wrinkled dress was unbuttoned. Realizing that Oline and Martin were staring at her, Inga pulled back her hair and clutched her dress. "I'm sorry, Oline. I was resting and forgot about your lesson."

"Do you want me to go home?" Oline asked in a low, frightened voice.

"No! No, of course not. Come in."

The children followed Inga into the kitchen. She turned to Martin. "Are you going to have a lesson too?"

Martin shook his head. "No, ma'am."

"Mr. Lyngen asked me to bring Martin today," Oline said.

Inga slumped slightly and put her hands on a chair as tears filled her eyes. "I don't think you should see him today, Martin. He had a very bad night. I had to use the wooden spoon twice."

Martin was unable to keep the disappointment from showing.

Talking with Mr. Lyngen was exciting. It made him feel important. But he attempted a smile and said, "I hope he feels better soon."

"So do I, Martin." Two tears escaped, flowing slowly down the same path taken by thousands. "He was doing so well. I was hoping … it doesn't matter what I was hoping. Oline, you go do your scales while I make myself presentable."

Before any of the three had time to move, Karl Lyngen called from his room, "Who is there, Inga?"

"Oline Branjord has come for her lesson."

"Is Martin with her?"

"Yes."

"Send him in, please."

Inga paused before asking, "Are you sure?"

"Yes. I want to talk with him."

A genuine smile spread across Martin's face. He started for the front hall. Inga stopped him. "Martin, he … he might look very bad."

The smile remained on the boy's face. "I don't mind. He's my friend."

Inga smiled through her tears and watched the boy disappear into her husband's room.

Karl stood by the heavily draped window, gazing intently at the single ray of light that had fought its way into the room. A candle flickered on the dresser. Martin closed the door and waited. He somehow knew he should not speak. This was another of his gifts: the knowledge of when to talk and when to remain silent, knowledge that many adults never acquire. Finally, Karl turned to the boy. "Come, Martin, sit on the end of the bed."

Martin did so. Karl settled into his chair. The undamaged side of his face was haggard. The scarred side glowed an incandescent red, punctuated by almost invisible metallic dots.

"Did Mrs. Lyngen tell you I had two seizures?"

"Yes, sir. Are you feeling better?"

"I'm feeling tired, but I'm glad you came."

Martin studied Karl's wound. The man saw it was a look of curiosity, not horror. "When you were leading your men in battle, were you a general?"

Karl laughed. "Generals don't often lead charges. I was a captain."

"How did you get to be a captain?"

Karl thought for a moment. "The answer is a big word, Martin. Attrition."

"What does that mean?"

"It means those who ranked above you were killed or wounded. I enlisted as a private. In the first battle, our sergeant was killed. My company captain knew I had been a teacher, so he promoted me to sergeant. Then the lieutenant was wounded, so I became a lieutenant. About a year later, the captain was killed. I replaced him."

"How long were you in the army?"

"Almost three years. The last six months were spent in several different hospitals. But enough about the war. How is your reading coming?"

Martin looked down at his bare toes, ashamed to look at Karl. "I cheated," he whispered.

"Cheated?" Karl said, surprised at the answer. "How did you cheat?"

"By not reading the English. The book became so exciting, I stopped reading the English and finished the Norwegian."

An amused smile exposed a dimple on the undamaged side of Karl's face. "I wouldn't call that cheating. I'd call that getting caught up in the story."

Martin returned the smile. He had thought Karl was going to be angry. "I tried to read a chapter in Norwegian and then the same one in English. My reading in English was so slow, I stopped."

"What did you think of the book?"

"It was terrific! But I didn't like the ending."

Karl placed his finger tips together and quoted, "'It is a far, far better thing that I do, than I have ever done; it is a far, far better rest that I go to than I have ever known.'" Karl smiled at Martin. "You don't agree with that?"

"Sydney Carton should not have had his head cut off. He wasn't even an aristocrat."

"Aristocrat! My, that is a big word. Did you look it up?" Karl asked with admiration.

"Yes." Martin grinned. "It means someone of high birth."

"Good for you! As for Sydney Carton, he died willingly. Why?"

"To save Charles Darnay, who was an aristocrat."

"That's right. But why did he want to save Darnay?"

"Because of Lucy."

"Right again. Sydney Carton was in love with Lucy, who was married to Charles Darnay. Carton switched places with Darnay so Lucy could be happy."

"But what about Carton's happiness? The two men looked just alike. Maybe if the husband had died, Lucy would have fallen in love with Sydney Carton."

Karl sat back in his chair and studied Martin's earnest face. "That is quite adult thinking for someone of your age. Do you feel Carton should have been more selfish?"

"Is it selfish to want to live? I wouldn't want to die just because I loved some girl."

"That last part may change when you get a little older." Karl chuckled. "As for the first part, no, it is not selfish to want to live. Everybody wants to be happy, but that's not the way life is. I think what the author was saying was what the Bible states: 'Greater love has no man than this, that a man gives up his life for his friends.'"

Martin again stared at his toes. He had no answer, but was unconvinced. "I still don't think the ending is fair."

"I see you are not a romantic," Karl said, knowing full well that, unlike Martin, he was. Had he not been a romantic, he would not have become a teacher or wanted to write himself; had he not been a romantic, he would not have enlisted in the army; had he not been a romantic, he might not be sitting in a dark room discussing *A Tale of Two Cities* with an eight-year-old boy. "Martin, the ending may not be fair, but Sydney Carton made a choice. We all have to make choices. Don't be one of those people who go through life expecting it to be fair. You will be constantly disappointed. When I was young …"

Karl's body stiffened; the handsome side of his face contorted in pain; the damaged side glowed a deeper red. He groaned. Martin jumped from the bed. "Do you need the spoon, Mr. Lyngen?"

"I … I don't think so, Martin. Just bring me the bottle and glass."

Martin quickly grabbed both and placed them on the table.

"Would you pour me some, please?"

The bottle shook as Martin poured the whiskey. He handed the glass to Karl, who took several gulps. "Thank you again, Martin."

"Should I get Mrs. Lyngen?"

"No. I just need to rest. You had better go."

Martin fled to the door. He was about to open it when Karl said, "Martin, most of the reading you will do in the future will be in English.

I want you to finish to the English version of *A Tale of Two Cities*. Will you do that for me?"

"Yes, sir."

"Thank you for coming. I enjoy our visits."

Martin gazed through tears at this wounded man he so admired. "I'll come back when I'm finished."

"Thank you. I'll look forward to it."

Martin quietly left the room. Karl finished the whisky the boy had poured, and then refilled the glass.

In the library, Inga was giving Oline her lesson. She was now presentable and in control. "Remember to keep your fingers bent. Let them float across the keys."

Oline sighed. "My fingers don't float. They sink."

Inga smiled, thinking what a joy it was to give this child lessons. "Nonsense. Your fingers are just fine. Play the D scale for me again. Work on giving each key the same touch."

"Scales are boring."

"Yes, they are. But when you can play the scales well, you can play almost any piece of music."

Like every child who has taken piano lessons, Oline sighed, then played the scale.

"That's better, but your thumbs are still too strong and your little fingers too weak. It is important to strike the keys with the same strength. It should sound like a kitten running up and down the keyboard."

Oline thought about the kitten and played the scale again.

"Better! Much better. Do it again and try striking the little finger with more force."

The lesson was interrupted by a loud knock on the front door. "Now who could that be? Nobody ever comes to the front door," Inga said, getting up from her chair. "You continue practicing. I'll see who it is."

Inga hurried from the library, closing the door behind her, and opened the front door. Hanna Signaldahl stood on the porch, a frozen, fake smile painted on her face. Beside her stood an unhappy daughter.

"Mrs. Signaldahl … Elsa. What a surprise."

Indeed it was a surprise. Hanna only spoke to Inga if it was absolutely necessary. She usually just presented the same phony smile and regally passed by. Inga was guilty of two unpardonable sins: living in a house slightly larger than Hanna's, and enjoying the company of Helena Branjord.

"Won't you both come in?" Inga continued, stepping back into the hallway.

"Thank you," Hanna said as she sailed into the house, followed by Elsa.

Inga closed the door. "To what do I owe this visit?"

"Elsa and I have been talking …" Hanna stopped abruptly when she heard scales being played in the library. "Are you giving a lesson?"

"Yes."

"Well, that's why we're here. Elsa would like to start taking lessons. Wouldn't you, dear?"

"Yes, Mama," Elsa replied, with all the enthusiasm produced by a trip to the dentist.

Inga smiled at the girl. She, of course, had seen it all before. One look at Elsa's face told her this was another case of a mother dragging her unwilling daughter to the piano teacher. "I think that could be fun, Elsa." She then turned to Hanna. "Won't you both be seated in the parlor until I finish the lesson?"

Hanna arched her eyebrows, which only served to elongate her face. "I'm sorry, but I don't find that acceptable. I'm in a hurry to get home."

Inga's eyes narrowed, but her lips smiled. "Well, then you had better be on your way. I believe it is my responsibility to give any student her allotted time." She stepped to the library but paused at the door. "If you choose to wait, make yourselves comfortable in the parlor."

Before Hanna could speak, Inga entered the library and closed the door. Hanna was livid. "The nerve of that woman," Hanna thought. "How dare she decide that a piano lesson to some girl was more important than talking to me! That is what is wrong with this country. People don't know or have forgotten how to act to their betters!"

"Are we going home, Mama?" Elsa asked hopefully.

"No!" came the sharp reply. "We'll wait in the parlor."

Elsa reluctantly followed her mother into the parlor, where Hanna sat in the middle of a needlepoint loveseat which was positioned under the front bay window. "Sit in that chair!" Hanna ordered, pointing to a Queen Anne chair in the corner next to a round walnut table. Elsa did as she was told.

"Sit like a lady, Elsa, and spread out your dress as I have," Hanna snipped. Again Elsa followed instructions, knowing that not to do so meant instant retribution in the form of verbal abuse or a slap in the face. She actually preferred the slap. To the average observer, the girl's submission was complete; but inside a rage was incubating that one day would explode like a keg of black powder.

Mother and daughter wore matching ivory-colored cotton dresses with dark green sashes. Their straw bonnets were tied with ribbons that matched the sashes. Hanna's neckline was more daring, which she had requested so as to draw attention away from her face.

Hanna fumed as she looked over the room. She was forced to admit it was tastefully done. The walls were covered with delicate, flowered wallpaper. The ceiling was a plain white plaster, which helped reflect the light from a crystal chandelier that, much to Hanna's disgust, was larger than the one in her parlor. She would have to do something about that. In the center of the room, sitting on a Persian rug in front of the fireplace, was a sofa and two facing Queen Anne chairs. A highly polished walnut coffee table sat in front of the sofa. Above the fireplace, a large mirror reflected two landscape paintings on the opposite wall that looked to be originals. Hanna had no original paintings. That was something else she would have to correct.

The minutes passed. The scales continued, flowing more smoothly with each run. "She plays good," Elsa said.

"Yes." Hanna sniffed. "She probably has been taking lessons for some time."

Having to listen to the scales made Hanna more angry. She was not musical. The only time she enjoyed music was when she was dancing. Listening to a concert or recital bored her to death. Of course, back in Norway she had regularly attended both. Attendance was expected and, more importantly, such events were a chance to show off the latest fashions.

Elsa was not musical either, although, unlike her mother, she could stay on pitch when singing the hymns in church. And, she had made it clear to Hanna that she was not interested in taking piano lessons. So why were the two sitting in Inga Lyngen's parlor? Because of that Branjord woman!

Two weeks ago, Hanna had overheard that Oline Branjord was taking lessons and was doing exceptionally well. The possibility of Oline outshining her Elsa at anything was unthinkable. The very idea of having to attend an event where Oline received applause made Hanna's skin crawl. She had obsessed about this for days, until arriving at a plan that would end the lessons for Oline and begin them for Elsa. The fact that Elsa was not interested was of no importance. Also, it was of little import whether or not she learned to play well. Stopping Oline from succeeding was all that mattered.

The grandfather clock in the hall struck the half hour. Hanna jumped to her feet. Waiting any longer was out of the question. She almost ran to the library door, and was about to knock when the door opened, revealing Inga and Oline.

"You!" Hanna snarled, glaring at Oline. "I waited for your lesson?"

Oline looked up at Hanna, first with surprise, then fear. Inga put her arm around the girl's shoulder. "Go on home, dear," Inga said. "You did very well."

Oline took a step forward, but was blocked by Hanna, who suddenly feigned fear and jumped back, almost knocking Elsa down.

"Don't you touch me!" Hanna cried.

Now it was Inga's turn to be surprised. "What on earth is the matter with you?"

"Nothing is the matter with me. But she is probably diseased!"

"Oh, that's ridiculous!" Inga said.

"It is not! What her mother did was ridiculous! She could have spread diphtheria throughout all of north Story County!"

Inga felt Oline tremble and drew her close. "What Helena did was noble. She went to the aid of a dying friend."

"Noble!" Hanna shouted. "What she did was reckless and stupid!"

"My mama is not stupid!" Oline cried.

Hanna glared down at this girl who was too smart, too talented, and too pretty. "Your mother is something I can't say in front of a lady."

Oline burst into tears. Inga said, "That's enough! Oline, go home." The girl did not hesitate. Her path was clear. She ran to the kitchen and out the back door. Inga watched her go, then turned to Hanna. "I think you and Elsa should leave."

"Leave?" Hanna said, arching her back in an attempt to intimidate Inga. "We haven't discussed Elsa's lesson."

"I'm sorry, but I don't have time for any more students."

"Oh, you will have time. I insist you drop all of your other students and devote your time to Elsa. For that, I will pay you seven dollars per week."

Inga's jaw dropped. "Seven dollars! That's more than a hired man makes per week."

"Seven dollars." Hanna nodded smugly. "I am sure that will compensate you for your lost income."

"It is far too much," Inga answered, growing slightly flushed. "But I must refuse your offer. I will not give up my students. Especially Oline Branjord."

Hanna was surprised and angry. No one refused her anything. "Why not? They are just simple peasant girls. I'll pay you ten dollars!"

"I don't care if you pay me twenty!" Inga replied. "I will not take Elsa as a student for two reasons. First, I can tell from her expression that she is not interested in lessons. And second, I do not like you, Mrs. Signaldahl. Now please leave!"

Hanna exploded. "How dare you talk to me like that! How dare you! My father is a banker and mayor of our city!"

"I don't see what that has to do with me giving piano lessons to Elsa," Inga said between clenched teeth. "Please leave."

"My husband will hear of this!" Hanna roared. "So will Reverend Amlund. So will the church elders. You won't be church organist for long!"

"Are you threatening my wife?"

Hanna whirled to see Karl standing in front of his bedroom door. His clothes were disheveled, his hair mussed, and because of the light, his good eye was a slit of rage.

Elsa screamed. She had only heard of this strange, disfigured man who lived in the dark. Seeing him would give her nightmares for years. She fled out the front door.

Hanna backed herself into the wall, feeling the same fear as her daughter. She too had never seen Karl Lyngen's wound. The sight made her sick. "Don't you come near me."

Karl did just that. When he stopped, his face was only inches from Hanna's. "Don't you come into my house and threaten my wife."

Hanna was now trembling. The smell of his oozing wound and whisky breath made her knees buckle. "Don't … don't you touch me."

"I wouldn't think of it," Karl whispered. "On second thought, you don't seem to like my face. Perhaps I should put what is left of my cheek against yours."

"No! No! I will report you!"

"To whom?" Karl asked, moving even closer. "Your husband? How many men has he killed?"

All the color drained from Hanna's face. She was too frightened to say a word.

Karl stepped back. "If you cause my wife any trouble, you and your husband will deal with me. Understood? Now get out of my house!"

Hanna stumbled twice on her skirt, but somehow made it to her buggy, where Elsa waited, face in hands.

Tears welled in Inga's eyes. Karl gently wiped them away with his hand. "She won't bother you again," he said softly, and then returned to his room.

Inga retreated into the library and sat on the piano bench. Silent tears continued to fall. The looks of horror on the faces of Hanna and Elsa were like knives to the heart. They considered her sweet husband a monster. But that was not why she was crying. She was crying because a part of her agreed with them.

Chapter Thirty

Saul Jaeran stomped away from the Twedt family toward Saint Petri Church. Hans Twedt, his face red, his fists clenched, and the veins in his neck bulging, glared after him. The only thing keeping him from chasing the departing man down was Julia's firm grip on his arm. Ole and Hattie had stepped back into the family wagon, expecting an eruption of their father's famous temper. Able, Joseph, and Jane were hiding behind a rear wheel. Two-year-old Sam clung to Julia's skirt. Carl, wide-eyed in Julia's arms, was wise enough, although just one, not to utter a sound.

Julia whispered, "Please don't hit him. He isn't worth it."

"He isn't worth a pile of shit!" Hans snarled, louder than he intended.

The older children gasped. Such language was not allowed in the Twedt household.

"Hans!" Julia hissed. "We're at church."

"I don't care. It's God's truth!"

Julia frowned, but actually was glad for the outburst—not only because she agreed with her husband, but because she felt his body relax.

Jonas Duea hurried up to the Twedts. "Good morning, Julia, Hans. I'm sorry. I heard what he said."

"And so did everyone else! I swear, Jonas, if that man calls me a papist one more time, I'm going to pound him in the ground and use him as a fence post."

"I understand. Thank you for not hitting him."

Julia pointed her finger at Jonas. "That man is a menace! He walks around under a cloud named trouble."

"I know. I know." Jonas sighed. "He just makes matters worse."

Hans spat on the ground, barely missing Julia's shoe. "How can they get any worse? Half the congregation isn't talking to the other half. And look at all the missing wagons! People are staying home. I wish I had."

Jonas kicked a rock, sending it flying. "There has to be an answer. If only Amlund wouldn't be so stubborn."

"You're wrong, Jonas. He's between a rock and a hard place. If he stops wearing the robe and reading the absolution, one group will be happy and the other will be madder than a flock of ruptured ducks!"

Jonas kicked another stone. "I suppose you're right, Hans. Maybe Elling Eielsen can straighten it out."

"Is he coming for sure?"

"Yes. Three weeks from Friday. He'll be speaking at the Shaldahl School, Seven seven o'clock. Will you come?"

"I don't know. From what I hear, he's a pot-stirrer, not a peacemaker."

"Come on, Hans! Keep an open mind. Give him a chance."

Julia felt the tension return to Hans's arm. She quickly asked, "Are women invited?"

"I don't see why not," Jonas replied.

Hans was surprised. He looked at Julia. "Do you want to go?"

"Of course. He's a famous preacher."

Jonas grinned. "I think you're going."

"So do I," Hans grunted.

Julia patted her husband's arm. "Oh, don't be that way. It might be fun."

"That's what I'm afraid of," Hans replied.

"We'll talk about it after the service," Jonas said as he started toward the church.

The Twedt family looked expectantly at Hans, who in turn stared at the church he had helped build. Finally, Hattie asked, "Are we going to church, Papa?"

Hans looked down at Julia, who gave a slight nod. "Well, we're here," he said. "Let's go."

As the Twedts moved to the church, the Branjords approached the property at a fast trot. They were late. Helena hung on to her bonnet with one hand and the seat with the other. The children stood, clinging to the wagon's sideboards, grinning with delight. Ole was not grinning. He hated not being on time.

It had been one of those mornings where anything that could go wrong, did go wrong. One of the cows, probably Maud, had knocked down a fence rail, and both had wandered out onto the prairie. The calves and sheep had followed, but the sheep decided the cornfield was much more to their liking. Thankfully, Doll and Lady had stayed in the pasture. With the help of the horses, the escapees were rounded up. But, by the time the fence was repaired and the cows milked, Ole was muttering words under his breath that Martin pretended not to hear.

Helena confronted the next crisis. While starting the fire to prepare breakfast, she heard cries coming from inside the chimney. She had Oline crawl into the fireplace and look up. The girl screamed. Beady eyes stared back at her. A raccoon had come to call ... again. Ole was summoned. He put a ladder up against the chimney, climbed up, and reached down. Naturally, since it was one of those days, the animal was stuck just beyond his reach. Ole retreated down the ladder, took the broom, and pushed up from inside the fireplace. The upward force somehow enabled the raccoon to turn around and scamper out of the chimney. The chimney was now clear, but breakfast was delayed, and Ole was covered with soot. He looked like a minstrel-show performer covered in blackface. Berent was the first to laugh. He was soon joined by his siblings. Helena almost succeeded in not laughing. Ole looked in the mirror. Yes indeed, it was one of those days.

Ole pulled the horses to a halt by the Twedt wagon. Everyone piled out and Ole tied Doll and Lady to a hitching rack. They all hurried to the church. Inga was just settling herself at the organ when they reached the door.

Since this was a Lutheran Church, all of the back pews were taken, forcing the Branjords to parade to the front. Four members of the family were embarrassed, one was proud. Berent had a huge grin on his face as he swaggered down the aisle, thumbs tucked into the waistband of his new pants. Smiles followed his progression like a wave washing up to the shore. Ole found a place by Jonas Duea. Helena had to walk to the third pew from the front, where she, Oline, and Martin quickly sat down.

Berent did not. Much to Helena's horror, her four-year-old continued to the front and up the three steps to where Reverend Amlund sat by the pulpit. "I've got pants!" he said loudly.

Reverend Amlund succeeded in keeping his smile from becoming a laugh. "I see that. Congratulations."

"My mama made them."

"They're very nice, Berent. Now I think you should go sit down."

Berent turned to the congregation. "I've got pants!" he repeated before hopping down the three steps.

An almost unheard-of event then occurred. The members of the Saint Petri congregation laughed. It was as rare for Norwegian Lutherans to laugh in church as for a blizzard to strike in July, but that is what happened. Some even applauded.

Blushing furiously, Helena grabbed Berent and sat him down on the pew. However, Berent was not quite finished. He spied Joseph Twedt at the end of the pew. "See, Joseph? I have pants too."

"I see," Joseph replied, standing up on the pew. "Mine are better."

It was Julia's turn to blush as more laughter rocked the church.

Inga Lyngen settled things down by playing the introduction to the first hymn. As the congregation rose to sing, Reverend Amlund marveled at the change in atmosphere. The tension in the building before Berent's announcement had been almost painful. It had been as if the church were ready to explode. Now the tension had disappeared, along with the grim faces and mistrustful eyes. Reverend Amlund felt himself relax. He joined loudly in the singing. It would be a good service. He glanced down at Berent and thought of the Bible verse, "A little child shall lead them."

The hymn ended. The service began. The absolution was given. No problem. The liturgy was completed. The lessons were read. Reverend Amlund gave his sermon. Most of the congregation felt it was thoughtful, appropriate, and well delivered. Two women sat with hands folded, eyes raised, and comprehended not a word.

Helena

Well, it has happened again. The Branjords are going to be the talk of Story County! Why couldn't he have just sat down? Oh, no! Not Berent! He is snuggling next to me and being as good as gold. Every time I look at him, he gives me that angelic smile. Lord, help me survive this … this … absolutely adorable scamp!

He is so happy. A single pair of pants can banish all the clouds and storms from his little world. Was I ever that happy as a child? No. There were too many dark days in my world. Too much dread. Too little food. Certainly not as a young woman. Norway was one trial after another.

I didn't know what happiness was until it arrived in the form of a shy Norwegian man. And to think I have Hanna to thank for it.

Hanna! That miserable witch! She made Oline cry. What was it the witch said about me? Oh, yes, not only was I stupid, I was something she couldn't say in front of a lady! Talk about the kettle calling the pan black! I have no doubt she and Ingvald are making the two-backed monster. Rooster may be a worthless snake, but he told the truth about that!

Should I confront Hanna? Tell her what Rooster said? Do it in front of her followers? It would be grand revenge, but would it just make matters worse? Probably. She always wins. What was it Papa used to say? It was crude but true. "Never get in a pissing contest with a jackass." That's what he said. And he's right. Especially if the jackass has money. No, Hanna would just twist everything around so that it would hurt me more than her. That is her great talent.

Keep your mouth closed, Helena. Swallow the bile. Confronting her will just cause pain for your family and hers. Poor Emil. He has to live with her. I wonder if he regrets following her around like a puppy before they were married. All she did was ridicule him, then poof! She married him. I'll never understand that! And then there's Elsa. I think she has it in her to be quite nice. And pretty too. Luckily, she has not been cursed with Hanna's face. Emil's either, for that matter. God was good to her. I think her best features are her eyes. She has beautiful dark-brown eyes ... almost black. Her eyes remind me of someone else. Who could it be? Not her grandfather. Not her uncle. Not her ... "Oh!"

Everyone is looking at me. Did I say that out loud? Oh my! Lord, forgive me for not listening to the sermon. Oh my! Oh my! Now I understand. I understand it all! It all makes sense.

Hanna

That woman! She has done it again! Made herself the center of attention. I'm sure she put her son up to it. Of course! She told Berent to go up to Reverend Amlund. It was her idea. The boy would never have thought of it by himself.

The whole congregation loved it! The woman next to me whispered, "Isn't he adorable?" I smiled and nodded. What else could I do? He was adorable. I glanced over at Emil. I saw him laughing. He would love a son. I know he wonders why we have had just one child. Little does he know, and he's too stupid to suspect.

He knows nothing about Elsa's birth in Chicago. I never told him about the pain, the endless labor, all the blood I lost. The doctor thought I was going to die. I did too. I actually wanted to die. Oh, God! The pain! And then she came ... along with half of my insides. No more children for me. Not that I really wanted them. Children are a bother. Emil still talks about having a large family. The fool! How can he not know I can barely stand to have him touch me? Even if I were still fertile, there would be no more children. At least by him! He is such a mouse. The only thing he's good at is making money. I suppose I should be thankful for that.

There is a big plus side to not being able to conceive. You can have all the sex you want, whenever you want, and not have to worry about getting a fat belly. It is very freeing. Especially if you have a dull husband like Emil. Not that Ingvald is much more exciting. But he has a wonderful, hard body. That's all I am interested in. He feels so good inside of me!

Whoo! Careful, Hanna, you're in church. Don't get all in a state. That will have to wait until tomorrow. I will have to think of way to make Emil go to Nevada and take Elsa along. Ingvald and I will have the farm to ourselves. Maybe we'll use the bed. No, I don't want Ingvald to get any ideas. He already is too familiar with me when Emil is around. The haymow is better. Besides, there is a delicious naughtiness about doing it there. And now that I had Rooster fired, we don't have to worry about him sneaking around.

Rooster! He's even more worthless than my brother. Neither one could manage a simple rape. And Rooster had to tell Helena about me and Ingvald. I know everyone in the settlement has heard the story. I'm sure she's the one spreading it. Thank heavens there is no proof. I just say it is a lie started by that Finnish woman. No one will believe her rather than me. At least, no one who means anything.

What was that? Helena made some sort of sound. I look over my shoulder and see she is staring at me. Her eyes are large ... like she just discovered a secret. I turn forward again. My heart is thumping. It is about me! I know it is. There is no way she can prove anything about me and Ingvald. No way! Relax, Hanna.

Oh, how I hate that woman! Why did she have to come here? Just to torment me, that's why! She and her talented, adorable children. I hate her! And to think some are saying she's a saint for going to help her friend. She's no saint. She's a fool! No one in her right mind would risk getting diphtheria to help a friend. Perhaps a family member; certainly not just a friend. Unless … unless she was more than a friend. What if they were lovers? Yes! That's it! They were lovers. Oh, I can't wait to tell someone!

What? Oh, people are standing. It is time for the closing hymn. It is time to sing praise to our Lord. Thank you, Lord, for the insight about Helena. I wonder what the sermon was about?

A large group of women, including Bertha, Julia, and Martha, were gathered about Helena. All were laughing. "Thank you for being so kind," Helena said. "I was so embarrassed I wanted to crawl under the pew."

"How about me?" Julia said. "When Joseph stood up and said, 'Mine are better,' I could have died."

This produced a new round of laughter.

Martha shook her head. "I have never seen a boy so happy to get his first pair of pants. Have any of you?"

All agreed they had not. Julia said, "I thought Joseph was proud, but Berent has him beat."

Helena sighed. "I don't know about that boy. Berent is … well, Berent is just Berent."

More laughter. More nods. "He's a charmer, that's what he is," one of the women said. "Can you imagine what he'll be like when he is a man?"

Eyes rolled and lips smacked.

"I don't want t even think about that." Helena laughed.

But some of the women did. Those with little girls could not help but think about the beautiful grandchildren he might father.

Hanna stood with her followers nearby. The gales of laughter infuriated her. She also noticed her group was smaller than the one gathered about Helena. This she could not endure. She strode over to confront Helena, almost knocking Bertha over in the process. There was no apology, only angry words. "Helena, I know you think what your son did was cute, but I found it to be disgusting. That is no way to behave in church!"

Helena stepped back, too surprised to respond.

Martha Tjernagel was not. "Oh, don't be such an old stick! He was adorable and you know it."

"Perhaps you think so. I thought he was sacrilegious!" Hanna bore in on Helena. "As for you, Helena, I know you put him up to it. You told him what to do."

"I did not! I was embarrassed. I had no idea he would do that!"

"If that's true, Berent has no manners. I suggest you teach him some!"

"You're a fine one to talk about manners," Bertha shot back. "You almost pushed me to the ground. Maybe you should learn some manners."

"How dare you!" Hanna blurted. "My manners are impeccable. You were in my way!"

Now Helena was angry. "I realize Berent's manners are not impeccable, Hanna. Neither are mine. We'll both work to reach your lofty level."

Hanna stepped back as if she had been slapped. "Don't you call me Hanna. You will address me properly. I am Mrs. Signaldahl to you!"

"I will call you Hanna until you call me Mrs. Branjord."

"You were my maid!"

"No. I was your aunt's maid. And even a maid deserves to be treated with respect."

Hanna took another step back. She saw the hostility in the other women's faces, even the faces of her friends. She realized she had crossed a line. Many of these women had once been maids. "I … I agree that maids deserve respect. I am angry with you because you have been spreading nasty rumors about me and Ingvald."

A gasp came from the women. Helena glared at Hanna as she took a step forward. "I have said nothing about what Rooster told me. Martin was there. He told Big Per. I am sorry that Big Per told others."

Hanna snarled, her face contorted like a rabid animal. "Oh, of course! Blame it on Big Per! You're so saintly you wouldn't think of gossiping."

"I am not saintly, Hanna. But I am closer to it than you are."

Helena turned to leave, but Hanna yanked her around by grabbing her shoulder. "Why? Because you went to help a dying friend. That was stupid! You put us all at risk."

"Perhaps it was stupid. But it was something I had to do. In Hardin

County I became very sick. For weeks Emma came every day. She nursed me and took care of Oline. Without her, I would have died."

Hanna sneered at Helena. "How touching. I still can't see anyone risking her life for a mere friend. But for a lover? Now that's another thing."

The women gasped again, all putting a hand to their mouths. Helena turned pale. "What are you saying?"

"You know perfectly well what I'm saying." Hanna turned to the other women. "Oh, don't be so shocked. I've heard that's not unusual for Finnish women."

Tears of anger appeared in Helena's eyes. Hanna took this as a sign of weakness and smile contemptuously. Helena took two steps forward, putting her face only inches from Hanna's. "You and I are going to have a private conversation, Hanna. I'm going to walk to the back of the church. You will follow!"

"Why should I have a private conversation with the likes of you?"

"Because if you don't, I'll say my piece in front of all these fine ladies. It concerns Norway." Helena paused, then whispered, "I know."

Hanna's stomach twisted into a knot of churning acid. She could taste the bile as she watched Helena stride, head up, shoulders back, to the rear of the church. "What could she know?" Hanna thought. No one in America knew Hanna's darkest secret. No one! Yet Helena knew something. Had she found out? The question struck fear deep into Hanna's soul, fear she hid by manufacturing a phony smile and saying, "I suppose I need to go find out what lies she intends to spread about me."

When Hanna reached Helena behind the church, she had regained some of her composure. "Make this quick, Helena. I want to get home."

"I will. Elsa is not Emil's child."

Hanna turned pale. Her worst fears were realized. "How dare you! You can't prove that."

"I think I can, Hanna. I never could understand your marriage to Emil. When I worked for your aunt, I often heard you making fun of him, laughing at him, calling him your lovesick lap dog. You said you could not stand him. At the same time, you were praising Johannas to the skies. You were madly in love with him. Then, in February, Johannas disappeared. He had a very good job at the bank, yet just left town. A month later you married Emil, and a month after that left for America."

"That proves nothing."

"Not yet. When you arrived in Chicago, you stayed there and Emil came here to build your home. He was not in Chicago when Elsa was born. She told me her birthday was December twenty-eighth. I happened to mention that to Julia Twedt. She said that was not possible because when you came in April, the baby was at least six months old."

Hanna's lips trembled. "That is not true. She was three months!"

"Oh, no! Emil may not know the difference between a three-month-old baby and one that is six months, but Julia Twedt knows, and so does every other mother in Story County." Helena paused for a moment, enjoying the fear written in bold type across Hanna's face, then continued. "Elsa was conceived in January. You knew you were with child in February. Johannas wouldn't marry you. He left. You married Emil in March and sailed for America in April, before you began to show. I'm sure you told Emil that Elsa was a honeymoon baby."

Hanna appeared about to faint. She leaned against the church. "How ... how did you find out?"

"Elsa's eyes. She looks nothing like Emil, but she does look like Johannas. She has his eyes. Those beautiful dark eyes."

"What are you going to do?"

"That depends on you. You have spread lies about me here and in Norway. You told your brother and Rooster that I like rough sex. Both tried to rape me. If you stop lying and gossiping about me, I will do nothing. I will say nothing. But if you continue, I swear before God I will stand in front of the Saint Petri congregation and tell the whole sordid story."

In a last, futile effort to save what little dignity she had remaining, Hanna whispered, "You have no real proof."

"Your daughter is living proof. And if Emil decides to investigate, I'm sure the doctor in Chicago has records of Elsa's real birthday."

Hanna sagged like a leaking sack of grain. Tears rolled down her cheeks. Her reputation lay in the hands of the woman she hated most.

"One more thing," Helena added. "From now on you will address me as Mrs. Branjord. Understand, *Hanna*?"

Hanna nodded. Helena walked to the wagon where Ole and the children waited. Other wagons were leaving the churchyard. On some of them sat women who stared at Helena with unrestrained curiosity.

"What was that all about?" Ole asked.

Helena climbed up to the seat. "Something between Mrs. Signaldahl and me."

Ole slapped the reins. Doll and Lady stepped out for home. "Something that is none of my business."

"Correct," Helena said, smiling and patting his arm.

The two were silent until they reached the ford. Then Helena began humming in her off-key fashion. Ole said, "You seem pleased with yourself."

"I am."

Ole laughed. "Sort of like … what is that old saying? Oh, yes. Like the cat who swallowed the canary."

"I did not swallow a canary." Helena grinned. "I swallowed an old crow!"

Helena

Dear Sister,

I have not received a letter from you since April. I hope everyone is well. Please write as often as you can. I do so miss hearing from you.

It is now September. The summer heat is gone, which is good, but the coming of fall means my flowers are dying. The prairie is beginning to turn a golden brown. Winter is not far off. I know what you are thinking! Your winters in Finland are much longer than ours. But I think ours are colder. You have those beautiful, huge trees to break the wind. The only thing between the North Pole and us is grass!

Praise the Lord, we have had a good year. The oat and wheat crops were excellent. I will have more flour than I need. We almost lost the corn, but rain came in time. Potatoes and squash look good. In another month, we will be butchering a hog. There will be no hunger in the Branjord home. We are truly blessed.

The children are well and growing like weeds. Oline and Martin are back in school. They both like their new teacher and are doing well. Oline is taking piano lessons from our church organist. She loves it. I am told she is quite good. I wish we could afford a piano so I could hear her. Martin is reading a long book … in English! Can you believe it? They are teaching English in school, but he is way ahead of everyone else. He is also getting good at understanding and speaking English. About a week ago, a Yankee stopped by and asked directions. Ole and I couldn't understand a word. Martin jabbered away and pointed to Ames. The man thanked him and gave him a penny! Ole and I decided then and there that this winter Martin will teach us some English. I hope he is patient with us.

As for Berent, that little stinker has been more of a stinker than usual. In my last letter I told you he had been pestering me to make him pants. Well, in July, a friend of his got pants. Berent created such a scene in church that Ole took him outside and spanked him. I have never been so embarrassed. After that, I had no choice but to make him pants. The first time he wore them to church, he walked right up to Reverend Amlund and told him and the whole congregation that he had pants. Everyone laughed. Some even applauded! As I have said before, it is good thing God made that boy so cute, otherwise he would never survive!

Speaking of children, you are about to have another niece or nephew. Delivery should be in late March or early April. Oline wants a sister. Berent wants a brother. Martin doesn't care much which it is. Ole and I would like a girl, but we'll both be happy if it is just normal and healthy. There has been no morning sickness this time. I guess my body is getting used to having babies.

July was a very sad month for me. I lost my dear friend, Emma. She and her entire family died of diphtheria. I was able to be with her at the end. She had such a hard life, living out there on the prairie in a dugout. She was alone so much. Being a settler is harder for women than men. Even though I live only two miles from Fairview, I often get lonely. Many times I go from Sunday to Sunday without talking to another woman. I don't know how Emma stood it. Life is so unfair. I do not understand how our loving God could allow such a sweet, giving person like Emma to live such a wretched life. But then, you and I know all about wretched lives. Put some flowers on the family graves for me.

My, this letter is getting long. I wish we could sit all night and talk and talk … in Finnish! I haven't spoken Finnish for so long, I don't know if I remember how. I hope you are still thinking about coming to America. I would love to have you close.

I am enclosing ten dollars. I know you can use it.

I love you,
Helena

P.S.

I just reread your last letter. You asked about washing clothes. Most women wash clothes three to six times a year. They wash in the spring, summer, fall, and at Christmas. I am considered a Clean Queen because I wash every month during the summer. However, my neighbor Bertha is worse than me. She washes once a month all year! Even I think that is excessive.

Love,
H.B.

Chapter Thirty-One

Ole ripped the husk halfway down the ear of corn. He grunted his approval. It was well formed and solid. The crop was made. He pushed the husk back over the golden kernels and said a quick prayer of thanks. If the good Lord saw fit not to send a hailstorm or strong wind, this crop would be better than he had expected. It might even be the best he had planted.

The good Lord. Saint Petri. The quarrel. Ole spat on the ground. He and Helena seldom had words, but the previous night had been one of those times. The argument was the reason he was in the cornfield as the sun set on what had been a glorious early September day, instead of sitting on the bench smoking his pipe. Helena had barely spoken to him all day, and had glared at him during supper. The usual warmth of the cabin had turned to glacial cold. The children did not know what to think or how to act. It was all that damn Elling Eielsen's fault!

Ole had no desire to go to the Shaldahl School, but Helena wanted to hear the famous itinerant lay preacher, and he had promised Hans and Julia Twedt that he would attend. The two couples had sat squeezed together, but felt fortunate to have seats. The back and side walls were lined two and three people deep.

Eielsen was older than people expected. He was in his mid-sixties, rather stooped, with graying hair and beard. There was nothing really special about the man until he began to preach. Then his body straightened, his voice thundered, and his eyes flashed. It was a true "hellfire and damnation" sermon. Drinking was a sin. Dancing was a sin. Attending the theater was a sin. All worldly pleasures were the playground of the devil. The only hope for salvation was to repent and beg for mercy from an angry and just God.

Eielsen vented nothing but disdain on the Norwegian Lutheran Church. It was a hypocritical organization run by power-hungry clergy, who dressed themselves in fancy vestments and believed they had the power to forgive sins. These men, he bellowed, were false prophets, whose aim in America was to create a state church. There was no need for ordained clergy, he cried. Everyman is a minister. Everyman can spread the gospel. Everyman can administer communion. And if a congregation calls a minister, the congregation should dictate what it wants the man to do, not some bishop in Norway. He closed by heaping scorn on the liturgy as an outdated remnant of the Roman Catholic Mass and a tool of the pope.

When Eielsen sat down, Saul Jaeran jumped to his feet and applauded. Most of the people joined him. At that moment, Ole knew any hope for compromise at Saint Petri was dead.

The quarrel with Helena began as a discussion on the journey home, but quickly turned into an argument. The argument became more and more intense, spreading like a virus to other grievances, some dating back to the voyage from Norway. It ended with Ole snarling and Helena in tears. The last words belonged to Helena. "You don't care what I think and never listen to me!" She spent the rest of the way home in stony silence, thinking dark thoughts about Norway, the Lutheran church, and Ole Branjord.

Ole kicked a clod of dirt and started back for the cabin. He reached the porch oblivious of the full harvest moon rising with regal grace in the east. He noticed his pipe and tobacco had been placed on one end of the bench. Was this a peace offering? He hoped so.

The cabin was quiet. Too quiet. Ole knew the children were getting ready for bed. Usually, they would be laughing, squealing, and causing a fuss. Not tonight. They were upset by the quarrel. "Well," Ole thought, "they are not alone." This blasted church business was now breaking up families in addition to friendships.

A disgusted scowl spread across Ole's face as he filled and lit his pipe. He brushed some tobacco from his overalls and attempted to blow a smoke ring. He failed. Too much wind. He crossed his legs, feeling the stiffness of the denim. The overalls had taken some getting used to, but now he liked them. So did a growing number of men in Story County. Some even wore them to church.

Ole attempted another smoke ring, failed again, and pretended not to see Doggie inching toward him on his belly. When the wolf-dog was less than six feet away, Ole said, "Are you finally going to let me touch you?" Doggie froze, then retreated nearly a foot. "I guess not. You're mad at me, too."

Three little heads popped around the doorframe. "Good night, Papa," they said in unison.

"Good night." Ole replied. "Say your prayers."

"Yes, Papa," Oline said.

Berent saw Doggie and dashed for the wolf-dog, throwing himself onto the animal. "Hi, Doggie!"

Doggie wagged all over and licked the boy's face. Oline and Martin looked on with envy, but made no effort to touch the wolf-dog. They knew he would just back away.

Berent looked up at his father. "Are you still mad at Mama?"

"No. I'm not mad at Mama."

"That's good. But I think she's still a little mad at you. Not so much, though."

Ole grinned. "I'm glad to hear that."

Helena appeared in the doorway. "Oh, Berent! I just washed you. Get away from that dirty wolf!"

"Doggie is clean!" Berent protested.

Helena groaned. "Doggie has never been clean. Get into the cabin. I'm going to have to wash your hands again." Berent kissed Doggie's head. The wolf-dog in return licked the boy's face. "And now your face!" Helena continued.

Berent hopped like a jackrabbit onto the porch and into the cabin. Helena attempted to give him a love tap on the bottom as he passed, but failed. "Missed me!" Berent laughed.

Helena also laughed. No matter how angry she became, Berent could always make her laugh.

Ole listened with pleasure as the final preparations for bed were made and the children climbed the ladder to the loft. "Say your prayers," Helena called from the foot of the ladder. In unison the children prayed:

> "Now I lay me down to sleep,
> I pray the Lord my soul to keep.
> If I should die before I wake,
> I pray the Lord my soul to take."

There was a slight pause, then Berent added, "And please help Mama not be mad at Papa."

"Good night!" Helena snapped.

Ole smothered a laugh.

"I heard that!" Helena grumbled.

Ole did not respond. He re-lit his pipe and waited. They had performed this dance before. After several minutes, Helena came out of the cabin with a bone for Doggie. The wolf-dog stood as she approached, but did not retreat. Helena dropped the bone, which was immediately snatched up. For this treat, she was allowed to pet him several times before he backed out of reach.

"That is no way to say thank you," Helena said before turning to the porch and sitting on the bench beside Ole.

Neither said anything. They just sat and watched Doggie gnaw away at his bone. Now it was a matter of who spoke first. Since Helena had sat down next to him, Ole knew this task was his. He took a puff on his pipe and said, "You and Doggie have something in common."

"Oh?" Helena replied. "What's that?"

"I can't touch either one of you."

Helena looked at him sharply. "Is that so? Maybe it would help if you threw him a bone now and then."

"I do. But it doesn't help. Will it help if I throw you a bone?"

"Ha!" Helena answered, crossing her arms. "It would help if you weren't such a stubborn Norwegian."

Ole nodded thoughtfully. "And it would help if you weren't a terrible-tempered Finn."

"I do not have a terrible temper," Helena said, turning directly to her husband.

Ole turned to Helena, their faces only inches apart. "And I am not stubborn."

They both laughed. Helena uncrossed her arms. Ole took her hand. She did not withdraw it. The war was over.

"Did you put Berent up to that prayer?" Helena asked.

"No. The children don't like it when we argue."

"I know." Helena put her head on Ole's shoulder. "I don't like it either."

"Well, include me in that too. I hate it."

There was no need for further words. They sat close together and watched the harvest moon, which was so bright that the thousands of stars seemed to flicker and hide from its brilliance, leaving a black velvet sky.

"I don't think I've ever seen such a large, bright moon," Helena murmured.

"It is bright. Look, you can see all the way to the river."

Helena did not bother to look. She did not want to move her head from Ole's shoulder. "I believe you," she whispered. Ole kissed her hair. "I like that."

"So do I."

Helena sighed. "The only good thing about fighting is making up."

Ole kissed her again. "Amen," he said.

They sat for several minutes without saying a word, each enjoying the closeness of the other. Then Helena sat up straight. "Is there any hope for the church?"

"Not as it is now. One side or the other will leave."

"I suppose you're right. Why is it that religion brings out the best and the worst in people?"

Ole looked at his wife with admiration. "That is a very profound question, Mrs. Branjord, and one I have no idea how to answer. Perhaps you should ask Martin."

"Good thinking, Mr. Branjord." Helena laughed. "And you know, one day that boy might be able to answer it."

"He just might. He is scary smart."

A cool breeze drifted across the prairie and onto the porch. Helena shivered. "I think it is time to go in."

Ole banged the dead ashes from his pipe. "So do I." They got up from the bench, still holding hands, and entered the cabin. Ole closed the door.

In his dream, Ole was back on the family farm in Norway, standing by the barn and looking down the slope to the fjord. A full moon bathed the familiar landscape. But there was something wrong. There was a dog barking. "How strange," he thought. "We don't have a dog."

Ole snapped into a sitting position. There was a dog barking. It wasn't a dream. He jumped out of bed, almost tripping over his boots as he ran to the door. A nervous horse and rider were down by the pasture gate, facing a barking, growling wolf-dog. "Get away from my barn!" Ole yelled.

The rider whirled his horse around to face Ole. In his hand was a long-barreled revolver. "Get back into the house, farmer, or I'll kill you!"

Ole did not understand the words screamed at him in English, but there was no mistaking their meaning when the man fired a shot at Doggie. The bullet landed between the wolf-dog's paws, sending dirt into his face. Doggie had been shot at before. He darted to the left and raced to the crib.

The man turned back to the cabin as Ole slammed shut the door. The rider laughed and fired, sending a round into the log above the door.

Inside the cabin, the children were crying and Helena sat wide-eyed on the bed. Ole ran to the fireplace and grabbed the Henry rifle from the wall.

"Ole! What is happening?" Helena cried.

"Horse thieves!"

"Papa! Papa!"

"Lie down! Don't move!"

Ole threw himself on the floor in front of the door. "Helena! When I tell you, open the door and then get under the table!"

Helena, pale as the moonlight that filtered into the cabin, raced to the door. Ole chambered a round into the Henry. "Now!"

The door flew open and Helena dove under the table. The outlaw must have been expecting the action because a bullet screamed through the doorway and buried itself in the back wall

Ole fired. The shot was high, but the noise frightened the outlaw's horse, which reared, almost unseating the rider. Cursing, the rider grabbed the horn of the saddle and fired a shot that shattered the edge of the porch bench.

Much to his surprise, the shooting actually calmed Ole. He took careful aim and fired. Again he was high, but close enough that the rider heard the round whistle by his head. Ole chambered another round and fired. This bullet sent the outlaw's hat flying. The man cursed and yelled with surprise. He had not expected a farmer with a repeating rifle. The outlaw fired a third time, missing the cabin completely.

Ole had found the range. His next shot did not miss. The outlaw screamed when the bullet ripped through his upper thigh and into the saddle. He wanted no more of this. He yelled something to his companions in the pasture and spurred his horse west to the open prairie.

Ole was about to shoot at the fleeing man when he saw a second rider coming out of the open pasture gate. In his hand was a rope. Attached to the other end was Doll, who was fighting the lead. The man was cursing. Ole took aim and pulled the trigger. The horn on the outlaw's saddle shattered, causing his horse to shy and Doll to snap back her head. The rope fell from the outlaw's hand. He clawed at his horse's mane to keep from falling off. The horse bolted to the west, carrying the half-mounted rider out onto the prairie.

Doll trotted back into the pasture and was almost run over by a third outlaw leading Lady. The man was riding hard, the lead rope wrapped around the saddle horn. He charged out of the pasture. Ole fired but missed. Before he could chamber another round, a snarling mass of fur hurdled himself at the rider. Doggie's powerful jaws clamped shut on the man's leg just above the knee. The outlaw screamed and beat at Doggie with his fist. The wolf-dog dangled in the air until a large chunk of human flesh gave way and the animal dropped to the ground.

The outlaw drove his heels into the horse's side as he looked in terror at the cabin door. His narrow, thin features were clear, his ugly face unmistakable. Rooster! The third horse thief was Rooster!

Ole leaped to his feet and ran out onto the porch, screaming, "Rooster, you bastard! I'll get you this time!" He fired three quick shots, but Rooster did not fall from the saddle. Ole rushed back into the cabin, threw his rifle on the bed, and began pulling on his overalls.

Helena looked out from beneath the table and trembled at the fury in Ole's face. She did not know this man. She did not want to know this man.

Ole slammed on his boots, grabbed his rifle and a box of shells, and started for the door. Helena's heart was suddenly in her throat. "You're not going after them, are you?"

"Yes. They took Lady."

"We can buy another horse!"

"I don't want another horse! Helena, it was Rooster. He's not getting away this time!"

In less than five minutes, Doll was bridled, the Henry reloaded, and Ole was mounted. He was met at the pasture gate by Helena. "Please, Ole. Don't go. We need you."

"I know that," Ole answered softly. "And I love you and the children more than anything in the world. But I can't just let them ride away. Especially Rooster."

Ole kicked Doll into a trot, waved to the children who were huddled on the porch like frightened lambs, and rode west. Only Berent, who did not fully understand what was happening, waved back.

The feeling of vastness the prairie created during the day was magnified tenfold at night. A terrifying loneliness gripped his soul. It was as if the prairie became a living, breathing organism, patiently waiting to devour any foolish enough to venture into its endless sloughs and challenge its countless ways of snuffing out life. The settlers called the feeling "prairie panic." Ole's stomach began to knot. He fought the fear by keeping Doll at a steady trot, which was uncomfortable but was a ground-covering gait. The outlaws were running their horses hard. They would have to stop and rest or slow to a walk. A steady pace should close the gap between them.

Then what?

The adrenaline rush that had fueled Ole's actions was draining out of him like a boy's confidence when he approaches the girl of his dreams. Ole now had to face the question of what he would do if he caught up with the horse thieves. At least two of them had pistols. Even if wounded, they could still shoot.

Doubt began to gnaw at Ole like a rodent trapped in a box. What was he doing out here? He was a farmer, not a lawman or a gunfighter. He did not even know what direction the thieves had gone in. There might be a trail to follow, if he could read it. But he was no Indian. He was just a poor Norwegian immigrant farmer trying to retrieve a stolen horse.

A large cloud obscured the moon, plunging the prairie into a fearsome darkness that added to Ole's unease and self-doubt. He slowed Doll to a walk, unable to see ten feet ahead. Even though it was September, he began to sweat. He hated the dark. All his life he had dreaded the long Norwegian winters, when the sun had hidden itself like a pouting child for months at a time. The same feelings he had then now returned. The only thing missing was the cold.

Questions began buzzing in his head like angry wasps. Was he going west? Were the outlaws even heading in that direction? What could he do to get Lady back if he did find them? He could not just say, "Please, give me back my horse." What if they had turned around? What if they were waiting to ambush him? A single bullet could end his life.

He desperately wanted to turn back, but kept moving forward into the darkness. He thought, "Would Big Per run for home? No! He would be riding at a gallop, bellowing like a wounded bull." But Ole was not Big Per. He was just Ole Branjord.

Without knowing it, Ole had brought Doll to a halt. His fingers gripped the Henry as if he were trying to strangle it. Tears came to his eyes as he thought, "What a fool I am. What a damn fool! I rode out like an avenging angel and will return like a whipped dog. What will Helena think of me? Some protector and provider I am!"

Ole slumped forward and said aloud, "I'm sorry, Doll. Lady is gone and I don't even know the way home."

A quiet voice from behind and to his right said, "I can help you with that."

Ole froze, waiting for the life-ending bullet. The voice continued, "Relax, Ole. It's me, Karl Lyngen."

Ole took a deep breath, almost dropping the Henry as Karl walked up beside him. Karl was dressed in black and wearing his army uniform hat. On his hip was an army holster containing a Navy Colt revolver.

"Karl," Ole said, shaking his head, "you scared me half to death."

"I didn't mean to," Karl answered. "What are you doing out here in the middle of the night?"

"Chasing horse thieves. One of them was Rooster. They took Lady."

"I thought I recognized that horse."

"You saw them?"

"Yes. They passed by me about ten minutes ago. Two of them looked to be in bad shape. They were screaming at each other and cursing up a storm. Did you shoot them?"

"I think I shot one in the leg. Rooster was bitten by Doggie."

"That's your wolf-dog, right? Martin told me about him." Karl chuckled. "I'll bet they wish they hadn't chosen your farm."

Ole grunted. "They still got Lady."

Karl pointed to the rifle. "Is that a Henry?"

"Yes. Our friend who died in Hardin County gave it to me." Ole handed him the rifle.

Karl examined the Henry like a man who was used to handling weapons. "Very impressive. I'm sure the thieves thought you were a small army."

"Did you have one during war?"

"No. A few were issued toward the end of the fighting. I was in the hospital." Karl handed the Henry back to Ole. "Are you going after them?"

Ole sighed as he looked out into the darkness. "I was. I was all riled up. But it is stupid. I'm a farmer, not a gunfighter."

"I saw a lot of farmboys become gunfighters."

"That was in the army. I'm alone."

Karl tipped back his hat. "You don't have to be. I'll come with you."

Ole was surprised. "Why?"

"Oh, I don't know. Hunting down horse thieves would make for an exciting night. I haven't had many of those lately. But before I join you, I have to know whether or not you're willing to use that Henry."

"I think I already proved that. I wasn't aiming at the man's leg."

"You probably weren't thinking at all. You were just shooting," Karl said sharply. "Thieves were stealing your horses and you reacted. This is different. Now you'll be hunting. You may have to shoot to kill, because those three men will kill you without a second thought."

At that moment, the moon escaped the cloud bank, bathing Karl's upturned face in light. Despite himself, Ole cringed at the sight of the man's shattered face. Karl did not show the pain he felt. He simply replaced his hat squarely on his head, putting his face in shadow.

Ole turned his face away, embarrassed. This good man was offering help. He looked down at the rifle. Could he kill a man? Ole had never thought about it before. Never had a reason to. Now he did. He did not think long. The image of Rooster leering at Helena made the decision easy. "Let's go hunting."

Karl smiled. "Good. Give me a hand up."

With a little help from Ole, Karl swung up on Doll's back. The horse started forward without urging, as if she knew they were going to find her partner. Ole asked, "Am I going the right direction?"

"A little to your left," Karl answered. "It's been a long time since I have ridden a horse. It feels good."

"Well, Doll is no saddle horse. She's a little rough on the trot, but she'll go all night."

"There's no hurry. We'll catch them."

"Why do you say there's no hurry? They must be riding hard."

"No, they were hurting too much to ride hard. My guess is they'll make camp as soon as they feel safe and try and patch themselves up."

"How long do you think that will be?"

"The way they were cursing, I'd say about an hour. They won't be expecting you to chase them."

"What will we do when we find them?"

Karl paused before answering. "Let me think about that. Just keep Doll pointed in the way we're going."

They rode for several minutes without speaking. Ole prayed no more stray clouds would cover the moon. Karl broke the silence by saying, "Ole, you are to be congratulated. You have delightful children."

"Thank you. It is good of you and Inga to be so kind to them. Oline and Martin talk about you all the time."

Karl chuckled. "Well, that's only fair. We talk about them. Martin has an amazing mind."

"I know. He takes after his mother. I hope he's not bothering you."

"No, no. Just the opposite. I was a teacher before the war. The greatest joy for any teacher is a bright student who is hungry to learn."

Ole nodded his head. "That sure fits Martin. He loves your library."

"I've seen that. Tell him he can read every book I have."

"He probably will. Is there a chance of you getting back into teaching?"

Karl's response was a raw, mirthless laugh. "About as much chance as seeing pigs fly. Children don't like dark rooms, and one look at my face sends them screaming in fear."

"My two aren't afraid of you."

Karl answered in a whisper. "That's what makes them so special."

"They are special to me," Ole said with pride. "But then, I suppose all parents think their children are special. You and Inga should have some."

Karl stiffened and Ole knew he had made a mistake. There was a long pause, then Karl sighed and said, "You're right. We should have children. The problem is we can't."

Ole bit his lip with embarrassment. "I'm sorry, Karl. Sometimes I put a big foot in my mouth."

"Don't apologize," Karl replied. "The good Lord has seen fit not to bless us. We'll have to make do with visits from Oline and Martin. Inga loves your girl. She is so proud of her. And do you know I call her my little angel?"

"Yes. She reminds you of a little girl who saved your life."

"That's right. She gave me a drink of water." Karl looked up at the moon. "It was a night much like this. A touch of fall in the air. I was lying in a meadow near an apple orchard. I can still smell the apples. I can still hear the moans of the wounded."

Ole did not know what to say, or if he should say anything; so he did what most do in such a situation, made an inane comment. "War must be terrible."

Karl was kind. He did not laugh. "War is what it is. Unless you have experienced combat, you can't imagine what it's like."

"I'm happy I will never know. I probably would have made a very poor soldier."

"I disagree, Ole. I think you would have been a good one. It is the loudmouths and the braggarts who make poor soldiers."

Ole did not answer. He was pleased by Karl's remark, but believed him to be completely mistaken. Ole was not brave. He hated confrontation. And he jumped at loud noises.

Karl appeared to read Ole's mind. "I take it you don't agree with me."

"I don't," Ole answered. "I could never charge an enemy line like you did."

"I must disagree again. You would do it for the same reason all soldiers do. Can you guess what that it is?"

Ole thought for a second before answering. "To show courage? For glory?"

Karl laughed scornfully. "Wrong! Every man charging a line is pissing in his pants. And as for glory, there is no glory in war. War is a gigantic slaughterhouse. The only place you'll find glory in war is at the opera house. A soldier charges the enemy because the men around him are charging—the men he marches with, eats with, shares a tent with, laughs with, cries with, and dies with. He charges because losing the respect of these men is worse than dying. Shakespeare called soldiers a band of brothers. He was right. There is a brotherhood among …"

Several distant pistol shots stopped Karl in mid-sentence. Ole pulled Doll to a halt. He looked over his shoulder and saw the Colt in Karl's hand. "Do you think those shots came from the horse thieves?"

"Had to be," Karl replied. "But I don't understand the shooting."

"How far away are they?"

"Hard to say. I'd guess well over a mile. Ole, this is it. Do you want to turn back?"

Ole answered by urging Doll forward. He actually wanted to turn back, but could not. It had become a matter of respect.

Karl checked his revolver, then holstered it. Ole asked, "Do you always carry a gun on your walks?"

"Always. You never know what you might find out here."

Both men peered anxiously ahead, wishing now a cloud would turn down the light. "Do you have a plan?" Ole asked.

"Yes. But I need to see their camp before I finalize it. We'll ride a little farther, then stake Doll and go the rest of the way on foot."

Doll shied as a jackrabbit darted out from a patch of milkweed, almost throwing both men. Ole grabbed Doll's mane and Karl grabbed Ole. Somehow they stayed on the horse's back. "Maybe we should start walking now," Ole said.

"Not yet," Karl said. Then, after a short pause, he continued. "Ole, I want to give you some advice. If there is shooting, don't think of those three as men. Think of them as dirty, rotten bastards who deserve to die. It's the secret of killing. In the war, we didn't kill southern boys with parents, wives, and children. We killed no-good rebs. And the rebs killed damn blue bellies. It makes it all much easier."

Ole nodded. He felt strangely calm. Shooting would be no problem. All he had to do was think of Rooster attacking Helena in the river. He chambered a shell into the Henry. Karl took out his Colt from the holster.

Doll walked slowly, her neck arched, her ears perked forward. She felt the tension of the men on her back. After traveling about two hundred yards, the desired cloud blanketed the moon, making it impossible to see more than a few feet in any direction. Ole's eyes began to water from the strain. His calmness lessened with each of Doll's steps. His heart beat so loudly, he was sure Karl could hear it.

"Relax, Ole," Karl whispered. "You're doing fine."

Ole took a deep breath.

So did Doll, who then trumpeted a loud whinny that destroyed the prairie stillness.

"Damn!" Karl hissed. "Stop her, Ole."

Ole jerked on the reins as Doll's whinny was answered by one not that far away.

Karl slid from Doll's back. "Get off and get down, Ole! Someone is coming."

Ole leaped off and both men flattened themselves into the damp grass. "That was Lady," Ole said softly.

"Then it's probably Rooster coming. Get ready!"

Ole heard the hoof beats approaching. His finger tightened on the trigger. He reminded himself to aim high. The last thing he wanted to do was shoot Lady.

"Just one horse," Karl whispered.

He was right. Within seconds, Lady trotted into view and went directly to Doll. The two horses greeted each other with low, joyful whinnies. The rope was still around Lady's neck, but there was no rider.

Ole began to rise. Karl stopped him, saying, "No. Stay down. It could be a trap."

The two men waited, staring into the blackness, while the horses nuzzled each other's necks. Finally, Karl stood. "There is no one out there."

Ole gave a sigh of relief as he stood and uncocked the Henry. He happily patted Lady's head. "It's good to see you, girl," he said, and then turned to Karl. "What do you think happened?"

Karl holstered the Colt. "My guess is there was a falling out among thieves. I think they were shooting at each other and Lady got away."

"God works in mysterious ways," Ole said. "Thank you, Lord."

As if on cue, the clouds parted, allowing light to flood the prairie. Karl chuckled. "I do believe he just said you're welcome."

"It could be." Ole grinned. "Yes indeed. It could be!"

Karl turned serious. "Ole, Rooster is still out there. Do you want to get him?"

Ole looked in the direction from which they had heard the shots. "Do you think he'll come back?"

"After being shot at by a Henry and bitten by a wolf-dog? Not a chance."

"Then I've had enough of playing lawman. Let's go home."

"You are a wise man, Ole Branjord."

Ole jumped on Doll's back. "You can ride Lady."

Karl looked at Lady and then shook his head. "I think I had better ride double. I feel a headache coming on."

Ole held out his hand and Karl mounted Doll. "Which way?" Ole asked. "I'm turned around."

Karl pointed east and they started off at a walk. Lady fell in beside Doll. After all, they were a team. Doll fought the bit. Both horses wanted to go faster. They knew they were going home. Ole held firmly on the reins.

"Are you going to need something to bite on?"

Karl snorted. "I see Oline has been talking to you. No, I'm not having a seizure. Just a headache."

"I'm sorry."

"Don't be. I've actually enjoyed it."

"I haven't," Ole said. "I would have turned back without you. Thank you."

"You're welcome. I'm glad I could help," Karl replied as he snapped shut the flap of his holster. "I don't think I'm going to need any more firepower tonight."

"Hopefully not," Ole said. "Have you ever had to use that pistol on your nightly walks?"

"No. But I hope one night I will be brave enough to use it."

Ole frowned. "I don't understand."

"It is very simple. I don't carry this weapon to protect myself. I just say that if I happen to meet someone. I carry it in hope that one night I will have the courage to finish what the rebs started."

Ole did not respond. He was too surprised it speak.

"Are you shocked, Ole?" Karl continued. "Think about it. Think about how I live. What would you do?"

Ole did not know what to answer. Finally, he said, "The Bible tells us suicide is a sin."

"Yes, it does. It also says destroying another person's life is a sin. The question is, which sin is the greater?"

Ole avoided the question. "You're not destroying anyone."

"Oh, yes, I am. I'm destroying the life of the person I love most. Inga desperately wants children. I can't give her any. For some reason the doctors cannot explain, this wound has made me impotent. My soldier won't salute anymore. So, instead of having children to love and care for, she has … me."

"She loves you, Karl."

"Yes, that's the pity of it. She is trapped. The greatest gift I can give her is her freedom."

The men rode in silence for over a minute. Ole took a deep breath and let it out slowly. "I wish I had an answer, Karl. I don't."

Karl gave a rueful laugh. "There is an answer. It's resting on my hip." He then groaned. "Let's try and go a little faster, Ole. The headache is getting worse."

Ole allowed Doll to break into a trot. The gait was rough, but Karl

309

did not complain. His only response was to grip Ole more tightly around the waist.

The sun was giving notice that a new day was about to begin when they reached the Lyngen home. Karl slid off Doll's back, but hung on to Ole so as to steady himself.

"Do you need help getting into the house?" Ole asked.

"No, I can make it."

"I don't know how to thank you."

Karl smiled. "You already have … twice. But I wish to thank you. For the first time since I was wounded, I felt useful. It is a wonderful feeling."

Karl squeezed Ole's hand, then slowly, like an old man, walked to the back door and entered the house.

Ole watched with a mixture of pity, admiration, and guilt, then turned his horses for home.

Helena

He is asleep, back to me, snoring softly. What a lovely sound. I lightly touch him. I really want to snuggle close, but that will wake him. He is so warm. I took that warmth for granted. Not anymore. I put my face next to his back. I want to smell him, breathe him into me, make sure he is next to me. Oh, Ole! Never leave me again!

It has been three nights since those evil men came. It is the first night he has really slept. I still can't sleep. Will I ever be able to sleep again? Every noise frightens me. Even the wind. I hear footsteps approaching the door! I hold my breath.

Nothing.

I snuggle next to Ole. I can't help myself. He mumbles something but does not awaken. This is better. I feel safe. Oh, Ole, I wish I could crawl inside of you and peek out.

I know I'm being silly. Helena, get a hold of yourself! Those thieves are not coming back. Turg told me some men coming from Boone had found their bodies. All three of them. They had shot each other. Good! I hope they're burning in hell! Especially Rooster. I'm sure he's the one who brought them here.

When Ole rode after them, I thought I would never see him again. The children were crying. I've never seen Oline so pale. We all knelt by the table and prayed. I told God I would never ask for anything again if he would protect Ole. And, thank you, God. You did. When Ole came home leading Lady, I was the happiest woman in America.

What would I have done if he had not come back? I don't want to think about that. I can't lose Ole. He is my rock, my life. Oh, dear God, never take Ole from me.

How can I thank Karl Lyngen? I believe God sent him to protect Ole. What a strange guardian angel. Poor man. How awful it must be to live in the dark and have that horrible face. The one time I saw him up close, I cringed inside. How does Inga stand to live with him? I don't think I could. But the children don't seem to mind at all. They both enjoy being with him. Children are so accepting. Maybe I can be accepting too. I'll have to try. Ole said that without Karl, things might have turned out very differently.

I have to sleep. Inga asked us to come early to church tomorrow. She wants to show Oline something on the organ. Oline is so excited. I wonder if she is sleeping. Of course she is. She goes to sleep as soon as her head hits the pillow. Like Ole. Oh, it so good to hear him snore.

Chapter Thirty-Two

Mathea Amlund pushed back a stray lock of hair from her face, picked up a fresh hot iron from the kitchen stove, and returned to ironing her husband's clerical ruff. She really did not hate the task; on the other hand, it was not one of her favorite things to do. As she ironed, she noticed the outer edges were becoming frayed. Nils would have to order a new one from Norway. Of course, if the church broke apart, that might not be necessary. They could return home and her husband could buy one in a church store. She finished, held up the ruff, and shook her head. Such a fuss over what was nothing but a piece of cloth.

"There! That's done," Mathea said, carefully placing the ruff on the hall tree next to Nils's robe.

"Thank you," Nils said absently as he sat at the kitchen table making last-minute changes in the sermon he would deliver in less than an hour.

"Would you like some coffee?" Mathea asked.

Nils looked up. There were dark circles under his eyes. "That would be nice. Thank you." He went back to working on his sermon.

Mathea poured a cup of coffee for Nils and one for herself, and then joined him at the table. She said nothing, but while Nils studied his sermon, she studied him. The anger and tension in the congregation was aging him. His face was haggard. He slept poorly and was often up in the night, pacing, trying to find a solution to the growing rift. These stiff-necked Norwegians were his sheep and they were scattering in all directions. He looked so sad. Mathea reached out and lovingly clasped his hand.

Nils gave her a smile and sat back in his chair. "You know, preparing a sermon is hard enough without having to worry that any word or statement might be taken out of context and used as a club against me."

"Maybe it's better if the split happens," Mathea said. "Get it over with."

Nils sighed. "I can't believe that. These people called me. They built this church. They want to be a thriving congregation. There has to be an answer."

Mathea patted his hand. "If there is an answer, you'll find it."

"With God's help."

Nils returned his attention to the sermon. Mathea drank her coffee, not at all sure that Jesus himself could keep this group together. After several minutes of silence, Mathea took her cup to the sink and looked out the window at Saint Petri Church, which stood about fifty yards to the west. The clouds were heavy and rolling, almost menacing. A gust of wind stripped more leaves from the two small elm trees she and Nils had planted in the spring of 1865. The color green was fighting a losing battle with the golds, browns, and yellows. Winter was not far away.

Mathea dreaded the winter. Although it was not as long as in Norway, and the days not nearly as short, it was still cold and lonely. The settlements went into hibernation. Whereas in Norway there were parties and socials, here the people hunkered down in their homes and counted the days until spring.

Mathea was about to turn away when she saw several wagons entering the churchyard. She glanced at the kitchen clock. "That is strange."

"What is?" Nils asked.

"A number of families have arrived for church," Mathea answered. "They are forty minutes early. Here comes another wagon."

Nils got up from the table and joined his wife at the window. They watched as the women and children trooped to the church and the men gathered in a group by the wagons. "What do you think it means, Nils?"

Nils frowned. "Trouble. I've heard they've had several meetings since Elling Eielsen stirred things up."

"You should have gone to hear him, presented the church's side."

"No, that's what he wanted. He would not have debated. He would have just paraded all the failings of the Norwegian Lutheran Church."

Nils sadly shook his head. His tall frame slumped. He turned back to the table, picked up his sermon, and went into the small bedroom he used as a study. Mathea's heart went out to him. She had tried to help by talking to the wives of the men who most wanted change. They either completely agreed with their husbands or did not want to start trouble in their own homes.

Another wagon approached the churchyard as Mathea turned away from the window. It was time for her to get ready for the service; time to put on her best smile and become the perfect preacher's wife; time to greet everyone warmly, although there were a few, like that horrid Saul Jaeran, that she would rather hit over head with a cast-iron skillet!

Ole drove Doll and Lady into the churchyard, surprised to see a line of empty wagons and a group of men who seemed to be arguing.

"What do you make of that?" Helena asked as she wrapped herself more securely in her gray cape. The children were snuggled under a blanket in the back. It really was not that cold, but the wind was raw and damp.

"Definitely a meeting. I can hear Saul Jaeran from here," Ole replied.

"About the service?"

"Most likely." Ole pulled the horses to a halt. "You and the children go on into the church. I'll tie off the horses."

Helena climbed down from the wagon. The children tumbled after her. They were wearing hand-knit wool sweaters over their usual church clothes, plus heavy socks and wooden shoes made for them by Big Per.

Ole slapped the reins, and the horses ambled down to the other wagons. He was well aware he had not been invited to the meeting, but he was still going to park his wagon with the others. As for the men, most were friends and, with the exception of Saul Jaeran, solid souls who happened to disagree with him on how to worship their God.

The discussion ceased and Saul scowled as Ole pulled his wagon next to that of Lars Sheldahl. "What are you doing here, Branjord?" Saul demanded.

Ole stepped down from the seat. "I suspect the same as you, Jaeran—going to church."

"You're a little early, aren't you?"

"That's true," Ole answered, tying Doll and Lady to a hitching rack. "Inga Lyngen wants to show Oline something on the organ."

Saul Jaeran spat on the rear wheel of Ole's wagon. "You expect us to believe that?"

"I don't care if you believe it or not. It's the reason we're here early."

Jonas Duea glared at Saul. "There's no need to be rude."

"I'm not being rude! He came to spy on us!"

Ole laughed. "Now Saul, why would I do that?"

"Because you're a papist!"

The other men groaned. Jonas Duea's face turned red. "Don't start that again!"

Saul turned on Jonas. "Why not? It's the truth! You just want to pussyfoot around, not hurt anyone's feelings. Well, I call a spade a spade!"

The two glared at each other and clenched their fists. Jake Jacobson stepped between them and attempted to lessen the tension by saying, "Saul, you'd better be careful what you call Ole. He has a Henry rifle."

That brought nervous laughter from the men. Saul turned to Ole. "That's right. Not only is he a papist, he's a killer!"

Ole had had enough. He walked to within two feet of Saul. "I'm not a papist, and I killed no one. The horse thieves killed each other. You can ask Karl Lyngen."

Saul stepped back. He blustered to cover his fear. "Why should I talk to a weird freak like Lyngen?"

Ole closed the space between himself and Saul and spat the words into the man's face. "Because he is a thoughtful and brave man who was badly wounded leading men into a real battle! Not just one of words." Ole turned to the other men. "I'm sorry I interrupted your meeting, fellows. I won't stay where I'm not wanted." He brushed by Saul, knocking him back into the wagon box. Ole did not excuse himself as he left the group.

Jonas Duea called out, "I'm sorry, Ole."

Ole stopped. "So am I, Jonas. So am I."

As Ole continued to the church, he heard Lars Shaldahl say, "Then it's settled. We'll call a meeting after the service."

Ole kicked a stone. The boil was about to burst. Perhaps in the long run the rupture would lead to healing, but for now, there would be a lot people covered with pus.

When Helena and the children entered the church, a hush fell over the wives of the men outside. Written on their faces was, "What is she doing here?"

Helena smiled and nodded to them, then turned to her boys. "Martin, you and Berent go sit in the back on the men's side until Papa comes."

"Is that permitted?" Martin asked with astonishment.

"You are little men, aren't you?" Both boys nodded. "Then go sit down and act like little men."

Martin and Berent marched to the back row and sat tall and straight, deeply aware of their awesome responsibility.

Helena and Oline continued on down the aisle to where Inga was softly practicing the prelude. Inga stopped playing and smiled as the pair reached the organ. "Mrs. Branjord, Oline, it is so good to see you."

"What are you going to show me? Oline asked, her face alive with anticipation.

Inga's smile faded. "I was planning to show you some stops on the organ and have you play some scales while I pump. But I expected us to be alone. Usually, there is nobody here at this time."

Oline's anticipation turned to disappointment. "You're not going to do it?"

"I don't think I should," Inga answered, nodding to the women in the back, who had resumed their conversation.

"I agree," Helena said. "Now is not the time."

Inga saw the tears come to Oline's eyes. "Oh, Oline, I'm so sorry."

Helena gave her daughter a half-hug. "It's not Mrs. Lyngen's fault. These things happen. You'll have plenty of time to learn about the organ."

"You mother is right, Oline. And next year, if you keep up your lessons on the piano, I'll start teaching you how to play the organ."

A huge smile replaced Oline's tears. "Really? You promise?"

"I promise," Inga replied.

Voices suddenly became louder in the back. The discussion had turned heated. Inga looked up at Helena and whispered, "Do you know what is going on?"

"No. But some men are having a meeting outside. They are planning something."

"I almost hope something does happen. I'm so sick of this tension every Sunday."

"Aren't we all? I would be so thankful to have a happy church again."

"Oh! That reminds me," Inga said, with her eyes glowing. "I have a request. Would you and your family join us for Thanksgiving dinner?"

Shock registered on Helena's face. An invitation was the last thing she had expected.

Oline was also surprised, but recovered quickly. "Please, Mother. Please!"

"Yes, please," Inga continued. "We haven't had anyone to dinner since Karl came home from the war. He never wants to see anyone. But this was his suggestion! I almost fainted. Please come."

"Well … well …" Helena stammered. "I don't see why not. We would love to come. What can I bring?"

"Goody!" Oline cried.

Inga laughed. "I don't know. I've never planned a big dinner in my life."

"Well, I have," Helena said. "Why don't I come over with Oline tomorrow, and while she practices, we can decide everything."

"Wonderful!" Inga said. "This will be such fun!"

Helena suddenly put her hand to her mouth. "There is a problem. I've invited Big Per Larson to have Thanksgiving with us."

"That's no problem! Bring him along. And tell him to bring his violin."

"He'll come, Mama!" Oline said, grabbing Helena's hand. "I know he will."

"I'm certain of that." Helena smiled. "But only if we insist."

Mother and daughter broke into laughter so loud they drew the attention of the women in the back.

"I don't understand," Inga said.

"It's a family joke. I'll explain it tomorrow," Helena replied.

The church door opened and Ole entered. The boys ran to him.

"Goodness!" Inga said. "I have to get ready for the service."

"We'll talk tomorrow," Helena said as she and Oline turned to meet Ole and the boys, who were coming down the aisle.

"We were good, Mama," Martin said proudly.

Berent added, "We sat like men!"

"I'm proud of you." Helena's questioning eyes met Ole's. He shook his head. "Bad."

"What's bad?" Martin asked.

"Nothing that concerns you. Go sit with your mother and don't cause any trouble."

Ole sat in a pew about halfway down the aisle. Helena herded the children into one directly opposite. They were still standing when the

Hans Twedt family entered. Hans and his eldest son joined Ole, while Julia and her brood entered the row with Helena. The two women smiled at each other and then began seating the children. Joseph and Berent were immediately banished to opposite ends of the pew.

"What is going on?" Julia whispered as she sat beside Helena.

"I don't know," Helena answered. "There was a meeting outside. Ole thinks it is bad."

Julia groaned. "I knew we should have stayed at home. I hope Hans holds his temper."

The church began to fill. People entered with a few smiles, an occasional nod, and a sea of furtive, questioning looks. They were as far as one could get from a congregation that is entering a house of God to make a joyful noise unto the Lord.

Inga began to play the prelude. The people began to settle. Some prayed. Reverend Amlund, wearing his robe and freshly ironed ruff, entered and took his chair by the pulpit. Closing his eyes, he too said a prayer; a prayer for guidance and peace. When he opened his eyes, he noticed his hands trembling. Angry at himself, he looked out at the congregation. Eyes, some friendly, some not, gazed back at him. What they all had in common was apprehension. He wondered if they saw the same emotion in his.

The prelude ended. None present would ever remember hearing it. There was silence. It was if the people were afraid to breathe.

Reverend Amlund forced himself to rise. He walked to the center of the chancel and faced his flock. The congregation stood.

Reverend Amlund said, "In the name of the Father, and the Son, and the Holy Ghost."

The congregation responded, "Amen."

Reverend Amlund said, "If we say we have no sin, we deceive ourselves, and the truth is not in us."

The congregation responded, "But if we confess our sins, God who is faithful and just will forgive our sins and cleanse us from all unrighteousness."

Reverend Amlund knelt at the altar. "Most merciful God, we confess that we are by nature sinful and unclean. We have sinned against you in thought, word, and deed, by what we have done and by what we have left undone. We have not loved you with our whole heart; we have not loved our neighbors as ourselves. We justly deserve your present and eternal punishment. For the sake of your Son, Jesus Christ, have mercy on us.

Forgive us, renew us, and lead us, so that we may delight in your will and walk in your ways to the glory of your holy name. Amen."

Reverend Amlund stood and faced the congregation. "Almighty God in his mercy has given his Son to die for you and for his sake forgives you all your sins. As a called and ordained servant of the Word, I therefore forgive you all your sins in the name of the Father, Son, and Holy Spirit."

The absolution hung in the air with a stillness filled with dread. No one breathed. The dread was fulfilled when Saul Jaeran shouted out, "Who are you to forgive my sins?"

An audible gasp escaped the collective lips of the congregation. Reverend Amlund froze in his turn to the altar. The boil had burst. Pus was about to flow. Saul continued, "Only God can forgive my sins! Not you! Not any preacher!"

Reverend Amlund turned to face Saul, his face as pale as the ruff around his neck. "This is a worship service, Mr. Jaeran, not a debating society."

"Are you afraid to answer the question?" Saul roared.

"No!" Color returned to Reverend Amlund's face along with anger. He made the sign of the cross and gave a quick benediction. "Now, the service is over. Everyone please sit down." The stunned parishioners sat like frightened children. "Not you, Mr. Jaeran!" Saul defiantly remained standing, although much of his confidence and bluster sat with the others.

Reverend Amlund glared at Saul. "I do not forgive your sins, Mr. Jaeran. God does."

"Not true! You just said I forgive your sins."

"What I said was, 'As a called an ordained servant of the Word, I forgive you all your sins in the name of the Father, Son, and Holy Ghost.'"

A voice from near the back called out, "But you're still doing the forgiving."

"That's right!" Saul added, the bluster returning. "How can you forgive my sins? Does wearing that fancy robe and that silly collar make you less of a sinner than us?"

"No, I am not less of a sinner. But I am a called and ordained servant of the Word. Jesus said to his disciples, 'Sins that you forgive are forgiven. Sins that you maintain are maintained.'"

Saul pointed a finger at Reverend Amlund. "Are you comparing yourself to the chosen twelve?"

"No. I am quoting Scripture. I am giving you the reason ministers are permitted to give the absolution. I am in need of forgiveness as much as any of you. The absolution is a part of Lutheran liturgy."

"The liturgy is papist!" Saul yelled.

An angry murmur spread through the congregation. Hans Twedt turned red and glared at Saul.

Reverend Amlund held up his hand to regain quiet. "The liturgy is taken from the Roman Mass. Martin Luther selected the parts he felt were the essence of the Mass and that became the Lutheran liturgy. It has been used by the Lutheran Church for hundreds of years."

"Times change!" Saul answered. "The liturgy should change."

A man behind Ole asked, "Can't you just stop saying you forgive our sins?"

Reverend Amlund threw up his hands in frustration. "I am not forgiving your sins. God is forgiving your sins. I am just his instrument. Perhaps the wording should be changed, but I cannot change it. That is up to the church leaders."

"No!" Saul cried. "Nothing should be up to the bishops in Norway. Every congregation should decide what parts of the liturgy to use."

"Is that so?" Reverend Amlund shot back. "Then do you also think each congregation should decide what portions of the Bible to follow; what words Jesus spoke are to be believed and which are to be discarded; what commandments are to be taken seriously and which are to be winked at? Are we in Saint Petri so brilliant we can decide all that ourselves?"

There were scattered answers of "No, no." Some were women's voices. A number of them, Helena included, wanted to speak but could not. That would not have been acceptable to either side. This was men's work.

Saul Jaeran gripped the back of the pew so hard his knuckles turned white. His eyes bulged and his face turned crimson. "You're twisting my words! You're like all the clergy in Norway. You use your fancy education to put us down and control us!"

Reverend Amlund paused a moment before answering. A slight smile played at his lips. "If I am controlling you, Mr. Jaeran, I'm doing a very poor job of it."

Laughter filled the church. Even those who agreed with Saul joined in. Tension dropped noticeably. Some relaxed enough to sit back in their pews.

"This is not funny!" Saul sputtered "The church is trying to control us just like it did in Norway!"

The laughter ceased. A man sitting by Jonas Duea said, "He's right. I heard the Norwegian church is planning to buy up all the open prairie in Iowa."

Heads nodded and voices of assent were heard.

"I've heard that rumor too," Reverend Amlund said. "It is pure foolishness. The Norwegian church has no interest in buying land in America. Even if it did, it does not have the money. We all know the Lutheran Church is the largest landowner in Norway. That can't happen here. There is no state church. If you don't like the Lutheran Church, you can join some other denomination."

"There are no other denominations in north Story County," Saul answered.

"That is true," Reverend Amlund said. "But there are in Nevada and Ames."

"They don't have services in Norwegian."

"Again, that is true. Perhaps, Mr. Jaeran, you should start one in Fairview that does."

Giggles and snorts were the responses from the congregation.

Before Saul could answer, an old man in the very back row stood up and pointed a bony finger at Reverend Amlund. "I am told you said we should have services in English and not Norwegian."

Reverend Amlund was surprised. This was a rumor he had not heard. "Why in the world would I say that? There is not a person in this church who understands more than a handful of English words. It would be impossible for me to lead a service in English."

"Good," the old man said as he sat down. "The service should be done in the language the Bible was written in."

Many nodded their heads. Reverend Amlund bit his tongue. Now was not the time for a history lesson on the Bible.

Saul was not satisfied. "I heard you say something about doing the service in English."

"Yes, I did. Our children are learning English. In the future, they or their children might want to hold services in English."

"The Norwegian church will never allow it," Saul said.

"The Church of Norway will have nothing to say about it," Reverend

Amlund answered. "Neither will we! We'll all be dead. My friends, you do not need to fear the Norwegian state church. It can't make you do anything."

"It makes you wear that robe and silly collar!" Saul said.

Reverend Amlund's words came back at Saul like the crack of a bullwhip. "This garb is to show I'm a trained and ordained minister of the Word. These vestments are an outward manifestation of my dedication to the teachings of Jesus Christ and that I am called to be your pastor here at Saint Petri. They are not silly!"

"Fancy words for fancy clothes!" Saul responded. "You wear that robe and collar just to show how important you are. To lord it over us! To make us all bow and scrape! It is also why we have to call you Reverend."

Ole Branjord jumped to his feet. "That is insulting! He is a man of God!"

"Papist!" Saul roared.

Hans Twedt leaped up, turning to face Saul. Thankfully, they were separated by three pews. Within seconds, all the men in the church and some of the women were standing. Most were pointing fingers, shaking fists, and shouting. No one was listening.

"Stop it!" Reverend Amlund ordered. "Sit down! This is still a house of God! You will treat it with respect. Sit down!"

Saint Petri Church became quiet. The congregation sat. These stolid Norwegians avoided looking at each other, embarrassed by this emotional outburst. Saul joined them, shaken by the ferocity of the anger directed at him.

"This has gone far enough," Reverend Amlund said, his voice breaking. "I do not think I am more reverent than any of you. Reverend is a title of respect; like calling a physician Doctor, or a teacher Professor. If you do not want to address me as Reverend, then call me Pastor. My friends, if you no longer wish me to be your pastor, then write to the bishop to have me recalled …"

Immediately there were shouts of, "No! No."

Reverend Amlund held up his hands. "Until I am recalled, I will conduct the worship service as I have been trained to do. I will use the liturgy. I will give the absolution. I will wear these vestments. If this is a problem for you, I respectfully suggest you form a new church and worship as your consciences dictate. God bless you all."

The congregation sat in silence as Reverend Amlund gave the sign of the cross and departed into the small room to the left of the pulpit.

All knew the die had been cast. A living organism they had created lay bleeding on the floor of the building they had constructed with their own hands.

Jonas Duea slowly rose to his feet. "Reverend Amlund is right. This can't go on. We should start our own church."

"The building should be ours!" Saul said.

Jonas shook his head, weary of the bickering. "The bishop will never recall Reverend Amlund, and more than half of the congregation is happy with the way things are. It is time to go."

With that, Jonas motioned for his family to follow and left the church. Others with like minds followed, never again to set foot in Saint Petri Lutheran Church.

Those who remained waited several minutes in silence. Many of the women were in tears. Then, family by family, they left, feeling as if they had attended a funeral.

They had.

Ole backed Doll and Lady from the hitching rack and started for home. He was stopped by Emil Signaldahl grabbing Doll's bridle. He was obviously nervous and angry.

"Branjord, what did your wife say to mine? Hanna hasn't been herself for weeks. She hardly leaves her room."

"I don't know, Emil. And I don't want to know," Ole replied. "Let go of the bridle!"

Emil addressed Helena. "What did you tell her?"

Helena pulled her cape more tightly around herself. "If she wants you to know, she can tell you."

"You're spreading lies about her!"

"I am spreading no lies. I am not even talking about her."

Ole slapped the reins. The horses jumped forward, causing Emil to release the bridle. Ole said, "Your wife has been telling lies about Helena ever since we moved to Story County. Drop it, Emil! It is between the two women."

Emil watched in frustration as the Branjord wagon pulled away. He clenched his fists, angry that he had learned nothing, yet at the same time relieved. In his heart, he knew the answer he sought would be deeply hurtful.

A cold rain began to fall on the wagons rolling out from Saint Petri. The one thing that all the adults in those wagons could agree on was that the weather was appropriate.

Chapter Thirty-Three

The door to the cabin flew open and Oline, her face an ocean of youthful excitement, rushed in. "Mama! Mama!"

"Shut the door!" Helena called from her rocking chair, where she was knitting a wool scarf that would be a Christmas present for Ole. "It's November, not July!"

Oline slammed shut the door. "Mama, can you have my new blue dress finished by Thanksgiving?"

"That gives me only three weeks."

"I know. But I want to wear it to Mrs. Lyngen's house. Please!" Oline said as she dropped to her knees beside the rocking chair.

Helena gave her daughter a questioning look. "The dress is for Christmas."

"I know that. But Mrs. Lyngen and I have something special planned."

"Are you and Inga plotting?"

"Yes!" Oline cried, jumping to her feet. "Please, Mama. Please!"

Helena could not help but laugh. "If it is that important to you, I'll try."

"Thank you!" Oline said, taking off her cape and hanging it on a peg by the door. "Mrs. Lyngen told me that we are bringing the turkey."

"That's right. The turkey men come by every year. Inga is preparing everything else."

Oline's face sobered. "Aren't you bringing the dessert?"

"Oh, I forgot. I am bringing the krumkake and the hagletta."

Oline's smile returned. "Wonderful! It will be the best Thanksgiving ever!"

"Well, it will be the Branjord family's first Thanksgiving with the turkey and trimmings. I hope it goes well."

"Oh, I'm sure it will," Oline said, then looked around the cabin. "Where are the boys and Papa?"

"Martin is milking and Papa is picking the last of the corn. Berent is driving the horses for your father."

Oline rolled her eyes. "Oh, is he going to be strutting around like a little rooster."

"I'm sure of that." Helena laughed. "But right now, he is a cold little rooster."

Berent stomped his cold feet, his wooden shoes making a clomping sound on the wagon floor. "Are we done yet, Papa?" he asked for the third time in as many minutes.

"No, Berent," Ole answered, throwing an ear of corn into the half-filled wagon. "We have to get to the end of the row."

"All the way down there?"

"That's right. Now don't ask again."

Berent frowned as he wiped his runny nose on a home-knit mitten. The end of the row looked to him like it was in the next county. Ole glanced to the end and saw there were about one hundred yards left. One hundred yards and the crop would be safely in the crib. He smiled. Considering the drought, it was an excellent crop. The Lord had indeed blessed them. "You can move up the wagon, Berent."

Berent slapped the reins. "Giddy up!" he called with what he considered great authority, and much to his delight, Doll and Lady obeyed. The wagon moved forward until Ole yelled, "That's good."

"Whoa!" Berent cried as he pulled on the reins. The horses stopped. "I drive good, don't I, Papa?"

"Yes, you do. You're a big help."

Berent grinned proudly and stood a little taller.

Ole meant what he said. The boy was doing well, and his driving of the horses made the picking easier and faster. "Maybe," Ole thought, "Berent will be a farmer like me." It was obvious Martin was destined for a career where he would be surrounded by books. Ole shook his head. "Reverend Amlund thinks he should go to Luther College and become a minister. Reverend Branjord … my, wouldn't that be something!" Ole laughed out loud.

"What's so funny, Papa?"

"Oh, nothing. Do you like farming, Berent?"

"I sure do, Papa," Berent replied. "But I want to farm with horses, not those big oxen Mr. Larson drives."

"Good for you!" Ole laughed. "You tell him that the next time he comes over."

"Maybe he'll get mad at me."

"He might pretend to, but don't be afraid of Big Per. He thinks you are quite the little man."

Berent stuck out his chest. "That's because I wear pants!"

"I'm sure that's it." Ole chuckled. The thought struck him that he was going to enjoy working with Berent. The boy was always able to make him laugh.

A gust of wind blew through the field, making the brown, dry stalks sway and bow to each other like they were preparing to dance. Berent pulled up the collar of his coat, which had buttons missing and had served Oline and Martin before him. Ole noticed the movement and looked down at the homemade sheepskin coat he wore over a heavy sweater. It was then he decided to purchase winter coats for the family on his next trip to Nevada.

The spring pigs were almost ready for market. Three gilts and a boar had been sold to a Yankee neighbor for thirty dollars cash money. The rest could bring in sixty to seventy dollars, perhaps even more. Ole smiled and picked faster. The Branjord farm was thriving.

"Are we done now?"

Ole looked up. They were at the end of the field. "Yes, we are," Ole answered as he picked the last ear and climbed into the wagon. "Can you drive us home, Mr. Branjord?"

Berent made a face. "Oh, Papa. You're Mr. Branjord. Not me."

"Well, one day you will be. Let's go home."

Berent slapped the reins. There was no need to do so. The horses were already moving. As soon as Ole climbed into the wagon, they knew where they were going, and no driving was required.

Dusk was introducing itself when Ole took the reins from Berent and drove the horses into the crib. The wagon had no more than stopped when Berent scampered down the rear wheel and raced for the cabin. Ole unhitched and unharnessed the horses. The unloading could wait for another day.

The temperature was dropping fast as Ole led Doll and Lady to the barn. It would be well below freezing by morning. In the barn, Ole provided his team with oats, hay, and fresh bedding of straw. He noticed that Martin had spread new straw for the cows, calves, and sheep. "Well done," he thought. "The boy may never be a farmer, but he knows how to take care of livestock."

The hog house also had fresh bedding, Ole saw as he stepped around and over the snoozing pigs on his way to the back, where he had gated off two small farrowing pens. In the first, the sow with six piglets lay on her side, allowing the little ones to hungrily nurse. "Still six," Ole thought. "Good. She hasn't lain on any."

A groan came from the second pen. Ole saw the sow there had dilated and was beginning labor. He would have to check on her after supper. It could be a long night.

Ole left the hog house, pausing at the artesian well on his way to the cabin. He bent down and took a drink of the cold, clear water. Wonderful! Not even in Norway had he tasted better water. He saw a thin layer of ice forming on the tub and lifted out the nearly full can of milk. Frozen milk was not on the Branjord menu. The can could sit on the porch tonight and be churned into butter tomorrow.

The door of the cabin flew open, revealing Berent standing with hands on hips. "Are you coming, Papa? I'm hungry!"

Ole grinned and called back, "You're always hungry. I'll be right there."

"He's coming, Mama. We can eat," Berent shouted as he slammed shut the door.

Candlelight flickered in the cabin windows as Ole carried the milk can to the porch. Much to his surprise, emotions welled up within him, causing tears to blur his vision. He was overwhelmed with the same feelings he had experienced as a young man when seeing the harbor lights after a fishing voyage. Those lights had meant a hot meal, a warm bed, and safety. So too did the light shining through the windows … and so much more. Everything he cherished, everything that made his life complete, was bathed in the soft light beckoning him inside.

When Ole entered, the children were seated at the table and Helena was placing a bowl of steaming boiled potatoes beside a platter of leftover ham from the previous Sunday dinner. Thanks to the cold weather, the meat had kept nicely in the large crock located in the cellar.

"I worked hard today, didn't I, Papa?" Berent said as Ole took off his coat and walked to the sink to wash his hands.

"Yes, you did. I'm proud of you."

"See!" Berent said to Martin. "I told you!"

Martin wrinkled up his nose. "All you did was drive Doll and Lady."

"That's work. Isn't it, Papa?"

Ole poured water into the washpan. "Yes, it is. And I remember when Martin thought so too."

The eight-year-old squirmed. He also remembered how proud he had been to drive the horses. "Well," he said defensively, "Berent talks like he picked the whole load by himself."

"I do not!" Berent said.

"That's enough out of both of you," Helena stated.

Ole finished washing his hands and dried them on the towel. "Martin, I saw that you put fresh straw down in the barn and hog house. That was good thinking. I'm proud of you."

Martin blushed slightly and grinned. He gave Berent a big brotherly, superior look. Berent responded by sticking out his tongue.

"I said, that's enough!" Helena snapped.

Both boys bowed their heads. That tone of voice meant they were getting near a greeting from the wooden spoon.

Ole took his place at the table. "I'll say the blessing tonight."

The children's eyes widened. Papa saying grace was special. "Heavenly Father, thank you for this meal you have provided for us. Thank you for the bountiful crops. Thank you for my wonderful wife and children. Bless them and keep them safe. Amen."

When Ole opened his eyes, he discovered the family staring at him. There were tears in Helena's eyes. The love on their faces made his insides turn to mush. He covered his emotions by picking up the platter of ham and saying, "I thought everyone was hungry. Let's eat!"

"Finally!" Berent said.

They all laughed and loaded their plates.

When the meal was half devoured, Ole asked Oline, "How are the Lyngens?"

"Fine. I think Mr. Lyngen is getting better. He hasn't had a major seizure in over a month."

"That's good news," Ole said.

Oline continued, "Mrs. Lyngen is all excited about Thanksgiving dinner. Mama, did you know she has china made in England?"

"That makes no sense," Martin said, giving his sister a disgusted look. "Don't you know China is a country? It can't be made in England."

Oline returned Martin's look with a superior one of her own. "I'm talking about dishes, silly. Not countries."

Helena laid down her fork "Oh my! Is she planning to serve us on fine china?"

"Yes." Oline nodded happily. "She showed it to me. It is beautiful."

"What is china?" Berent asked.

"It is ceramic plates and dishes that break very easily," Helena answered, a worried frown on her face.

Berent lightly tapped his plate. "Our dishes don't break."

"That's because they are pewter," Helena answered. "Oh, dear. I'm going to have to talk to her."

"Please don't, Mama," Oline begged. "They are so pretty and she wants to use them. She said they haven't been used in years."

"But what if something breaks?"

"Then it breaks," Ole said. "It's Inga's decision, not yours. We can all be careful."

Martin asked his father, "Have you ever eaten on china?"

"Not the kind Mrs. Lyngen has."

Berent's face became solemn. "Then you're going to have to be careful too, Papa."

Ole laughed. "You are so right, son."

Helena sighed. "We are all going to have to be careful. From now until Thanksgiving, we'll practice being careful and minding our manners. Is that clear?"

The children answered in unison. "Yes, Mama." After a pause, Berent added, "I don't think I like china."

Ole laughed as he pushed back his chair. "I think that will change as soon as you see what is served on it. Martin, Oline, help Mama clean up and then get to bed. I'm going out to check on how many new pigs we have."

"Can I help you?" Berent asked.

"No, you've helped me enough for one day," Ole said, putting on his coat. "Get ready for bed. Working men need their sleep."

Oline and Martin groaned. Berent grinned.

When Ole reached the hog house, he was disappointed. There were just three piglets, all dry and hungrily sucking a nipple. This was a bad sign. Either the sow was finished or having trouble. Ole had his answer when the sow groaned and pushed. No newborn appeared. She groaned again, breathing heavily. There was no doubt in Ole's mind what needed to be done. He ran to the cabin.

"Oline!" Ole cried as he opened the cabin door. "Come quick. I need you, and bring a towel."

Ole hurried back to the hog house. Oline grabbed a towel and her cape and ran after her father. She was right behind him when they reached the struggling sow. "It is just like last year," Ole said, lifting Oline into the pen. "Do you think you can do it?"

"Yes, Papa," Oline answered calmly, kneeling behind the sow.

The previous year, a sow had been near death. At his wits' end, Ole had asked Oline if, with her small hands, she would reach into the birth canal and clear the obstruction. She had done so and, although the piglet was dead, the sow had been saved.

Oline did not hesitate. She easily entered the birth canal, and as her arm disappeared, the sow raised her hind leg and moaned. "Can you feel anything?" Ole asked,

"Not yet." Her arm was now in past the elbow. "Wait! There! I think it is sideways."

"See if you can turn it so the head comes out first."

The whites of Oline's eyes shone brightly in the darkness. She bit her lip as she concentrated. Precious seconds passed. Ole held his breath. And then Oline smiled. "I turned it, Papa!" She pulled back her arm and almost immediately, out popped the newborn. Ole was ready, catching the piglet in his hands. He snatched up the towel and began cleaning and massaging the limp, tiny animal. It was not breathing. Ole forced open the mouth and blew his breath into it.

"Is it dead?" Oline asked.

"I hope not."

Ole continued the mouth to mouth, gently rubbing the piglet at the same time. He was about to give up when he was rewarded with a shudder and a squeal. "She's alive!"

"Is it a little girl pig?" Oline cried.

"Yes! And she's breathing on her own." Ole grinned, massaging her more vigorously. "She might make it, Oline! Thanks to you." He wrapped the piglet in the towel. "Take her up to the cabin and have Mama wipe her off with a hot washcloth and then put her in the oven. When she starts to wiggle, bring her back so she can eat."

As Oline left the hog house, the sow delivered another healthy newborn. Ole picked up the piglet and placed him near a free nipple. Nature did the rest.

Bursting into the cabin, Oline said, "Mama, the pig needs a hot bath!"

Helena poured warm water into the wash basin. "I thought it might." She took the newborn from Oline and dipped her in the water. The piglet thrashed about briefly, then relaxed. Helena gently rubbed her with a washcloth. "See?" Helena said to the children who had gathered around the sink. "The little one likes it."

"It's a little girl pig," Oline said. "Is she going to be all right, Mama?"

"I think so."

Berent grumbled. "I want it to be a little boy pig."

"Well, it's not." Helena laughed. To Oline she asked, "Was she turned backward?"

Oline shook her head. "No. She was sideways."

"Oh, dear!" Helena replied. She could not help but think of her own deliveries which, thank the Lord, had not been overly difficult.

Martin looked at Oline with new respect. "How does it feel in there?"

"Real soft and sort of squishy," Oline answered, growing more proud of herself by the minute.

Helena took a fresh towel, dried the newborn, and wrapped it like she would a small child after a bath. "Oline, wash your hands and arm. You smell like pig."

Both boys held their noses. "Pew!" Martin said. Oline responded by sticking out her tongue and then did what she was told. Martin and Berent followed their mother to the stove, where Helena placed the piglet just inside of the oven.

"Are you going to roast it, Mama?" Berent asked with alarm.

"No, Berent. I'm just going to keep her nice and warm."

The boys knelt by the oven. Helena sat in her rocking chair and resumed her knitting. The piglet did not move. "I think she's dead," Berent whispered to Martin.

Martin lightly poked the animal. The towel moved. "No. She's just sleeping."

Oline joined the boys. "Papa said to bring her back when she begins to wiggle."

The children watched. As the minutes passed, their expressions turned from curiosity to concern. Maybe Berent was right. Maybe she had died. Oline bit her lip. She remembered that the little pig she had tried to save last year had died. Two large tears rolled down her cheeks. Then the towel began to do a slow dance.

"Mama! She's wiggling!" Oline said with both delight and relief.

"You saved her, Oline." Helena smiled. "Take her back to her mother. She needs to eat."

Oline tied on her cape, gently picked up squirming newborn, and ran to the hog house. The sow was resting comfortably when she reached the pen. "Is she done?" Oline asked.

"I think so," Ole answered with satisfaction. "She has twelve. How is your little one doing?"

Oline unwrapped the towel. The piglet's four little legs were pumping and she was making soft gurgling sounds. "Is she doing good, Papa?"

"I'd say she's doing great," Ole replied, taking the newborn from his daughter. He placed her on the pile of wiggling flesh near an unused nipple. She was soon sucking the life-giving milk. One of her siblings attempted to claim her nipple. She would have none of that! She pushed the other piglet away and resumed her nursing.

Ole grinned. "She is going to do just fine." He then pointed to a white mark like the letter V on the back of the piglet's neck. "See that mark? She is the only one who has it. That is how you will know which pig is yours."

"Is she really mine?" Oline asked.

"Yes, she is. And we'll keep her so she can have babies of her own."

Oline smiled mischievously. "Are they going to be mine too?"

Ole laughed. "No, you can't have them all."

At that moment, the sow raised her leg, and out slipped another little pig. "She's not done!" Oline cried.

"Apparently not. You go to bed now. Tell Mama I'll be here until I'm sure the sow is finished."

They both stood. Ole gave his daughter a big hug that made her giggle and kissed the top of her head. "Thank you, sweetheart. You did good work tonight. All but three of those little wigglers owe their lives to you. And so does their mama."

Oline wrapped her arms around Ole's waist and hugged him back. Praise from her father was precious.

Thirty minutes later, Ole entered the cabin. Helena was still in her rocking chair, knitting. "I thought you would be in bed," Ole said, hanging up his coat.

"I wasn't sleepy," Helena said. "How many?"

"Thirteen," Ole answered, and then continued in a louder voice, "thanks to Oline."

"That makes a total of nineteen."

"Yes, it does," Ole said, walking to the sink. "Eight of them are gilts. If I could breed them, we would have quite a herd."

"You wouldn't have enough corn to feed them."

"I know," Ole said. He washed and dried his hands. "Forty acres isn't enough. We'd have to have at least eighty to produce enough for that many."

"Maybe someday."

Ole took his pipe and tobacco from his pocket and pulled up a chair beside Helena. "Maybe someday is closer than you think."

Helena dropped a stitch. "Oh? Why do you say that?"

"There's a farm about a mile north of the Randall Road that could be for sale."

"What do you mean by 'could be'?"

"Well, according to Big Per, the farm is owned by a widow who is thinking about selling and moving to Nevada. The farm is eighty acres. Forty of them are tilled. The rest is prairie."

Helena dropped another stitch. The thought of moving again was not appealing. She had grown to love this land and being so close to Fairview. "Have you been looking at this land without telling me?"

Ole blew a perfect smoke ring. "No, but I have been thinking about it. You know we're boxed in here. All the land around is owned by someone, and we are going to need at least eighty. The farm I'm talking about has the eighty and the surrounding land is mostly prairie. Within a few years, we could expand to a hundred and twenty or even a hundred and sixty acres."

"One hundred and sixty acres! You can't farm that much by yourself."

"Of course not," Ole answered, his eyes sparking with excitement. "But the boys are getting older, and there are single men coming from Norway all the time. They all are looking for work."

"We don't have the money," Helena protested, laying the knitting aside. Ole's excitement was frightening her. They had spoken often of

Ole's big dreams, but those conversations had been pie in the sky. This was serious.

Ole pulled his chair closer to Helena and lowered his voice. He did not want little ears to hear what he was about to say. "We don't have enough yet, but we are close. Tilled land up there is going for three dollars to five-fifty an acre. Prairie is one twenty-five. I think Albert Hindberg will give us six for this farm. With that money and the money from the spring pigs, we just might make it!"

"Have you seen this farm?"

"No, but Big Per has. He was friends with the widow's husband. Big Per said the land is good, the outbuildings are about the same as here, and the cabin is solid and bigger than this one. He is going to ask her to give us first chance to buy if she decides to sell."

Helena's eyes were wide. "Oh my!" she whispered.

"You can say that again." Ole laughed. "Just think, Helena. If this happens, in a few years you could have your house and I could have my barn. I could have ten to fifteen milk cows, over one hundred hogs, a herd of sheep, feed cattle, and four or five teams of horses. We might even have a high-stepping road team and a fancy buggy like Emil has. That is definitely an 'Oh my!'"

"I can hardly believe it," Helena cried, then covered her mouth and looked up at the loft. There was no sound. The children were still asleep.

Ole grinned after blowing another perfect smoke ring. "Believe it! I know you have planned the house, but you've never told me what it will look like."

"That's because I never thought it would happen."

"Will you tell me now?"

A broad smile spread across Helena's lovely face. "Yes! In front will be a wide, covered porch we can sit on in the evenings. In the back will be a kitchen with windows on three sides. I want a kitchen filled with sunlight. There will be a small porch and entryway at the back door, and steps that lead down to the cellar." Helena jumped up from her chair. "The dining room is next to the kitchen, and next to it, connected by an archway, is the parlor."

"Don't you want sliding doors between the dining room and parlor?"

"No! Absolutely not. I want to use the parlor, not show it off. That's where Oline's piano will be."

"Oh, now we have a piano."

"Of course. And I want a fireplace in the parlor."

Ole wrinkled his nose. "Are you sure? Fireplaces are so messy."

"I know they are, but I love to sit in front of a fire on nights like tonight."

"Then a fireplace you shall have. Is there an upstairs?"

"Naturally, but there is one more room downstairs. Our bedroom."

A slow, sly smile played at Ole's lips. "That sounds good to me. We can make as much noise as we like."

"Ole Branjord, shame on you!" Helena giggled, feigning disgust; however, if the truth be known, that was exactly why she wanted a bedroom downstairs. "Upstairs, there will four bedrooms and an attic."

"Four bedrooms!" Ole's eyes became mischievous as he scratched his beard. "My, my. It sounds as if the downstairs bedroom is going to be a busy place."

"Ole, stop it!" Helena said, actually blushing, which made Ole laugh.

"What color will this mansion be?"

"White. But I want green shutters on the windows. And outside, I want lilac bushes and flowerbeds and trees. Lots of trees!"

"Yes, I agree," Ole said. "I do miss trees. We'll have a pine grove to the north and west of the house. It will serve as a windbreak during the winter."

"And an orchard! I want apple and cherry trees and all kinds of berry bushes. Just think of all the wonderful fruit we'll have to eat."

Helena's eyes were shining as only dream-filled eyes can shine. Ole got up and took her in his arms. They swayed slightly, enjoying the touch of their bodies as their minds imagined the future. It was one of those magical moments that sustain a marriage for a lifetime.

"Are we being foolish?" Helena whispered.

Ole gave her a squeeze and answered, "It is never foolish to dream when you can make those dreams come true." He kissed her lightly. "Let's go to bed."

Chapter Thirty-Four

The spitball, which had a tiny pebble at its core, struck Martin behind his left ear. "Ouch!" he cried.

All eyes, including those of the teacher, Elmer Fjelstad, turned to Martin. "What happened?"

Marin rubbed behind his ear. "Nothing," he muttered.

"If nothing happened, why are you rubbing your ear?" Mr. Fjelstad asked. He was a tall, clean-shaven man with a strong, angular face, blond hair, and, at the moment, angry blue eyes. Needless to say, this single twenty-five-year-old was a popular topic of conversation among the women of the community, both single and married. His good looks, plus the fact he was a veteran and a graduate of Luther College in Decorah, made him quite a catch.

Mr. Fjelstad walked from the right side of the one-room frame school to the center, where Martin sat a table with three other boys. The school was set up with small tables for the first and second grades on the right; slightly larger tables in the center for the third, fourth, and fifth grades; and full-sized tables for the sixth, seventh, and eighth grades on the left. In the front were a desk and a potbellied stove sitting on a slightly raised platform. Elmer's black suit coat hung on the back of the desk chair. A blackboard dominated the front wall, under which were shelves that contained pitifully few books and supplies. Bright, late-morning light streamed through the four windows—two on the left, two on the right.

Martin sat very straight, but was fighting back tears when Mr. Fjelstad reached him. The teacher looked carefully at the welt behind

Martin's left ear. "That 'nothing' gave you quite a nasty red bump, young man. I'm sure it hurts."

Martin looked down at the table as two tears rolled down his cheeks. Mr. Fjelstad patted Martin's shoulder, the tears making him more angry. He then spied the spitball by Martin's chair, picked it up, and unwrapped the paper. The pebble fell to the floor. Mr. Fjelstad's anger turned to fury. "Some idiot doesn't know you can put an eye out with one of these!" He picked up the pebble, wrapped it in the paper, and put the spitball into his pocket. "Some idiot's parents are going to hear about this!"

It did not take a detective to see the projectile had been shot from the left rear. At that table sat Ernst Hindberg, Sam Anderson, and Seth Jaeran, none of whom would meet the teacher's cold, steady gaze. Mr. Fjelstad knew the culprit was not Ernst. Not only was he a good boy, he blushed every time he came within five feet of Martin's sister, Oline. Sam was a mischievous sort who shot his share of spitballs, but would never put a rock in one. That left Seth Jaeran.

Mr. Fjelstad focused on the squirming boy, who was busily studying his reading book. Elmer thought, "The apple does not fall far from the tree." Because he attended Saint Petri Church every Sunday, Emil was well aware of Seth's father. Young Jaeran, who was twelve, had the same narrow-set eyes, weak chin, and sour countenance of the senior Jaeran. And, like his father, Seth was a loudmouth bully.

"Mr. Jaeran, would you stand, please?" Mr. Fjelstad ordered in a hard, flat voice.

Seth looked up with frightened eyes. "It wasn't me! I was just sitting here reading."

"Do you always read with your book upside down?" Mr. Fjelstad asked. "If so, it might explain your poor grades."

Seth blushed to the point that his face almost turned purple. He looked down at his book, but did not do the natural thing and turn it. Elmer Fjelstad noticed this and that the left-hand side of the book did not lie flat on the table. "Ernst, please close Seth's book."

Ernst hesitated, then reached over and shut the book, exposing a five-inch copper tube. Seth stared at it in horror. The other children held their breaths. Mr. Fjelstad picked up the tube and pensively examined it, rolling it over and over in his hand as if it were some strange foreign artifact. When he spoke, it was to the entire school.

"I try to treat people with respect until they prove they do not deserve my respect. And, as you know, I am not a great believer in corporal punishment. For you younger ones, that means spankings. But I am a firm believer in discipline. No one achieves anything without it."

With that, Mr. Fjelstad strode to the front of the room, slammed the tube down on his desk, and picked up a willow switch from the chalk tray. "Come forward, Mr. Jaeran!"

Seth was shaking. "You can't prove it was me! You didn't see me do it!"

"That is true. But Ernst and Sam did. Boys, did Seth shoot the spitball? And don't even think about lying to me!"

Ernst and Sam did not hesitate. Their heads were nodding before Mr. Fjelstad finished speaking.

"Thank you, boys. Mr. Jaeran, front and center!"

Seth's face was now the color of frost as he struggled to his feet. "If ... if you hit me, I'll tell Pa!"

"That won't be necessary. I'll tell him myself. Get up here!"

Tears were already rolling down Seth's cheeks as he began the long walk of the condemned. Like all bullies, his bravado collapsed when confronted with real strength.

"Put your hands on the desk and bend over!" Mr. Fjelstad ordered.

Seth obeyed, tears dripping like falling rain on the desk.

Mr. Fjelstad brought the switch down in a high arc. The willow sang through the silent room, ending its tune with a chord on Seth's bottom. "Ouch!" he cried. After five more encores, he was sobbing.

Elmer Fjelstad stepped back. "Go to your seat!"

As Seth stumbled back to his table, Mr. Fjelstad struck his desk with the switch. "I trust you now understand that I know how to use this willow and will use it if necessary. It is almost noon and we have been blessed with a beautiful, warm, Indian summer day. Eat your lunches outside And, Mr. Jaeran, don't do anything out there that will get you into more trouble."

The children quickly grabbed their lunch pails and fled the school like colts released from long confinement in a stall. The food was momentarily set aside so they could run around the school yard, releasing the pent-up energy created in their young bodies by the unnatural act of sitting still for seemingly endless hours. Wooden shoes and darned woolen socks were abandoned, permitting bare feet to crush the dry prairie flowers and grass that surrounded the building. Games of tag swiftly developed among the older children, whereas the younger ones simply ran, hopped, skipped, and jumped for the pleasure of it.

When the release frenzy abated, food beckoned. Oline and Martin sat cross-legged on the ground, sharing a lunch of flatbread and butter, two leftover pork chops, and one piece of cornbread, which both eyed with desire.

"I'll flip you for it," Martin said.

Oline gave Martin her big sister look. "Mama said we're supposed to go half and half."

"Mama isn't here."

"You'll just cry if you lose."

"I will not," Martin replied, pulling a flat rock from his pocket. He had planned for this on the walk to school. "Wet I get it. Dry you do."

"All right. But no crying."

Martin rubbed the rock for luck. He was certain he would win. This was his lucky rock. The day before he had won a marble and a piece of licorice. He spat on the rock, or at least tried to. Most of the saliva ran down his chin. He spat again, with much better results, and then flipped the rock into the air.

"I won!" Oline cried, grabbing the cornbread.

So much for lucky rocks. Martin's lower lip quivered.

"I said no crying!"

"I'm not," Martin answered, a quiver in his voice. He had been so sure.

Oline took a huge bite, giving a loud smack of her lips as she did so. Martin hung his head. He couldn't bear to watch. Life just wasn't fair,

Before Oline could take a second bite, shadows fell over the two Branjord children. Martin looked up to see Seth and two younger would-be bullies glaring down at him.

"You got me in trouble, Branjord!" Seth snarled. He was not big, but he was twelve and looked threatening to Martin.

"You shot me," Martin replied, the cornbread forgotten.

"Yeah, but you didn't need to squeal like a stuck pig!"

"It hurt. You hit me with a rock."

Seth snorted. "It was just a little pebble. I took a whipping because you yelled. I'll give you one after school."

Oline angrily crushed the cornbread into crumbs. "Mr. Fjelstad told you to leave him alone."

"Mr. Fjelstad won't be there, Miss Tattle-tale. And if you get in the way, I'll whip you too!"

A fourth shadow appeared. "You're not whipping anybody," Ernst said, easing himself in between Seth and the Branjord children.

Seth stepped back. The two hangers-on fled. Ernst was just a few months older than Seth, but was a good four inches taller and much stronger.

Seth swallowed hard. "Well, if it isn't Mr. Tattle-tale."

"I just told the truth. What you did was wrong."

"I've seen you shoot spitballs!"

"Not with rocks in them! Just remember, if you beat up Martin, I'll beat you up."

Seth took another two steps back. "Oh, the big protector! Why? Because you're sweet on Oline?"

Ernst blushed and clenched his fists. "No! Because Martin is just eight and didn't do anything to you!"

Seth attempted a contemptuous laugh, but took several more steps away from Ernst. "You win for now, Branjord. But I can wait. Someday your protector won't be around."

It took Ernst four long strides to be in Seth's face. "And if that someday comes, I'll be looking for you!"

Seth quickly retreated. "I'm not afraid of you!" he lied. "You're just sticking up for Martin because you're sweet on Oline."

Now it was Ernst turn to lie. "That's not so!"

"Yes, it is!" Seth taunted, then began the sing-song chant, "Ernst likes Oline … Ernst likes Oline … Ernst likes Oline!" But as he continued, Seth was smart enough to turn his back to Ernst and walk away. He was soon joined by his two followers, who were now far enough away to have regained some courage.

Ernst's face was a crimson portrait of anger and embarrassment. He wanted to pound Seth into the ground, but knew the joy of doing it would produce a whipping at school and another at home. He took a deep breath and, without a word to the Branjords, stomped back to where he had been eating with Sam.

The chant continued for a few more seconds, but when no other children joined in, Seth and his followers lost interest.

Oline was blushing almost as deeply as Ernst. She stared down at the cornbread crumbs as if they were the most fascinating objects on earth. This, however, did not keep her from peeking at Ernst out of the corner of her eye. Even though embarrassed, she recalled the electric touch of his hand when they had been lost on the prairie, and secretly hoped the chant was true.

"He's mean. Just like his papa," Martin whispered.

"You're right," Oline answered. "Don't be scared. Ernst won't let him hurt you."

Martin picked up the flat rock and threw it down hard. "He talks about someday. Well, someday I'll be bigger than him. Then we'll see who is scared!"

"I want to be there when that happens." Oline smiled.

Martin returned the smile with a humorless and promising grin. "I'll tell you first," he said, then jumped to his feet and walked to the school doorway.

Oline watched him go, thinking, "He already walks just like Papa." Her attention was then drawn back to the school yard by Seth Jaeran's taunting voice. Angry that he had been thwarted in intimidating Martin, he had found a second victim … Elsa Signaldahl.

As usual, Elsa was sitting by herself on her own private campstool. She never sat on the ground. That would get her dress dirty, which, to her mother, was a cardinal sin. Besides, the same source had told her, only peasants sit on the ground. This made her a rather queen-like figure on the school ground, a figure the other children resented.

Elsa rarely smiled and seldom spoke to her fellow students. This, of course, meant they avoided speaking to her. The girl's isolation was further exacerbated by her being driven to and from school in the family buggy, arriving just before the bell rang and departing immediately after dismissal. To Mr. Fjelstad, her loneliness was obvious and painful, but he could think of no way to break through her carefully constructed shell.

"Hey, everybody! Look!" Seth yelled, pointing at Elsa's feet. "The Princess has another pair of new shoes."

Elsa attempted to hide her feet behind the stool. "They're not new," she said softly.

"They're not? Wow!" Seth laughed. "Then you better run down to Nevada and get some new ones. These have dirt on them. We can't have the Princess wearing dirty shoes, now can we?"

A number of children giggled. Seth's followers roared with laughter. Encouraged by the response, Seth continued. "I know! We can shine

341

them for her. Let's all get in a line and kiss the Princess's shoes so they will be all pretty!"

More laughter.

Elsa said nothing. Her head was bowed, her face rigid. Two tears rolled down her cheeks.

"Are those tears I see?" Seth asked with mock surprise. "I didn't know Princesses could cry."

Oline also saw the tears. She jumped up and walked to Elsa, having had quite enough of Seth Jaeran for one day. "Leave her alone! She's done nothing to you."

Seth was truly surprised. No one had ever stood up for Elsa before. "Stay out of this, Branjord!"

"I won't. You're just being nasty."

"What do you care? Her mother hates yours!"

"That makes no difference. You're just a mean boy, Seth Jaeran!"

"I am not!" Seth snapped, his face reddening. "And you had better watch your mouth!"

To Seth's surprise, Oline did not retreat. Instead, she took a step forward. "Oh, you're big and brave with a girl or little boys, but I see you run real fast from bigger boys."

Seth became furious. Being challenged by a girl could not be tolerated. He balled his fist and took a menacing step toward Oline. What he did not consider was that Oline was her mother's daughter. She did not flinch.

"Go ahead! Hit me! Then we'll get to see you whipped with your pants down!"

Seth raised his fist but did not swing. There was no doubt in his mind that Oline was right. Also, Ernst had jumped to his feet, and there was no doubt what he would do if the girl was struck. "Your … your father is a papist!" Seth sputtered as he spun on his heel and hurried away. No one followed him, not even his two shadows.

Oline suddenly felt a little weak and plopped down on the ground beside Elsa. The other children relaxed, returning to whatever they had been doing. Elsa turned to Oline. "Thank you," she whispered.

"You're welcome," Oline replied. "He's a mean bully just like his papa."

"I hate him."

"Me too."

Oline looked up at Elsa and the two girls smiled. Then they

remembered their mothers and the smiles faded. Oline prepared to get up.

"Don't go!" Elsa pleaded, desperately searching for something more to say. "Are … are you still taking piano lessons?"

Oline settled back down. "Yes. Are you going to start?"

"No. At least not with Mrs. Lyngen." Elsa sighed. "But Mama is making Papa buy me a piano."

"Really?" Oline said with awe. "Oh, I wish I could have one."

"I wish I could give you mine."

Oline did not know how to respond. The thought of owning a piano boggled her mind. The conversation ended. An invisible wall began to grow, brick by brick, between the girls as each desperately tried of think of something to say. Finally, Oline blurted, "Those are new shoes, aren't they?" Elsa nodded. "I thought so. They are very pretty."

"I know," Elsa answered, as she stuck out her legs and examined the shoes. "But I hate them. I wish I was wearing wooden ones like the rest of you."

"Why?" Oline asked with surprise. "We all wish we had leather ones."

"Because maybe then everyone wouldn't hate me," Elsa answered, two more tears escaping her sad eyes.

"Nobody hates you," Oline said, not at all sure she was right. "You … you just never want to play with us."

"I do!" Elsa cried, pounding her fists on her lap in frustration. "But I can't! I might get my dress dirty. Oh, I wish I was wearing your dress!"

Oline stared in amazement at Elsa's beautiful green dress that only six months ago had been her Sunday dress, and then down at her own faded one which was at least one size too small. "Your dress is beautiful."

"I know that! All my dresses are beautiful. But because of them, I can't run! I can't play! I can't do anything that's fun! All I can do is sit like a lady!"

Elsa began to cry.

Oline began to understand what it must be like to be the daughter of Hanna Signaldahl. "I'm sorry" was all she could think to say.

"It's not your fault." Elsa wiped her eyes with the sleeve of her dress. "It's Mama. She thinks all the people in Story County are peasants. Especially your mother."

"Why does she hate Mama so?"

"I don't know. She says terrible things about her."

Oline became defensive. "They're not true!"

"I believe you," Elsa answered quickly, not wanting the conversation to end. "Your mama is always nice to me. I think whatever the reason, it goes back to Norway."

"I think so too. I think it was because she was a maid to your mother's aunt."

A sad smile accompanied a shake of Elsa's head. "There's more to it than that. What did your mama say to mine after church a few weeks ago?"

"She didn't tell me. She won't tell anybody, not even Papa."

Elsa made a face. "Whatever it was made Mama so upset she didn't come out of her room for days. And now," she added bitterly, "she treats Papa worse than ever."

Again, Oline did not know how to answer, but realized she had to do or say something. Tears were streaming down Elsa's face.

Out of nowhere came an idea. Oline came to her knees and, with a grin, pushed Elsa off of her stool onto the ground.

"Why did you do that?" Elsa cried.

Oline's grin widened. "Now your dress is dirty. I'll race you to the fence."

The shock on Elsa's face transformed into a mischievous smile. The tears abruptly stopped. Her dark brown eyes turned from dull to sparkling. "I'll win!" she cried, scrambling to her feet.

Both girls ran like a hound chases rabbits, screaming and giggling down the hill, their swirling dresses providing splotches of color against the prairie's earth tones. The other children looked at them in disbelief. The Princess could really run!

Martin silently entered the school. He saw Mr. Fjelstad sitting at his desk, concentrating hard on the Nevada newspaper. Not wanting to disturb the teacher, Martin stepped as lightly as he could to his seat. Mr. Fjelstad did not seem to notice. Martin saw there were four sentences written in English on the blackboard. The boy took out his writing pad and began copying the work. Martin loved English.

Of course Elmer Fjelstad had noticed Martin; however, his coming in early from the noon break was not unusual. Elmer continued to study the paper, but thought about what an enigma this boy had become. Martin Branjord was obviously bright, but his grades were just good, not excellent. He appeared to quickly absorb everything he was taught, yet on tests he missed simple questions that Mr. Fjelstad was sure the boy knew.

Elmer had been warned about Martin in a letter, filled with bad grammar and worse spelling, written by his predecessor. The letter had said Martin was a loudmouth smart aleck who thought he knew more than the teacher. Elmer found the boy to be just the opposite: quiet, respectful, and unwilling to put himself forward. Martin never volunteered to answer a question, but when called upon, always knew the answer. The question in Elmer's mind was how smart was this boy? Was he just a bright child or much more?

Mr. Fjelstad turned a page of the paper, continuing to ignore Martin. He studied the paper religiously each week so as to improve his own reading of English. In the army, he had learned to speak and understand the language fairly well, but he felt deficient in both reading and writing English. He hoped to improve his own skills while teaching the children the basics.

Two girls went screaming by the window, causing him to check his new pocket watch. It had been a gift from his proud parents for graduating college. He thought, "Almost time to start the afternoon classes." A trip to the outhouse was in order.

Elmer rose from his chair and smiled. "I'm going to stretch my legs, Martin. You're in charge."

Martin blushed and mumbled, "Yes, sir."

The children paused as they saw Mr. Fjelstad come out of the door, thinking he was going to ring the bell. They were pleased and relieved when he walked to the outhouse. It was still playtime.

On the way back to the school, Elmer detoured to the front east window and peeked in. Why? He did not know. His feet just moved him in that direction. To his surprise, he saw Martin standing behind the teacher's desk, looking at his newspaper. No, looking was the wrong word. The boy was *reading* his newspaper. There was no doubt about it when Martin suddenly burst out laughing. Elmer knew exactly why he was laughing. There was a story about some boys trying to catch pigs on Main Street in Nevada and ending up dirtier than the porkers.

Elmer was stunned. He had no idea Martin could read English. What else did he not know about this boy? He hurried to the door and stealthily entered the school. Before Marin could move, Elmer was inside staring at him.

Martin turned pale. "I … I wasn't doing anything bad," he stammered.

"I can see that," Mr. Fjelstad replied, walking to his desk. "I also can see you were reading my paper."

"No!" Martin gulped. "I was just sort of looking at it."

Mr. Fjelstad smiled. "The story about the pigs loose on Main Street was pretty funny."

Seeing the smile, Martin grinned. "Yes. I wish I could have seen it." The words escaped before he realized what he had done. His hand flew to his mouth as if trying to push the incriminating words back in.

"When and how did you learn to read English?"

Martin could not meet Mr. Fjelstad's steady gaze. "I … I don't read so good."

"If you can read the newspaper, I'd say you read quite well. How did you learn?"

"Mr. Lyngen gave me a book," Martin answered.

Mr. Fjelstad was surprised. "The husband of the church organist?"

Martin nodded. "Oline is taking piano lessons from Mrs. Lyngen. Mr. Lyngen invited me to see his library. He has a whole wall of books! He was a teacher before the war."

"Is that so? What book did he give you?"

"*A Tale of Two Cities*."

Mr. Fjelstad's jaw dropped. "You read the whole book in English?"

"I read it in Norwegian first," Martin said, almost defiantly. "He has the book in both languages. He told me to read a chapter in Norwegian then the same chapter in English. It took me a long time, and I still don't know a lot of the English words."

"That is incredible," Mr. Fjelstad said, more to himself than to Martin. He then looked at the simple sentences on the blackboard. "Martin, read what I wrote on the board."

Martin read, "Mary went to town. John jumped into the river. Tom went to by a horse. I love kumla." Martin laughed. "I love kumla too."

"Well now," Mr. Fjelstad said, scratching his chin. "Maybe you should teach the students English."

Martin's eyes grew wide. "Oh, no! I don't know that much."

Mr. Fjelstad laughed at the response. "All right. But during class, just sit quietly. Go take your seat."

"Yes, sir," Martin replied. He stepped from the platform, glanced back at the blackboard, and hesitated.

"Is something wrong, Martin?"

Martin again looked at the board. "No, nothing," he said, then walked to his seat.

"Martin, don't you lie to me! What is wrong?"

The boy bit his lip. He slowly turned to face the board. Correcting a teacher was how he had gotten into trouble last year. He gulped, took a deep breath, and answered in a small voice, "You used the wrong 'by.' It should be b-u-y."

Elmer looked at the board, then at the boy, and then back to the board. "You are absolutely right. I thank you," he said, crossing to the board and making the correction.

Martin slid into his chair. Mr. Fjelstad picked up the bell and walked to the door. His question about Martin Branjord had been answered. But a much greater question now loomed like a summer thunder storm on the horizon. What was he going to do with this boy?

Later that afternoon, Elmer Fjelstad approached the Lyngen home with the trepidation of a boy about to pick up his first date. His mouth was dry, his palms damp. Since that first Sunday at Saint Petri, when he had first seen Inga Lyngen, he had thought her to be the most attractive woman he had ever seen. Every Sunday he had moved a pew forward so that he could be closer to her.

Elmer paused at the steps to the front porch. Should he knock on the front door or the back? He had not been introduced to either of the Lyngens, and this was not a casual visit, which meant the front door was the proper choice. However, he was young, Norwegian, and Lutheran, so he walked around to the back. He brushed off his suit coat, took a deep breath, and knocked.

Within moments, Inga appeared and opened the door. She was surprised and more than a little taken aback to see Elmer standing there, black felt hat in hand. Inga was well aware who this handsome young man was, and had noticed the long looks he gave her in church. She had no interest in him, but was vain enough to be flattered by his attention and, at that moment, wished she looked more presentable.

Inga was wearing a simple housedress and apron. There was a smudge of flour on her right cheek and traces of flour on her neck. Her hair hung loose, tied with a ribbon in the back to keep it from her face;

however, one strand had escaped and dangled over her left eye. She brushed back the strand. "May I help you?"

Elmer thought she looked absolutely gorgeous. He stammered, "I'm … I'm … Elmer Fjelstad, the new schoolteacher."

Inga smile. "Yes, I know who you are. I've seen you at church."

"I've seen you too," Elmer said, realizing, much to his consternation, that he was blushing. "You … you play the organ beautifully."

Inga's smile widened, not only because of the compliment, but because of the boyish blush. "Thank you. I've heard good things about your teaching."

Elmer grinned. "Thank you. For the most part, the children are a joy to teach."

"For the most part," Inga mimicked.

They both laughed.

"It is because of a student that I'm here. Is it possible for me to talk with Mr. Lyngen for a few minutes?"

Inga's face sobered. Karl did not welcome visitors. "Well … I don't know. I can ask him."

"Would you please? I need some advice."

"Won't you come in?" Inga replied.

Elmer followed her into the kitchen. On the table were flour, bread dough, and bread pans. The aroma told him some loaves were already in the oven.

"As you can see, I'm baking bread."

"It smells wonderful. I love the smell of baking bread."

"So do I," Inga said. "Wait here. I'll see how Karl is feeling." She took a step to the hallway, then paused. "You are aware of his wound?"

"Yes. I know about his injury."

There was sadness in her eyes as Inga left the kitchen.

Elmer took several deep breaths just for the pleasure of absorbing the different scents of the room: burning wood, coffee, flour, dough, spices, baking bread, and her. This was a woman's kitchen, not a college boarding club or an army mess hall. A woman's kitchen. Since leaving home, he had been in few. Until this moment, he had not realized how much they meant to him and how much he missed them. Loneliness grew in him like a cancer. This kitchen radiated a woman's love. Elmer was suddenly struck with the knowledge that without love, life would be a long, cold journey.

Inga returned. "He's waiting for you in the library."

She led him down the hall and gestured to the open door. Elmer entered. Inga closed the door, leaving the two men alone.

It took a moment for Elmer's eyes to adjust to the semi-darkness. The drapes were drawn, the only light being provided by two candles. Karl stood in profile in front of the bookshelves, the undamaged side of his face visible. He was wearing dark pants, a white shirt, and a gray wool sweater. To Elmer, Karl looked completely normal, handsome even. Then Karl turned and faced him.

Elmer thought he had prepared himself for the carnage that had been described to him. He was wrong. His jaw dropped and he audibly sucked in air. He immediately was ashamed. "I'm sorry."

"No need," Karl answered. "I'm used to it. Won't you sit down?"

"Thank you," Elmer said, crossing to Karl with his right hand extended. "I'm Elmer Fjelstad, the new schoolteacher."

Karl took his hand, the result being a firm handshake which pleased both men. "The community is very happy with you," Karl said, sitting in one of the Queen Ann chairs. Elmer sat in the other.

"Thank you. I'm told you were a teacher."

"Yes. In Illinois before the war." Karl chuckled softly. "Have you noticed, Mr. Fjelstad, everything is either before or after the war?"

Elmer nodded. "I think, for our generation, that's the way it will always be."

"Did you serve?"

"Well, yes and no," Elmer answered, squirming a little in his chair. "I was drafted in sixty-three, after my first year at Luther College. I was sent to Saint Louis and spent the rest of the war in a supply depot."

"Lucky you."

"I know that now, although during the war I kept trying to transfer to a fighting unit."

Without realizing it, Karl touched the disfigured side of his face. "You didn't miss anything."

"Respectfully, sir, I must disagree. I will never know if I could have done what you did. That's why I answered yes and no. I was in uniform, but you were in the war."

The candlelight reflected in Karl's good eye as he gazed steadily at Elmer. "I like you, Mr. Fjelstad. To hear some desk riders talk, you would think they won the war all by themselves. But don't minimize what you did. An army can't fight without supplies."

Elmer snorted and his eyes narrowed. "It is a wonder the boys on the line got anything at all! I've never seen so much graft, corruption, and stupidity in my life."

This brought a rueful laugh from Karl. "Those words pretty well describe the whole idiotic war. But you didn't come here to swap war stories."

"No, I didn't. I was told you were a teacher, and I need help with a student."

"Martin Branjord."

Elmer, who had been leaning forward, sat back in his chair. "How did you know?"

"That's easy. I can see you would have no trouble with discipline, so it has to be just the opposite. And Martin is the only really special student you have."

"He reads English better than I do. He said you gave him *A Tale of Two Cities* to read in both Norwegian and English."

It was now Karl's turn to lean forward. His good eye sparkled. "I did. I thought he would bring both back in a week, saying they were too hard. But he read the Norwegian translation like it was a third-grade reader, and struggled through the English version. It is one of the most remarkable things I have ever seen."

"I don't think I could read that book in English."

"Well, I did, but it was a real fight."

Elmer threw up his hands. "What do I do with him? I can't just put him in the eighth grade."

"No, that would be bad. Emotionally, he is still a small boy. Has he been acting up in class?"

Elmer shook his head. "No, he has been very quiet. Now I see he has been bored out of his mind."

"How is he in math?"

"Good, but not exceptional. It is just in reading and English that he is miles ahead. Did you ever have a student like this?"

Karl smiled as he sat back and tapped the ends of his fingers, remembering. "One. I was teaching high school algebra. I caught a boy doing problems at the end of the book when I was teaching the first chapter. I assigned him extra work, but by the end of the first semester, he was creating math problems I could not understand."

"What did you do?"

"I was fortunate. There was retired college professor living in our town who had taught advanced math. I talked to the boy's parents and then arranged for the professor to teach the boy math. It worked out very well."

There was a moment of silence, then Elmer leaned forward. "Would you teach Martin reading and English? I could arrange his other work so he could come here in the afternoons."

"The answer is yes." Karl smiled. "I was hoping you would ask. It will be a pleasure to work with the boy."

"Wonderful!" Elmer grinned, slapping his leg. "You have no idea what a relief that is to me."

"I compliment you, Mr. Fjelstad. You care about your students. I predict you will be a master teacher. But I am curious as to why you are teaching in our school. You are very over-qualified."

"I thank you for your compliment. I hope you are right," Elmer answered. "As to why I am here, that is because of tardy decision making on my part. When I graduated from Luther in May, I intended to go to the seminary in the fall. But in August, I decided I would rather teach than preach. By that time, all the teaching jobs in the academies were taken. I asked President Larson at Luther if he knew of any teaching jobs. He had just received a letter from Reverend Amlund stating that the teacher they had chosen was moving west. So I came down and was hired."

"To the benefit of our community," Karl said. "The Lord works in mysterious ways."

Elmer laughed. "I don't think the Lord had much to do with it."

"You never know."

Both men laughed, each enjoying the intellectually stimulating company that he had sorely missed.

They were interrupted by a timid knock on the door. The door opened and Inga entered. Gone were the flour smudges and the apron, and her hair was now brushed and up in a twist. "Can I interest you gentlemen in some coffee and fresh bread?"

Both men immediately stood. "Indeed you can," Karl answered.

"But only if you join us," Elmer added.

Inga smiled and gave a short curtsy. "It's on the table."

When Elmer Fjelstad walked away from the Lyngen home, it was almost dark. Inga and Karl watched him go.

"What a delightful young man," Inga said.

"Yes, he is," Karl agreed. "And I think you have made another conquest."

"Oh, Karl, don't be silly. He is just a boy."

Karl laughed and kissed his wife's forehead. "That boy is just three or four years younger than you are."

Chapter Thirty-Five

"Mama! I'm ready. Look at me!"

"After I finish basting the turkey, Oline," Helena answered as she knelt by the open oven.

The turkey had been roasting since before dawn, filling the cabin with the mouth-watering aromas of meat and stuffing. It was a beautiful golden brown, which made Helena smile with pleasure and relief. It was her first roast turkey, but not her first roasted bird. She had prepared a number of geese when she worked for Mrs. Lessing in Norway.

This whole celebration of Thanksgiving was new. President Lincoln had declared it a national holiday, but to the Norwegian immigrants in north Story County, it was considered a Yankee holiday and mostly ignored. Had it not been for the invitation from Inga Lyngen, the meal would have been far more modest.

Helena pushed the pan back into the oven, closing the door as she rose to her feet. Oline stood by the window to the left of the door. Sunlight streamed through the glass, creating a pool of stage lighting in the shadows of the cabin. Whether by choice or chance, she had selected the perfect place to model her dress. Seeing she had her mother's attention, Oline smiled, her eyes shining, and turned a pirouette, which caused the full, ankle-length skirt to flare.

"Isn't it pretty, Mama? I think it is perfect! Thank you."

"You are welcome," Helena replied, admiring her handiwork with both dress and daughter. The soft blue wool had made up into a dress with three-quarter length sleeves and a high ruffled neck. It was fastened in the back with hook and eyes and was set off at the waist by a white sash.

Oline looked down at her feet and did a little dance. "My shoes are perfect too."

"Well, you can thank your father for them, and for the sash and the blue ribbons in your hair."

The week before, Ole had taken a load of hogs to Nevada and had come home with buttoned leather shoes (a size too big so that Oline could grow into them), the sash and ribbons (picked out with the help of Mrs. Hammerdahl), and a fancy tortoiseshell comb for Helena, who had feebly scolded him for his extravagance and poorly hidden her pleasure.

"Oh! I can't wait for Papa to see me!" Oline squealed.

"Well, it won't be long. He and the boys are hooking up the wagon." Helena laughed. "One more thing," she added as she crossed to the big chest. She removed her box from the chest, opened it, and removed her solje. In doing so, her fingers brushed the lock of Nettie's hair. A sudden ache surrounded her heart. She should have been readying two girls, not just one. "Don't forget this." Helena smiled, putting the box back into the chest.

Oline's eyes grew wide. In the excitement of putting on the dress and shoes, she had forgotten about the solje. Helena pinned it to the throat of the dress. "There! Now you are ready."

Oline's hand trembled as she caressed the solje. Helena watched her with pride and sadness. It was obvious her daughter would someday be much more than just pretty.

"Oh, Mama. It is beautiful."

"Like you." Helena gave Oline a kiss on the cheek.

The door opened and Ole stepped inside. "The boys are in the wagon. Are you ready?" He was wearing his black suit and Sunday hat.

"Almost," Helena replied. "Give me the box."

Ole handed her a wooden fruit box that had once held peaches. "Do you need my help getting the turkey out of the oven?"

"No, I can manage."

In exasperation, Oline cried, "Papa, look at me!"

Ole looked but was not prepared for what he saw. The creature in blue with sparkling eyes was his daughter, but not his little girl. Perhaps it was more the solje than the dress; or, more likely, the combination of the two that made Ole's heart skip a beat. Oline was neither child nor woman. Rather, she was something magically suspended between—a flower about to open, a promise about to be kept.

"Mama let me wear her solje. Am I pretty?"

Ole swallowed, attempting to clear the lump from his throat. "Yes. Yes, you are pretty." Then, to cover his emotions, he raised his eyebrows and gave Oline a quizzical look. "Who are you?"

"Oh, Papa! It's me!" Oline laughed.

Ole slowly shook his head. "Mrs. Branjord, you must introduce me to this charming young lady."

"Papa! Stop!"

Helena set the box by the stove and nodded to Ole. "Mr. Branjord, I would like you to meet Miss Oline Branjord."

"I am honored," Ole said, as he removed his hat and gave Oline a sweeping bow. "May I escort you to your carriage?"

"No!" Oline blushed, grabbing her cape and darting around Ole. The spell was broken. The child had returned. She ran out the door, thoroughly satisfied with the impression she had made.

Her parents watched her. Ole sighed. "She's growing up."

"And there is nothing we can do about it," Helena said, placing a towel in the box. She then took two quilted hot pads and placed the turkey pan in the box.

"Oooh, that smells good," Ole said, his mouth watering.

Helena placed several towels over the bird. "I hope it tastes as good as it looks." She removed her apron, folded it, and placed it on the towels. She was wearing her Sunday best, a navy blue wool with long sleeves and a white collar. The dress was almost too tight for her around the waist.

"May I say, Mrs. Branjord, that you also look very pretty?"

Helena closed the oven door and placed the box on the table. "You mean pretty for a woman who is five months with child."

"No, I mean beautiful."

Helena gave her husband a peck on the cheek. "Thank you, even if it is not true. Take the box to the wagon."

Ole did so as Helena put on her gray bonnet and cape and the new black gloves Ole had purchased with the comb. She checked to make sure there was nothing on or close to the stove, then walked out into a beautiful late fall day.

Doll and Lady perked their ears as they neared the Lyngen home and saw a familiar wagon waiting. Ole halted the horses beside Buck and Pride. "Why are you waiting here?" Ole asked.

"Waiting for you," Big Per answered.

"There was no need of that," Helena said. "You know the Lyngens."

"Not really. I've hardly talked to Inga and I've never met Karl." Big Per shook his head and groaned. "I should have stayed home."

"Nonsense," Helena scolded. "Inga invited you. She would be hurt if you didn't come."

"But they live in that big, fancy house. I don't belong in big houses."

Ole laughed. "Of course you do. They are just your size." He slapped the reins. "Come on. I'm hungry."

Doll and Lady started off and Buck and Pride decided to keep them company. The two wagons rolled along side by side. Helena took a deep breath. "Per, can you believe this wonderful weather? This is the longest Indian summer I have seen."

Big Per grunted and spat on the left front wheel. "It will change, then watch out. A long Indian summer means a longer Norwegian winter."

"Who said that?"

"I did."

"My, my," Ole said. "Big Per has become a big grump."

"I am not grumpy. I'm just … Oh, I just shouldn't have come."

Helena fumed at Big Per. "Well, if you feel that way, turn around and go home. But I warn you, you'll be missing a real feast: turkey, mashed potatoes, dressing, squash, blackberries, and pumpkin pie topped with whipped cream."

Big Per did not turn around, but Oline suddenly jumped to her feet. "Mama! You forgot to make the hagletta!"

"No, I didn't, Oline. Inga and I decided to make this an all-Yankee dinner. Pumpkin pie will be the dessert."

"I would have rather had the hagletta," Big Per grumbled.

"Oh, Per, stop complaining," Helena said. "I'll bet you a big bowl full of hagletta that you eat two pieces of pie."

Big Per could not help but smile. He did love pumpkin pie. "Well, only if Inga insists."

All laughed, and Big Per's grumpiness slithered away into a prairie hole. Helena smiled at Big Per and her voice softened. "You are looking very nice today, Mr. Larson."

This brought a twinkle to Big Per's eyes. He was wearing his black coat, a store-bought white shirt, and brand-new overalls. "Thank you, Mrs. Branjord. Alderman finally got in some overalls that fit me."

"Not really," Ole deadpanned. "All they did was sew two regular sizes together."

Helena failed at smothering a laugh. Even Big Per had to grin, but said, "Funny, Branjord. Very funny."

Berent stood up behind Ole, poking him lightly in the arm. "Is that true, Papa?"

Big Per and Ole both laughed, but Helena answered the question. "No, Berent. Papa was just teasing Mr. Larson." Her voice then became serious. "Now, we are almost there. Remember what I said about Mr. Lyngen's face. It was hurt in the war. Don't stare at him." Helena's gaze then took in the other two children. "All of you be very careful when you eat. Mrs. Lyngen is using her fine china. Don't break anything."

"I don't like china," Berent said.

"I'm with you, boy," Big Per moaned. "I should have stayed home."

Ole and Big Per drove their teams to the hitching posts by the side of the house. After helping Helena down from the wagon, Ole tied off the team. Big Per didn't bother. Buck and Pride would not move until ordered to. The boys scrambled from the wagon while Oline carefully climbed down. New dresses would make a girl do that. Helena checked the turkey, which had made the journey without mishap and was still warm. Ole came to the back of the wagon and picked up the bird, and they all trooped to the back door, where they were greeted by a smiling Inga Lyngen.

"I'm sorry," Inga said, "but guests go to the front door."

"What?" Big Per asked with astonishment.

Inga laughed at the expressions on the faces looking up at her. "This is a holiday and you are my guests. Please go to the front door."

"But I have the turkey," Ole said.

"Then give it to me."

Ole handed Inga the box. "Oh, this smells delicious. I'll meet you on the front porch."

Inga disappeared into the kitchen, leaving the Branjords and Big Per looking at each other. Helena laughed. She loved what Inga was doing. "You heard the lady. Let's get moving."

The children ran ahead as Helena led Ole and Big Per to the front door. Big Per shook his head. "I've never entered a house through the front door."

Helena glanced back over her shoulder. "Then it is about time you did."

Big Per muttered, "I should have stayed home."

When the three reached the porch, Inga and the children were waiting. Inga was wearing a full apron over a saddle-brown, high-neck dress. Her hair was wound in a French twist. Helena had never seen her look so beautiful or so happy.

"Oline," Inga cried, placing her hands on the girl's arms, "Your dress is perfect!"

"Thank you." Oline blushed, then held out her right foot. "I have new shoes too."

"How nice! You are so pretty. And look!" Inga added, touching the solje at her own throat, "we are both wearing soljes."

"Mama let me wear hers," Oline proudly answered.

"It is beautiful. Just like you." Inga turned to the adults. "Welcome! Isn't it a gorgeous day?"

"That it is," Helena said. "And thank you for inviting us."

"Come in! Come in!" Inga said, holding open the front door. "Hang your wraps on the hall tree. Karl is in the parlor."

As they entered the home, the boys and Big Per removed their wooden shoes. Inside, the bright light of the sun gave way to the soft light of flickering candles. Heavy drapes covered the windows, but the house was far from gloomy. There was a festive, almost romantic air about the rooms. On a table in the entryway was a large vase of cattails, surrounded by colorful gourds and red and yellow maple and elm leaves. On the coffee table in the parlor, reflecting the tongues of flame, was a mirrored tray on which was a bowl filled with yellow and red apples and another filled with various kinds of nuts. The dining room glimmered with crystal, silver flatware, and china. To Big Per, it was overwhelming. Had there been any graceful way to exit, he would have fled faster than a jackrabbit running from a prairie fire.

"You men folk make yourselves comfortable in the parlor," Inga said. "Helena, you and Oline follow me."

There was swishing of skirts as the females hurried with purpose to the kitchen, while the males hesitated, shifting from one foot to the other, uncertain of what to do. A deep voice, filled with humor, rescued them. "You have your orders. Come in."

Karl stood at the far end of the parlor, his body turned so that he was almost in profile to his guests, the uninjured side of his face visible. He was wearing a freshly pressed black suit, a white, high-collared shirt, and a black cravat. Martin led the group into the parlor. Berent clung to Ole's hand.

Big Per was surprised. He had expected to see an invalid. Oh, he knew of Karl's nocturnal ramblings, but in his mind, he thought of Karl as frail cripple. Instead, in front of him stood a tall, well-built young man.

"Martin." Karl smiled. "It's good to see you. How is school going?"

"Pretty well. Mr. Fjelstad is a good teacher."

"I'm glad to hear it." Karl affectionately tousled the boy's hair, then said to Ole, "Been out chasing any outlaws lately?"

Ole shook Karl's hand and laughed. "No. Once is enough for me."

Karl turned to Big Per, extending his hand. "And you are Per Larson. It is about time we met."

Big Per shook Karl's hand, but his eyes stared in horror at the man's now exposed face. He could not speak. His mouth hung open in disbelief. The disfigurement was worse than he had been told, but he understood why. No words were adequate to describe the carnage.

Karl released Big Per's hand. He had known this reaction was coming. It was the same at every first meeting. But the horrified looks still stung. "Not very pretty, is it?"

Big Per blushed as he dropped his eyes and swallowed hard. "I'm … I'm so sorry."

"Don't be. I'm used to it," Karl lied. He would never be used to it, but he broke the awkward tension by looking down at Berent. "And you are Berent. Oline and Martin have told me a lot about you."

Berent hung tightly to Ole's hand, all the while staring with unblinking eyes at Karl's face; however, his look was different than that of Big Per. There was no horror in it, just curiosity. Karl immediately saw the difference. He knelt down to the boy. "I also was told you got new pants."

Berent grinned and grabbed the legs of his pants with both hands. "Mama made them for me."

"They are very nice."

"I'm too big to wear a dress."

"Yes, you are." Karl smiled.

He was about to get up when Berent asked, "Does it hurt?"

The smile faded. "Most of the time."

Berent took a step closer to Karl. "Can I touch it?"

"Berent!" Ole snapped.

"It's all right, Ole," Karl said. "If he wants, he can touch it."

The boy took another step forward and lightly caressed the scar tissue. Karl realized that, other than Inga, Berent was the first person to purposely touch his wounded face since he had left the hospital. Oddly, the small fingers felt soothing. "Did you fall down?"

"No. My face was hurt in the war."

Berent dropped his hand but continued to stare at the wound. His small face became much too serious for one so young. "I don't think I like war."

"I don't like war either," Karl answered, rising to his feet. Then he smiled. "Do you like books?"

Berent quickly nodded. "But not as much as Martin."

"Well," Karl said, "maybe someday you will. Martin, why don't you show Berent the library?"

Going to the library was exactly what Martin was hoping to do. "Yes, sir. Come on, Berent."

The adults watched the boys run from the room. Ole turned to Karl. "I'm sorry about Berent."

"Don't be. Your children have taught me something important. Children look at my face, see that it is ugly, and then forget about it. Oline and Martin don't even seem to notice anymore. Adults can't do that. They always see the wound."

"Like me," Big Per muttered.

"Yes, like you, Mr. Larson. And like Ole and Helena and Inga and everybody else. Adults can't get by the disfigurement. They put themselves in my place. They ask, 'How would I feel?' The answer is written on their faces every time they look at me." Karl ruefully shook his head. "Don't feel badly. I would react the same way. Please sit down. Enough of this pain and suffering. This is going to be a happy day."

Karl sat in the wingback chair, while Ole and Big Per shared the sofa, which promptly sagged under the weight. Karl chuckled. "The sofa usually holds three."

"I hope I don't break it," Big Per said, making as if to get up.

"Sit," Karl said. "I wouldn't be that sad if you did break it. Between the three of us, I don't especially like it."

The three men laughed and relaxed. Ole looked around the room. "You have a beautiful home, Karl."

"Thank you. It's a little fancy for my taste. But it is what Inga's mother wanted, and her father had the money from the sale of his farm in Illinois to build it. So here we are."

Big Per snorted. "The price of land in Illinois is ridiculous. I heard some land is selling for twenty to thirty dollars an acre. At those prices, only the rich can afford to buy."

Ole answered. "I don't see how a man can make a living at those prices."

"Well, I think you will see how," Karl said. "When the prairie is all bought up around here, you're going to see the same kind of prices. If you can afford it, now is the time to buy."

Ole and Big Per nodded. Then Ole added, "Like the man says, they are not making any more of it."

The conversation was interrupted by the sound of the piano being pounded, not played. Ole had no question as to the identity of the would-be pianist. "Berent! Get away from the piano!"

The concert stopped.

Karl said drily, "I don't think he has Oline's talent."

"I don't either." Ole grinned. "If he plays anything, it probably will be the drum."

The three men laughed.

"That reminds me," Karl said, looking at Big Per. "I hope you brought your violin. Inga says you are quite good."

Big Per replied with a little embarrassment, "Well, I don't know how good I am. But I brought it."

"Wonderful! Martin told me you played for the Indians."

Big Per laughed. "Yes, that was up in Wisconsin. A group of us were on our way to Iowa."

"It's a great story, Karl." Ole chuckled.

"Then I must to hear it."

Big Per needed no more encouragement. The only thing he liked more than playing his violin was telling stories. "Well, we had hired this no-account steamboat captain to take us down ..."

Inga tied the strings of the full apron around Oline's waist. "Put this on. We don't want anything to spill on that beautiful dress." Oline smiled broadly. The apron was too big, but it made her feel very grownup. "There!" Inga continued, tucking up the apron. Then she bent down and whispered loud enough for Helena to hear, "Are you ready for after dinner?"

Oline's smile became a giggle. "I think so."

"What are you two cooking up?" Helena asked, putting on her own apron.

"You'll see." Inga laughed, then turned back to Oline. "Do you know a girl named Lea Wicks?"

"Yes. She's new at school. She sits by me."

"I thought she was your age. Her mother talked to me yesterday. Lea is going to start taking piano lessons next week."

Oline clapped her hands. "Oh, that's good! She didn't tell me."

"It means you have to share your practice time."

"I don't mind. I like her." Oline paused for a moment, then continued. ""I know why she didn't tell me. She was home sick yesterday. Her brother says she has a cold."

Inga looked over at the stove. "Oh! The potatoes are boiling over!" She ran to the stove and removed the lid from the pan.

"What else needs to be done?" Helena asked.

Inga brushed back a loose strand of hair. "Let me think. We have to mash the potatoes, make the gravy, slice the bread, whip the cream, and fill the water glasses. Would you make the gravy, Helena? Mine is always lumpy."

"I'll be happy to, although mine can also get lumpy." Helena laughed. "Oline, take the pitcher and fill the water glasses."

Conversation ceased as the kitchen became a ballet of swirling skirts and expressive, busy hands. Oline filled the pitcher, thinking how wonderful it would be to have a pump in the kitchen, and carried it into the dining room. Inga whipped the cream while Helena stirred the gravy.

Inga glanced at Helena with a broad happy smile on her face. "Doesn't this kitchen smell wonderful?"

"It does," Helena answered. She momentarily stopped stirring, and said, "Oh."

"Is something wrong, Helena?"

"No," Helena replied as she resumed stirring. "The baby decided to give me a kick."

Helena did not notice the smile fade from Inga's lips. "When are you due?"

"In March or early April. She'll be a spring baby."

"Do you think it's a girl?"

"I hope so. Oline wants a sister. And I know Ole would like a girl. I'll be happy if the baby is healthy and normal."

The whipping slowed, then stopped. "How does it feel to be pregnant?"

Helena glanced over at Inga and saw she was being studied by large, intense blue eyes. "That depends on whether it is early, middle, or late. Right now, I feel terrific. There is something magical about having a new life moving around inside of you. In February, I'll feel like I'm lugging around a whale! Maybe someday soon you'll know what I'm talking about."

Inga resumed whipping. "Maybe," she lied. Unless God decided there was a need for a second virgin birth, there was no chance.

"Well, I think the gravy is almost done," Helena said. "Now, where is that … Oh! There she goes again. I think she can't wait to eat this wonderful food!"

Inga set the bowl of whipped cream on the table as she got up from her chair. "Helena, would you let me feel your stomach?"

Helena laughed. "Certainly. But I have to warn you, children are often uncooperative, even in the womb."

Inga placed her hand on Helena's midsection. After a long pause, Helena laughed again. "I told you." Inga was about to remove her hand when she felt a firm thump. "There!" Helena said. "Did you feel that?" Inga nodded as her eyes filled with tears. "Inga, what's wrong?" The younger woman's lips began to quiver, but before she could answer, Oline entered from the dining room.

"Is the baby kicking again?" Oline asked.

Inga nodded. "Yes, have you felt it?"

"Three times," Oline replied. "I hope it's a girl. I have enough dumb brothers."

Helena and Inga both laughed. Inga wiped away her tears. "Well, for your sake, I hope it is too. Now, let's get the food on the table. I'm starving!"

Chapter Thirty-Six

They all had taken their places at the heavily laden table, Karl at the head, Ole, Martin, and Big Per on one side, Helena, Oline, and Berent on the other, when Inga brought in the platter of sliced turkey.

"Oh, Helena, this turkey looks absolutely delicious!" Inga said, setting the platter on the table and taking her place at the end opposite Karl.

"So does everything," Helena replied. "I haven't seen so much food on one table since leaving Norway."

Big Per sighed. "I don't think I've ever seen so much food on one table."

There was a pause as all looked at the steaming food. Besides the turkey, there was squash, corn stuffing, mashed potatoes, gravy, cranberries, butter, and freshly baked bread. Helena could not help but think of her childhood when, at times, a kettle of birch bark soup was all that sat on her parents' table.

"Yes, indeed," Karl admired. "This is a real Yankee feast."

Inga beamed. "It is! But according to what I read, the man of the house is supposed to carve the turkey at the table."

Karl raised his one eyebrow at his wife. They had discussed him carving the bird earlier in the day. "That may be true in a Yankee house. But this is a Norwegian house, and since the man of this house has never carved a bird in his life, the woman of the house carved it in the kitchen."

They all laughed. Inga wiggled a finger at Karl. "But you promised you would learn how to carve so that next year we can do it the Yankee way."

"I did." Karl nodded. "My, aren't we becoming Yankeefied."

"Well," Ole said, "If eating like this means becoming Yankeefied, I'm all for it."

"Amen!" Big Per said.

Again laughter filled the room, the adults enjoying the warmth and fellowship that encompassed the table like steam in a sauna. However, children are more interested in food than fellowship. Berent pulled at Helena's sleeve. "Aren't we going to eat soon?" This brought more laughter, which Berent did not understand.

"You are right, Berent," Inga said. "The food is getting cold." She turned to Ole. "Would you say the blessings, Mr. Branjord?"

Ole bowed his head and then looked up. "I do believe this is Karl's task."

Inga looked at Karl with a mixture of surprise and fear. The last thing she wanted at her table was a tirade against God.

"Ole," Karl said, softly, "I haven't had much communication with God these last few years."

Ole smiled. "I don't think that matters. I'm sure He is listening."

Karl and Ole gazed at each other for a long moment, then Karl bowed his head. "God, I ask your blessing on this food you have provided. Protect the people around this table. And I thank you for their presence. Amen."

"Amen" was said by the others. Heads were raised. Ole gave Karl an approving nod. There were tears in Inga's eyes.

"Now!" Karl continued, rather brusquely. "It's time to eat!"

"And again I say amen!" Big Per said.

The food was passed, dished, and devoured. There was much smacking of lips and many mutters of "Mmm" and "Delicious." Conversation mostly consisted of "Please pass" and "Could I have more of …" interspersed with compliments to the cooks that made Inga and Helena blush with pleasure. Inga encouraged second helpings, and her pride grew as the bowls and platters emptied.

Big Per took the last of his bread and wiped his plate clean. "I do believe that is the finest meal I have ever eaten."

Helena raised an eyebrow and tilted her head in mock displeasure. "Oh, is that so, Mr. Larson?"

"Ah!" Big Per said quickly. "Except for your kumla, Mrs. Branjord."

Everyone laughed.

Ole put down his fork. "I ate too much."

"That makes two of us," Karl sighed.

"I'll make it three," Big Per added, then looked across the table at Berent. "How about you, Mr. Branjord, are you going to make it four?"

"I am four!" Berent answered proudly.

There was more laughter.

Helena tousled her son's hair. "What Mr. Larson meant was, did you eat too much?"

"No," Berent answered solemnly. "And I didn't break anything, either."

Berent did not understand the reason for the resulting laughter, but joined in anyway.

"I hope you all saved room for pie," Inga said.

Ole rolled his eyes. "I don't think I did, but I suppose it would be impolite not to eat at least one piece."

"I agree," Karl said.

"Only if you insist," Big Per added.

"I do." Inga laughed, rising from her chair.

Helena also stood. "Oline, Martin, help clear the table."

"How about me?" Berent asked.

"Don't press your luck." Helena smiled. "Stay where you are."

Half an hour later, Oline and the women were in the kitchen doing dishes, Martin and Berent were exploring the Lyngen barn, and the men were standing in the living room.

Big Per patted his stomach. "My, such a feast. I won't have to eat for a week."

Ole chuckled. "Per, you'll be nibbling before you go to bed."

"No, not tonight. But I just might take a bite or two tomorrow."

"I would call that a safe bet." Karl laughed. "Would you gentlemen like to light up your pipes?"

Big Per answered, "Yes, I would. Will Mrs. Lyngen allow it?"

"Yes. But, she would prefer you smoke on the porch."

"Then the porch it is," Ole said. He took a step toward the front door, then stopped. "Wait. Karl, you can't go …"

"Outside?" Karl completed. "Yes, I can. The porch is in the shade and it has gotten cloudy. I'll just put on my snow goggles."

Karl pulled from his pocket two pieces of glasses-sized leather, with a slit in the center of the right patch, and tied together with string. On each end were black ribbons, which Karl proceeded to tie around his head.

"Can you see through that?" Big Per asked.

"Well enough not to stumble over things," Karl answered, leading the men to the front door. "They keep most of the light out."

The three settled into wooden armchairs on the porch, and Ole and Big Per lit their pipes. Big Per blew out several puffs, then asked Karl, "Mr. Lyngen, don't you smoke?"

"Not since I was wounded," Karl replied. "I still miss a good cigar."

"You're probably better off," Ole said, blowing a smoke ring. "Putting smoke into your lungs can't be good for you."

"I'm sure you're right. But I envy you both."

Big Per asked, "Does our smoke bother you?"

"No. It smells good. Puff away."

Ole blew another ring. "Too bad tobacco doesn't taste as good as it smells."

Karl grinned. "Inga found that out. When we were first married, she would sneak puffs of my cigars. One day, I gave her a cigar and dared her to smoke it."

"What happened?" Big Per asked.

"She turned green, got sick as a dog, and didn't speak to me for two days."

Ole and Big Per howled, trying to picture their gracious and lovely hostess with a big cigar in her mouth. The laughter ended abruptly when Karl gripped his chair and became rigid.

"Are you all right, Karl?" Ole asked.

Karl relaxed and nodded as he took a handkerchief from his breast pocket and wiped the drool from his mouth. "Sorry you had to see that. Actually, the seizures have become less severe and fewer. That was just a little one."

"Do you want to go in?" Ole asked.

"No, no. I'm fine. Can you believe this weather we've been having?"

"It is something," Ole answered. "Per, you've been here since the early fifties. Have you seen anything like it?"

Big Per scratched his beard. "Not this long. But my right knee tells me this Indian summer is about to go to the happy hunting ground."

"The clouds agree with you." Ole nodded. "We could be tromping around in snow tomorrow."

The three men were looking up at the clouds when Martin came running around the side of the house and charged up on the porch shouting, "Ha ha! You're still it!"

Berent, angry and red-faced, followed. He stopped at the porch steps. "Papa! Martin won't let me catch him!"

"Well, he's not supposed to." Ole grinned. "You have to run faster."

"But he's bigger and can run faster than me."

Big Per reached out and wrapped a massive arm around Martin. "I'll bet you can catch him now."

"That's not fair!" Martin cried, attempting to break free.

Big Per laughed and tightened his grip. Martin continued to struggle, but would have had a better chance of escaping from the clutches of a giant octopus than from the grasp of Big Per. Berent dashed up the steps and touched Martin. "Ha! Now you're it."

Martin stuck out his tongue at his little brother. Berent reciprocated.

"That's enough, boys," Ole ordered. "Sit down!"

Big Per released Martin, giving him a playful slap on the rear end. Martin grinned. He remembered when Big Per had held Oline so that he could catch her.

"Know what, Papa?" Berent said. "Mr. Lyngen has an outhouse with a door. It even has a hook inside so no one can come in."

This exciting piece of news was heard by Helena, who along with Inga and Oline was coming from the house onto the porch. "I have been promised a door since we moved from Hardin County. Isn't that right, Mr. Branjord?"

Ole hung his head in mock shame. "That is true, Mrs. Branjord. And you will get your door."

Helena turned to Inga. "I am not going to hold my breath."

Inga laughed. "Come inside. It is time for our surprise."

The men rose from their chairs. Ole furrowed his brow. "Inga, have you been smoking cigars lately?"

"Have I what?" Inga answered, a shocked look on her face. Then she noticed the grins appear. She looked at Karl. "You didn't!"

"He did." Big Per nodded. "Told us you smoked like a chimney."

"I did not! Karl, how could you?"

"It just sort of slipped out."

"Oh, now it will be all over Fairview and the East Settlement."

"Not if you don't tell." Ole laughed. "I won't say a word."

"Neither will I," Big Per added.

Helena failed at smothering a giggle. "Did you really?"

"One time," Inga replied with her own giggle. "And I've never been so sick in my life."

Both women laughed along with the men. Helena leaned over to Inga. "I know how you felt. I did the same thing with my father's pipe."

"I didn't know that," Ole said.

"You don't know everything about me, Ole Branjord," Helena replied with a smirk. Then she noticed the grins on her children's faces. "Oh, dear." The smirk was replaced with a stern frown. "Now, don't let me catch any of you with your papa's pipe. I'll take the wooden spoon to you! Is that understood?"

The reply was in unison. "Yes, Mama." However, it was not heard because of the laughter that traveled all the way to the coach road.

Big Per wiped his eyes as he looked down at the children. "The important words to remember are 'don't let me catch you.'"

"Per Larson, don't make it worse than it is." Helena giggled as she swirled back into the house.

The others followed.

Inga had set up chairs in the library. Everyone except Inga and Oline took their seats. Karl, of course, sat in his wingback, leaving the other for Inga, who put her arm around an excited but nervous Oline. "I have the privilege of presenting to you Miss Oline Branjord in her first public recital."

Big Per led the applause. Oline blushed.

"She has practiced hard and advanced remarkably," Inga continued. "I am truly proud of her."

Inga took her place by Karl as Oline settled herself at the piano. The music to a simplified version of *Romanze* by Beethoven was open on the music rack, but she really didn't need it. Oline took a deep breath, placed her hands on the keys, and began to play.

The first phrases were awkward and uneven, but as Oline gained confidence, the notes began to flow and became music. Her shoulders squared and her bowed head came up. She was feeling the music, not just playing a collection of notes.

Inga, who had been sitting nervously on the edge of her chair, relaxed and sat back. Like anyone with talent, Oline had risen to the occasion. She was performing at her best. There were mistakes, of course, but much more important was the musicality displayed and the promise. Tears of pride welled in Inga's eyes.

To say Ole and Helena were proud was like saying the Atlantic Ocean was wide. They stared at their daughter in disbelief. Neither had ever heard her play. Although they had guessed the surprise would be Oline playing the piano, they were not prepared for the quality of music they were hearing. They watched her fingers fly with assurance over the keys and wondered, "Is this our daughter?"

There was a moment of silence when the final notes faded, then applause led by Big Per's mammoth hands erupted. It was not the usual polite "Oh, you did so well, dear" type of clapping often heard after a child's performance. This was a real, meaningful, excited show of appreciation. Even her "dumb" brothers were impressed.

Oline faced her audience, blushing with pure delight, and gave a deep curtsy that Inga had taught her. This brought laughter and more applause.

Helena gushed, "Oline, that was just wonderful!"

"I don't know what to say," Ole added.

"Well, I do." Big Per grinned. "You play like an angel."

Karl nodded, a faraway look in his eye. "That's because she is one," he said softly.

"I agree!" Big Per exclaimed, not realizing the depth of meaning in Karl's words.

Inga bounced out of her chair and almost ran to Oline. She gave the girl a big hug. "I'm so proud of you!"

"Thank you," Oline whispered as happy tears blurred her vision.

"We have something else for you," Inga said, turning to the group while keeping one arm around Oline. "This is a little Mozart for four hands."

Oline sat on the stool and Inga pulled a chair up to the piano. Inga arranged the music and smiled at Oline. They began to play, Oline doing the bass line, Inga the treble. The spirited music filled the room, bringing smiles to the faces of all. Berent even tried to clap along until Helena grabbed his hands.

Inga could not have chosen a better selection. The festive mood, the warmth of fellowship, their full stomachs, and the flickering candlelight were woven into the delightful phrases, creating a magical, never-to-be-forgotten memory.

The conclusion of the piece brought more applause and hugs. "More! More!" shouted Big Per.

"We don't have any more." Inga laughed. "Now, Mr. Larson, it is your turn. Where is your violin?"

"It's in the wagon. But after such great music, I don't think I should play."

"Oh, we do!" Inga said. "You're not getting off that easy."

Ole pointed to Martin. "Go get Mr. Larson's violin."

Martin jumped up and raced from the room. Berent followed, yelling, "I'll help!"

"Some help you'll be," Big Per said with a laugh.

"Anything for an excuse to run," Helena said with motherly pride as both sons banged out the front door.

Moments later they returned, and Big Per took the instrument from the case. He bowed a few notes, adjusting first one string, then another. He winked at Inga and said, "I do this to make people think I know what I am doing." Inga and the others laughed, then Big Per tucked the violin under his chin and tore into a lively jig. Within seconds, everyone was clapping in rhythm.

Berent, followed by Oline, leaped from their chairs and began an improvisational dance which consisted mostly of jumping around. Martin, taking his cue from the adults, remained seated. Helena swayed to the music, wanting to get up and dance, but was unsure of how Inga and Karl would react, which was a shame because Inga felt exactly the same way.

Big Per increased the tempo and began stomping his left foot to the beat, which in turn caused the floor to shake and the empty piano stool to join in the dance. Oline squealed with delight. Berent attempted to stomp his left foot in unison with Big Per. In doing so, he lost his balance and fell on his bottom, causing the adults to laugh and the clapping to get off the beat. Big Per finished with a flourish, his face red and his brow moist.

"That was wonderful!" Inga said as she applauded. "Play another!"

Big Per wiped his face with a large farmer's handkerchief. "Give me a chance to catch my breath."

Ole chuckled. "You're getting too old to stomp like that."

"Never too old to stomp," Big Per growled.

Helena said, "Play something slow and soft."

"A folk song," Inga added. "The one about the moonlight on the fjords. Oh, I can't remember the name."

"This one?" Big Per asked, playing the first couple of measures.

"Yes, that's it!"

Big Per stuffed the handkerchief back into his pocket and began to play. The mood instantly changed. Stillness came over the room as the long, singing phrases described a lone bird ascending and descending over a moonlit fjord on a still, quiet winter night. The music stirred in each of the adults memories of a land that had once been home, but now had assumed the properties of myth. Ghosts of persons long dead and past events in which they had played important roles were summoned, relived, and enjoyed. The memories rode on the notes with the grace of a hummingbird flitting from branch to branch. As the last note faded, they reluctantly returned to the silent shadows of the past.

"Oh, that is so beautiful." Inga sighed. "It almost makes me cry."

Big Per beamed. "Well, I certainly would not want you to do that."

"Why don't you two play something together?" Helena suggested.

Inga smiled. "I would love that!"

"So would I," Per said glumly. "But I can't read music."

Oline looked at Big Per with surprise. "Then how do you learn the notes?"

Big Per scratched his beard. "I just hear a song and sort of fiddle around until I learn it."

"Which is a great talent," Inga said. "It is called playing by ear."

Karl agreed. "Per, you may not be able to read music, but you certainly know how to make it."

Big Per blushed slightly as he accepted the praise. He loved to play. He loved it more than farming. But sadly, he could not make a living with his violin, and he loved to eat more than anything!

At that moment, the grandfather clock in the hallway struck four.

"Four o'clock already?" Ole said, getting up from his chair. "We have to start for home. I have cows to milk."

"So do I," Big Per said, putting his violin in the case.

"Oh, can't you stay a little longer?" Inga begged.

"Cows wait for no man," Ole replied.

"And it's going to be dark before I get home," Big Per added.

By now, all were standing and Ole and Big Per were waiting in the hallway. After putting on her cape and bonnet, Helena gave Inga a hug. "It was so much fun. Thank you for inviting us."

"The pleasure was all ours," Inga answered, tears coming to her eyes. "Wasn't it, Karl?"

"Indeed it was." Karl paused for a moment, then swallowed hard and continued. "I thank you all for the happiest day I have had since being wounded."

There was a moment of silence before Big Per spoke. "Karl, remember what you said about children looking at your face, accepting it, and moving on? I think adults can do that too, if you give them a chance."

Again there was silence, this time broken by Karl. "Thank you, Per. I'll think about that."

"Well," Ole said with a smile, "while you think about that, Per and I will think about cows."

They all laughed, and Inga turned to Helena. "Let's do this again on Christmas Day!"

"Oh, that's so much bother for you," Helena replied.

"No, it's not! Please say yes!"

Helena looked at Ole, who smiled and nodded. "We'd love to come," Helena said, "and let's have a Norwegian Christmas ... lutefisk and lefse."

"That's a wonderful Idea!" Inga replied. "Come over and we will make the lefse together."

"I'll do that. And I'll bring my little helper with me." Helena smiled, giving Oline a half-hug.

Big Per joined in. "I'll get the lutefisk. They sell it in Nevada at Christmas time."

The smile on Inga's face was something to behold. "Oh, thank you so much!"

Ole opened the door. "Come on, Helena. We do have to go."

As they trooped out onto the porch, Inga stopped. "Your turkey, Helena. Don't forget your leftover turkey."

"You and Karl eat it."

"No. It's yours."

Inga fled back into the house. Karl slipped on his snow goggles and put his hand on Martin's shoulder. "Are you ready to study English with me tomorrow?"

"Yes, sir," Martin answered. "What are we going to do?"

"That is my surprise." Karl chuckled.

Helena lightly touched Karl's arm. "It is so good of you to help him. Thank you."

"Once again, the pleasure is mine. It will be a joy and honor to teach the boy."

"Teach him well, Karl," Ole said. "Because he is going to teach Helena and me."

"Oh, Papa," Martin mumbled.

"I'm serious. I want to be able to talk with Mr. Alderman when I go to Nevada." Ole turned to Big Per. "Want to join us, Per?"

"No." Big Per laughed. "I had enough trouble learning Norwegian."

Inga returned with the turkey and handed the box to Helena. "Enjoy the leftovers."

Helena looked at Big Per. "Mr. Larson, would you like to come over for supper tomorrow evening and enjoy the leftovers with us?"

Big Per frowned and scratched his beard. "Well, only if you insist, Mrs. Branjord."

"I do."

There was more laughter and the first "good-byes." In true Norwegian fashion, there were three more "good-byes" before the wagons were rolling out of the yard.

Karl and Inga waved as they watched their guests leave. "It was a wonderful day, Karl," Inga whispered.

"The way things should be," Karl replied.

Inga hugged her husband fiercely. "Tell me everything will be fine."

Karl took her in his arms. "Everything will be fine."

They clung to each other, attempting to smother the lie that snuggled between them.

Chapter Thirty-Seven

The ordeal began deep in the night with Oline's plaintive voice from the loft. "Mama, I have a sore throat."

Helena opened her eyes to complete darkness. No moonlight penetrated the low, dense clouds. Ole snored peacefully beside her. She sighed, wanting to return to her dream of a house with many rooms, each filled with vases of beautiful flowers.

"Did you hear me, Mama?"

"I hear you, Oline. How bad is it?"

"It hurts, Mama."

Helena sat up. "Come down. I'll give you something to gargle."

The snoring stopped. Ole groggily raised his head. "What's wrong?"

"Nothing. Oline has a sore throat," Helena replied. "Go back to sleep."

Few orders have so swiftly been obeyed.

Helena crawled from the warm bed and quickly grabbed a sweater to put over her long-sleeved, gray flannel nightgown. She also slipped on a pair of heavy wool socks. Old Man Winter had definitely chased Indian summer from Story County. She then filled a mug half full of lukewarm water from the teakettle, and added vinegar and two pinches of salt. The concoction was ready when Oline climbed down the ladder and crossed, sleepy-eyed, to her mother. She was wearing a smaller version of Helena's nightgown, made of the same material. "I can hardly swallow, Mama."

"I'm sorry," Helena said, feeling the girl's forehead. "You don't seem to have a fever. It must be just a cold." She handed the mug to Oline. "Gargle this over the sink. Try not to swallow any."

Oline gagged as she attempted to gargle and spat the liquid into the sink. "This tastes awful!"

"I know, but it will help. Try again." Oline made a face, but gargled with more success, finishing the cup. "Good girl. Now get back to bed."

"I'm cold."

"So am I. Put on some socks and I'll get you a sweater."

Within less than a minute, Oline was back in the loft and Helena, still wearing the sweater and socks, was snuggled close to Ole. She hoped Oline's sore throat would be better in the morning.

It was not.

When Oline climbed down the ladder, Martin and Berent were dressed and sitting at the table, gobbling down cornmeal mush. Helena stood at the sink board, slicing a loaf of bread Inga had hidden in the box with the leftover turkey. "How are you feeling?" she asked, knowing the answer by just glancing at Oline's red eyes and hangdog look.

"My throat still hurts, Mama."

"Well, that means there is no school for you today. Come over here. I fixed some more gargle for you."

Oline reluctantly crossed to her mother. "Do I have to? That stuff tastes bad."

"It is supposed to taste bad," Helena said, handing Oline the mug. "It's medicine."

Berent swallowed his last spoonful of mush. "Why is it supposed to taste bad?"

Helena replied with a smile, "So that you will hurry up and get well and not have to take it anymore."

Oline began to gargle as Helena carried the plate full of bread to the table. "Take just one slice. I want to have some left for Mr. Larson when he comes for supper." The bread was quickly buttered and even more quickly devoured.

Helena returned to Oline, who was spitting and twitching. "Do I have to finish this, Mama?" the girl asked.

"Yes," was the answer, as Helena felt Oline's forehead. "You have a low fever. It is probably the flu. Gargle and then try and eat some mush."

"It hurts to swallow."

"I know. But you have to keep your strength up." Helena turned to

Martin. "You had better start for school. Tell Mr. Fjelstad that Oline is sick."

Martin slid from the bench and stepped into his wooden shoes. "Should I ask him about any homework?"

"No. That will have to wait for a day or two," Helena answered, giving him a kiss as he struggled into his coat. "Where is your cap?"

"In my pocket," Martin said, pulling out the knit cap and jamming it on his head.

He looked so cute, Helena kissed him again. Martin made a face. "Aw, Mama," he said, pretending he was too old for the attention he dearly loved. Helena laughed as Martin opened the door. "One more thing," she said. "When you leave Mr. Lyngen today, ask Inga if she could give you some ice. Ice is good for sore throats."

"Yes, Mama," Martin replied, slamming the door as he started off for school.

Helena put a small amount of mush into a bowl and placed it on the table. Reluctantly, Oline sat in Ole's chair and began forcing small bites down her sore throat. Berent frowned at his sister. "You're sitting in Papa's chair," he scolded, sliding down the bench to Oline, whose response was to stick out her tongue, which had become a strawberry color. Helena, busy at the sink, did not notice.

"It's all right, Berent," Helena said. "Papa has eaten."

"She still shouldn't sit there," Berent grumbled.

Helena looked over her shoulder. "I said it is all right. You stay away from Oline. I don't want you getting sick too."

Berent walked to the sink. "What can I do?"

"Anything you want, as long as it is outside. Why don't you go help Papa? He's putting down fresh bedding for the animals. It turned cold last night."

"Do you think it will snow?"

"Papa does."

"Oh, goody!" Berent yelled, running to the coats hanging by the door. "I'll make a snowman."

"It hasn't snowed yet, silly," Oline croaked.

"I know that!" Berent answered, bringing the coat to his mother. "I'll make him tomorrow."

Helena buttoned the coat and placed his knit cap on his blond curls. She kissed him for the same reasons she had kissed Martin. "Put on your shoes."

Berent ran to the door, stepped into his wooden shoes, and raced outside, leaving the door wide open. Oline quickly slammed it shut, muttering to herself about the pain of having to live with little brothers.

Low, heavy clouds and a chilling wind greeted the boy. Although he did not know it, the temperature had dropped thirty degrees overnight. He ran to Ole, who was down by the pasture gate. "I've come to help you, Papa!"

"Glad to hear it. I need good help."

"What are we doing?"

"We're filling the hay bunks in the barn." Ole pitched a forkful of hay from the pile onto a canvas sling, four feet wide and ten feet long, with handles on both ends. The sling was now full. He put the handles together and swung the load up onto his back.

"What can I do, Papa?"

"You can stand by the gate and make sure the animals don't get out," Ole answered, starting for the barn. Berent ran ahead, planting himself with all the authority he could muster in the opening. "Good boy!" Ole grinned, then disappeared into the barn.

Berent glared at the animals, all of whom were down at the far end of the pasture and paying no attention whatsoever to the four-year-old guard. A cold gust of wind came close to knocking the boy over, causing Berent to question the need for his assigned task. He did not question long. Considering the animals were far away, the wind was cold, and Papa was nowhere in sight, Berent decided to abandon his post and darted into the barn.

Ole was putting hay into the cow's bunk when Berent arrived. The boy studied the overflowing bunk and said, "Papa, there already is hay in there."

"Yes, I know," Ole replied, not at all surprised to see the boy. "But I think we might have a snowstorm, so I want everything full to the very top. A good farmer takes care of his animals, correct?"

"Yes, Papa. I'm a good farmer too," Berent said, attempting to throw an armload of hay into the bunk; however, since the lip of the bunk was about two feet above the boy's head, most of the hay fell back onto his knit cap and shoulders. "Oh, pew!"

Ole laughed and brushed off the hay. "Better let me do that. You're still a little short in one end."

Berent looked up at his father. "Someday I'll be big like you."

"That's right. Then you can take care of your own animals."

"But no oxen," Berent said firmly.

"No oxen," Ole repeated, picking up the sling. He looked with satisfaction at his work. Fresh straw was down and the hay bunks were filled. If a storm did come, his animals would be as snug as he could make them. He sighed and thought, "Oh, for a real barn!"

"What do we do now, Papa?"

Ole patted the boy's shoulder. "Now we feed and bed the pigs and then take care of the chickens. Think you can do all that?"

"Yes, Papa. I'm a good farmer."

Inside the cabin, Oline was vomiting into the chamber pot. "I'm sorry, Mama," she whispered.

"Don't be," Helena said. "Vomiting is good. You're throwing up all the bad humors that cause the sickness."

Oline lay back on the pillow of her parent's bed, her face glistening with sweat. There was no doubt the fever was increasing. Helena, kneeling beside her, wiped her face with a damp cloth. The girl thanked her with a slight smile. "That feels good, Mama."

"I'm glad," Helena replied, kissing her daughter's forehead.

"Will that make me better, Mama?"

"I hope so," Helena said, masking her concern with a loving smile. She had been surprised and disturbed by the heat her lips had felt. "Do you think you can drink some more water?"

Oline slowly shook her head. "Not now. I just want to sleep."

"You do that. Sleep is the best thing for you."

Oline breathed heavily and closed her eyes, but almost immediately reopened them. "Yesterday was so much fun."

"Yes, it was," Helena agreed. "It was a wonderful day and you played beautifully. Your papa was so proud of you. I thought he would bust his buttons!"

"Were you proud of me too?"

"Yes, I was. Even more proud than Papa."

Oline's response was a real smile. "Do you think someday we can have a piano?"

"Without a doubt. When I get my real house, you'll get your real piano."

In spite of the fever and sore throat, Oline beamed. "Will we have a house like Mrs. Lyngen?"

"Oh, I don't think it will be that big and fancy, but there will be room in the parlor for a piano."

Oline fell asleep with the smile still on her lips. Helena continued to sponge the girl's face. She thought, "This is not exactly like the flu, but what else can it be?"

Outside, occasional lonely snowflakes, acting much like an army scouting party, survived long enough to touch the ground. Ole and his little shadow puttered around the farmyard for the rest of the morning, preparing the buildings and equipment for the storm Ole was convinced would come. And after a noon meal of cornmeal mush and salt pork, he and Berent walked to the river, where Ole cut down a small snag and sawed it up for additional firewood. Berent, being Berent, came close to falling into the water.

It was midafternoon when Ole approached the cabin with the last armload of wood. Berent trudged behind, dragging a dead branch which made a zigzag trail in the light dusting of snow.

"Are we done know, Papa?" Berent asked, in a voice that left no doubt that he was tired of working.

"Yes, and I thank you for your help," Ole answered, stacking the split logs on the pile that was now shoulder high.

"Can I go in to Mama?"

"Better not. Oline is sick. We'll go down to the barn."

Berent stamped his foot. "But I'm cold!"

"The barn will be warm. Maybe you can snuggle down with the sheep."

"Oh, Papa, that mean old ram will just butt me."

Ole laughed as he turned from the pile to take the branch from Berent. He looked down toward the stage road and was surprised to see Buck and Pride ambling up the hill. He was surprised because it was too early for supper and because of the threatening storm. Ole had not expected Big Per to come. No one with any sense wanted to be caught out in a blizzard.

Walking a few steps toward the approaching wagon, Ole called out, "You really must be hungry to come this early."

There was no jocular answer, only a wave of the hand. Big Per's face was grim. Something was wrong.

The oxen came to a halt. Big Per stepped out onto the front wheel and jumped to the ground. Ole gave him a questioning look. Big Per held up his hand and turned to Berent. "Mr. Branjord, I am so thirsty. Could you go down to the well and get me a drink of water?"

Berent looked up at his father, who nodded. "Go on. Get Mr. Larson some water."

"Yes, Papa," Berent answered, not understanding why Big Per was so thirsty on such a cold day.

As Berent ran to the well, Ole asked, "What was that all about?"

"I was just at Turg's store," Big Per said, taking off his mittens and untying a fox-skin cap that had the face of the animal still attached. "I was picking up extra supplies. I think we're in for a blow."

"So do I. I didn't think you would come."

"I wasn't planning to. But I heard in the store they are closing the school. Scarlet fever."

"Scarlet fever!" Ole repeated, turning pale.

"Yes. A girl who just moved here has it."

"Oh, dear God! Oline is sick. We thought it was the flu."

"Have you checked her tongue?"

"No, why?"

"If it is scarlet fever, her tongue will be strawberry red," Big Per answered as he and Ole walked to the cabin porch. "I know, because I had it as a kid. Believe me, it's no fun."

When they reached the door, Berent came running up with a tin cup half filled with water. The men ignored him as they entered the cabin, leaving the boy even more confused.

Helena was kneeling beside the bed, wiping Oline's face with a warm, damp cloth. She too was surprised to see Big Per. "I didn't expect you so soon."

"I'm not staying," Big Per answered, crossing to the bed. "Oline, can you stick your tongue out at me?"

Oline stared up at this gentle giant with fear-filled eyes. Her feverish mind was unsure who this person was. With his fox-skin cap, sheepskin coat, and grim countenance, he looked like a villain from a Brothers Grimm fairy tale. She stuck out her tongue, hoping that doing so would make the apparition go away. Her tongue was strawberry red. Helena sucked in air and turned pale. She realized what the color meant.

"Thank you, Oline. Try and sleep," Big Per said, and then turned to Berent, who had entered and closed the door. "Berent, you stay in here and watch your sister. I need to talk to your folks on the porch."

Helena jumped to her feet, grabbing her cape as she reached the door.

"Berent, don't go near her! Understand? If she calls out for something, come and get me."

The boy nodded, his eyes wide, absorbing the adult fear with trembling. He sat at the table, not taking his eyes off Oline, as Big Per and his parents hurried outside and closed the door.

"Scarlet fever!" Helena blurted.

"Yes," Big Per answered.

""The new little girl at school has it," Ole snapped, suddenly angry at the girl's family for moving to Story County.

"Oline sits right beside her," Helena said, her hand covering her mouth.

Big Per shook his head. "There's no doubt about it then. It's scarlet fever. Where is Martin?"

"He's with Karl Lyngen," Helena answered. "He should be home soon."

"Good. The school has been closed."

Helena wrapped the cape more tightly around herself. "What do I do for scarlet fever?"

Big Per sighed. "Just what you're doing, I guess."

Ole grabbed Big Per's arm. "You had it. What did they do for you?"

"I don't remember much. I was too young. But I know keeping the fever down is the most important thing. Just try and keep her cool and pray."

"Isn't there some medicine to give her?" Ole asked.

"I don't think so. If there is, it is new."

"What about quinine?" Helena asked.

"Definitely no," Big Per replied.

"I'm going to ride to Nevada and get the doctor," Ole said, starting for the barn.

Big Per grabbed him. "In this weather? Are you crazy? Besides, the old fool is drunk most of the time."

"Per is right, Ole," Helena said. "But Julia Twedt told me there is a new young doctor in Ames."

"Then I'll ride to Ames!" Ole said, breaking free of Big Per's grasp and running for the barn.

"Helena, stop him!" Big Per said.

"No," Helena whispered. "The doctor has to know more than we do."

The cabin door opened. Berent cried, "Mama! Oline is throwing up!"

"Oh, dear Lord!" Helena said, rushing into the cabin. "I didn't think there was anything left in her to throw up." Berent slammed shut the door.

Big Per stared at the closed door, not knowing what to do. He sighed. As much as he wanted to help, there was nothing more he could do. He looked to the heavens. Snow was now falling more heavily. Reluctantly, he climbed back into his wagon and turned Buck and Pride for home. "God," he prayed aloud. "Protect the Branjords."

Ole was saying the same prayer as he bridled Lady. Prayer was all he could do in confronting scarlet fever. He was well aware of how deadly the disease was for children. "Perhaps the doctor in Ames has new medicine," he thought, and added that to his prayer.

Lady was reluctant to leave the barn. Ole jerked on the reins. "I don't like this any better than you do. I'm sorry." Lady did the horse equivalent of a sigh, and followed Ole out of the barn and up to the cabin. Helena met him on the porch, a heavy sweater, two wool scarves, and his buffalo shoes in hand.

"Here," Helena said. "Put these on. They will help to keep you warm."

Ole did not argue. He took off his sheepskin, put on the sweater, and then, with Helena's help, struggled back into the coat. Next, he put one scarf around his neck and the other over his cap and ears and tied it under his chin. "I don't think I need the buffalo shoes."

"Put them on!" Helena ordered. "Don't be a stubborn Norwegian."

Ole grunted and slipped into the overshoes made of buffalo hide, hair out. They had been made for him by Emma's husband in Hardin County. "Get back inside," Ole said as he jumped on Lady's back. "You're freezing out here."

"Be careful," Helena said.

Ole forced a smile. "I'll be fine. All I have to do is follow the stage road. Have Martin milk the cows. Everything else is taken care of." He turned Lady and trotted down to the stage road.

Helena watched with both hope and fear. It was her turn to pray.

Chapter Thirty-Eight

Ole had been gone an hour when Martin entered the cabin, red-faced and glassy-eyed. One look at him made Helena's heart sink. "Are you sick, Martin?"

"I don't feel so good," he answered.

Helena, who was sitting in the rocking chair with Berent on her lap, leaned her head back and closed her eyes. "Dear Lord, give me strength," she muttered.

"Where is Papa?" Martin asked.

"He's riding to Ames to get the doctor."

"Is Oline bad sick?"

"I'm afraid so."

A shiver ran the length of Martin's body. He dashed for the sink. He did not make it.

"Oh, pew!" Berent said, jumping from his mother's lap.

Martin fell to his knees, disgusted with himself as he hovered over the pooling vomit. "I'm sorry, Mama."

Helena quickly snatched the chamber pot, knowing there was more to come. She reached Martin just in time to capture the second stream. She knelt beside Martin and placed her arms around his shoulders. "Don't hold it in. Vomiting is good." She looked back at Berent. "Bring me the towel by the bed and a damp washcloth from the sink."

Berent did as he was told and then retreated to the table bench. "Are Oline and Martin going to die?" he asked in a small, frightened voice.

"No!" Helena answered sharply. "Don't be silly! They are just sick." She gently wiped Martin's face with the cloth. He was burning with fever. She kissed his forehead. "Martin, I want you to stay just as you are. I'm sure you will throw up more. I'm going to get your pallet down from the loft. When I think you're done vomiting, we'll get you into your nightshirt."

"I can't," Martin said, still trembling. "I have to milk the cows."

"No, you don't. I'll milk the cows."

A surprised look came over Martin's red, moist face. "You don't milk."

"I do today," Helena answered, getting to her feet.

Berent ran to the ladder. "I'll get the pallet, Mama."

"Thank you, Berent. You can hand me down Oline's too."

After scrambling halfway up the ladder, Berent stopped. "Should I bring down my pallet?"

"No. Yours stays put."

Berent's mouth dipped at the corners. "Am I sleeping in the loft by myself?"

The first smile of the day came to Helena's lips. "That's right. If you're old enough to wear pants, you're old enough to sleep up there alone."

Berent blinked several times before setting his jaw and climbing into the loft, realizing for the first time that there were disadvantages to growing up.

Helena spent the next half hour settling Oline and Martin onto their pallets, placing the chamber pot between them. She had to mostly carry Oline from the bed, as the girl was only partially awake. The moment Oline laid her head on the pallet, she again was asleep. "Good," Helena thought. "Sleep is the best thing for her."

In an attempt to help, Berent grabbed a towel and began wiping the vomit from the floor. He had picked a dry towel, so he succeeded in making a bigger mess. Helena, tired as she was, could only shake her head and thank Berent for his effort.

"Am I a big help, Mama?" Berent asked.

"Yes, you are," Helena replied, rising from her knees after cleaning the floor. "I'm going to milk the cows. I want you to sit in Papa's chair and watch Oline and Martin. If either of them tells you to get me, you come running, understand?"

"Yes, Mama," Berent answered as he crawled up into his father's chair, feeling oh so important.

Helena put on her old work cape, picked up the milk pail, and left the cabin. The snow was now coming down hard, and as she stepped from the porch, the northwest wind caught her back and propelled her to the barn. There was no doubt a blizzard was preparing to release its fury.

The sheep were huddled together, the two calves were sleeping nearby, and Doll and the cows were contentedly munching hay. Helena approached the cows, surprised at how much warmer it was inside this flimsy building than outside in the wind. She touched Maud's back. The cow turned and perked her ears, as if to say, "What are you doing here?"

Helena patted the cow's neck. "Please don't kick me, Maud. It's been a long time since I did this." She then sat herself on the milk stool and put the pail between her legs. Pausing for a moment to take a deep breath, she put her hands on Maud's two front teats. The cow shivered and raised her right hind leg. Helena instantly released the teats. "Sorry, Maud. I forgot my hands were cold." She rubbed her hands together on her cape for several seconds before trying again. Maud's right hind leg stayed put. Milk began to stream into the pail.

Helena had not forgotten how to milk. If the truth be told, she was quite good at it. But she also had not forgotten why she avoided the task. The touch of the teats, the smell of the hide, the sound of the milk striking the bottom of the pail, all released a nightmare of repressed memories. With each squeeze of her hands, bile built in her stomach. A cloak of fear and dread wrapped itself around her. Tighter and tighter it became until she no longer could breathe.

He was in the barn! He was standing behind her! She could smell him. Smell his lust. She could hear him taking great gulps of air, making it impossible for her to breathe. Sweat broke out on her forehead. She attempted to scream, but only a childlike whimper escaped her lips.

Suddenly, Maud's right hind leg flashed, missing Helena by inches. Helena released the teats, trembling. She realized she had been jerking rather than milking Maud. The cow turned her head and looked angrily at her tormenter. Helena relaxed enough to reach up and gently stroke Maud's side. "I'm sorry, Maud. I didn't mean to hurt you." The cow turned her attention back to the hay bunk, and she too relaxed.

Helena sat on the stool for over a minute, doing nothing but trying to regain control of her emotions. She took a deep breath and forced herself to look out at the falling snow. Fear was replaced by anger. Anger at herself. "Stupid woman!" she snarled, and then thought, "Here I have two children sick with scarlet fever and a husband on the road in a near blizzard, and I'm having a nervous attack over something that happened when I was a girl!"

"Stupid!" she said aloud again, and returned to her milking, now concerned with what was really important. Where was Ole? Had he reached Ames?"

Almost.

By keeping Lady at a ground-covering trot, his rear end was sore, but he had reached the cutoff to Franklin, only two miles from Ames. Ole passed the cutoff and shook his head. Franklin was withering like a tree deprived of water. It had been a thriving little community, much like Fairview, until the railroad had decided the station should be two miles to the south.

The weather had worsened. Wet, heavy snow was now accumulating, making visibility a problem. Ole was thankful there was still daylight and that the increasing wind was at his back. He did not want to think of the ride home.

Ole passed Pressley Craig's cabin, almost missing it because of the snow. The sight of flickering light shining through the windows was comforting. He knew the Alexander Duff farm was next and then the Ames railroad station. He was almost there.

New false-front frame buildings huddled around the train station like kittens not wanting to stray far from their mother. Ole was surprised at the number. Ames was starting to look like a real town. Turg had told him that a man named Tilden was building a general store and that some damn fool was planning to build an apothecary on land that flooded every time there was even a moderate rain. Of course, since Ames was built on land surrounded by sloughs, this was true of much of the town. Ole could not see it, but behind the railroad station was the biggest slough of all. Locals said it was a great place to shoot ducks.

Lady was breathing hard as Ole brought her to a halt in front of the station. He was about to jump off and go inside for directions to the doctor, when a man, heavily bundled up because of the weather, stepped out of the long frame building.

"Excuse me!" Ole called. "Do you speak Norwegian?"

The man stopped, surprised that another human was out in such foul weather. "I don't speak anything else."

"I don't either," a relieved Ole continued. "I was afraid everybody in Ames was a Yankee."

"Most are, but there's a few of us Norskies. What's your problem?"

"I'm looking for the doctor. Do you know where he lives?"

"I do. But I don't think he's much of a doctor." He paused and then pointed to the Congregational church, barely visible through the snow. "See the church? Go two houses north."

"Thank you," Ole said, turning Lady in the direction pointed.

The man just waved as he began walking in the opposite direction, thankful he had only two hundred yards to his home and was not the poor devil on the horse.

Ole turned north at the church, a simple frame structure with a steeple, almost identical to Saint Petri. The second house was obviously new. There were still cans of paint sitting on the front porch. It was not fancy, but substantial. Through the lamp-lit windows on either side of the door, Ole could see the front of the home was a combination office and waiting room, which meant the living quarters were in the back and on the second floor.

Lady shook herself with relief when Ole slid off of her back, tied the reins to a hitching rail, and climbed the steps to the front door, where he rang a bell attached to the doorframe. There was no answer. Ole nervously shuffled his feet and then peeked in the right window. No movement. Ole returned to the door and rang the bell long and hard. Because of the burning lamps, he knew someone was home.

"I'm coming! I'm coming!" an angry voice called from inside.

After a short pause, the door opened, revealing a tall, thin man in his twenties, dressed in a black suit and white shirt, minus the collar. His black hair was slicked down and parted in the middle. His long face was punctuated by a Roman nose, under which was a perfectly trimmed mustache and goatee. One glance told Ole that this face was, under the best of circumstances, not pleasant, and under the current circumstances was next to hostile.

"What in the …!" the doctor said, then paused, taken aback by the snow-covered apparition standing before him. "My God, man! What are you doing out on night like this?" he said through a mouthful of food.

Ole's eyes blinked with confusion. The language spoken by the doctor was English. The only words he understood were "My God." He took a deep breath and asked, "Are you the doctor and do you speak Norwegian?"

The doctor's face scrunched like he had eaten an especially sour prune. In a false Norwegian accent he answered, "Ya, I am da doctor."

He then dropped the accent and said, "And I don't speak Norwegian!" To the doctor, Norwegians meant a language problem and the inability to pay for his services. He shouted over his shoulder, "Mrs. Helgeland, we have another Norskie here." Then to Ole he said, with a beckoning wave, "Well, don't just stand there. Come in and shut the door."

Ole understood and gladly entered the warm room, shutting the door behind him. The two men looked uneasily at each other until a stout, gray-haired, middle-aged woman, nearly the same height as Ole, entered from the kitchen. She wore a plain black wool dress covered by a full apron, on which she was wiping her hands. There was no doubt she was cook and housekeeper.

"What is your problem?" she asked Ole in Norwegian, her voice as tired as the look in her blue eyes. It was obvious that working for this doctor was no walk in the park.

"My daughter has scarlet fever," Ole replied. "I want the doctor to come see her."

Mrs. Helgeland stepped back, her demeanor softening. "Scarlet fever! Oh, I am so sorry. Are you sure?"

"Yes. She has a strawberry tongue."

"Where do you live?"

"Two miles south of Fairview."

The doctor understood "scarlet fever" and "Fairview" and knew what Ole wanted. "No, sir! There is no way I'm driving to Fairview in this weather. Besides," he added, his voice lowering to almost a whisper, "there is nothing I can do."

After the translation, Ole asked, "Are there no new medicines?"

The doctor had been asked this question before and did not wait for Mrs. Helgeland to translate. "No. I'm sorry to say there is nothing."

Ole visibly slumped. He understood the word no. "There is nothing?"

Again the doctor understood and shook his head. "There are five ways to treat scarlet fever. One, cold compresses to keep down the fever; two, sponge baths for the same reason; three, sweating out the bad humors; four, bleeding out the bad humors; and five, blistering. The body can contain only one disease at a time. The pain of the blistering drives out the disease. But this is a last resort."

While Mrs. Helgeland translated, the doctor disappeared into his office. Ole listened to the woman, his hope diminishing, his anguish growing. When Mrs. Helgeland finished, she asked Ole, "Can I get you some food?"

"No, no. I have to get home."

"Not in this weather! Fairview is too far. You and the horse could stay in the livery stable."

"Thank you, but no. My wife is expecting me."

Mrs. Helgeland frowned and touched Ole's arm. "You won't help your wife and family by freezing to death on the road."

"I won't freeze," Ole said, attempting a smile. He was about to leave when the doctor came out of his office carrying a glass tube and a small jar of sticks. He handed both to Ole. "The tube has leeches in it. They are good for bleeding. Just put some milk on the girl's arm or make a small cut. Either will get the leeches to sucking. Let each suck until you think it has taken enough blood. The jar has scented sticks. You and your wife put those under your noses when you work with the girl. The sticks help keep the bad humors from entering your bodies."

"Thank you," Ole said in English as he put the jar and the tube in his coat pocket.

The doctor hesitated, then asked, "You don't have fifty cents, by chance?"

Mrs. Helgeland gave the doctor a sharp look before translating.

Ole's eyes narrowed and he stiffened. "Yes, but I forgot to bring any money."

Upon hearing the translation, the doctor sneered, "How convenient." He then turned and returned to his living quarters. There was no need for a translation. A sneer is a sneer in any language. Mrs. Helgeland patted Ole's arm twice, as if to say she was sorry, and followed the doctor.

Ole wanted to throw the tube and jar on the floor, but forced himself to leave the house. The leeches and sticks may be of some help. He mounted Lady and turned her north into what was now a roaring blizzard. Ole promised himself he was not going to die on the road, if for no other reason than to make damn sure this doctor got his fifty cents!

A gust of wind rattled the cabin windows and whistled down the chimney, making the logs in the fireplace crackle and the flames sputter and hiss. Helena sat in her rocking chair, exhausted. One sick child had been difficult; two was a nightmare. Her back and knees ached from kneeling between Oline and Martin—comforting them, placing cold cloths on their heads, giving them sponge baths, having them gargle the vinegar mixture, giving them ice to suck on, attempting to get them to eat, cleaning up vomit, wiping away tears. She even made mustard plasters to put on their stomachs to help control the vomiting. That failed.

Another gust forced more frigid air down the chimney, carrying snowflakes which made the fire sizzle like fat in a skillet. The candle on the table flickered, then died, leaving only a thin layer of smoke to mark its passing.

Berent lifted his head from Helena's chest. "Is the fire going out, Mama?"

Helena opened her eyes. "No, Berent. We have plenty of wood. Besides, the stove is going too."

"I'm glad," Berent said, laying his head back on his mother's breasts. "I don't like being cold."

Helena kissed the boy's blond curls. "Don't worry. I won't let you get cold."

Ever since Ole had left for Ames, Berent had been like a second shadow, and had crawled into her lap the moment she sat. Helena knew his clinging was more than wanting attention. He was frightened. So was she.

"When is Papa getting home?"

"Soon. Real soon."

There was a long pause, then Berent asked, "Is he lost in the snow?"

"No!" Helena said, with much more conviction than she felt. "He's not lost. Lady knows the way home."

Berent sat up smiling. "That's right! Lady knows the way home." He lay back down. Helena felt his body relax. She wished hers could. To herself, she prayed, "Bring my Ole home safe. Please don't let him be lost."

Ole was not lost. Thanks to the stage road running next to the river, he was able to keep moving in the right direction. The road itself was invisible, covered ankle deep in blowing, swirling snow. Ole trusted Lady to secure a firm footing. In truth, she was guiding him, not the other way around.

He was in a whiteout, doggedly swimming against the current in a sea of snow. He could not see ten feet in any direction. Only the shadowy trees on the right and the north wind kept him oriented. Had he been on the open prairie … Ole shuddered at the thought. Had he been on the open prairie, he would not only have been lost, he would have been dead.

Ole bent low over Lady's neck. Even though only his eyes were uncovered, the flakes struck his face like miniature shrapnel. The scarf over his face had become a frozen mask. It burned his skin, but he dared not remove it. He put his left cheek next to Lady's hide. Warmth … beloved warmth. He patted her. "You are a blessing, Lady. Keep going. We are more than halfway home." The words were blown back into Ole's face, never reaching the horse's ears. But the touch encouraged her on.

Because there had been a brief break in the snowfall, Ole had seen a light inside a cabin. He knew the farm was four miles south of his own. He had no idea how long he had traveled since the sighting. He knew only that each step his faithful Lady took made him one step closer to those he loved most.

Ole looked up, straining to see anything familiar. Nothing. Just snow, which now was blowing into sizable drifts. He was so cold. Never, not even fishing in the North Sea as a young man, had he been so cold. He felt his body growing numb. His mind began to float. He saw his mother at the fireplace, cooking. How strange. His eyes closed. He swayed. Sensing he was falling, he grabbed Lady's mane. His eyes opened. He was halfway off of Lady's back.

Adrenaline saved him. He clung to Lady's mane, then righted himself. Fear gripped him with the force of an angry grizzly. He had almost fallen. Falling meant sure death. Ole struck his legs and flapped his arms. As his head cleared, anger replaced fear. What a wasted trip! He was risking his life in a blizzard for what? Leeches and scented sticks and information he already knew! And then there was the doctor. He had the gall to ask for fifty cents! What was his name? Ole realized he didn't know. Just as well, he thought. He would never darken the man's door again except to throw fifty cents in his face!

Ole's own face actually felt warm. Anger was good. He swore, something he seldom did, and felt even warmer. Thinking of the doctor, he said every swear word he knew, shouting them into the wind. Lady heard and broke into a trot. Ole bellowed a crazed laugh and cried, "We're not going to die, Lady! That damn doctor is going to keep both of us alive!"

Helena's eyes snapped open. She thought she heard something. Perhaps Ole was home! She listened carefully, but heard only the wind. Sighing, she looked down at Berent, who was sound asleep in her lap. She kissed the curls she loved and then gently shook him awake. "Time you went to bed, Berent." The boy snuggled closer, warm and secure in his mother's arms. "Come on, sleepyhead. Wake up."

Berent reluctantly opened his eyes. "Is Papa home?"

"No," Helena answered, trying her best to sound reassuring. "Stand up. Let's get your clothes off and nightshirt on."

More asleep than awake, Berent stood as Helena prepared him for bed. The nightshirt had just fallen over the boy's shoulders when the door banged open and a snow-covered, half-frozen masked figure stumbled into the cabin. Both Helena and Berent screamed. Berent clung to his mother.

"It's just me," Ole mumbled as he closed the door and collapsed into his chair.

"Ole?" Helena asked in disbelief.

Ole nodded, unable to do anything more.

Helena pushed Berent aside, jumped to her feet, and ran to Ole. She put her hands on his face.

"No!" Ole cried. "I … I think the scarves are frozen to my face."

"Oh, dear Lord," Helena said, stepping back, not knowing how to help this poor man she hardly recognized. Icicles hung like miniature glistening snakes from the scarf covering his mouth. Snow melted from the top of his cap, forming drops that fell like a light mist into his eyes, which in turn made them shimmer with the blue of a deep mountain lake.

Helena knelt beside him and clutched his still-gloved hands. Berent remained by the rocking chair, still not sure this was really his father. Ole groaned, closed his eyes, and allowed himself to relax. Behind the frozen scarf, his cracked, chapped lips turned up at the corners. He was well aware that this night, he had cheated death.

His wife knew she had to get the scarves from his face. She soaked a fresh towel in warm water and applied it to the frozen material. The icicles hissed as if protesting their demise. Ole moaned. Helena ordered, "Hold still! I'm being as gentle as I can." She kept soaking the towel and applying it to his face until she was certain all the ice had melted. She then walked behind his chair. "Lean forward so I can untie the scarf covering your face."

Ole did so, and Helena began working the knot, which also was frozen. By the time she had the scarf loose, her hands were freezing. The ends fell free, but the cloth still clung to Ole's face.

"This may hurt," Helena said as she carefully began removing the scarf, beginning with the portion that covered his nose. Ole winced. "I'm sorry," Helena whispered, "But this has to come off."

And, eventually, it did, falling into Ole's lap, along with facial hair and pieces of frostbitten skin. The scarf that covered his ears and tied under his chin came off with little damage, as did the cap. When bare, Ole's face resembled a red dress with irregular white polka dots.

Helena again soaked the towel and placed it over Ole's face. Ole sighed. "That feels so good." Helena did not bother to answer. She was busy removing his mittens and placing his hands in a pan of warm water.

"The hands shouldn't be too bad," Ole mumbled. "I was able to keep them inside the sheepskin much of the way."

"I think you're right," Helena answered with relief. "Let's see about the feet."

Thanks to the buffalo boots, Ole's feet appeared to be a healthy pink. Helena rubbed them vigorously. "They're good," she said.

Berent eased his way to Ole and tapped him lightly on the arm. "Is that really you under there, Papa?"

"It's me, Berent," Ole said, without removing the towel.

The boy stood for a moment, not really convinced. Then he picked up a corner of the towel and peeked, his face only inches away from Ole's. Berent grinned. "It is you!"

Ole could not help but smile, even though doing so made his face feel like it was going to crack apart like a dried clump of dirt. "I told you so."

"Go to bed, Berent," Helena ordered, continuing to rub Ole's feet. "Your papa needs to rest."

"Can I sleep down here?"

"No. Now get up in the loft."

Berent's mouth turned down, but he obeyed, careful not to step on his sleeping siblings. Halfway up the ladder, he paused. "Are you sure there are no trolls in America?"

"I'm sure," Helena answered with exasperation. "Besides, trolls live under bridges, not in lofts. Get to sleep and don't forget your prayers."

Berent scampered up the ladder, dove under the covers, and curled into a fetal ball, just in case his mother was wrong about trolls.

Helena leaned her head against Ole's knee. "Thank God you're home."

"That's who to thank," Ole said. "I don't know how we made it."

"Did you find the doctor?"

Ole snorted. "Yes, but what a waste. There is nothing new. He gave me some silly scented sticks for us to wear under our noses, and a tube of leeches. And for that he wanted fifty cents!"

"No!"

"Oh yes! And, by God, he'll get it, too!" Ole replied, pulling the towel from his now angry face.

Helena stood, biting her lip to keep from tears. "I was so hoping there would be some new medicine."

Ole placed the basin of water on the floor, sagging slightly with the effort. "Well, there's not. I risked my life and that of a wonderful animal for scented sticks and leeches."

"How is Lady?" Helena asked, picking up the basin and placed it on the stove.

"I think she will be all right. I pray so. I would have ridden by the cabin if she had not turned off the road on her own. I couldn't see a thing."

"I love that horse," Helena whispered, fully realizing the debt she owed Lady.

"So do I. After I rubbed her down and gave her some water, she lay down on the straw and was asleep before I left the barn."

"Doll will watch over her."

Ole nodded. "I'm sure of that. So will Doggie."

"Doggie! He never goes near the barn."

"He did tonight. He's curled up not ten feet from the sheep."

"I can hardly believe it," Helena said, shaking her head. She then remembered a Bible verse. "'In that time, the wolf shall lie down with the lamb.' Or was it the lion?"

"I don't remember." Ole yawned. "I've heard of things like that happening on high ground during floods, but I never thought I would see it."

Helena placed her hands on Ole's shoulders. "You need to get up and get out of those wet clothes."

Ole answered by struggling to his feet. Helena steadied him and, much like she had done with Berent, helped him out of his clothes and into his nightshirt. She next steered him to the bed, where he fell asleep as soon as his head hit the pillow.

Helena returned to her chair. She wanted desperately to lie down herself, but she knew there would be no bedtime for her. She closed her eyes and rocked, thankful the cabin was quiet and she could listen to her husband snore.

The quiet ended with a cough, a hack, and uncontrollable gagging that brought Helena out of her chair and over to Oline's pallet. The girl's eyes were wide with fear, and her face was turning blue when Helena knelt beside her.

"Sit up, Oline! Sit up!" Helena cried, boosting her daughter into an upright position. She pounded on Oline's back. "Vomit! Don't try and breathe! Throw up!"

Oline's eyes responded with terror. She could not vomit. She could not breathe. Unable to think of anything else to do, Helena reached over and struck Oline in the diaphragm with her fist. A wad of phlegm shot from the girl's mouth, almost striking Helena in the face. Oline gulped for air. Her color returned to normal.

Helena held the girl tightly as Oline panted and then began to cry. There was nothing else she could do. She then kissed her daughter's tangled, sweaty hair. "Everything will be all right, sweetheart. You will be fine."

Oline's sobs lessened as she pressed herself closer to her mother. After they had ceased, she whispered, "I don't want to die, Mama."

"You're not going to die, Oline," Helena replied, tightening her hug. "I won't let you."

There was a long pause before Oline said, "I feel so awful."

"I know, and I'm so sorry. But I think this is the worst of it. You'll be better in the morning."

"You promise?"

Helena kissed her again. "I can't promise, but I think so."

Oline's nightgown was open enough for Helena to see that her neck and shoulders were covered with an angry red rash. Now there was no doubt the disease was scarlet fever.

When Helena was sure Oline was asleep, she leaned her head and shoulders against the loft ladder, closed her eyes, and prayed, "Dear Lord, please make her better. Don't take my little girl from me."

Chapter Thirty-Nine

Helena awoke with a stiff neck and sore back, confused because she was both hot and cold. She looked down at Oline and understood. Her chest and arms were heated by the fever. Her back was exposed to the drafts produced by the relentless, howling wind.

Dying embers in the fireplace provided the only light. Helena had no idea what time it was, wished she knew, but concluded it didn't matter. What mattered were the fires in the stove and fireplace. Both were nearly out. The cabin was becoming cold. That was unacceptable. Cold was her enemy. Cold must be fought.

A low moan escaped Helena's lips as she eased herself from behind Oline and laid her flat on the pallet. She paused, waiting to see if there would be a choking spasm. There was none. Oline whimpered but did not awaken. Helena put a damp, folded towel on the girl's forehead before getting up and tending to the fires.

Minutes later, Helena had both the stove and fireplace blazing, but she was still cold. She tried rotating, as if on a vertical spit, in front of the fireplace. It did not work. One half of her was always cold. In desperation, she wrapped herself in her work cape and settled into her rocking chair.

The shivering increased. Helena was not surprised. She had been through this many times, and at the moment was too tired to fight it. Cold gripped her body in frigid arms dripping with icicles, and flooded her mind with pain—pain that only would die when she drew her last breath. Nettie…sweet little Nettie. Nettie was why she hated the cold.

Helena

She dies in my arms. Just stops breathing. I feel her tiny body relax. She had tried so hard to live.

We have stopped for the night. The raw, cold wind fans the small campfire. The moon is full. Oline is asleep in the wagon. I sit on a stool by the tailgate. Ole spreads our sleeping tarp near the fire. He looks up at me and somehow knows. "She's gone," he says. I nod. He gets up and gently takes her from me. He rocks her in his arms like he has done countless times when she cried and could not sleep. His tears fall onto her half-closed eyes. Neither of us says a word. He stands there for nearly a half an hour and then hands her back to me and takes a shovel from the wagon.

The grave does not take long to dig. Nettie was not yet one. Ole returns and reaches out for her. I clutch her to me. "She's still warm," I say. Ole drops his arms and sits down beside me, his back against the rear wheel.

That is the way we spend the night. I hold her until the moon sets and there is pink in the eastern sky. Ole rises, taking her from me. I do not resist. She is now cold. He takes a step toward the grave. "Wait!" I say. I go to my rosemal box, where I keep my needlework, and get my scissors. I cut a lock from her fine, almost transparent, baby hair, tie it with a yellow ribbon, and put it in the box. We kiss her one last time, then Ole wraps her tightly in her blanket and secures it with two small ropes.

I carry her to the grave. It wasn't a proper grave, just a hole in the ground. Ole takes her from me. He then lies on his stomach and lowers her into the hole. His arms are not quite long enough, so he is forced to drop her the last few inches.

Ole gets up, removes his hat, and prays. "Lord, we don't know why you took our Nettie from us. We loved her. We know she is in a better place. Have your angels care for her." He pauses, choking back his tears, then adds, "The Lord giveth, the Lord taketh away. Blessed be the name of the Lord."

Ole's grief turns to anger as he grabs his shovel and begins to fill the grave. I feel a tug at my dress. Oline is standing there, looking into the hole. She sees Nettie's blanket. "Don't throw dirt on Nettie, Papa," she says. Ole begins to sob. I snatch Oline up in my arms and run to the wagon.

When the grave is filled and a makeshift cross is stuck into the soft earth, Ole hitches Doll and Lady to the wagon and we move on to the west. Oline sits on my lap. She looks up at me. "Don't leave Nettie, Mama. She'll be cold." Three-year-olds do not understand death. I hold her close to me and weep.

We just drive away. That's all we can do. We drive away and leave Nettie alone and cold on the endless prairie.

Chapter Forty

"I'm cold, Mama," Martin moaned.

Helena opened her eyes and saw that Martin had kicked off all of his blankets. She quickly knelt beside him and tucked the blankets under his chin. He shivered as she wiped the sweat from his face. To her surprise, he suddenly sat up, looked around, spotted the chamber pot, and vomited. Helena supported him as his stomach emptied. It was not surprising to her that not a drop was spilled on the blankets. That was just Martin being Martin.

He lay back down on his pallet. Helena wiped his face. "Is Papa home?"

"Yes," Helena replied. "He's sleeping. Do you think you can drink something?"

"No. My throat hurts."

"I'll get you some ice."

Helena unlatched the door. She opened it slightly and carefully. Even though the door faced south, she knew from experience that a strong north wind could catch it and blow it open. The snow swirled around her feet as she reached into the box of ice and chipped off a piece. She did not bother to look into the blackness. Her ears told her the blizzard was getting worse.

Back with Martin, Helena moistened the boy's lips with ice, then put a small piece in his mouth. "Suck on it and try to swallow." Martin did as asked. "Is that better?"

"Yes," he murmured. "More."

Helena continued to feed him pieces of ice until the chunk was gone. "Do you want more?"

Martin shook his head and closed his eyes. "Make it go away, Mama," he whispered.

Helena bit her lip. Two tears rolled down her cheeks. Only once before in her life had she felt so helpless. She took a deep breath. "I'll try, Martin." Her back straightened. "I'll do more than try. I'll make it go away!" Martin smiled before falling back to sleep. Helena stared at him. Her fists clenched. One was enough. She would not lose these two. That she would not allow!

Ole's growling stomach forced the rest of his body awake. His eyes opened to see Helena standing at the stove, frying potatoes and meat. The smells made him realize he had not eaten since the previous noon. He reluctantly swung his legs out of the bed and onto the cold floor.

Helena gave him an exhausted smile. "I thought you would be hungry."

"I am," Ole said, getting to his feet. "How are they doing?"

"No real change. I was hoping Oline's fever would break, but it hasn't. Your clothes are hanging on the peg by the sink. They are dry."

Ole crossed to the sink, drank a dipper of water from the pail, and looked into the mirror. "Well, I'll never win a beauty contest, but I think I'll be all right."

On most days, such a remark would have brought a quick retort from Helena. Not today. She was much too tired.

"Did you get any sleep?" Ole asked as he dressed.

"Not much."

"You should have woken me up."

This brought a snort from Helena. "Thor's hammer wouldn't have awakened you last night."

"What time is it?"

"Early," Helena replied, dishing up a plate of hash and setting it on the table. "The sun is up, but with this awful storm, you can hardly tell."

Ole looked out of the window. Black had turned to dull gray, but because of the blowing snow, he could not see ten feet beyond the porch. He sat down at the table. "This smells delicious."

"It's the leftover turkey from Thanksgiving," Helena said, dishing up a plate for herself. "I made a lot. I'm afraid this will be breakfast, dinner, and supper."

"That's fine with me," Ole answered, his mouth full.

Ole wolfed down the food and was working on his second plateful when Helena brought two cups of coffee and sat down herself. She too had not eaten since the previous day, but discovered she had little appetite. She drank the coffee as she picked at her food. "I'm worried about the children lying flat. Oline almost choked to death."

A forkful of hash hung in the air in front of Ole's open mouth, forgotten. "What did you do?"

"I pounded her back and punched her in the stomach. A wad of phlegm came out. How can we prop them up?"

Ole remembered the food and swallowed it before answering. "There are some boards in the crib. I can bring in extra fire logs, prop the ends of the boards on them, and pull the pallets on the boards."

"That sounds good," Helena said, relieved that Ole had thought of a solution.

An excited voice from the loft interrupted the conversation. "Mama! My quilt is all white!"

"What?" Helena asked in disbelief.

"There's snow on my blanket. See?" Berent dangled his quilt down from the loft, creating his own miniature snowstorm.

"Oh, for goodness sake!" Helena said, watching the flakes fall on Oline and Martin. "Bring the quilt down so I can dry it."

The boy scrambled down the ladder, dragging the quilt with him, and greeted his parents with a big smile. "Can I build a snowman today?"

"Not today, Berent," Ole said, after emptying his coffee. "It is still a blizzard out there. You'll have to stay in and help Mama."

Berent's smile turned south. He dragged his quilt to Helena. "Can I play with Oline and Martin?"

"No, they are still sick," Helena said, taking the quilt and giving him a kiss. "How are you feeling?"

"Hungry."

"Good! I'll help you get dressed and then you can eat breakfast."

Ole put on his sheepskin, knit cap, and buffalo boots. "I'll be right back with the boards."

It took him longer than he expected. After he put on his mittens, he stepped off the porch and was nearly blown over by a gust of wind. The snow was not falling. It was riding the north wind with a vicious glee that struck Ole's raw face like an invading swarm of stinging wasps. He put both hands to the right side of his face as he stumbled through thigh-high snow to the crib.

A six-foot drift greeted him on the north side of the building. All that could be seen of the wagon was the box and the top rims of the rear wheels. He glanced at the chicken house and thought for a moment that it was gone, but then saw the roof. He hoped the chickens had survived. He would check later.

Ole fought his way into the crib alley and out of the storm. He paused to catch his breath before looking through his small collection of cut lumber. There were fewer pieces than he remembered; only three short one by six boards would be of any use. He then spied the folded wagon tarp and had an idea.

Inside the cabin, Berent was eating and Helena was giving Oline and Martin ice when Ole entered with his load. Smiling down at the children, he dropped the boards and tarp on the floor. "Are you feeling better?" he said with a cheerfulness he did not feel. Both shook their heads. "Sorry to hear that." He turned to his youngest. "Berent, I'm going for firewood. Open the door when I kick it."

Within less than a minute, the kick came. Berent opened the door, and Ole came in and set the wood down behind the two sick children. "I'm going to need you two to sit up," he said.

The children did so with Helena's aid. Ole stacked the wood into three equal piles, placed the top end of the boards onto the piles, and then partially unfolded the tarp on top of the boards. When he was finished, he pulled the top half of the pallets up onto the tarp, so that when the children lay back down, they were lying at nearly a thirty-degree angle.

"Is that better?" Ole asked.

Oline and Martin smiled. It was better—much easier to breathe.

"Thank you," Helena said, once again impressed by her husband's ingenuity.

"Good!" Ole said to Helena as he got to his feet. "I am going out to do the chores. When I come in, you are going to bed." Ole grabbed the milk pail and left the cabin.

Helena did not argue. She only hoped she could stay awake that long.

Ole's walk to the barn came close to being a run, as the wind was to his back. Twice he almost fell. Through the snow, he saw the hog house which, like the chicken house, was buried up to the roof. He climbed over the pasture gate—there was too much snow to open it—and ducked out of the wind into the barn. What he saw brought a smile to his lips. The sheep and calves were still contentedly lying in the straw. Lady was standing beside Doll, munching on hay. And Maud and Mabel eyed him reproachfully, as if asking, "What took you so long?"

The barn was remarkably comfortable. Ole was able to unbutton his coat, take off his mittens, and pull the knit cap above his ears. He crossed to the horses, giving Lady several pats on the neck and a hug. "I love you, girl. Thank you." Lady ignored him. It was not going to be that easy for him to get back in her good graces. Not after what she had been through! However, Doll was jealous and nuzzled Ole. "I love you too," he said, patting her neck. "If there is a next time, and I hope there won't be, it will be your turn."

Ole opened the horse chest and pulled out a tin of horse liniment. He spread some on his frostbitten nose, cheeks, and forehead. He did not know if would do any good, but it felt soothing. "And," he thought, "if it is good enough for Doll and Lady, it is good enough for me."

The milking came next. Since there would be no churning, and the milk can which now sat on the porch was full, Ole dumped the milk into the hog trough. The pigs, being pigs, rushed out into the storm and gobbled it up. Ole then cleaned the ice from the water troughs. Ole smiled at the artesian well. No matter what the weather, that beautiful well just kept flowing.

His last stop was the chicken house. He approached it with concern. It was the least substantial building on the place. He shoveled the snow from the door, thankful that the previous owner had had the sense to place the door on the south side. As he scooped, his hopes rose. There was movement inside, and there appeared to be little damage.

The doorway was only four feet high, forcing Ole to stoop as he entered. To his relief, most of the chickens were comfortably squatting on roosts. Three were on the nests. All were quietly clucking away. None had frozen. In fact, thanks to the large snowdrifts surrounding it, the building was verging on being warm.

From the pail he had carried with him, Ole poured water into pans that usually sat outside. He then checked the round tin feeder and was satisfied there was enough corn for at least one more day. Since he was there, Ole decided to pick the eggs. He removed his mittens and picked four eggs from the empty nests, putting them in the pocket of his sheepskin coat. Two of the occupied nests had nothing. From the third, he picked a still-warm egg and, for his trouble, received a painful peck on his hand. Ole retaliated by swatting the chicken out of the nest. She flew to the roosts, squawking her indignation. Once there, she ruffled her feathers and continued to scold Ole, who was sucking the back of his hand and glaring at the bird. "I'll remember you the next time Helena wants to fry a chicken." The hen was still in full voice when Ole ducked out of the chicken house, making sure the door was securely shut.

Carrying the pail and scoop shovel, Ole walked to the cabin. He noticed the snowfall was lightening. He could see all the way to the river. Maybe the worst was over … inside the cabin as well as out.

It was not.

Martin was vomiting into the chamber pot while Helena supported Oline, pleading with her to drink some water.

"It hurts, Mama," the girl croaked.

"I know it does, but your body needs water." Oline took a deep breath and swallowed. "Good girl! Drink as much as you can." Oline took several more gulps before pulling away from the mug, causing water to drip down her chin and onto her nightgown. "Oh, Oline!" Helena cried out in frustration. "Now you're all wet."

"I'm sorry, Mama," the girl moaned, lying back on the pallet. "I hurt all over."

Helena put down the mug and picked up an almost dry towel. She dabbed Oline's nightgown, seeing that the rash now covered much of Oline's arms, neck, and chest. "I'm sorry I shouted at you," she said. "The fever will break soon, then you'll feel better. I promise." Oline closed her eyes. Helena replaced the damp towel on her daughter's forehead, praying that what she promised would be true.

"Mama," Martin whispered, "I missed some."

Helena looked. The boy had missed. For the first time. She cleaned it up with the almost dry towel. "I'm sorry," Martin continued.

"It's not your fault, Martin," Helena said with a weary smile. "Do you think you can drink some water?"

"I'll try."

Martin forced himself to sit up. Helena held the mug to his lips. He took several painful swallows, held up his hand, but did not pull away. No water was spilled. He lay back and looked at Helena with those old, thoughtful eyes. "Do we have scarlet fever, Mama?"

Helena was startled by the question. She had not wanted the children to know. But the old eyes already knew the answer. There was no sense lying. Yet she could not bring herself to say the words. She just nodded.

"People die from that, don't they?"

"Yes," Helena answered, hurriedly adding, "But most recover good as new."

The old eyes stared up her as if they knew she had not told all; she had not said the most likely to die were small children.

Helena turned away and scrambled to her feet, not wanting to look into the old eyes that seemed able to read her mind. She swayed, almost falling. Could he see the fear she desperately was trying to hide?

Martin

Mama is scared. She's been crying. I'm scared too. I've never felt so bad. I go from being hot to cold. I'm thirsty, but it hurts so much to swallow. Mama wants me to eat. I can't. All I do is throw up. It tastes awful. The ice helps. The wet towel on my head helps some. I don't have to pee. I don't have to do number two either. I wonder why?

Oline looks awful. She is sicker than me. Do I look that bad? I'm glad nobody at school can see me. I'm sure Oline is glad too. Especially Ernst. She likes Ernst. She says she doesn't, but I know she does. The school was closed because of the storm. At least I'm not missing school. I don't understand why some people don't like school. It will be fun to have Mr. Lyngen teach me. We're starting a book in English on the American Revolution. It was almost one hundred years ago. There are some long words, but Mr. Lyngen knows them all.

Oh! I have to throw up again! "Mama!" It tastes so bad. But I didn't miss. I didn't make a mess. Mama is giving me ice. It tastes good. I look up at her worried face. "Mama, are there books in heaven?" She looks at me funny. Now she is covering my face with a wet towel … my eyes too. I wonder why she is covering my eyes? I don't want to die. I can't die. I have so much to read. I have to teach Mama and Papa English.

Chapter Forty-One

When Ole entered the cabin, Helena was sitting in her rocking chair, a pensive Berent snuggling on her lap. He sat up. "Is it still snowing, Papa?"

"Yes," Ole replied, hanging up his coat and cap and removing his buffalo shoes. "But I think it is beginning to let up."

The boy brightened. "Can I go out and play?"

"No. What you can do is get off your mama's lap and go sit by the table. Mama is going to bed."

"It's daytime, Papa."

"I know. But Mama was up all night," Ole said, picking the boy up and setting him down on a table stool.

Helena sighed. "I can't, Ole. They are not any better."

"You can and you will," Ole said, gently pulling her from the chair. "I can give them ice and sponge baths and keep damp towels on their heads." He guided her to the bed. Before Ole could cover her, Helena was asleep.

"Are you kissing her good night, Papa?" Berent asked.

Ole chuckled. "That's a good idea, Berent." He bent down and kissed Helena on the cheek.

After checking that Oline and Martin were both asleep, Ole sat in his chair. Berent was onto his lap before he could get settled. The boy frowned and wrinkled his nose. "You smell funny, Papa."

"That's the liniment I put on my face."

"Does your face hurt?"

"Not so much. It is getting better."

Satisfied, Berent leaned his head against Ole's chest. "I heard Mama praying. She asked God not to let Oline and Martin die."

"I've been praying that too," Ole said, putting his arms around the boy.

"I don't want them to die. I would have nobody to play with."

"They're not going to die, Berent." Ole kissed the boy's forehead. "They'll be up playing with you in no time."

Berent sat up, smiling. "Me and Martin will have snowball fights!"

"What about Oline?"

"She throws too hard."

To his surprise, Ole laughed out loud. Doing so hurt his chapped lips, but gave a momentary lift to his worried mind.

Berent continued. "Do you think we can ride down the hill on the scoop shovel?"

"Do you think you're big enough?"

"Yes! Oh, that will be fun!"

Ole gave Berent a hug. It was enjoyable listening to the boy's excitement. But the joy ended abruptly when Oline moaned and cried out. Ole plopped Berent onto a stool and was at her side in seconds. He slipped his left arm under her neck and lifted her into a sitting position. Oline's eyes flew open, filled with terror. In a raspy, raw voice, she cried, "They're taking it! Don't let them take it, Papa!"

"Taking what, Oline?"

"The sound. They're taking away the sound!"

Ole held her close. "No one is taking anything, Oline."

"Yes, they are!" Oline clutched Ole's arm. "I can't hear it! Don't let them take it away. Please!"

"I won't," Ole replied, his voice quivering. "I won't let them. I promise."

Oline's body relaxed. Her eyes closed. Ole lowered her back onto the pallet and stared down at his daughter, more frightened than he had ever been. "Dear God. Please don't take her from me."

Not knowing what else to do, Ole wrung out two towels, putting one on her glistening forehead and using the other to bathe her neck, shoulders, and chest.

Oline

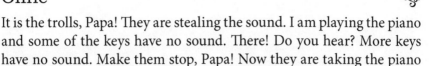

It is the trolls, Papa! They are stealing the sound. I am playing the piano and some of the keys have no sound. There! Do you hear? More keys have no sound. Make them stop, Papa! Now they are taking the piano out into the prairie. Stop! Pianos don't belong on the prairie. I'll catch you! I'll make you put it back! I'm running. I'm running as fast as I can. I can't catch them! Papa, they're taking my music!

Oh, no! There is a girl walking to school. She is wearing my blue dress and my shoes. She can't wear my clothes! I tell her to give them back. She says the dress and shoes are hers. She says Mama gave them to her when I died. I didn't die! I'm still alive! Give me back my clothes!

What is happening? I am rising above the ground. I can see the entire farm. I can see Fairview. I'm rising higher. It is beautiful! I can see for miles and miles. Now I can see trees, huge trees! Great, tall, evergreen trees that go on forever.

Now I am going down, down into a clearing. There is an old woman standing there. She is smiling at me. It is Grandma Rahto! She is telling me to lie down and rest. I do as she says. The meadow grass is soft, but it is blue … blue like my dress. Grandma tells me to sleep. Yes, Grandma. I will sleep.

Chapter Forty-Two

By noon, Ole's neck, back and knees ached. He placed a fresh towel on Oline's head, then stood and crossed to his chair, from where he studied his two sick children. Both were now covered with red rash. There was no more vomiting, but the fever had not broken. Oline worried him the most. Twice he had been forced to hold her down because of frightening hallucinations. Her sweet face was constantly contorting in pain and was so pale that the rash glared like tiny red beacons. "Please God," he silently prayed, "don't let her suffer. Break the fever."

"Papa, I'm hungry."

Ole looked down at his youngest, who was standing by his chair. He put his arm around Berent and gave him a hug. The boy had been remarkably good all morning, sitting in his mother's rocking chair, watching but saying little.

"I'll dish up some dinner," Ole said, crossing to the stove.

From the black, cast-iron skillet, Ole scraped two plates of turkey and potato hash. He was not really hungry, but knew he must eat. Berent carried his plate to the table, while Ole brought his and the coffeepot. After pouring himself a mug of coffee, he filled Berent's mug with milk from the pitcher. Both of them sat, and Ole picked up his fork.

"Aren't we going to say blessings?" Berent asked.

Ole set down the fork. ""Yes, we are. Thank you for reminding me." He folded his hands. Berent did the same and bowed his head. "Lord, bless this food you have so bountifully provided. And please, make Oline and Martin well. Amen."

Father and son ate in silence, the father only picking at his food, the son gulping it down.

"Should I wake Mama?" Berent asked after cleaning his plate and wiping a milk mustache from his face.

"No. She needs to sleep."

Berent looked out the window. "I think it has stopped snowing. Can I go outside?"

"Still too windy, Berent. You'll have to wait until tomorrow."

Berent's lower lip protruded. "I have nothing to do."

"I know," Ole said, tousling the boy's hair. "I'm sorry, and I thank you for being so good." Suddenly, Ole grinned. "I forgot," he said, reaching into the top pocket of his bib overalls. "Look what I found in the feed chest this morning."

Berent's eyes lit up, the uncertainty and worry dispelled by the object dangling in Ole's hand. "My whirligig! The one Mr. Larson made for me!"

"That's right. Someone must have lost it."

"Me!" Berent shouted as he snatched the button on a string from Ole. Within seconds, Berent was pulling the string in and out, making the button sing.

Ole's attention, however, was drawn to Martin, who groaned and kicked off his blankets. He quickly knelt beside the sick boy. "Are you awake, Martin?"

There was no answer. Ole covered the boy and put a damp towel on his head. He then turned to Berent. "I know you haven't taken a nap in a long time, but since there is nothing to do, why don't you go up to the loft and see if you can sleep."

Much to Ole's surprise, Berent did not argue. As the boy climbed the ladder, Ole thought, "He really must be bored to take a nap without a fuss."

The afternoon was a repeat of the morning. It was also the longest afternoon of Ole's life. Martin's rash became worse; Oline's breathing more labored. His repeated attempts to get them to drink failed. They only accepted small pieces of ice, which gave momentary solace. When the ice was gone, he used fresh snow. He bathed them and kept damp towels on their heads, but nothing diminished the fever. It continued to rage in the children with all the heat and fury of a gurgling sulfur pit, causing cries and whimpers that seared Ole's soul.

When it was time for the evening chores, Ole felt both relief and guilt; relief that he could escape to the barn, guilt because he had to awaken Helena. He crossed to the bed and gently shook Helena. Her eyes flew open, filled with dread. "Who died?" she demanded.

"Nobody died," Ole answered, giving her a reassuring squeeze. "I have to go milk."

Helena relaxed, putting her hand over Ole's. "Are they any better?"

"No. They are still burning up."

"What are we going to do?"

Ole sighed. "I'm thinking we should try the leeches."

Helena's fingers tightened on Ole's hand. "I don't like bleeding."

"Neither do I. But the doctors say it releases the bad humors in the blood."

"I still don't like it."

Ole removed his hand from her grasp and stood up straight. "We have to do something, and the doctors must know more than we do. We'll talk more when I come in."

Ole almost ran to the door, where he put on his coat, cap, and buffalo shoes and fled. Helena watched him go, knowing exactly how he felt. She too wanted to run. Instead, she rose from the bed and attended her sick children.

The snow had ceased. There were patches of blue in the western sky; however, the wind was still strong, blowing small whirlpools of dry flakes across the white surface like dust devils in the desert. Ole took a deep breath. The tension of the day was swept away by the cold, crisp air. His spirits rose. "Storms do end," he thought. "Clouds do give way to sunshine. Children do get well as fast as they get sick." He took another deep breath and smiled. The ending of the storm was a good omen.

Another positive sign was the empty barn. The sheep were pawing at the snow, while the calves were bouncing stiff-legged through it. Doll, Lady, and the cows were standing at the water trough, attempting to lick up the water that flowed over the hard, frozen ice. Ole broke up the ice in the trough and then did the same for the hogs. When the cows had drunk their fill, he led them back into the barn. Ole saw the straw was becoming damp and soiled. He made a mental note that tomorrow he would have to put down fresh bedding and fill the hay bunks. While he milked, he thought of other work that needed his attention. Doing work was good. It kept his mind off the children. Tomorrow, he promised himself, Oline and Martin would be on the mend and he could get back to farming.

As he had done in the morning, Ole fed the milk to the hogs. He then checked the chickens and, for no special reason, took the scoop shovel and cleared the snow away from the wagon. It felt good to use his muscles. It felt good to work up a sweat.

All too soon, he was finished. He looked around for other jobs that could not wait, jobs which required they be done now. There was only one. It was inside the cabin.

Ole stuck the scoop shovel into a snowbank with a sigh. His mood darkened as he trudged toward the cabin. Outside was freshness and hope. Inside was sickness and fear.

Berent, who was wearing his nightshirt, stood hands on hips. "I'm not tired! I slept all afternoon!"

Supper was over, night had fallen. Berent had been told to go to bed.

"I know," Helena said, bathing Oline's neck and shoulders. Ole was doing the same to Martin. The children responded with whimpers but did not wake up. "Papa and I have to take care of your brother and sister. Please go to bed."

"It's not fair, Mama!"

Ole answered. "No, it is not fair. Get used to it. Now go to bed!"

Tears rolled down Berent's cheeks as he walked to the ladder. Helena gave her husband a "how could you?" look. Ole groaned. "I'm sorry, Berent. But Mama and I are tired. You can go outside with me in the morning when I do chores."

"You promise?" Berent sniffed.

"I promise."

With something to look forward to, Berent climbed the ladder to the loft.

"The poor little boy just wants some attention," Helena said.

"And that's something he won't get until these two are better," Ole answered, more gruffly than he intended. "Have you thought about the leeches?"

"Yes. Oline is getting weaker. I think we have to try it."

"So do I," Ole agreed, rising to his feet and taking the tube of leeches from the shelf. He cringed as he looked at the ugly little things. Each was a small, dark, flattened worm with a segmented body and suckers at both ends. The thought of putting them on his children's bodies came close to making him sick.

"I can't watch this," Helena said, fleeing to her rocking chair.

Ole knelt beside Oline. He pulled the hem of her nightgown up to her knees, then took out a folding knife from his pocket.

"What are you going to do with that?" Helena cried.

"I thought you weren't going to watch."

"I can't help it."

Ole found a vein in Oline's leg and pricked the skin. "I'm making an opening for the leech."

A trickle of blood appeared among the red blotches on Oline's tender skin. Ole quickly opened the tube, placing it an angle next to the wound. A leech responded to the feast by slithering down the tube and attaching itself to the tiny opening. Oline did not seem to feel a thing. "Is it working?" Helena asked.

"Yes," Ole answered, desperately wanting to snatch the bloodsucker from his beloved daughter's leg. Instead, he moved to Martin and repeated the process. When he finished, he got to his feet and sank into his chair by the table.

"How long do we let them suck?"

Ole shrugged. "I don't know. Maybe until they get full."

Both parents stared in disgust at the leeches. Helena slowly shook her head. "I don't see how this does any good."

"The leeches suck out the bad blood."

"How do they know the good blood from the bad blood?"

Ole looked at his wife. What a good question. He had no answer, so just shrugged again.

They watched in silent fascination as the worms gorged themselves, hoping and praying that by some miracle the bad blood would be sucked out and the fever along with it.

The miracle did not occur.

After half an hour, the parents had seen enough. Helena spoke for them both. "Get those wretched creatures off my babies."

Ole took a small bowl of salt from the table and sprinkled some lightly on the leeches, causing them to stop sucking and back out of the wound. He quickly put them back into the tube, aware that doctors used the same leeches numerous times. Helena washed away the blood and put pads on each wound, securing them with strips of cloth.

Again husband and wife stared at each other, neither making any attempt to hide the exhaustion and fear they felt.

"What do we now?" Helena asked.

"Wait," Ole answered. "Then wait some more."

Helena returned to her rocking chair. "No. I'll wait. You sleep."

Ole nodded and stumbled to the bed. He did not remove his clothes. "Wake me if you need help," he said, pulling the quilt over himself.

"I will," Helena replied.

She did, an hour before dawn.

"Ole! Ole! Wake up!"

Groggily, Ole sat up, turning his blurred eyes to the children. Helena was holding Oline in her arms. "She's not breathing, Ole!"

With three quick strides, Ole was kneeling beside his daughter. He grabbed her by the shoulders and shook her. Oline's head wobbled like it was not connected to her body. Getting no response, he braced her head with his left hand and slapped her right cheek.

"Ole!" Helena cried.

He was about to repeat the slap when Oline's eyes fluttered open and she coughed up a wad of phlegm. She gulped for air and then began to cry. Helena held her close, kissing her as she wiped the phlegm from her mouth.

"I'm so sorry, Oline," Ole said.

"Don't be," Helena replied. "She's breathing."

Ole sat back on his heels as all color drained from his face. "Dear God," he thought, "we almost lost her." His heart was pounding. He too gulped for air.

When the crying subsided, Helena put the mug of water to Oline's lips. "Please try and drink, sweetie."

Oline's eyes were clear, and she drank five swallows before turning her head to the side.

"Good girl!" Ole smiled.

"It hurts so much, Papa," Oline mumbled, laying her head on Helena's chest.

"I'm so sorry," Ole replied, gently touching the girl's matted hair. In return, Oline gave her father a sad smile.

Helena held her close. As she kissed Oline, she noticed Martin staring up at her.

"Oline almost died, didn't she, Mama?" the boy asked matter-of-factly, as if he were commenting on the weather.

The old eyes knew the truth. There was no sense in lying. "She is very sick, Martin," Helena replied.

Tears came to the old eyes. "I think we're both going to die."

"Don't say that!" Helena cried. "Don't you ever say that!"

The old eyes closed.

Helena squeezed Oline so hard, the girl winced. "You're hurting me, Mama."

"I'm … I'm so sorry," Helena whispered, easing her grip. Tears fell on Oline's hair.

Ole stared at his wife and daughter in stunned silence, facing for the first time the reality that death truly was stalking the Branjord home.

"Mama," Oline said in an exhausted voice. "Don't let another girl wear my blue dress."

Helena inhaled sharply, fighting to control her emotions. "Nobody but you will ever wear that dress."

"Promise?"

"Promise."

After a pause, Oline added, "I saw Grandma Rahto. She waved at me and told me to rest."

Oline's eyes closed. Ole's eyes widened. "Your mother is dead," he said in a breaking voice.

"I know," Helena answered, looking up at Ole. Her tear-filled eyes pleaded, "Do something!"

Ole could not bear Helena's plea. He looked away, stumbling to his feet. The cabin seemed to sway. His legs felt as if they would collapse. He leaned against the wall for support. There was nothing he could do. He could not magically make his children well. He didn't know anything. He was just a dumb farmer! In frustration, Ole pounded his fist against the wall.

Seeing his anguish, Helena asked, "Do you think sweating would help?"

Sweating!

Ole grasped at the word like a falling mountain climber lunges for a safety rope. "Yes! When I was a boy, I had the flu and my mother sweated me. It broke the fever." Ole became all business, thankful for a plan. "We need to get the cabin as hot as possible. I'll bring in firewood and water from the well. You put the double boiler on the stove and find two old sheets or blankets."

"Do you think it will work?"

Ole grabbed his sheepskin. "It has to!"

One hour later, as a streak of pink colored the eastern sky, smoke billowed defiantly from the cabin chimney, a signal to death that it would not enter easily into this home. Inside, Ole used wooden stakes to extract two blankets from the steaming double boiler. Water drained onto the floor, forming miniature rivers that flowed in all directions. Neither Ole nor Helena paid the least bit of attention. Ole dropped the blankets in a heap. Helena reached out, but was stopped by Ole. "No! They are too hot!"

"They have to be hot."

"Hot, yes, but not scalding. Wait a bit."

They waited in silence. There was nothing to say, no words to ease the desperation both felt. The two stared at the soggy pile of material, praying that, somehow, it had the power to save their suffering children. Finally, Ole reached down, touched one of the blankets, then nodded to Helena. "Take the other end. Let's wring out some of the water."

After they had wrung both blankets, they carried them to the children. Ole knelt beside Oline, who curled into a fetal ball when he removed her covers. "I'll pick her up. Spread out the blanket over the pallet." When this was done, Ole laid the girl back down and tightly wrapped the hot blanket around her. He then lifted Martin and the procedure was repeated. "Now," Ole said, "we pile on as many quilts and blankets as we can find."

Ole replaced the children's covers as Helena stripped the bed and piled the additional sheets and quilts onto the children. "Is that enough?" she asked.

"I think so," Ole replied, getting to his feet. "Now, we wait some more."

Helena turned to the stove. "I'll make some coffee and breakfast."

The last of the turkey and potato hash was sizzling in the skillet when a sleepy voice was heard from the loft. "Mama, it's hot up here."

Ole answered. "It's hot down here too. Come down and eat."

Berent scrambled down the ladder and was surprised by all the covers on his brother and sister. "Are Oline and Martin cold?"

"No," Ole answered. "We are trying to sweat the sickness out of them."

"Can they go out and play?"

"No, but you can. Get your clothes. I'll help you get dressed."

Helena smiled as she watched Ole help Berent into his homespun shirt and a patched pair of pants Martin had outgrown. They were a little big, but Berent did not mind. They were pants. Her idea of keeping him in a dress around home had been a complete failure.

"I'm hungry," Berent said, as Ole finished putting heavy wool socks on the boy's feet.

"I'm glad to hear it," Helena replied, wishing her other two felt the same. "Sit down at the table. Breakfast is ready."

Ole and Berent ate. Helena grabbed bites in between placing damp cloths on the foreheads of the sweating children and keeping the blankets tightly wrapped around them.

After breakfast, Ole helped Berent put on leggings made of deer hide, a heavy sweater, coat, cap, and mittens, and then wrapped a wool scarf around his neck. On the boy's feet were muskrat shoes. Ole had trapped the muskrat the previous winter and, using his buffalo shoes as an example, had made fur shoes for the Helena and the children.

"When I come in, you're going to bed," Ole said to Helena as he put on his sheepskin.

"Don't hurry. I doubt if I'll be able to sleep anyway," Helena said, then nodded to Berent. "He needs to play. Wear him out a little."

Ole gave Berent a squeeze on the shoulder. "I'll do that."

Berent and Ole stepped out of the overheated cabin into a cold, clear, beautiful winter morning. The boy squealed with delight as he raced by Ole and promptly fell face forward into a snowbank. He jumped up grinning, and attempted to make a snowball out of the dry snow.

"Wrong kind of snow." Ole laughed. "This is sliding snow."

"We don't have a sled."

"You don't need one," Ole replied, taking a deep breath of the sweet, fresh air. "We have a scoop shovel. Remember?"

Berent grinned. "Yes! Can we do it now?"

"After we finish the chores. You have to work before you play."

Ole walked to the barn. Berent followed, trying to match his father's stride. He failed and proceeded to fall about every five steps. Ole helped him up after the first two falls, but then realized from the happy grin on Berent's face that the falls were accidentally on purpose.

"Aren't you going to help me up, Papa?" the boy asked from the prone position.

"No. If you're big enough to wear pants, you're big enough to get up by yourself."

Ole reached the barn gate, then turned and waited for Berent. The boy had almost reached him when he suddenly stopped, his eyes wide and shining. "Angels!" he cried. "I remember!"

"Remember what?"

"Angels! Me and Oline and Martin made snow angels!"

"So you did." Ole smiled. "Do you remember how?"

"Yes!" Berent cried, as he fell back on a patch of virgin snow and made a perfect angel.

"Good job!" Ole said, pulling the boy to his feet. "You can make more while I milk."

Berent did just that. He also played tag with the calves and lambs and tried to ride the sheep, all to the delight of his father. By the time Ole finished milking, Berent, red-faced and panting, plopped himself down on the straw. "I'm tired, Papa."

"Too tired to go sliding?" Ole asked.

"No!" Brent answered, jumping to his feet and recovering from being tired as only a child can.

"Go get the scoop shovel by the wagon." Ole laughed.

Berent ran to the wagon. When he returned, dragging the wide shovel behind him, Ole had finished the necessary chores. There was still much he could do, like carrying in more hay and putting down fresh bedding, but that could wait one more day. Tomorrow Oline and Martin would be better.

"I've got it, Papa," Berent yelled.

"Do you remember how to use it?" Ole asked, meeting his son at the gate.

"No."

"That's not surprising. You were pretty little last year. I'll show you."

Ole took the shovel from Berent and the two walked to where the pasture began to slope down to the river. "You turn the shovel backward, sit on it, put your legs up, and hang on to the handle with your hands."

Berent looked down at what appeared to him to be a very steep hill. He took his father's hand. "You come with me, Papa."

"Me?" Ole laughed. "I haven't been sliding in twenty years."

"Please, Papa. I don't know how."

Ole looked down at Berent's pleading eyes. There was no way he could decline. "Me and my big mouth," he sighed, sitting down on the shovel. Berent scooted down in front of him, the fear banished by excitement.

"Here we go!" Ole said, digging his heels into the snow.

The shovel wobbled, then began to move. Ole dug once more with his heels and then lifted his feet. Gravity took over. Berent squealed.

The shovel skimmed over the snow. Faster and faster, father and son careened down the hill. Because of Ole's weight, the shovel took on the characteristics of a toboggan. The wind they created stung their faces. Ole clung to the handle, trying to steer, but mostly just hanging on for dear life. Twice they almost tipped over before running full speed into a snowbank at the bottom of the pasture.

"Wow!" Ole said, brushing off the snow. He looked down at Berent, wondering if he had frightened the child out of year's growth. His answer was an upturned, grinning face. "Let's do it again, Papa!"

And they did, both of them laughing and yelling all the way down.

The third time up the hill, Ole said, "This time, you go by yourself." Berent was more than willing. Ole gave him a shove. Berent made it close to halfway down before flipping over and skidding to a stop, the shovel riding him.

The boy jumped up laughing. "I tipped over, Papa!"

"I see that. You'll have to learn to guide better."

Berent dragged the shovel up the hill and prepared to go again. "This is fun!"

"Yes, it is," Ole agreed, giving his son a push. It was fun. In fact, it was the most fun Ole had experienced in years. He watched Berent swerve and bounce down the hill and remembered a sled he had seen in the back of Alderman's store in Nevada. It was an extra-long sled, one that could easily carry three children. Ole grinned. The sled would make a great Christmas present.

Berent completed the run by hitting the snowbank at the bottom of the pasture. He jumped up in triumph. "I did it, Papa!"

"You sure did!" Ole yelled. "I'm proud of you."

When Berent reached Ole at the top of the hill, he was huffing and puffing. Ole asked, "Had enough?"

Berent shook his head. "Let's go together one more time."

"That sounds good to me," Ole answered.

Down they went and, for few moments, Ole was a carefree child again. He could not know as he and Berent slid down the hill, but in his long life of eighty-seven years, this would be the last time he would experience the thrill of youth.

Ole and Berent laughed as they trudged up the hill. Their laughter continued until Ole opened the cabin door. Helena was kneeling beside Oline and Martin, wiping sweat from their faces. Both were crying. Ole was shocked by Helena's haggard look. She appeared to have aged ten years.

Berent pulled off his cap and scarf. "We slid down the hill, Mama. It was fun!"

Helena gave Berent a half smile. "I saw you."

Quickly removing his outer clothing, Ole knelt beside Helena. "I'm sorry. I should have come in sooner."

Helena sighed. "No. Berent deserved some fun. So did you. There was nothing you could have done in here."

"I could have relieved you. Come on. You need sleep." Ole rose and helped Helena to her feet. Too tired to reply, Helena allowed Ole to half-guide, half-carry her to the bed, where she collapsed into a fetal position. There were no blankets to cover her.

Berent called, "I can't get my muskrats off."

Ole crossed to his son and removed the outdoor clothing. "Berent, I played with you. Now I have to take care of Oline and Martin. Find your whirligig and go sit by the table."

"Can I sit under the table?"

"Sit anywhere you like. Just stay out of the way."

Ole took Helena's cape from the peg by the door, but before he could take it to her, Martin began choking. Ole threw the cape on his chair and knelt beside the boy. He propped up Martin, pounding his back until a wad of phlegm dribbled out of his mouth. Martin gasped for air, then said, "Papa, I'm so hot."

"I'm sorry," Ole answered, wiping the boy's face. "We're trying to sweat out the fever. It won't be much longer."

The old eyes closed, but not before telling Ole they knew he was lying.

While Ole was helping Martin, Berent carried Helena's cape to the bed, where he carefully covered her. He paused for a moment, then kissed her cheek as she had countless times kissed his, before retreating to his safe place under the table.

The hours moved with glacial speed. Ole's back and knees ached from kneeling beside the children. When they cried, he comforted them; when they fitfully slept, he wiped the perspiration from their faces. Numerous times, he attempted to have them drink. More water dribbled down their chins than down their throats. There was no sign the fever was breaking.

At noon, Ole fed Berent but ate nothing himself. Fear left no room for food. Sweating had just made the children weaker. The only reason he continued it was because he did not want to consider the last alternative. While Berent ate, Ole rested his head in his hands and prayed. It was a simple prayer. "Dear Lord, save Oline and Martin. I'll do anything you ask. Don't let my children die."

Time passed. Ole did not notice Berent slide from the bench and climb the ladder to the loft. He did not notice the fires cooling in the stove and fireplace. He did not notice Martin free himself from his blanket cocoon. He did not notice any of these things because he sat slumped over the table, his head resting on his folded arms.

"Ole! Ole! Wake up!"

Disoriented, Ole leaped to his feet, knocking over his chair. "What? What's wrong?" He turned to see Helena kneeling beside Oline.

"She's hardly breathing," Helena cried, frantically removing the stack of blankets.

Ole dropped to Helena's side and ripped away the soaked blanket. Oline's nightgown was a tangled mess up around her shoulders. Her skin was so red from the heat that it blended with the scarlet rash.

"Lift her up, Ole!" Helena ordered. "Let me get her nightgown off."

The girl's body felt almost weightless in Ole's arms. He hardly recognized his daughter. She looked like a shriveled old crone.

"Help me bathe her," Helena said, after removing the nightgown. "We have to cool her down."

Ole laid Oline back on her pallet, grabbed a damp towel, and began washing her face, neck, and arms while Helena bathed her chest and legs. "Did she call out?" Ole asked.

"No. I just woke up," Helena answered. "I somehow knew she needed me."

"And like a damn fool, I fell asleep," Ole muttered angrily.

"Don't be too hard on yourself. I did the same thing when you were out with Berent."

Martin moaned but did not awaken. Only then did Ole see that the boy was uncovered. Helena said, "He may be having chills. Cover him with a dry blanket. No more sweating."

Ole tucked a quilt around Martin. The moaning stopped.

Oline's skin had cooled so that the rash was now visible. Gooseflesh appeared like miniature moguls on a ski slope. She began to shiver. Helena covered her with a dry blanket, then looked at Ole, hopelessness in her eyes. "She's dying, Ole. What can we do?"

Ole sat back on his heels. The unspeakable words had been uttered. Tears watered his beard. "There is one thing we haven't tried. Blistering."

Horror replaced hopelessness. "No! Not that!"

"I don't like it either. But the doctors say the body can contain just one illness at a time. Maybe the blistering will drive out the fever."

Helena looked from her husband to her daughter. She lightly caressed the girl's cheeks and listened to her shallow breathing. Helena sighed. It was impossible to do nothing. "There really is no choice," she whispered. "Like you said, the doctors have to know more than we do."

Ole struggled to his feet. He walked to the fireplace, where he placed the poker into the flames and threw more logs on the fire.. The poker was damp from condensation, due to the overheating in the cabin.

Neither Ole nor Helena spoke. They both just stared at the poker as the tip began to redden and give off hissing belches of steam. When it glowed, Ole wrapped a wet towel around the end, removed it from the fire, and crossed to Oline. Helena lifted the blanket. "Do it high on her leg. It will leave a scar."

Ole's hand trembled. Causing his beautiful little girl more suffering was the last thing he wanted to do. But it might work. It might drive out the fever. It might save her life. The doctors might be right. He swallowed hard and touched the angry heat to the girl's thigh.

Oline's eyes flew open. She half sat up, her arms flailing. The burned leg sprang up, kicking Helena in the shoulder, as the girl's anguished scream reverberated off the cabin walls.

Ole stepped back, filled with self-loathing. Helena covered the burned flesh with a wet towel. The water sizzled. Oline fainted, falling back onto her pallet. "I'm so sorry," Helena repeated again and again as she applied water to the burn.

The scream had awakened Martin. He stared up at his father, fear in the old eyes. "Don't burn me, Papa!" he pleaded.

Ole threw the poker into the fireplace, fled out the door, dropped to his knees in the snow, and vomited. Several minutes passed, then Helena came out of the cabin and bent over him. "Come inside, Ole. I can't lose you too."

"How is she?" Ole asked, getting up from his knees and entering the cabin.

"I think she's breathing easier," Helena replied, closing the door.

Ole picked up his overturned chair and sank into it. "I'll remember that scream as long as I live," he said, burying his face in his hands.

Helena squeezed his shoulder. "So will I. But we had to try. I'll get you some coffee."

"No, I don't want any," Ole said, placing his hand over hers. "Just go sit down. You need to rest."

Helena sighed as she stumbled to her rocking chair. There were no more words. Both were physically and emotionally exhausted. They sat in silence, too tired even to pray.

Neither heard Berent come down from the loft. He patted Helena lightly on her knee. She opened her eyes and sighed. "Not now, Berent. Go back up to the loft."

The boy did not move. "Mama," he said softly. "I have a sore throat."

Helena grabbed Berent by his arms. She saw the fever in his eyes. "No!" she cried, pulling the boy into her lap, hugging him furiously.

Ole stared in disbelief at mother and son. "Not Berent too," he whispered as Helena's uncontrolled sobs, which tore at his soul like threshing knives, filled the cabin.

Berent put his arms around Helena's neck and placed his face next to hers. "Don't cry, Mama. I'm not so sick. Don't cry."

Chapter Forty-Three

Big Per carried the small coffin into the cabin, placing it on the table. Ole followed with the lid. It was not a real coffin, just a box the two men had nailed together. Ole leaned the lid against his chair and picked up Berent's quilt, which was neatly folded on the bench. He carefully lined the box with the quilt, then turned to Big Per. "I can't do it."

Per understood. He walked to the bed where Berent lay, dressed in his best shirt and beloved pants. With eyes blurred, Big Per picked up "Mr. Branjord" and carried him to the box. He and Ole placed the boy in the coffin, folding his hands across his chest. Ole took the whirligig from his pocket and intertwined the string through Berent's fingers. Big Per picked up the lid.

"Wait!"

Helena's voice startled both men. She had not spoken a word since Berent died. Nor had she taken any part in preparing the body for burial. Ole and Big Per had washed and dressed the boy. After Berent's last breath, Helena had retreated to her rocking chair, treasure box in hand, and had not moved. There had been no tears. Dry-eyed, she had just stared into space.

Helena got up from the chair, placing her box on the table. From it she took a pair of scissors. Lovingly, she looked down at the curls she had so often tousled and snipped a lock of hair. She tied the hair with a blue ribbon and, without a second look into the coffin, placed the lock of hair into her box with the others. Helena then picked up the box and returned to her chair.

Tears streamed down Ole's face. "Let's close it outside."

On the porch, Ole nailed the lid to the box. Each stroke of the hammer made Helena flinch.

Big Per carried the coffin to Ole's wagon, where Doll and Lady stood placidly waiting. Ole entered the cabin, gently taking Helena's hand in his. "It's time to go," he said softly, looking into her eyes. What he saw made him want to fall to his knees and weep. Helena's eyes were not just dry; they were empty. Dead eyes in a living face. Ole fought back the tears and pulled Helena to her feet. She did not resist. Nor did she resist when Ole dressed her in her bonnet, cape and gloves; however, she did nothing to aid him. She simply stood like an uninterested, uncomprehending small child.

When Ole and Helena were seated on their wagon, Big Per climbed into his own and urged Buck and Pride into motion. The two wagons rattled down the hill to the stage road, beginning the two and a half mile journey to the Fairview Cemetery.

This was not the first trip to the cemetery by these two wagons. Three days before, they had traveled the same route with two small coffins in Ole's wagon. Oline and Martin had died within hours of each other on the day after Ole and Berent had enjoyed the snow. On the same day, Big Per had fought his way to the Branjord cabin to find Ole in shock and Helena desperately nursing Berent. He then went to Turg's store to buy lumber for the coffins, wisely purchasing enough for three.

By nightfall, word of the children's deaths had spread throughout Fairview, but because of the scarlet fever, no one came to the cabin. Big Per constructed the coffins as Ole and Helena washed and dressed the children: Martin in his Sunday best, Oline in her new blue dress.

Later in the evening, Karl Lyngen, obviously drunk, entered the cabin without knocking. He ignored the living and gazed without speaking at the two small boxes. The other adults in the room were wise enough to remain silent. Tears dripped like soft rain into the two coffins. After several minutes, he placed Oline's piano book into her box and the two copies of *A Tale of Two Cities* in Martin's. He then turned to Helena. "Angels belong in heaven, not down in this shit hole." He took two steps to the door, then paused. "I want you to know that when I heard the children were sick, I prayed for their recovery. It just shows you what God thinks of my prayers." Karl stumbled back out into the night without bothering to close the door.

Helena did not attend the burial service for Oline and Martin. She insisted on staying home to care for Berent. Inga and Karl were there,

Karl wearing his goggles to protect his eyes from the bright sunlight. Inga had tried to make him stay home, knowing the pain he would suffer. But he had insisted on attending. Karl stood at attention while the coffins were lowered. He had seen countless graves, but this one caused something inside of him to break. Upon reaching home, he filled a glass with whisky. He had been drunk ever since.

A small group of people were standing apart from the gravesite when the wagons arrived at the cemetery. Some people from the East Settlement, including Hans and Julia Twedt, were there, as were the Tjernagels and Bertha and Albert Hindberg. Mathea Amlund stood next her husband.

Big Per carried the coffin to the open grave. Helena and Ole followed. Mrs. Amlund hardly recognized the woman walking beside Ole. For perhaps the only time in her adult life, she was glad she had no children of her own.

Reverend Amlund took a step forward, addressing Ole and Helena. "I have no words of my own to comfort you. I do not pretend to understand the depth of your grief or the reason for these untimely deaths. But we have to believe God had a reason for taking the lives of your children." He paused, gazing at the coffin. His thoughts were the same as those of all who gathered there: "It is such a little box."

Opening his Bible, Reverend Amlund began the service. "The Lord giveth. The Lord taketh away. Blessed be the name of the Lord." He then read the Twenty-third Psalm and concluded by saying, "Ashes to ashes. Dust to dust."

When Reverend Amlund closed his Bible, there were only two dry eyes. Helena stared as if made of stone at the two fresh mounds of earth next to the open grave.

Ole and Big Per lowered the coffin by ropes into the grave. As the box neared the bottom, it scraped against the inside wall, exposing a corner of Oline's coffin. The sight made Ole smile through his tears. Somehow, this gave him comfort. His children would rest eternally the way they had slept in the loft: Oline in the center, Martin on the left, and Berent on the right.

The ropes were retrieved. The service was over. Everyone just stood, staring into the hole. No one came to give their condolences. Fear of scarlet fever prevented grieving friends from getting too close.

"I'm so sorry," Reverend Amlund said. "We'll close the grave."

Ole nodded, took Helena by the arm, and led her to the wagon. Big

Per climbed into his own wagon, turning Buck and Pride for home. As he traveled across the snow-blanketed prairie, he gave God a tongue lashing that made the angels in heaven cringe. Doll and Lady pulled a wagon carrying two empty people toward an empty cabin with an empty loft.

Two yellow eyes had watched the service from the safety of a thicket. Doggie lay motionless as the grave was filled and the people departed. He did not move until a full moon bathed the cemetery in its soft light. Cautiously, Doggie crept up the hill to Berent's grave. He circled it several times, then began to dig. He dug frantically for several minutes, until the futility of the task overwhelmed him. For an hour he lay panting in the hole he had made. He then rose to his haunches, pointed his scar-marked face to the moon, and howled. Those who heard him said it was the most mournful sound they had ever heard.

Doggie was never again seen at the Branjord farm.

Chapter Forty-Four

The congregation of Saint Petri shaded their eyes as they exited the church into a glaring sun high in a sky punctuated by soft, fluffy clouds. Three weeks had passed since the blizzard, which was now mostly forgotten. The remaining snow was struggling to survive in two small drifts down where the horses were tied.

This had been the first service since the scarlet fever scare, and had been one of celebration and thanksgiving. With the exception of the Branjords, few had suffered any loss. All agreed that the blizzard, which most saw as a direct gift from God, had saved them from an epidemic. The East Settlement had not been touched at all.

Julia Twedt and Bertha Hindberg walked out into the balmy weather, their younger children racing ahead. Julia handed one-year-old Carl to Hattie. "Take him down to the wagon. He needs changing." The young girl wrinkled her nose as she took the baby.

Bertha took a deep breath. "Can you believe it is just four days until Christmas? It must be fifty degrees."

Julia shook her head. "And to think a week ago we were walking around in knee-deep snow."

"Well, I think we had better enjoy it. Albert's knee is hurting. That means cold weather is coming."

"I don't doubt it," Julia said." I have never seen a country for such changeable weather. Oh, Bertha, it is so good to have you back in the congregation."

Bertha smiled and touched Julia's arm. "It is good to be here. Albert had a big argument with that awful Saul Jaeran and we decided that Saint Petri was the place for us."

Joseph Twedt, his face flushed from running, arrived at Julia's side. He looked up at her, his bright blue eyes questioning. "Mama, why isn't Berent here?"

Julia gave a quick glance to Bertha. Both women swallowed hard. "I told you, Joseph," Julia said, gently. "Berent died. He won't be here anymore."

"Never?"

"No, never."

Joseph sighed as he walked away, hands in his pockets.

"He doesn't understand," Julia whispered.

"Why should he?" Bertha replied, angrily crossing her arms. "I don't understand either. Dear Lord, losing all three. I can't imagine how Helena feels."

Tears came to Julia's eyes. "Nor can I. When I lost Carrie last year, I cried every day for six months. Have you been to see Helena?"

"Yesterday. I decided there was no more danger of catching the fever. I had been sending food over for the past two weeks."

"How is she holding up?" Julia asked.

"She's not. She looked awful. I think she has aged ten years. All she does is sit in her rocking chair, staring at nothing. Ole said she doesn't talk, doesn't eat, doesn't cry. Just sits. I tried to get her to eat some of the johnnycake I brought. I told her to think about the baby she's carrying. She turned to me with a look that just broke my heart. She said, 'It will just die anyway.'"

Julia snatched a handkerchief from her cape pocket and dabbed her eyes. "Oh, the poor thing."

Bertha wiped her own eyes. "Ole told me later those were the first words she had spoken since Berent's funeral."

Big Per walked up to the women, hat in hand. He had come to church today after deciding he might owe God an apology. "Good morning, ladies."

"Good morning, Mr. Larson," both women said, more than a little intimidated by this huge male figure. Bertha continued, "Have you seen the Branjords?"

"I stopped by this morning. There is no change," Big Per answered. "I want to thank you for all the food you have sent over. But I think they have more than enough."

"Yes, I saw that yesterday," Bertha said. "But I have a big roast in the oven. I'll send Ernst over with some dinner later this afternoon."

Big Per smiled at Bertha. "You are a good woman. I know Ole appreciates it."

"How is Ole doing?" Julia asked.

"Badly," Big Per replied. "Most of the time he walks around in a daze. He's worried sick about Helena."

"Oh, the poor man," Julia said, dabbing her eyes. "It is so tragic."

The conversation was interrupted by Hanna Signaldahl storming out of the church and bumping Julia into Big Per's arms.

"What in the Sam Hill ..." Big Per said as he caught Julia.

Hanna did not seem to notice. Her angry face was the color of her matching maroon cape and bonnet. "Emil! Emil! Get in the buggy! We're going home!"

"What is wrong with her?" Bertha said, watching Hanna stomp toward the horses.

"I can tell you that," Martha Karina Tjernagel said, joining the group. She too was flushed, and her eyes were as hard as her childhood had been. "Some of us were talking about Helena and Ole, and she butted in by saying the deaths of the children were God's punishment for Helena being a wicked, sinful woman."

"No!" Julia and Bertha said as one.

"Yes." Martha continued, "That was too much for me. I told her she was the nastiest woman on earth and should be horsewhipped. I also called her Horse-Face."

Big Per heard no more. Fists clenched, he started for the Signaldahl buggy. Martha attempted to catch the sleeve of his coat but failed. "No, Per! Don't!" she cried, knowing how deeply Big Per cared for the Branjords and how volcanic his temper was when it erupted. "Oh, my God! What have I done?"

By now, all eyes were on Big Per. He reached the buggy just as Hanna was getting settled on the seat and Emil was untying the horses. "Have you no feelings, woman? Helena Branjord has lost three children and you say it is because she is sinful? You have the gall to say that? You, who spread your legs for any man in Story County!"

Hanna was shocked but still furious. "How dare you talked to me like that, you ... you peasant! I'm the daughter of a banker!"

"You're the daughter of the devil!" Big Per roared.

Shaking with fear, Emil approached Big Per. "Now, see here ..."

Without taking his eyes off of Hanna, Big Per lifted Emil off the ground with one hand and threw him nearly ten feet into the slush.

Hanna took this opportunity to stand up, grab the buggy whip from its holder, and slash at Big Per. The leather thongs caught Per on his coat sleeve, ripping the fabric and drawing blood. But Hanna was slow in taking back the whip, allowing Big Per to snatch it from her grasp. She cried out, and for good reason. The fury on Big Per's face would have frightened the bravest Viking.

"Don't you touch me!" Hanna pleaded, her face as pale as the white lace around her collar.

Her plea went unheeded. Big Per expertly flicked his wrist, sending the business end of the whip encircling Hanna's hips. Thanks to her cape, woolen dress, and undergarments, only cloth was damaged. She screamed. The frightened horses lurched forward, sending Hanna sprawling half on and half off the seat.

Big Per leaned forward, his face only inches from Hanna's. "Helena Branjord is worth a thousand of you, banker's daughter. You are a sinful bitch who is going straight to hell!" With that, he tipped the buggy on its side, causing Hanna to fall headfirst into a dirty snowbank. The whip followed, almost hitting Hanna. "The whole county knows about your Ingvald. How many other men are there?"

Emil struggled shakily to his feet. Big Per glared at him. "If you want to make more of this, you know where I live. I do feel sorry for you, Emil. No man should have to live with this piece of crap!" Emil stood, unable to say a word, as Big Per climbed into his wagon. Buck and Pride knew their owner's mood. They left the churchyard at a trot.

Hanna screamed at Emil in frustration as she struggled to her feet. "My dress is ruined! You worm! He struck me and you did nothing!"

An exasperated Emil fired back, "What was I supposed to do? He threw me down with one hand."

"Anyone can throw you down with one hand!" Hanna spat.

Emil swayed slightly, attempting to hold as much dignity as possible. He was thankful that Elsa was home with a bad cold. "Can I have some help here?" he shouted to the thunderstruck congregation.

Several of the men helped Emil right the buggy, but none assisted Hanna up onto the seat. Neither did Emil. Hanna climbed up, ripping the hem of her skirt in the process. Emil slapped the reins before she was settled, causing her to fall back onto the leather cushions. She glared at Emil, who returned her glare with one of his own. He quickly drove away from the church.

When the buggy was on the road, Emil asked, "What did you say about Helena Branjord?"

"The truth! I said God was punishing her for her sins."

Emil looked at Hanna with undisguised disgust. "You can say that after what you have done with Ingvald?"

Hanna stared straight ahead. "I have done nothing with Ingvald."

"Nothing? You call rolling in the hay nothing? After I fired him, he laughed in my face!"

Hanna turned slowly to face Emil. The look on her face was one of complete contempt. "At least Ingvald was a real man."

Emil felt as if he had been slapped in the face, but he did not turn away. He stared at Hanna as if seeing her for the first time. "A real man, you say. Like the real man who fathered Elsa."

Hanna's lips turned into a sneer. "Yes," she answered. "So you finally figured it out."

They drove the rest of the way home in silence. Hanna knew her marriage was over. Oh, they would continue to share the same house, but there would be no pretense of love. To her surprise, she was relieved. There was no longer a need to endure his incompetent sexual advances.

The silence in the Branjord cabin was so loud it was painful. The only sound Ole heard as he sat in his chair was the squeak that had developed in Helena's rocking chair. He stared at the dying embers in the fireplace. The stove was stone cold. He knew he should get up and put wood on the fire, but he couldn't bring himself to move. Moving required effort. Moving required energy. He had neither.

Ole could not make himself look at Helena. That would only bring on a fresh flood of tears. His beautiful, vivacious wife was now an empty shell, a shell without emotion. No anger; no sorrow; no hate; no bitterness; certainly, no love. Looking at her was like entering a house where no one was home.

People called it nervous fever. She had suffered from it in Hardin County, but not this seriously. There, she had fought it. She had talked to him; she had cried; she had been angry; she had railed against God. Now … nothing. Since Berent's funeral, she had been as docile as a sleepy lamb. Only three times had she shown emotion: once when he had tried to take away her box; the second time when he had suggested she put on her nightgown to sleep—she had not been out of her dress since Oline complained of a sore throat; and the third this past morning, when Big Per had begun to play her favorite tune on his violin. She had screamed and covered her ears.

"Hello in the house!"

Ole forced himself out of his chair and opened the door. Ernst stood about fifteen feet from the porch. He was still afraid of getting too close.

"Mama sent over some leftover roast from dinner," Ernst said. "I put the basket on the bench."

Ole looked down at the towel-covered food. "Thank you, Ernst. And thank your mother. But tell her we have enough food to last a week. Will you tell her that?"

"Yes, sir."

Ole picked up the basket but saw that Ernst had not moved. The boy stood looking at the ground, hands in pockets, shifting from one foot to the other. "Is there something else?" Ole asked.

Ernst raised his head, tears in his eyes. "I … I want you to know I thought Oline was real nice. When I found out she was sick, I prayed for her. I prayed God would make her well." He paused for a moment, then blurted, "God didn't listen. I hate God!"

Ernst turned and ran for home. Ole watched him until he was out of sight. "That makes two of us," Ole sighed.

Ole

I walk into the cabin, placing the basket on the table. "Bertha sent over more food," I say. Helena does not respond. I don't expect her to. The basket contains pork roast, potatoes, carrots, cornbread, and four cookies. Wasting such good food is a sin, but I am not hungry, and I know Helena will eat nothing. "More treats for the hogs," I mumble, surprised that I have spoken out loud. Helena stares into space.

The cabin is now quite cold. I see that I have neglected to shut the door. I stare at it, thinking, how many times did I yell at the children for doing the same. A hundred? A thousand? The number doesn't matter. I will never do it again. The doorway becomes a blur.

I wipe my eyes as I walk out to the woodpile. The temperature is dropping fast. Heavy clouds cover the late-afternoon sun. There will be more snow tonight. Good. I hope it's a blizzard. The worse the weather, the better I like it. I used to like the sun. I don't anymore. I hate the sun almost as much as I hate God.

After three trips to the woodpile, I put logs on the fire and light the stove. I watch the flames in the fireplace awaken and the fire in the stove come to life. When I am sure both fires are burning well, I put on my sheepskin and cap. "I'm going out to do chores," I say. Helena looks at me like I am not even there.

It feels good to be outside. Thank God for chores. How stupid. Why? Why should I thank God for anything? He doesn't give a damn about me. He doesn't care. He doesn't listen! Thanks for nothing, God!

I walk to the barn. It is a mess. What little bedding there is, is damp and sour; the horse and cow areas badly need cleaning; hay bunks are as empty as a politician's promises. The cows give me accusatory looks. Doll and Lady snort their disgust. They are not used to being neglected. I feel guilt but also resentment. "Why are you looking at me like that?" I yell. "Am I your goddamn servant? You're not tied in here! Go out and eat some grass. Shit somewhere else!"

The yelling is as foreign to the animals as the neglect. Doll and Lady trot out of the barn, more than a little afraid of this stranger who resembles their owner. The cows are unsure what to do. They are nervous, but know it is time to be milked. So they do what cows always do when confused ... nothing.

Watching my horses run from me makes me cringe. Why am I taking my pain out on them? They are not to blame. I thought there was no way I could feel worse, but the miserable condition of my barn sinks me even lower. How many times did I tell my boys that a good farmer takes care of his animals? What would they think of me now? Oh God! I miss them so. I can't think about the children. I'll go crazy if I think about them. Work, Ole! Do something! Don't just stand here crying like a schoolgirl!

I carry hay in from the stack. The chaff runs down my neck. It feels good. I then give the cows and horses a measure of oats. Doll and Lady quickly return. I pet their necks as they eat. "Sorry I yelled," I say. Lady stops eating long enough to nuzzle me, as if to say I am forgiven. I put my arms around her neck and cry into her mane.

I have to stop this crying. I've never cried like this, not even when Nettie died. Stop it! Stop crying you damned old Norwegian! Men don't cry. Men work!

I pick up the pail and sit down to milk Maud. She turns and gives me the eye. That makes me mad. "I just fed you, you ungrateful bitch! You swish me in the face with your tail and I'll break your goddamn back!"

It feels good to swear. It shows what I think of God. "Do you hear me, God?" I say as I begin to milk. "I'm breaking your damn Second Commandment! I'm taking your name in vain! Why should I keep your commandments? Why should I give a damn about you? You don't give a damn about me or Helena! What are you doing up there, having a good laugh? Well, you can go to hell, God! Hear me? Go to hell! Go down to your friend the devil and have a party! You're no more caring than he is! You say ask and it shall be given to you. What a damn joke! I asked! I prayed! Helena prayed! Big Per prayed! We all prayed you would spare my children. Did you listen? Hell, no! You squashed their lives like they were nothing more than cockroaches! Well, have your good laugh! I'm telling you I will never pray to you again! Never! So help me God, you will never hear another prayer from me!"

I lay my head against Maud's flank. Tears drip from eyes into the pail. I don't care. I don't care about a goddamn thing!

Helena

Ole is telling that woman in my chair that he is going out to do chores. Why does he keep talking to her? She can't answer. I could, but I am staying up here where it is safe. It is much better up here as long as I don't look into the loft. I can't look into the loft. That would bring back the pain.

I wonder how I stay up here? I am just floating around looking down at that woman sitting in my chair. That's not right! She should not be sitting in my chair, holding my box. But I am afraid to go down to her. We must keep separated. If we don't, the pain will come back.

Ole is crying again. He cries often. I had only seen him cry once before … before what happened. That was when Nettie died. But that was just once. Men aren't supposed to cry. I don't like it when Ole cries.

The woman in the chair doesn't cry. I do. Especially if I look into the loft. I don't like that woman in my chair. She smells bad. And that hair! It hasn't felt a brush in weeks. She should be ashamed. Her dress is the worst thing of all! How can she sit there in that dirty thing? There is vomit from all three children on the front. Ole tried to take it off. She would have none of that! I know why she won't take it off. She can smell the children. As long as she wears the dress, they are not gone. They still need her. If she takes it off, they are gone forever.

There is food on the table. Everyone tries to get her to eat. She won't. She wants to die. She wants the baby inside of her to die. Why go through the pain of giving birth just to have the child die later? I think it is good that she wants to die. Ole would be better off if she died. He could find a new wife. He could father more children with her, children who would live and grow up and have children of their own. The children of the woman in my chair always die. She knows that God does not want her to have children. He is punishing her for having them against his wishes. God hates her. Yes, Ole would be better off if she died. Me too! Then I could have my box and chair back.

Look! She is getting up. She is picking up a folded quilt. She is walking to the door. Oh my! That foolish woman is going outside without a cape or bonnet! She's not even putting on shoes. Well, good! Good riddance. No one loves her. No one even likes her. She is just a stupid Finnish serving girl! Now I can have my ... Wait! Don't take my box! You can't have my box! Please, don't take it!

Chapter Forty-Five

Ole poured milk into the hog trough; there were no children to drink it, no one to churn it into butter. The thought brought fresh tears. He turned toward the cabin. What he saw through the blur made his jaw drop. He wiped his eyes. The door to the cabin was wide open. Ole dropped the pail and raced toward the cabin.

Soft, dry snowflakes were beginning to fall through the still, cold air when Ole reached the open door. A quick look inside told him the folded quilt was missing from the bed and that Helena's cape was still hanging on the peg. There was no doubt in Ole's mind where she was headed. He grabbed her cape, shut the door, and ran toward the north—toward Fairview, toward the cemetery, toward the graves.

As Ole ran through the early twilight, he prayed. "Oh God, please don't take Helena. She is all I have. She is my life. Please, don't take her! I'm sorry I swore. I'm sorry for all the things I said. Please, God. Don't take her!"

His breath came in gasps, but he continued to run. There was no sign of her. Had he guessed wrong? Had she gone in another direction? The river. Oh God! Not the river! He was about to stop when he stumbled over a small rise and saw her walking serenely through the corn stubble about one hundred yards ahead.

"Helena!" Ole cried.

She did not even pause. Either she did not hear Ole or chose to ignore him. It did not matter. He could see her. Ole sprinted forward, quickly covering the ground that separated them. When he reached her, he grabbed her arm. "Helena, stop!"

Helena tore herself from his grasp and continued walking. Ole followed, putting his hand on her shoulder. She whirled and faced him, her face a frozen mask of hatred and anger. "Don't you touch me!" she snarled. "Don't you ever touch me again!"

"Helena, put on your cape."

"I don't want my cape! And I don't need you! This is all your fault. You brought me here. You brought me to this God-forsaken, blood-sucking land. God damn this prairie! God damn you, Ole Branjord! God damn you to hell!"

Ole was stunned. He did not know this woman. All he could say was, "Helena, put on the cape. You are freezing cold."

"It is the children who are cold. I have to cover them."

"Oh God, Helena!" Ole cried, tears running down his cheeks. "The children are dead."

Deranged fury filled Helena's eyes. "And it is your fault! You brought us here!" With a howl, Helena dropped the quilt and her box and sprang at Ole like a rabid, snarling beast, her fingernails searching for his eyes. Ole held up the cape and sidestepped much of the threat.

"Stop it, Helena!"

"God damn you, Ole Branjord!" Helena screamed, and with the quickness of a cat, attacked again.

Ole attempted to hold her off with the cape, but she had the strength of the insane. Her nails raked his right cheek, drawing blood. Ole broke free, but the sight of the blood added to Helena's fury. Roaring obscenities, she flung herself at Ole, her claw-like hands hungry to inflict the pain consuming her. He stopped her with a stiff arm, then, out of desperation, slapped her hard across the face with his right hand.

Helena staggered but did not fall. She stared at Ole as if she had just seen him. Her frozen face began to crack like ice on a pond in springtime. The fury in her eyes dissolved into a bottomless ocean of sadness. She dropped to her knees. From her mouth came a primal cry of loss that shook Ole to his core. Soul-wrenching sobs followed.

Ole fell to his knees in front of Helena and took her in his arms. She collapsed against him, her strength spent. His sobs joined hers, creating a harmony of sorrow known only to those who have lost children.

As the sobs subsided into whimpers and moans, Helena fell to her side, pulling Ole down with her. They lay on the cold earth, snowflakes melding with their tears. Neither attempted to rise. It was so peaceful, so quiet, so free of pain. To free themselves from their anguish required nothing more than falling asleep. Ole kissed Helena's hair and closed his eyes, giving up, welcoming eternal rest. Together they would join their beloved children. That was good. Children need parents. A smile softened the deep fatigue lines on his face. He had fought the good fight. His race was over. Death was a welcome friend. Let the fresh snow be their shroud.

"Ole," Helena whispered. Her husband did not reply. "Ole," she repeated with more urgency.

Ole heard her voice as if coming from a great distance. He mumbled gibberish.

"Ole, listen," Helena said. "The baby is kicking me."

Ole opened his eyes and gazed into Helena's clear, tear-filled ones. The insane creature was gone. His wife had returned. "Did you hear me, Ole? The baby is kicking. It wants to live."

Neither moved. They just looked into each other's souls as they struggled with the most important decision of their lives.

"Perhaps God wants the child to live," Ole said. Helena answered with a slow nod. Ole continued, "Do you?"

"Yes," Helena answered as fresh tears spilled down her face.

Ole forced himself to sit up. The uncertainty and pain of life had been chosen over the finality and peace of death. Groaning, he rose to his feet, his limbs complaining at being awakened and asked to function, and discovering that it is more terrifying to live than to die.

Ole weaved, almost falling, then steadied himself and held out his hand. Helena grasped it and, with his aid, stood. Ole drew her into his arms. They remained that way until Ole felt Helena shiver. Her fury had kept her warm. Now she stood trembling with cold. Ole snatched up Helena's cape and tied it around her neck. He then wrapped her in the quilt. She smiled her thanks.

Ole took her hand and was about to turn for home when Helena's eyes filled with fear. "My box! Where is my box?"

Helena pulled away from Ole and darted to where the box lay open, its contents scattered. She fell to her knees, scooping up the precious locks of hair.

Ole joined her search. "Do you have them all?" he asked.

"All except Berent," Helena answered, her voice filled with panic.

Ole began sweeping the ground with his fingers. "I found your solje!"

"I don't care about that! Help me find Berent. Oh, dear God, I can't lose Berent!"

With growing fear, Ole crawled through the stalks. He knew this could bring back the insane creature.

"There!" Helena screamed, diving as if into a pool at the barely visible blond lock of hair, which lay pinned against a fallen cornstalk. "I have him! I have him!"

With the locks of hair safely back in the box and the box clutched tightly beneath Helena's cape, against her breasts, Ole wrapped his wife in the quilt and began to lead her home. After just a few steps, Helena stumbled. Ole caught her and, noticing her bare feet, swept her up in his arms. He was not a big man, but this night he could have carried Helena all the way to Nevada.

Helena laid her head on Ole's shoulder, then noticed the blood on his face. "Ole, you're bleeding."

"It's nothing."

"Did I do that?" she asked, gently touching Ole's cheek.

"It will heal," Ole said. "Don't concern yourself."

"I'm so sorry," Helena whispered. "Oh, I am so sorry. I love you, Ole. I'm so sorry."

Ole kissed Helena's forehead and carried her back to the warmth of the cabin.

Helena
(1917)

I am sitting in a rocking chair on my front porch, wrapped up like a mummy. Well, it is not really my front porch anymore. My son Oluf and his family live here now. When Oluf married and Ole grew too old to work the farm, we moved to a house in Ellsworth, Iowa, just a few miles away. The house is a nice, cozy little place, but this farm will always be home. It is two hundred and twenty acres of the best farm land in Iowa. We named it Elm Lawn Farm because of all the elm trees we planted around the front yard. Look at them now! They are magnificent. They give wonderful shade in the summer and the grandchildren love to hide behind them when playing hide-n-seek.

It is a beautiful farm, a real showplace. All the buildings are painted white. The house sits on a small rise and is just as I planned it. To the south is the barn, Ole's pride and joy. It is just as he planned it. West of the barn is a large corncrib and a machine shed. Ole also built a hog house, chicken house, milk house, smokehouse, and outhouse … with a door. On the side of the door, he hung a small plaque that read: "Helena's Door. Please Close." The words have faded but the plaque is still there.

North and west of the house is a grove of pine trees, which acts as a windbreak in the winter, and an orchard of apple, plum, and cherry trees, plus blackberry and gooseberry bushes. I love the orchard. It has produced such wonderful fruit. Of course, it also has meant countless hours of work. Once we started canning, I spent much of every summer putting up preserves and canning all sorts of fruits and vegetables. What a blessing! In the dead of winter we could have applesauce, peaches, pears, and vegetables from the garden. No more mushes and salt pork! Up until last summer, I would come out to the farm and help Oluf's wife, Anna, with the canning. But not last summer. Ole was doing poorly and I wasn't doing much better. Old age is the pits.

"Grandma! Grandma! Donald isn't playing fair!"

I look down the porch steps and see Vernon standing there, hands on hips, breathing hard. He turned five in August. Donald, who will be seven in a month, is standing a few feet behind him, grinning from ear to ear. Both boys are wearing overalls and cotton, store-bought shirts. No one wears homespun anymore.

"What is the problem, Vernon?"

"We're playing tag and Donald won't let me catch him!"

I laugh. "I think I've heard that one before."

Vernon sticks out his lower lip. "It's not funny, Grandma. He's bigger than me!"

"Don't listen to him, Grandma. He's just slow."

"I am not!"

"Are too!"

Vernon quickly dashes at Donald, catching him by surprise, touches him, and runs. "You're it!"

"Cheater!" Donald yells, and both boys disappear around the side of the house.

I laugh again. It is good to see little boys run. I turn my attention to the tree line, where Oluf's two girls are taking turns on the sack swing. Olive is eleven and Myrtle is nine. They both have long brown hair and are as pretty as they can be. Oluf adores them. Ole doted on them. All they had to do was smile and he would buy them anything they wanted. The girls are wearing matching blue dresses Anna made for them. She is very handy with a sewing machine. The dresses were made for school, but now are a little small. The girls are growing so fast.

When I first saw them in those dresses, my heart skipped a beat. Olive did a pirouette and asked, "Isn't it pretty, Grandma?" I told her it was, then hurried to the kitchen and shed a few tears. Little girls in royal blue dresses have that effect on me.

Oh! There is a car coming down the road. "Olive! Myrtle! There is a car coming. Get away from that swing!"

The girls just stand there and look at the oncoming machine. I grip the arms of my chair. The car whizzes past them, creating a cloud of dust. The driver honks. Olive and Myrtle wave. It must be a neighbor. When the car is gone, Olive looks at me like I am a crazy woman. "Grandma, we're twenty yards from the road. The cars aren't going to hurt us."

"I don't care," I answer. "You be careful."

I hate cars. They go too fast and make too much noise. When you ride in them, you go so fast that everything is a blur. You can't see anything! The car that just passed had to be going thirty miles an hour! I like the horse and buggy. It is quiet, and you can look for wildflowers in the ditches along the roadside.

Oh, I know cars are convenient. Oluf owns one. I don't know what kind it is. He calls it a touring car. It has a top that folds down if the weather is nice. He goes to Randall or Story City in no time. Why, last spring, Oluf drove Ole and me to Nevada. It did not take us half an hour. It used to take half a day.

My, how things have changed since those days. The land is laid out in six hundred and forty acre sections, with at least four farms to each section, and sometimes as many as eight. The farms are all fenced. There is no more open land. Ole was right about the prairie. None of us missed it until it was gone. Ole told me many times that he wished he had saved a couple acres of prairie. Just enough for us to walk through. But those beautiful flowers no longer exist, at least not around here. So many things disappeared with the prairie. It was almost as if they vanished into the tall grass. Poor little Fairview was one.

When the railroad arrived, the tracks ran about a mile west of Turg's store. The new town, called Story City, grew up around the train station, and Fairview just faded away. Turg closed up his store and spent all of his time fishing. Story City has grown to a town of over one thousand people. It really is a wonderful town. There is no longer any need to go to Nevada or Ames to shop. It even has a new picture-show theater. I haven't been there, but Oluf and Anna say it is quite nice.

I remember the first picture show Ole and I saw. It was in Nevada. We didn't know quite what to expect, but we were both excited. When the picture came on the screen, a piano player began to pound the keys. The show was all about a bunch of outlaws trying to rob a train. When the shooting started, some people ducked. It was exciting! At one point, the train looked like it was coming right at us. I grabbed Ole's arm and I thought he was going to jump out of his seat. We didn't go to many picture shows. Ole didn't like all the shooting and outlaws. I think it brought back memories of the night he chased Rooster and those other rotten men.

"Do you want to come in, Helena?"

I turn to see Anna standing beside me. She is a tall, handsome woman with a warm personality. She is three inches taller than Oluf, but neither seems to be bothered by it. They have a happy marriage. Praise the Lord! Anna is holding two-year-old Everett. He is giving me a wary eye. He knows I want to hold him, but he doesn't want to be held. I used to hold him all the time. Not in the past few weeks. I think I smell bad. In fact, I know I smell bad. I smell of death.

"No, Anna," I answer. "I love it out here."

"The kids aren't bothering you, are they?" she asks.

"Oh no! I enjoy watching them play. And I can watch for those speeding cars."

Anna smiles. She has heard this all before. "Helena, you worry too much."

"Well, you never know," I answer. "If the driver loses control, that car could be in the yard before you know it! I still say Oluf should put up an iron fence."

"I'll talk to him about it," she says, as she shifts Everett from one hip to the other.

I know she won't. They all think I'm a crazy old lady when it comes to cars.

"Isn't it a beautiful day?" Anna says, taking a deep breath. "It's hard to believe it is November."

"We're having an Indian summer," I say. "It's like the one in sixty-nine."

Anna pats my shoulder. She knows what 1869 means to me. "I'm taking Everett in for his nap. Call if you need anything."

"Thank you, dear," I say. Anna goes into the house. I drift back forty-eight years.

Thankfully, my memories of that winter are few and shrouded in a fog. Pain destroyed them. Ole and I clung together as we had never done before or since. I know we came close to drowning in our tears. I do remember Christmas Day. We did not go to Inga's home. We did not exchange gifts. Big Per came over and brought his violin. He played a few dance tunes to cheer us up. It didn't work. Every song he played reminded us in some way of the children. We all ended up crying.

Although we did not exchange gifts, we did receive a life-saving one. I believe it was a gift from God. Big Per told us the farm up near Randall, this farm, was definitely for sale. The next day Ole rode Lady up to the farm and bought it. Albert quickly bought our forty acres, and in March of 1870, we moved. I loved our place by Fairview, but when we drove away the last time, I did not look back. Neither Ole nor I have ever so much as driven by the place. I am told the cabin was torn down years ago. There is nothing there now but the land.

I don't remember the sun shining that winter. I'm sure it did. I just don't remember anything but gloomy, gray skies. But the sun came out again at the end of March. The child who saved our lives was born. It was a boy. Oline would have been disappointed. We named him Berent. That was a mistake. We should have named him Martin. He turned out to be so much like Martin. He graduated from the University of Iowa and became a lawyer. Ole and I were so proud. He was the first in either of our families to ever go to college. The only problem was that he moved all the way to Spokane, Washington. But, lo and behold, a few years ago he decided to become a Lutheran minister. He now has a church in Wisconsin. I wish he were closer. I hardly know his children.

Nettie lives close. She married John Sparboe and lives a few miles up the road. She was born in seventy-five. We were happy to have another little girl. She was so cute ... and smart. She attended the Lutheran Women's Seminary in Red Wing, Minnesota. I hope she comes to see me today.

When Oluf came, Ole finally got his farmer. What a surprise he was! He was born in eighty-three. I was forty-five years old. He is such a joy. Just like his father.

"Grandma! Grandma! Look!" Olive is pointing to the sky. "Airplanes! Three of them."

I look up. At first I don't see them. My eyes aren't what they used to be. I had to give up my needlework last winter. Then I see them. Three bi-winged planes flying close together. I wonder what it would be like to be up there. Ole said you couldn't get him in one of those contraptions with a team of horses. I did not agree. I would love to fly, to see what God sees, to see how insignificant we really are. Ole laughed at me. "It makes no sense," he said. "You hate cars because they go too fast, but you want to fly and go much faster." He is right. It does not make sense. But I still would like to do it. It must be wonderful to fly in and out of the clouds.

I suppose the three pilots are training for that awful war in Europe. It is such a stupid war! At some river over there, the British lost over fifty thousand men in one day. It is nothing but slaughter! How many of our boys will be killed? How many will be wounded like Karl Lyngen?

Poor Karl. During one of his nighttime walks in March of 1870, he drowned in the Skunk River. The water was high. Some say he was drunk and fell in. Others believe the bank collapsed. They didn't find his body for three days. Ole told me why he carried the pistol on his walks. I think he wanted to die so that Inga would be free to live.

So many of the pioneers are gone: Big Per, Hans Twedt, Bertha and Albert, Martha Karina, and dear Ole. Oh, sweet husband, you have been in the ground for just two weeks and I miss you so. He was eighty-seven. I'm told the funeral procession from the church in Randall to the Fairview Cemetery in Story City was over a mile long. So many people said such nice things about Ole. How could they not? He was such a thoughtful man.

Julia Twedt was there. She is still looking strong and healthy despite having had eleven children. She told me she has over fifty grandchildren and can't keep them all straight. How many do I have? Let's see, Oluf has five. Nettie has one. And Berent has five. No, that's not right. Margaret died in 1913. She was just four. Good heavens, if all of my children had lived, I might have had close to fifty. Ole used to like to bounce the grandchildren on his knees. He certainly would have had tired legs with that many!

At the cemetery, I saw tears running down Amos's cheeks. He loved Ole. He said many times that Ole put him on the right track. Then he would laugh because he became an engineer on the railroad. Starting in the eighties, he and his wife and family would come visit us at least once a year. Ole was real proud of him. After the service, Amos whispered to me that he still has the pants I patched for him and that old quilt. He says they are his most prized possessions. Can you imagine that? It just shows that money can't buy what is really important.

Inga and Elmer Fjelstad came up from Ames. Elmer said he was soon going to retire from teaching at Iowa State College. He has been a professor there for nearly forty years. Inga is looking frail. I noticed she walked over to Karl's grave. Elmer was wise enough to let her be alone. She married Elmer two years after Karl's passing. She had five children. All of them lived. She named her first girl Oline and her first boy Martin. She again reminded me of that wonderful Thanksgiving dinner in sixty-nine. She said it was one of the best days of her life. Mine too.

A cloud passes over the sun. I draw my shawl a little tighter. I'm dying. That is why I'm sitting on this porch. I asked Oluf if I could spend my last days on this farm. He granted my wish. I know I'm a bother to Anna, but I won't be here much longer. I can feel my body shutting down. I no longer can seem to get warm. It feels as if death has entered through my feet and is slowly coming up my legs. I don't mind dying. I find the process rather interesting. I suppose that is because I am in no pain. Not like the children. They died in great pain. Will I see them again? Will they know me? Will Ole be waiting? Will I go to heaven? Is there a heaven? I will know the answers very soon.

"Grandma?"

I look to my side. Olive and Myrtle are standing there. Myrtle is holding my box.

"Would you tell us some stories, Grandma?" Myrtle asks.

I take the box. It is old now. Like me. I open it. My solje is still here. It needs polishing. I touch the locks of hair. Tears come, as they always do, when I touch the hair.

"See!" Olive hisses at Myrtle. "I told you we shouldn't bring the box. Grandma is crying."

"No, it is all right," I say. "I enjoy telling my stories. I like to talk about the children."

Donald and Vernon come bounding up the steps. They are so full of life.

"Are you going to tell stories, Grandma?" Donald asks.

"Yes, I am."

"Tell us about Berent," Myrtle says. "He's funny."

Vernon reaches into the box and picks out a lock of hair. "Is this Berent?"

"No," I answer. "That's Nettie."

"Aunt Nettie isn't dead," Vernon says.

"That's not your Aunt Nettie," I say, putting the hair back into the box. "That is my first Nettie. She died coming from Illinois to Iowa."

"How come you kept using the same names?" Donald asks.

"It was a custom back then, a way of remembering the children who died."

Olive frowns. "If I die, I don't want someone else taking my name."

"You're not going to die!" I scold, the thought making my stomach turn into a knot. "Don't ever say that!"

"This is Berent," Myrtle says, picking up the lock of hair tied with a blue ribbon.

"That's right," I say, taking the hair and feeling the soft, silky texture. "Berent was four. He was the cutest little boy."

"Cuter than me?" Vernon asks.

"Aw, you're not cute at all," Donald replies.

Both tongues come out. Some things never change.

"Yes, Vernon. Even cuter than you," I say, as I tousle his hair. "But he was a little stinker. He used to hide from me."

The children laugh.

For the sake of the novel, I advanced the ages of the children. When they died in 1869, Oline was eight, Martin was four, and Berent was two. Also, the children died in July, not December.

It is doubtful that Ole and Helena knew Big Per Larson. He died in 1864. I included him in this novel because he was such a wonderful character. The feats of strength attributed to him in this book, with the exception of tipping over Hanna's buggy, are all based on fact, as is the playing of the violin for the Winnebago Indians. For more on Big Per, I recommend you read *The Follinglo Dog Book* by Peder Gustav Tjernagel, published by the University of Iowa Press, and *Store Per* by Peter Tjernagel Harstad, published by Jackpine Press.

The breakup of Saint Petri Church took place in 1868, not 1869. The reasons were as presented in this novel.

Ole Branjord died October 19, 1917. Helena Branjord died November 16, 1917. To this union, eleven children were born: Nettie died on the journey from Illinois to Iowa; Oline, Martin, and Berent died of scarlet fever in 1869; a second Oline, Marie, Christine, and Oluf died of diphtheria in 1882; a second Nettie, a second Berent, and a second Oluf lived to old age. Oluf Martin Christian Branjord was my maternal grandfather.

The Branjords are buried in the Fairview Cemetery, Story City, Iowa. After the deaths of Ole and Helena, the surviving children had stone markers with the names and dates of the dead children placed around the family plot.

My mother, Myrtle Branjord Twedt (1908—2007), remembered Ole as being a kind, gentle man who fed her cookies and crackers and patted her head, calling her his "lille duka," which is little doll in Norwegian. She remembered Helena as always being busy. Gardening and canning consumed her summers; needlework and quilting dominated the winter months. Mother recalled Helena's sister visiting from Chicago. The women rattled away in Finnish, a language no one else in the house understood. She also told me that Helena loved to tell her the story of riding with the Lapps on a reindeer-pulled sled. However, Mother's most vivid memory of Helena was her sitting in a rocking chair with her box in her lap. The old woman would slowly open the box and, as tears rolled down her aged cheeks, she would finger the locks of hair and tell stories about her dead children.

WORKS CONSULTED:
BOOKS:
Brown, Farwell T., *Ames*. Ames: Heuss Printing Inc., 1993

Fiske, Arland O., *The Scandinavian Heritage*. Minot: North American Heritage Press, 1987

Gesme, Ann Urness. *Between Rocks and Hard Places*. Hastings: Caragana Press, 2004

Nelson, David T., *The Diary of Elizabeth Koren, 1853-1855*. Northfield: Norwegian-American Historical Association, 1955

Tjernagel, Peder Gustav. *The Follinglo Dog Book, A Norwegian Pioneer Story*. Iowa City: University of Iowa Press, 1999

Torvik, Solveig. *Nikolai's Fortune*. Seattle: University of Washington Press, 2005

Zempel, Solveig. *In Their Own Words*. Minneapolis: University of Minnesota Press, 2003

OTHER SOURCES:
Christiansen, Christian Poul. *From Vejle Amt to Iowa, an Immigrant's Christmas Letter*. The Journal of Danish-American Heritage Society, Vol. 25, number two, 2002

Knutson, Carrie. *Pioneer Days*. Jewel, Iowa: Jewel Gem, 1881 to 1981

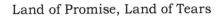
Severson, George J., *Reminiscences of Pioneer Life.* Slater, Iowa. A family history

Tjernagle, Nehemias. *Pioneer Iowa Soil Subjugation.* The Annals of Iowa, Vol. 31, October 1952

Voices from the Past – The Story of Nevada, Iowa. The Nevada Community Historical Society, 2003